Hero Ever After

Gibson Hollow
Book 1

Kait Nolan

Author's Note

Welcome to Gibson Hollow.

This is a town where love is love, families come in all shapes, and everyone gets to show up exactly as they are—without fear, shame, or explanation.

In these pages, you won't find homophobia, racism, ableism, or cruelty rooted in fear of difference. Not because those things don't exist in the world—but because they don't belong in *this* one.

Here, drag queens are fairy godparents. Queer joy is sacred. Neurodivergence and chronic illness are woven into the rhythm of daily life. And no one's humanity is up for debate.

Gibson Hollow isn't a fantasy. It's a blueprint. It's the world I believe we *can* build—one book, one conversation, and one community at a time.

Thanks for stepping into it with me.

Love,

Kait

P.S. This book is set in the Deep South. As such, it contains a great deal of colorful, colloquial, and occasionally grammatically incorrect language. This is a deliberate choice on my part as an author to most accurately represent the region where I have lived my entire life. This book also contains swearing and pre-marital sex between the lead couple, as those things are part of the realistic lives of characters of this generation, and of many of my readers.

If any of these things are not your cup of tea, please consider that you may not be the right audience for this book. There are scores of other books out there that are written with you in mind. In fact, I've got a list of some of my favorite authors who write on the sweeter side on my website at https://kaitnolan.com/on-the-sweeter-side/

If you choose to stick with me, I hope you enjoy!

Happy reading!

WAIT!

Did you read Alia and Ramsey's prequel, Hero After Midnight?

While you will certainly understand the events of this book without it, I promise you'll appreciate it more if you get their backstory! You can grab your copy for free!

Chapter 1

Alia

The thing about running a law practice out of your grandmother's diner is that sometimes your client tries to pay you in peach preserves.

And sometimes—like today—you accept. Not because you necessarily want jam, but because the only thing thinner than your patience is the town's collective wallet, and at least Mrs. Larrabee's homemade deliciousness won't bounce.

Mrs. Larrabee set the jar down as if it were something fragile and priceless, both of which were probably true. "I know it ain't much." She folded her hands over a worn vinyl purse with peeling corners and a safety pin holding the strap together. "But since that check from FEMA still hasn't come through, and the heater went out again last night, I figured jam was better than nothing."

I glanced down at the label. *Cinnamon-spiced peach.* It was dated last summer. Before the flood that had literally washed away half of our town. Back when the biggest thing any of us was worried about was who'd win the annual Gibson Hollow Great Griddle Games.

I tucked the jar safely into the corner of the table, beside my portable printer. "It's more than enough. And it's going to be really great on pound cake." I'd gotten one of those yesterday from Sue Meechum for helping draft a lease agreement for the garage they were turning into an apartment to rent.

Mrs. Larrabee's faint smile didn't reach her eyes. She looked tired in the way you got from treading water for too long and the shore still hadn't shown up.

It was where most of us were five months on from the disaster.

"Now, I'm guessing FEMA won't release the funds because you can't prove ownership of the property."

Her lined face crumpled in defeat. "Luther never got around to putting the deed in my name after his mama passed. And she... she never had a deed at all. We just—lived there. Forty-seven years. When he passed two years ago, nobody said I needed to do something to keep living in my own house."

"Of course they didn't. Heirs property is more common than you might think. Especially out here." I grabbed a form from the rack beside the printer and began writing. "FEMA's love language is bureaucratic delay. But we're going to get around it."

Her arthritic hands knotted together. "I'm real sorry to trouble you, Alia. I know you've got more important cases than me."

I reached out to lay one of my hands over hers. "There is nothing more important than keeping you in your home, Mrs. L." With a gentle squeeze, I resumed filling out the form.

I believed in the pen being mightier than the sword. I'd made a fine living at it—not that anyone knew about that. But I'd have given a hell of a lot to just attack FEMA with battle unicorns and dragons. I would be so much more satisfying. But the real world didn't resemble the ones I spun into fantasy, so I'd continue to do this the old-fashioned way.

Form complete, I slid her a pen. "Start by signing this affidavit of continuous residence. I'll get started on the title work and pull what records I can from the clerk's office. We'll piece it together."

Please God, let there be something on file at the county seat.

What remained of our own town records was in disarray or various stages of water damage. In the grand scheme of post-flood cleanup, they hadn't been a priority. Not when we'd needed to fully rebuild infrastructure to reconnect the town to the rest of the world.

Her fingers trembled a little as she took the pen, like she wanted to trust this lifeline but couldn't quite get there. "It's only a house," she murmured.

"No, it's not. It's where your grandbabies learned to ride bikes. It's where Luther built that chicken coop modeled after the Taj Mahal because it made you laugh. It's yours. We'll make sure the government knows it, too."

And this was why I hadn't written in months. Because people's real lives were hanging on by threads, and I could help keep them afloat.

She signed, and I filed the moment and the document away. Another crisis queued. Another thread in the town's unraveling tapestry that I was trying to stitch back together, one piece of bureaucratic red tape at a time.

"Now, let's move on to more immediate concerns. You said the heat went out. Have you got somebody to see to that yet?"

"Not yet. But I've got the wood stove. It heats the whole house pretty well."

I added more notes to the legal pad at my elbow. "I'm gonna have someone come by to make sure you're plenty stocked up on firewood. And I'll see that Fletcher or one of his crew comes by as soon as he's able to take a look at that heater." The last thing we needed was Mrs. Larrabee slipping and breaking a hip as she tried to carry wood into the house.

She rose with a quiet grunt, a soft sound that implied everything hurt but she was too proud to say so. "You're a godsend, Alia Gibson."

"Just doing what needs doing." My life motto.

I walked her to the door and didn't miss the way her knees wobbled as she stepped out into the midmorning chill. I made a mental note to send out a request on the group text with my brothers to see if one of them could swing by with some fresh logs and to make sure her steps were clear of ice.

The moment I sat back down, another folder slid into the open seat across from me, attached to a man who looked about one bad morning away from throwing a hammer at someone. I didn't even need to see his face.

"Morning, George." Instead of reaching for the breakfast I'd started on five clients ago, I grabbed the cup of coffee that had also long since gone cold. I needed the bracing support of caffeine. "What's broken now?"

"The generator we finally got working at the water station blew out again. Inspector came by this morning. Flagged the wiring as a hazard."

I stared at him for a full two seconds before answering. "Of course he did."

Because why wouldn't a piece of equipment we'd coaxed into functioning with borrowed parts and two Hail Marys decide to spontaneously combust the second someone with a clipboard showed up?

I jotted down a note below Mrs. Larrabee's name on the legal pad that served as my master list of town chaos. If this kept up, I was going to have to start color-coding by crisis type. "I'll call the inspector and the county permit office this afternoon. See if we can push through an emergency variance or at least stall enforcement until we get someone to do the necessary permanent repairs."

"Appreciate you." He gave me a tired smile and left me with the paperwork.

I glanced around at my makeshift office—two vinyl booth seats and a Formica tabletop wedged in the back corner of my grandmother's diner, surrounded by a fortress of manila folders and an elderly laptop that needed to be coaxed into submission more often than not. A battered portable printer hummed faintly, refusing to acknowledge its wireless capabilities. The entire space smelled like bacon grease, biscuits, and desperation.

This was never supposed to be permanent.

Five months ago, courtesy of an Atlantic hurricane that had stretched further inland than anyone expected, the river had crested higher than it had in a century, swallowing half of Gibson Hollow, and much of the rest of Western North Carolina, in a single, violent night. The law office I'd spent years building was literally washed away. Power lines down. Roads gone. More than half the bridges decimated. My dad— our beloved, bullheaded mayor—had pulled three people out of a collapsed foundation and ended up with a crushed pelvis, multiple broken ribs, and a shattered shoulder when he got caught by debris. Once he'd been stabilized, the doctors sent him to Nashville for multiple surgeries and rehab and told us not to expect him back soon.

So I'd stepped in. Temporarily.

Then temporary turned into taking FEMA calls at midnight, coordinating volunteer crews, filing damage assessments, arguing with state reps over funding that should've shown up two months ago, and mediating a fistfight in the hardware store over drywall.

My degree was in law, not miracles. But someone had to hold it all together, and around here, that someone always seemed to be me. Even if it meant putting my own dreams on hold.

I hadn't worn my heels in five months. But I had worn two pairs of work boots into the ground.

A fresh, steaming cup of coffee appeared on the table beside my elbow, as if summoned by my need alone. "Your blood, ma'am. Fresh and black as your mood."

I glanced up at Grandma Elsie, the unquestionable matriarch of our family, who once shooed a black bear out of her backyard with a broom and a disapproving glare. If I didn't watch my mood, she'd give me the same Eyebrow of Doom. "You're an angel."

"I'm a realist." She propped both hands on her generous, apron-clad hips. "And realism says if you're gonna keep running this town out of my booth, the least I can do is keep you caffeinated."

I sipped the hot coffee and corrected my assessment. "A saint, then."

"Don't be ridiculous." She leaned in a little closer. "Besides, if I leave you to your own devices, you'll forget to eat, run yourself into the ground, and make me look bad."

I snorted, the first genuine sound of amusement I'd made all morning. "Can't have that."

"Exactly." She glanced at my abandoned breakfast, noting with disapproval that I'd only made it through one egg and a half strip of bacon. "You want a fresh plate?"

There was no point. I'd get interrupted before I could finish again, and my appetite wasn't exactly stellar these days. No reason to waste any more food when supplies were still limited. "This is fine." To prove it, I picked up the other slice of bacon and nibbled.

She patted my shoulder and turned back toward the kitchen.

My twin brother, Bodie, strolled in a beat later in his standard Gibson Hollow PD khakis, a manila envelope under one arm and the weight of the town slung across his shoulders like part of the uniform.

He dropped the envelope on my stack of files like it belonged there. "Morning, Madam Mayor."

I shot him a withering stare and moved the envelope off my precisely organized stack. "Don't call me that."

He grinned down at me. "Power's back on at the west substation. Linemen wrapped up around four this morning. We're running patchy on coverage along Hollow Ridge, but most folks should have lights again."

That was a damned miracle.

"Anyone giving you grief?"

"Only Doug Milner. He's mad the internet's still spotty and says it's cutting into his online poker league."

"God forbid," I muttered. "I'll add it to the list."

Bodie leaned in slightly, studying my face. "You get any sleep last night?"

"Define sleep."

"That's what I thought."

Before I could fire back, the door opened again and in walked our next-youngest brother, Colter, dragging cold air and the scent of cedar smoke with him. He clapped Bodie on the back as he passed, then dropped into the seat Mrs. Larrabee had vacated not ten minutes ago.

"Did this one tell you about the west substation?"

"He did. Good news all around."

"Don't let him fool you," Colter said. "His idea of checking power lines is rolling by in a truck with his flashlight and pretending to squint meaningfully."

"I resent that," Bodie shot back. "I documented the whole inspection."

"You documented it with your phone while sitting on your butt."

"You know how cold it is out there? I'm preserving law enforcement assets."

"Emphasis on the 'ass'."

Ignoring their ribbing, I dove right in. "Colter, can you swing by Mrs. Larrabee's place today? Her heater's out again. She's using the wood stove, but I'd feel better if you made sure she's stocked up and doesn't have to hike down icy steps for firewood."

He sobered immediately. "I'm on it. I'll get by before my shift at the firehouse."

Before anyone else could settle, the door opened one more time and in came Dean, brother number three. He was still getting used to civilian clothes, but he moved like a man who didn't miss his uniform. His beard was new, his desert tan had started to fade, but the posture was still pure Marine.

He slid into the booth next to Colter and fixed his gaze on me. "Any chance you're free for five minutes today?"

I sipped the coffee Grandma Elsie had delivered. "For you? I can do four and a half. What's up?"

"I got my final separation paperwork yesterday. It's official. No more Uncle Sam."

My chest twinged in relief. No more worrying about where in the world he was and whether he was being shot at. "That's a big deal."

"Yeah. Feels weird."

"What's your plan?"

"I was hoping you'd tell me."

He'd predominantly been on debris cleanup for the few weeks he'd been home, but I could tell he wanted something a bit more constructive now. "Fletcher can for sure use another set of hands on the bridge crew. Just don't fall in the river."

He half grinned. "No promises."

Bodie glanced between us. "Is that the same bridge where the temporary scaffolding keeps washing out?"

"That's the one." I set my coffee aside. "We've got new materials coming, but it's slow going with the weather. If we get another snow, it's going to push everything back again."

Dean nodded. "Still. It'll feel good to build something. Even if it's one board at a time."

And wasn't that the whole town in a sentence?

We talked for a few more minutes—status updates, which roads were drivable without four-wheel drive, how many more comms towers were back up. The grocery had reopened last week with limited hours. The food pantry had gotten extra donations. The clinic was still operating out of trailers, and the town green—the part that hadn't turned into a sinkhole—was a mud pit, frozen solid most mornings and thawing enough by afternoon to swallow your boots. The library was a loss. The office strip where I used to work was down to slab.

But the lights were coming back on. Kids were back in school, even if it was in borrowed spaces. People were laughing again—tired, worn down, barely holding-on people—but laughing all the same.

It wasn't merely buildings we were rebuilding.

It was hope.

The bell over the door jingled again, and Blair swept in like she'd timed it for maximum disruption—coat unbuttoned, cheeks pink from the cold, and that unmistakable gleam in her eye that meant my day was about to get significantly more complicated.

She scanned the room, spotted me in the back corner, and made a beeline. As Colter and Dean were still parked like sentries, she dragged over a chair from the next table and dropped into it backward, chin resting on the top rail like a smug cat who'd knocked over something expensive.

I didn't even bother with pleasantries. "What did you do?"

Her smile suggested she had a secret she was dying to tell. "Now, is that any way to greet your best friend?"

"You're sparkling."

"I always sparkle."

"This is *that* sparkle. The one that means I should already be stress-sweating."

She leaned in slightly, voice dropping in a way that made my stomach tighten. "It's not something we can talk about here."

That got a slow blink from me. "So it's *that* kind of surprise."

"Nothing illegal, nothing dangerous." She lifted a hand in mock innocence. "No goats. No glitter. No engagements. No explosives. And no pop-up flash mobs."

Dean raised his brows over the plate of my breakfast he was shoveling in since I obviously wasn't going to eat it. "That's a weirdly specific list of things to rule out."

Blair only smiled wider. "Experience, darlin'."

I groaned. "Blair."

"Meet me at the house before dinner?"

I exhaled slowly. "Will I need wine?"

"I will provide it." She stood with a dancer's grace, brushing invisible lint off her coat. "Promise it's not bad. But you're definitely going to have feelings."

"Fantastic," I muttered.

She winked, tossed a cheerful "Bye, boys!" over her shoulder, and breezed out the door like she hadn't dropped a live grenade on my already overloaded mental to-do list.

I watched her go, a spark of dread burrowing in under my

ribs. Blair never meant harm. But she also never let minor details like boundaries get in the way of what she thought was a good idea.

I didn't have time for surprises.

But in Gibson Hollow, they didn't ask my permission.

They just kept coming.

Chapter 2

Ramsey

@CharlieCharlestonFan: That missed connection between Logan and DeShawn in the 4th quarter killed us! So close yet so far. Ramsey Shaw was the only one who showed up today. #SentinelsSeason #HeartbreakCity

@BlitzBreaker44: Marcus Logan had 3 quarters of brilliance and then completely fell apart when it mattered. That overthrow to Shaw in the end zone? UNFORGIVABLE. 👻 #SentinelsLoss #WeDeservedBetter

@NavyAndSilver: Tough ending but I'm still proud. Shaw was an absolute BEAST all season. Career high receptions! That sideline grab in the 3rd was insane! We'll be back. #SentinelsForLife

@GridironGrandma: DeShawn Sims showing some real promise! That kid's gonna be special. Logan needs to trust him more next season instead of forcing it to covered receivers. #RookieOnTheRise #Sentinels

@SentinelsOrDie: Heartbroken but hopeful. Logan's leadership kept us in it. Shaw was clutch as always. DeShawn showing flashes of greatness. We're building something special here! #TrustTheProcess #Sentinels

The hallway outside the press room buzzed with the usual end-of-season chaos—fluorescent lights humming overhead, cleats clacking on concrete, some poor intern sprinting past with a stack of fresh towels and panic in his eyes. The air reeked like sweat, Gatorade, and whatever industrial cleaner they used in here that never quite masked the funk of long hours and harder losses. We were three minutes out from the final press conference of the season, and all I could think about was how badly I wanted a burger with extra cheese and bacon. And an extra-large waffle fries.

I leaned against the cool concrete wall outside the door, towel slung around my neck, team hoodie damp at the collar. Across from me, DeShawn Sims—the rookie wideout with hands like glue and nerves like a hummingbird—was smoothing down the front of his warm-up jacket like he was about to walk a red carpet. Kid had only been on camera a handful of times this season, and he was still convinced one wrong word would get him cut. He didn't know yet that the press didn't need help twisting your words. They could do that fine on their own.

Next to him, Marcus Logan—the QB and captain of the we-will-win-it-next-year optimism committee—clapped him on the shoulder. "Don't puke, rook. That mic picks everything up."

DeShawn looked like he might actually consider it. I didn't blame him. The first time I sat behind those mics, I'd nearly cracked a molar keeping my jaw clenched tight enough not to say something I'd regret. That was ten seasons ago. Long time. A whole lifetime, if you measured it in yardage and injuries.

"Ready?" Our media liaison's voice was a little too chipper for a man who'd been yelling into a headset all night.

I straightened, rolled my shoulders once, and nodded. Marcus winked at me like we were about to go on stage for a talk show, and then we stepped into the light.

The barrage of camera shutters echoed like gunfire. Reporters leaned forward, pens poised, recorders blinking red. The room smelled like stale coffee and expectation.

I took my seat at the far end of the table at the front, adjusted the mic, and waited.

The moderator leaned toward the mic and gave the room his usual firm-voiced "Let's get started." That cut through the noise—barely—and the questions came fast and sharp like they always did after a season ender.

First up was Marcus. No surprise there. He was the face of the Charleston Sentinels, and he knew how to wear it. He kept his tone even, his shoulders square, his words carefully chosen. Talked about missed red zone chances, busted coverage in the third quarter, and that fifty-two-yard field goal that hooked left at the worst possible moment. He didn't blame anyone. Didn't dodge, either. Just laid it all out in that voice of his that was part analyst, part preacher, all performance.

Then they turned to DeShawn.

Someone lobbed a classic rookie question: "What was it like, your first post-season appearance?" and I swear, the kid's pupils doubled in size. But he leaned into the mic like he was bracing for impact and launched into a breathless answer about heart, hustle, and how much he'd learned from the veterans. Which was flattering, I guess, but he rambled for a solid minute too long, and started to circle back on himself, like he forgot how sentences worked.

Marcus shot him a grin. I gave him a single nod of quiet support—nothing that'd fluster him further. He needed to feel like he belonged up here, not like he was one mistake from the practice squad.

I kept my posture relaxed, hands folded on top of the table, eyes forward. Contained. I'd learned the hard way that giving too much in front of cameras had a way of turning into noise you couldn't take back.

So, I let Marcus handle the performance. Let DeShawn find his footing.

A voice from the back finally cut through the swirl of questions. "Ramsey, this is your tenth season. You've seen a lot of post-seasons. What's your read on this one?"

I leaned into the mic and kept my tone even. "This is football. Sometimes you win, sometimes you don't. That doesn't mean we didn't fight for every yard."

Pens scratched. A few nods around the room. That was plenty for most people, but one more question followed it up.

"From your perspective, how did the blocking hold up tonight?"

I didn't hesitate. "We held the line pretty well in the first half. The pocket stayed clean, and the run lanes were there. But in the second half, the defense started getting in quicker. Pressures landed a bit earlier than expected. We didn't break down—we just got slightly off rhythm. It wasn't about effort or execution. It came down to timing."

I didn't have to look to know Marcus was nodding beside me. He knew. He'd felt it, same as I had—those half-second shifts where a route broke late or a block landed a fraction too high. Cumulative rather than catastrophic. Enough to tip the balance the other way.

They asked me a couple more questions. Nothing too deep. I gave them straight answers. No dramatics. No shoulder-patting. This wasn't a confessional. It was a report. They didn't need more than that.

I wasn't here to sell soundbites. I was here to finish the season.

A hand shot up in the second row—a beat reporter I recognized, someone who'd been following us for years. His tone was lighter than the earlier questions, which meant we were shifting into the wind-down phase.

"Got a training plan lined up for the off-season?"

I took a slow sip from the bottle of water in front of me, then set it back down with a soft thud. "I always stay in shape."

That earned a few quiet chuckles from the front row. They'd heard variations of that line from me before and knew better than to push for more. I wasn't the guy who volunteered vacation plans or dropped hints about endorsements. I showed up. I did the work. I stayed healthy. That was the story.

Next to me, Marcus grinned and leaned into his mic. "He'll be back with calves like steel cables, as always."

The laughter got a little louder at that. DeShawn tried to smother a grin behind his hand.

Instead of responding, I folded my hands again and let the noise roll over me as Marcus played the room. He was good at that.

Whatever I planned to do with the off-season, it didn't concern anybody here.

DeShawn fielded the next one, something about the biggest difference between college and the pros. He gave a tight answer this time—quick, specific, more confident than before. His nerves had settled.

Good. He'd earned that.

Marcus got one more after that. Someone asked what he was reading now, and he flashed a smile like he'd been waiting for it. Said he was halfway through a biography on Vince

Lombardi. The press ate it up. Marcus had always known how to charm a room without looking like he was trying.

The moderator looked down at the tablet in front of him and gave the signal. "Last question."

A reporter near the front leaned into his mic. "Ramsey—you hit a career-high in receptions this season. Do you think this was your peak?"

I didn't flinch or smile or deflect. "I think I did my job."

I'd shown up, played hard, blocked like hell, made the catches that counted. Whatever that added up to didn't need my commentary. They could write what they wanted. I'd already done the work.

Things wrapped up quickly after that. We filed out the way we came in, the door swinging closed behind us with a soft click. The noise shifted from press chatter to hallway clatter. Cleats echoed again, distant shouts bounced off concrete, and another of the interns hustled past with a phone pressed to each ear and a look on his face like he was negotiating a hostage crisis.

Security nodded us through at the locker room entrance, barely glancing up. Inside, the noise was a different type of loud. Familiar. Comfortable. Towels snapped in the air. Someone yelled about a missed call in *Madden*. The Bluetooth speaker perched on top of a laundry cart blared a bass-heavy track that had all the lyrical depth of a toaster manual. It felt like home.

I shrugged out of my hoodie and tossed it into the mesh bin near the showers, then dropped onto the bench in front of my locker. The wood creaked, cool against my spine. I leaned forward, elbows on knees, letting my head hang for a second. After ten seasons, my body screamed a fair bit more when the adrenaline wore off, and I was looking forward to some ice.

Marcus flopped down beside me, already unlacing his

cleats. DeShawn hovered a beat longer, still buzzing with end-of-season energy.

"So what now, Ramsey?" He dropped into the open space to my left. "Jet to Dubai? Hit up a yacht?"

I cracked my neck. "Nah. I'm thinking downtime, a double cheeseburger, and some time visiting my mom."

Marcus snorted without looking up. "Man of culture."

"Man of cravings. My mama's been sending me pictures of meatloaf since October."

That got a laugh from both of them. Real ones. Easy ones. The kind that didn't come with a camera in your face or a head-line waiting to happen.

DeShawn launched into a monologue about Miami plans with his cousin and maybe booking a few weeks of offseason training in LA if he could swing the budget. Marcus asked if he'd packed sunscreen. I nodded along, half-listening, until the kid hit the five-minute mark without breathing.

I picked up a towel and chucked it at his head.

"Hey!"

"Catch your breath, rook. You'll need it for the layover."

He laughed and batted the towel away.

They didn't ask what else I had planned. Nobody did. Not because they didn't care, but because they understood the line. You said what you wanted to say, and the rest stayed yours.

Good thing, too.

Because if they knew I was about to spend part of my offseason at a fantasy romance book convention in a full custom cosplay of my favorite character? I'd never hear the end of it.

Chapter 3

Alia

@KellaHarmonAuthor: After months of radio silence (blame it on the muse 😴), I might have a little something special coming your way soon. No spoilers, but let's just say some of you might actually get to see me in the wild for the first time ever? ✨ ✦

Keep those notifications on, darlings. The wait might finally be worth it. #KellaHarmon #ComingSoon #MaybeImNot-DeadAfterAll

B y the time I pulled into Blair and Elena's driveway, the winter sun was already dipping behind the mountains, leaving the sky streaked in that bruised purple that came standard with January. The place looked like a Pinterest board had gotten drunk and decided to settle down—an old Craftsman with a wide front porch, strung-up café lights, and a vivid teal door that somehow never clashed with the season, no matter how gray the world around it got. Their porch light was on, warm and golden, throwing soft halos onto the faded welcome mat that proclaimed, *Come back with tacos*.

They'd been among the lucky ones whose houses had been on high enough ground and hadn't been impacted by the flood.

I climbed the front steps and had barely raised a hand to knock before the door swung open.

"Your presence is requested." Blair swept an arm out like a magician revealing the final trick. "Shoes off, coat on the hook, and prepare to be soothed."

I arched a brow but did as instructed. The moment I stepped inside, I was hit by the scent of chocolate and something floral, probably the essential oil Blair was obsessed with diffusing into every corner of her house. The living room was cozy chaos. A riot of textures and colors, mismatched throw pillows, and a blanket Elena's *abuela* had crocheted draped over the back of the couch. The heating vents hummed quietly, and I could already feel some of the cold working its way out of my toes, because this wasn't merely a friend's house. This was one of my safe places.

Blair led me to the couch like I might break if left to my own devices, then promptly disappeared into the kitchen with a shout. "Stay right there and don't make me put on a weighted blanket to keep you still!"

I snorted and dropped onto the cushions. The blanket was already warm from the vent behind it, and I curled it around my shoulders without thinking. Seconds later, Blair returned with two mismatched mugs—one in a chaotic pattern of hearts, one emblazoned with *Nevertheless, She Persisted* in glittery script—and handed me the latter.

It was hot chocolate. With a very generous splash of something that definitely wasn't milk.

I arched a brow. "I thought you were providing wine?"

"This seemed like a better idea." She sat down beside me and curled one leg beneath the other like a lounging cat in sparkly nail polish. "You look like you wrestled a power grid and lost."

"That's because I did. Figuratively." I'd gotten the delay on enforcement at the water station, and Fletcher had sent one of his crew over with another emergency generator to keep things going until we could get a proper electrician to deal with whatever was wrong.

She raised her mug. "To surviving the grid."

I clinked mine against hers. "Barely."

We sipped, and I soaked in the silence of being able to sit with someone I'd been best friends with for more than a third of my life. Then she casually tossed out, "They finally got the mud cleared out from behind the school cafeteria. Only took four months and an act of Congress."

"Elena still stuck in that meeting?"

"Yeah. District's still fighting over how to allocate the next round of grants. She's trying to get enough pushed through to put real money toward the rebuilding. You know, for things like walls. Roofs. Functioning plumbing."

I hummed. "Luxury."

"Mmm. Apparently, infrastructure is now considered bougie."

Her tone was breezy, but I caught the slight uptick in pitch. That little flare of brightness she only deployed when she was overcompensating. Her legs jittered faintly against the couch cushion, and she wasn't making eye contact. Classic signs.

I narrowed my eyes over the rim of my mug. "You've been laying groundwork for something all day."

Blair blinked. Once. Twice. The exaggerated innocent stare might as well have been a road flare.

Then I used the voice I'd honed since my mother died when I was sixteen and I'd become the de facto mom to my seven younger siblings. "Blair Alexandra Young. What. Did. You. Do?"

She winced with her whole perfectly fashionable body, then lifted her mug like a shield and mumbled into the steam, "Technically? A favor."

"A favor." Somehow I knew I was going to absolutely hate this favor. "What sort of favor?"

Blair's shoulders rose practically to her ears. "I signed you up for a panel at a fantasy romance book convention in Atlanta."

My brain stalled like it had thrown a rod.

There was a beat of pure, perfect silence—no heating vent hum, no diffuser whisper, no mug-clink. Just the sharp snap of my reality fracturing.

"You did what?" The words came out flat. Deader than my creative drive.

Blair winced again, teeth bared in a guilty grimace. "Okay, hear me out—"

"Oh, I cannot wait for this."

"You need the exposure." The words came out in a rush. "You haven't posted anything in months. People think you died or got kidnapped by your own protagonist."

My mouth dropped open. "You told them I was kidnapped?" This was what I got for letting her run my social media.

"Only in memes!" Her hands flailed in defense. "Which I didn't make. But I did share them, because the algorithm rewards engagement."

I stared at her, and the only thing keeping me from setting my mug down with lethal intent was the sheer absurdity of that sentence.

"It's good for sales." She steamrolled ahead before I could interrupt. "And readers are foaming at the mouth for the next book. You've seen the DMs."

"They're rabid," I muttered. "That's not the same thing as supportive."

"They're hungry," she corrected. "And justifiably so. It's been over a year since you released anything."

"I had a flood."

"I know. And a FEMA backlog, and a town half held together with duct tape and collective goodwill. Which is exactly why you need this. You need a break. You need to remember that you're a writer, Alia, not a crisis management robot in boots."

I opened my mouth. Closed it again. Because she wasn't wrong.

Which made me want to scream.

I stood, needing motion or oxygen or both. "I told you I didn't want anything public. That was the entire reason for the pen name."

She set her mug down slowly, carefully, like it might go off next. "Alia—"

I cut her off. "No. You don't get to soft-pedal this. I never wanted the spotlight. The writing was never supposed to be for anyone else."

"You left your laptop open." Her voice had gone quiet now. "I read that first book because you walked off to take a shower and forgot to close the file."

"And instead of minding your own damn business, you published it. Without asking." Because boundaries were only suggestions when my bestie thought she was doing something for my own good.

"Damned right, I did. Because it was too amazing to sit in a forgotten folder while you gave yourself ulcers over tort reform and bar exam hypotheticals."

My temper snapped as if the betrayal were fresh. "I was furious."

"You didn't take it down."

"No. Because people bought it and asked for more. Which I gave them, because I needed the money. Because law school is expensive, and I was already drowning in loans and stress."

Blair stood too, facing me now. "And then the second book sold better. And the third even better than that. And then the new series dropped and took off like it had wings. You remember what you said to me the night the BookTok stuff started exploding?"

I didn't want to. But I did. Clear as a bell.

"You said you were thinking about shutting down the practice and going full time as an author. That you finally wanted to choose the thing that made you feel alive."

She took a step closer, eyes shining, but not with tears. This was fire. "You *do* want this, Alia. Maybe not the spotlight, maybe not the fan cons or the panels. But the books? The stories? You've always wanted that. Don't rewrite the whole narrative now because the spotlight feels too bright."

I barked out one sharp, humorless laugh. "Yeah? And look how well that turned out. I decided to take a leap, chase something for me for once, and the universe responded by giving us a literal flood of Biblical proportions."

Blair's mouth opened. Then closed again. There wasn't a comeback for that, and we both knew it. Any dreams I had of pursuing something purely for myself were put permanently on the back burner because everyone needed me.

I ran a hand through my hair and looked away, suddenly exhausted. "I haven't written a word since the flood. And now you want me to sit on a stage and smile and pretend everything's fine?"

Blair didn't push. She waited with maddening patience.

I dropped back onto the couch, sinking into the cushions and half wishing they'd swallow me whole. "You want to know the last time I opened the manuscript file?"

Her continued silence gave me permission.

"Two days before the flood." My voice was low, tight. "Chapter fifteen. Half-finished sentence. Since then, nothing."

I stared down into my hot chocolate, the swirl of cocoa and whiskey catching the light like it might hold answers I didn't want to see. "The town is hanging on by a thread. I'm doing FEMA paperwork in triplicate, fighting red tape over every supply run, begging for grant money with one hand, and trying to rebuild infrastructure with the other. My brain is fried. I haven't written anything in five months, and now you want me to go play Author Barbie at a fantasy romance book con?"

Blair opened her mouth. I cut her off with a glare.

"I ended the last book on a goddamn cliffhanger. Because that's what you do. Readers are frothing. They want answers. And I've got nothing but static. And if I bomb in public? If I freeze or freak out or someone figures out who I actually am? It's over."

I rubbed a hand over my face, fingers pressing into my eyes until stars burst behind my lids. "The law practice is gone. I don't have an office. I don't have a legal secretary anymore, since Kim moved back to Raleigh with her sister. I'm literally running legal aid out of a booth in my grandma's diner. That writing income? It's all I've got right now. It's the only steady thing coming in."

Blair sat down again. Slowly. "Alia..."

"I've used that money to help keep The Commissary open. To pay for repairs nobody else could afford. To float utility shortfalls and fill pantry gaps and fix the goddamn water station generator. I've been plugging holes with royalties and hoping the dam doesn't break. If people stop buying the books because they think I'm flaky or ungrateful or just plain weird? If sales dip?" I shook my head. "Then we're screwed. Not simply me. The town."

It came out harsher than I meant it to. But it was true.

And terrifying.

Blair didn't come back at me right away. Only watched me for a second, her glitter-tipped nails tapping quietly against her mug. When she finally spoke, her voice was lower. Gentler. "I know you're scared. And I know you're exhausted. But you're not doing this alone. You never have."

I looked away and let the silence press in for a breath, then two.

Then she nudged my leg with her toe. "Look, this isn't some big red carpet reveal. It's a panel. Two, tops. You'll be on stage with a couple of other authors, you'll answer some softball questions, sign a few things, and then you're done. Two or three days, in and out. Your hotel room is already booked."

"*My* hotel room? You aren't coming with me to this insanity?" Another knot of panic wedged itself behind my breastbone.

"Darling, you know I absolutely would, but it's my and Elena's anniversary, and she can't get away from school just now. Besides, it'll be good for you to get away for a few days on your own, without anyone from home—even me—yammering in your ear. I promise the whole appearance will be easy peasy."

"That's not helping."

She smiled faintly. "I wasn't trying to help. I was trying to ground you in the reality that this isn't the circus you're building up in your head."

My jaw tightened, but she pressed on.

"Right now, your readers are buzzing. They're excited, engaged, talking about the books again because you've been quiet, and the mystery's fueling the fandom. But that only lasts so long. You can't give them a book right now, so give them a face."

I stared down at my mug. The hot chocolate had cooled, the booze mellowed into the mix. It tasted like something soft and slow and dangerous—like something I'd buried deep and hoped would stay that way. Ambition. For myself.

But Blair had always known how to dig. "You've spent five months holding this town together. Let this be one thing that gives something back to you."

I groaned and let my head drop back against the couch cushions, staring up at the ceiling like it might hold a better answer than the one already forming in my gut.

I hated this idea.

Every molecule of my overworked, overstimulated, burned-the-hell-out introvert self wanted to say no. To dig in my heels and build a barricade of manila folders and municipal chaos around myself and hide until the world forgot my name—both of them.

But Blair's logic was maddeningly airtight.

The exposure would help. The timing was strategic. The cost of staying invisible might finally be too high.

"Fine," I muttered. "But I'm not going as me."

The effect was immediate. Blair lit up like someone had flipped a switch behind her eyes. "Then you'd better call in the big guns."

I closed my eyes and sighed. "Oh, no."

"Oh, yes."

She smirked so hard, it practically radiated smugness. "It's time to let Uncle Dee do his thing."

I groaned again, louder this time. "This is going to be a disaster."

She bounced off the couch, already reaching for her phone to text my uncle, who loved nothing more than a makeover and could transform anyone into anybody. Then she called over her shoulder, grinning with wicked delight, and contradicted me in a way only Blair could. "It's going to be epic."

Chapter 4

Ramsey

From the front, Vivienne Marchand's tailoring studio looked exactly like it always did—polished, pristine, and terrifyingly expensive. Floor-to-ceiling windows, sleek navy awnings, and her name etched in brushed steel above the door like it was a couture house in Paris instead of a high-end Charleston boutique. You half-expected someone to valet your car for daring to park nearby. She'd been custom tailoring my clothes for five years now.

I stepped inside, the hood of my jacket pulled low, hands in my pockets. Not that it helped. I could've been wearing a paper bag and people still would've clocked me as That Guy From The Sentinels. Being six-four and built like a brick wall didn't exactly lend itself to subtlety.

But I wasn't here for attention. I was here for the pickup.

"Ramsey!" Viv's voice cut through the boutique's gentle hum like a champagne cork. She swept out from behind a display of Italian wools, sharp, purple-tipped blonde bob swinging, tailor's tape draped like jewelry around her neck. "You're early."

"I was in the neighborhood." I wasn't, but punctuality seemed like the only way to say thank you for what she'd pulled off.

She tilted her head, appraising me as if I were another project for her needle to refine. "Good. Come on back. I've been dying for you to see it."

The front of the shop was all glass cases and restrained elegance—muted lighting, racks of custom suits lined up like soldiers, the quiet hush of a place where money talked softly. But as she led me past the main floor, the vibe shifted. Subtly at first, an unusual mannequin here, a bolt of heavy leather there. And then all at once—

The back room was pure, glorious fantasy chaos.

Gone were the clean lines and muted colors of the front showroom. Back here, the walls were papered in concept sketches and color swatches that definitely hadn't come from any bridal catalog. A half-finished mannequin stood in one corner, arms akimbo like it was daring someone to cross it, while a nearby worktable was strewn with patterns, buckles, and enough heavy-duty thread to rig a mainsail.

Viv clasped her hands like she was about to present a Michelin-star meal. "You have no idea how happy I am to work on something that doesn't involve another damned lapel."

I raised a brow. "You're telling me you don't dream of tasteful charcoal suits?"

She snorted. "Please. If I have to match one more groom to the exact shade of his fiancée's Pinterest board, I'm going to start drinking during fittings."

She moved deeper into the room, practically vibrating with glee. "But this?" She spun on her heel to face me, eyes alight. "This is the good stuff. And I still can't believe you, of all people, came to me with this commission."

I jerked a shoulder. "Figured if I was gonna do it, might as well do it right."

"Oh, you're doing it *very* right." She grinned. "When your email came through, I had to triple-check it wasn't some prank. But then I saw what you wanted—and who you wanted to be—and I dropped everything. Cleared my whole week." Her green eyes glinted with delight. "And let me tell you, working with someone who actually has a budget? A revelation. You'd be amazed how often fantasy clients try to haggle like they're shopping at a medieval flea market."

I grinned back. "Happy to spoil you for the rest."

She wagged a finger at me. "Oh, you have. I'm ruined. Completely. I may never go back to regular tailoring again. I got to work with the most *amazing* artists for this project. I'm seriously considering taking time off to master leatherwork myself."

I fixed her with a mock-serious look. "I can't go back to off the rack, Viv."

"I wouldn't leave you hanging, darling." She turned toward the far side of the room, where a rolling rack was draped in a protective cover. Her hands poised dramatically at the edge. "Now, ready to meet your alter ego?"

"Bring it."

With a gravitas worthy of unveiling a holy relic, Viv tugged back the cover on the rack and revealed the armor beneath piece by piece.

The helm was sleek and ceremonial, styled less for war and more for the mythology that followed in its wake. Matte black from crown to jaw, it covered the entire head with a smooth, sculpted design that hugged close, sweeping back behind the ears in clean, aerodynamic lines. The eye slits were narrow but precise, with enough visibility to suggest keen awareness behind them. The lower half—left open to expose the mouth and jaw—added a strange intimacy to the otherwise faceless facade.

Etched into the temples and curving down toward the nape were faint sigils from the Lost Kingdom of Verethan, barely visible unless the light caught them just right. Like secrets whispered onto steel. Or leather, in this case. Elegant and grim, like the character they represented. They matched the map in the book exactly.

Viv held it up with reverence. "I wanted intimidation with vulnerability. Mystery, but still room for expression. The mouth being visible? That was a choice."

Excitement began to bubble, and because this was Viv, I didn't bother to moderate. "It's perfect."

Her grin grew wider. "Wait for the rest."

Next were the chest piece and pauldrons. Layered leather in deep slate, burnished and worn like it had seen actual battles. The stitching was precise, bordering on obsessive, with faint diagonal scoring across the front like someone had raked claws through it mid-battle. I knew that mark. It was from the wyvern ambush scene in Chapter Twenty-Six of the first book.

Viv smoothed her hand over it. "I used treated suede here. Lightweight but holds its shape. And the lining won't roast you alive under con lighting."

Then came the undershirt in a deep forest green.

"Not everyone notices it, but fans will. This is the color he wore in the oath scene, when he swore to protect the last heir of Selenne."

That scene had lived rent-free in my brain since the first time I read it. He'd knelt in that blood-soaked corridor, armor cracked, mask dented, and made a vow to her with a voice like a funeral bell. Every line was burned into my memory.

Viv lifted a pair of gauntlets next—reinforced at the knuckles, dark with brushed metal accents. Then the bracers. The boots. All reinforced but elegant, like they were made for a man who moved like a shadow, not a tank.

"Now, the sword." Viv practically bounced as she gripped the hilt to draw it from its sheath. "This beauty was made by a weapons master out of Asheville, who does limited fantasy commissions. It's balanced, edged for presence, and yes—con-legal. Barely."

She passed it over carefully. The weight settled into my palm as if it belonged there. Long grip wrapped in black leather, crossguard etched with the same sigils as the helm. No jewel in the hilt. No flash. A weapon with purpose. I backed up for room and swung it once. Slow. Deliberate. It whistled through the air.

I looked up. Viv was watching me like she already knew what I was thinking.

"It's him," I said.

"Soren." She whispered the name in hushed delight, as if saying it too loudly might break the spell she'd wrought from leather and metal.

"Can I try it on?"

"Hell, yes! I've been waiting for this all week."

I stepped behind the folding screen Viv had set up in the corner of the workshop and stripped down, relishing the buzz of anticipation I usually only felt right before going onto the field for a game.

"Ready?" Viv's voice floated from the other side of the screen like she was announcing a magic trick.

"Let's do it."

Her small hand appeared behind the screen with the dark forest green undershirt that would serve as the base layer. I tugged it on, appreciating how the soft fabric fit close to my skin.

"Trousers next." The disembodied hand appeared again, with leather pants.

I slid them on. The butter-soft leather was heavier than anything I was used to wearing, snug without being stiff.

"Come on out, and I'll show you how to adjust the closures."

I stepped from behind the screen.

Viv did up the hidden fasteners, then had me turn so she could check the fit at the hips. "Lift your knees. Do a squat or two. See how they feel."

I did as ordered, surprised by how the pants didn't restrict my range of movement. "Close, but not too tight."

Satisfied with that, Viv dragged over a stool so she could help me on with the chest piece. I held still as she guided it over my head and settled it onto my shoulders, securing it with a series of straps down the sides and back. The weight shifted my balance in a way that felt authentic. Which was exactly what I'd commissioned.

"Try moving your arms."

I rolled my shoulders, bent my elbows, and made a few slow movements like I was loosening up before a game. With each motion, I was aware of the armor, but I wasn't restricted.

"Good. Range is right where it should be." She passed me the bracers next, then the gauntlets. These I buckled myself, since I'd be on my own to actually dress for the con, and I wasn't unaccustomed to gearing up. The boots came last. Comfortable, yet sufficiently sturdy to feel like I could kick some serious ass, if needed.

Finally, the helm.

Viv handed it over with ceremony. "Moment of truth."

I turned it in my hands, letting the overhead light catch on the faint sigils etched along the sides. Then I slid it on. The interior fit like a glove, and the weight balanced perfectly across my crown and jaw.

I looked at her through the narrow slits.

She stepped back, arms folded, and tilted her head as she took me in from head to toe. "You're gonna break hearts and cause meltdowns."

I flexed one arm and shifted my weight again, listening to the creak of the leather. "Let's hope they keep it to meltdowns. I'm not signing any armor-related injuries." That might be worse than the cleavage I'd been asked—and politely declined —to sign in my football career.

Viv laughed, looping her tape measure back around her neck. "Seriously, though, I love that you went old school. Soren from the first series? That's proper fan behavior."

I shrugged. "Honestly, I don't even remember how I found the book. Probably insomnia and a digital sale. But that story hit me right over the head. I was obsessed. Stayed up all night to read it, even though I had practice the next day. Then I nabbed the second one and did it all over again. My ass was dragging the rest of the week, but it was so worth it."

"Stuck around for the slow burn, didn't you?"

"I mean, I had to know if he ever actually won Meriel's love."

Viv mimed a swoon. "Took for-freaking-ever, but that payoff? Chef's kiss. What do you think of the new series?"

"Strong. Different tone from that more classic fantasy vibe, but she pulled it off."

"Still no word on the next one, though. It's been over a year. There's not even a preorder up. You'd think with all the hype we'd at least get a title drop."

"They're big books. She's probably working to get it exactly right."

She groaned dramatically. "I need to know if the king lives

or dies. My group chat is in full civil war. Someone rage quit over a fan theory last week."

"Was it that one that suggested that Kane is her half-brother?"

"Yes! Maybe you'll find out at the con." Viv turned a circle and let out a squee. "Oooo, I can't believe you get to meet Kella Harmon!"

"Well, I'll get to theoretically be in a room with her for a panel. I don't know that I'll get to actually meet her."

"Still! That woman is a freaking ghost! No pictures of her online. No nothing! She's almost as much a mystery as the plot of the next book."

I chuckled. "If I can get her autograph, I'll have it made out to your entire book club."

Viv gave me a narrow-eyed glare. "Shaw, do I look like a woman who shares?"

I laughed. "Just you, then. Let 'em die of envy."

"Damn straight." She tapped the edge of the helm. "Alright. Soren's ready for the convention floor. Go ahead and get back in your street clothes, and we'll get him packed up for the trip."

In less than ten minutes, I'd changed clothes, and we'd gotten the costume carefully packed up, including the foam-lined case for the helm.

"I expect all the pictures of Soren in full glory."

Shouldering the bag and tucking the helm case under one arm, I gave Viv a salute. "Understood. And thanks again. I couldn't have done this without you."

"Please promise to continue to embrace your hidden nerd-dom, so I can do this again in the future."

I grinned. "I wouldn't trust anyone else."

As I stepped out of the shop and into the January chill, my phone vibrated in my pocket.

Fishing it out, I saw Bodie's name flashing on the display. I hit answer. "Hey, man. How are things going in your neck of the woods?"

"January's been a bitch, but we're holding. Power's mostly back, patching through the Ridge. Bridge crew's slogging on. Town green's still a mess—mud pit with ambition—but people are showing up as volunteers for boots-on-the-ground kind of stuff." Clear fatigue underscored his usual easy tone.

I forced a smile I knew he couldn't see. "That's good. And you?"

"I'm surviving. Not sure I can say too much beyond that. How about you? Season's through. Sorry about that last game."

"Win some, lose some. I was ready for a break, so I'm fine with this. We'll be back stronger next season."

"You had that double cheeseburger yet?"

I laughed as I unlocked the truck and set my cargo into the backseat. "I've had two. With bacon and Cajun fries."

"Priorities."

"How's the family?" I kept my tone easy and conversational.

"Oh, you know. Grandma Elsie's keeping the whole damned town fed. She's been keeping a big pot of community burgoo going on the daily, with donations from folks. Anybody who can't afford to pay still gets to eat. Colter's running all the electricians in town crazy about the fire code. Dean's finally losing some of the post-deployment jumpy. Fletcher and Gunner are both up to their eyeballs in infrastructure rebuilds and debris clearance. And Dad's keeping Everly and Hutton on their toes with his recovery down in Nashville."

I swallowed and did my best to maintain a polite tone of interest. "And Alia?"

"Alia's Alia. Single-handedly keeping the town from

collapsing. Burning the candle at both ends and in the middle. If there's a problem, she's found it—and fixed it."

My heart squeezed. Holding everything together had been Alia Gibson's default state as long as I'd known her. And damn if I didn't admire the hell out of that, even though I'd always wanted to be her shelter so she didn't have to.

And wouldn't her brother have plenty to say about that if he knew?

As far as Bodie was aware, I was just another brother to add to her already extensive collection. The reality was that I'd been carrying a torch for my best friend's twin for basically my entire adult life. She was the path I hadn't taken.

That didn't stop the wanting, though. Time hadn't dimmed it either. Our lives had been on diverging paths for more years than I cared to think about, so I'd kept my distance, as much to save my sanity as anything else.

But as Bodie finished giving me the update on the family and the rest of town, I considered that maybe, when I was done with this conference, it was high time I paid a visit to my friends to lend a hand. It sounded like they could use it.

Chapter 5

Alia

Dark had fallen by the time I slipped into the house. Strains of cheerful trumpets and sassy trombones playing classic New Orleans jazz drifted from the kitchen, along with the scents of spicy sausage and the mix of onions, bell peppers, and celery that was known as the holy trinity of Cajun cooking. Given the weather, I was betting on gumbo. Uncle Dee was either homesick for his former adopted hometown, or he'd had a good day and was feeling nostalgic. I hoped for the latter as I slipped off my boots and padded past an endless parade of colorful paintings from New Orleans street artists. I loved how he filled his house with all the things he treasured from his years in the Big Easy. The color and vibrance fit him down to the ground. But nothing was more colorful or vibrant than Uncle Dee himself.

His close-cropped salt-and-pepper hair gleamed under the kitchen lights, and his wire-rimmed glasses had a subtle purple tint that made him look both wise and fabulous. Accurate on both counts. A deep-plum sweater hugged his trim frame, sleeves pushed up to reveal forearms dusted with flour and spice. Dark jeans and the fuzzy leopard-print slippers I'd given him for Christmas completed the look.

As I stepped into the room, he turned from the stove, his narrow hips twitching in time to the music behind a kitchen apron that read *Slay Now, Simmer Later.* "Hey, Buttercup." His long fingers snagged my hand and, with an expert tug, he spun me into a dance.

I did not want to dance after the day I'd had. "Uncle Dee."

"You need to loosen up. C'mon, Sugar pie."

There was no refusing Uncle Dee in any mood, so I tried to find the rhythm to follow his lead. By the time the song ended, I had to admit he'd been right. I felt looser and lighter for the effort. More so for the giant squeeze of a bear hug at the end. I'd needed that most of all.

With a sigh, I set my head against his shoulder. "Thanks."

He stroked a hand down my hair and glanced past me. "No Blair? When I got her 911 text, I figured she'd be coming with you. I know she hates to miss a makeover."

"Just me. I wanted to talk to you on my own."

Some of his good humor turned to concern. "Everything okay?"

I sucked in a breath. "It will be." That was the other mantra I was living by these days.

"Did Elena feed you?"

My lips quirked. "No. She wasn't home yet."

"Then you'll have some gumbo. If I know you, the most you've eaten today is half a biscuit and a string cheese."

That was a bit too close for comfort. "Don't forget the coffee. Grandma kept me well supplied there."

Uncle Dee made a rude noise. "Baby girl, you cannot live on coffee alone, no matter how hard you try. Now sit."

He was just about the only person on earth who could order me to do a thing, and I'd do it without complaint. I took my seat at the table he'd painted chili pepper red, watching as he bustled about, filling bowls with the fragrant stew.

"Where did you even get andouille sausage? The market's only had the basics since they reopened."

Uncle Dee slid a bowl in front of me. "You aren't the only one who gets paid in food. I helped Dewey Walker salvage what was left of his late mama's hope chest after the flood. Poor thing was warped to hell, but I managed to clean and refinish the pieces that could be saved. Dewey was so grateful, he made some out of one of the deer he brought down last month. This is the first time I've tried it. You'll have to tell me if it passes muster."

"It smells fantastic." To echo the point, my stomach made a growl loud enough to be heard over the music.

With a laugh, he turned the stereo down a bit and joined me at the table with his own bowl and a few slices of sourdough on a plate. "Now, do you want to tell me what this 911 makeover text was about?"

"I need to work up to it."

His shrewd eyes studied me over the steaming bowl. "Would wine help?"

"Probably."

Without a word, he retrieved a bottle of Rioja from the small rack in the cabinet and poured us each a glass. Then he launched into tales of his day, which had been far more entertaining than mine—not a high bar. As he told me about helping Miss Loretta Caldwell salvage what was left of her mother's vintage wedding gown after the flood took out half her attic, talking her down from turning it into bunting for the rec center reopening, and convincing her to let him work some restoration magic instead, a bit more of my own day slid off my shoulders. This was why I'd moved in with Uncle Dee after the flood, instead of to my father's house or with Grandma Elsie or one of my brothers. I'd never be able to relax with any of the rest of them, because there'd always be something to *do* or take care of.

Uncle Dee took care of me. Insofar as I'd let him.

"I also wrangled most of the Sasspatch Society into assembling emergency glam kits for flood-displaced seniors ahead of the winter community dinner—just because you've lost your house doesn't mean you should lose your lashes, right?"

"Thank you." The words slipped out in a beat of silence as he paused to take a bite.

His perfectly shaped brows arched up. "For what?"

"For so many things. For letting me live here. For feeding me. For giving up your life and coming back here to help after Mama died. You were the only reason I survived it. The only reason I felt comfortable leaving for college and law school. Some days, you're still my only real tether to sanity. I can't ever repay you for that."

His hand reached out and covered mine. "You don't ever have to repay me for a thing. And I didn't give up my life, sweet girl. I up and changed it. In case you missed it, I'm happy to be home. Happy to be near the family. It's been a privilege to watch you grow into the woman you've become."

My throat went thick, and my eyes began to burn. "Damn it, don't you get me going. It'll get you going, and that eyeliner is too perfect to ruin, even this late in the day."

"You're not wrong about that. No tears for either of us." His fingers squeezed mine. "Now, are you ready to tell me what it is you need my help for?"

I used the heel of my bread to sop up the last of the roux from the gumbo. "You're sworn to secrecy. You can't tell anyone."

One brow lifted in clear insult. "You are aware of my policy of confidentiality. I can keep a secret."

"I know you can. I'm just saying that this can't go any further."

"Understood. So this isn't a glam-up or rebranding?"

"No. Not like you're thinking." I ate the last of the bread and washed it down with more wine. "I need to be less me."

His head tipped to one side. "You're gonna have to be more specific. What is this for?"

Suddenly nervous about admitting this out loud, I knotted my fingers together. "I did a thing."

"Like a signed-up-for-speed-dating-in-Asheville sort of thing?"

I blinked. "No."

"Too bad. Your love life is criminally sad."

"We are not here to talk about my love life or lack thereof."

Uncle Dee waved an imperious hand. "Sorry. Go on, baby."

Maybe if I said it fast, like ripping off a Band-Aid.

"I have a secret, surprisingly successful romantasy pen name, and I've got to appear in public at a conference."

Now Uncle Dee was the one blinking. "You've been writing books?"

Pressing my lips together, I nodded.

"How long have you been sitting on this?"

"Since law school. It was never supposed to be anything. I wrote for stress relief. But then Blair found them and self-published them without asking me. I didn't find out until she showed me the first check."

He whistled long and low. "Bet you were right het up about that."

"It's one of the few major fights we've ever had. It wasn't a ton of money, but every little bit helped in law school, so I left that first book up and wrote more. People liked them. And then they went viral and have stayed that way."

"Viral like...?"

"Viral like it's replaced my income as a lawyer, and I've been secretly funding projects around town, including keeping The Commissary open when things got really bad."

His mouth dropped open. "Does Mama know?"

"Are you kidding? Grandma would skin me alive if she knew I'd been putting my own money into keeping things going. Since Blair does the books, I've been able to keep it quiet."

"We're gonna set that piece aside for the moment. But, baby, this is incredible! Why wouldn't you tell any of us? I mean, not about funding The Commissary—I understand you value your hide—but the rest?"

"That's... complicated." I sipped more wine to give myself time to pull my thoughts together. "My whole life, I've been on display. On top of essentially stepping into Mama's role for my siblings when she died, I'm a Gibson in Gibson Hollow. I'm the eldest. The overachiever. People have expectations of me."

I rolled the stem of my glass between my fingers. "The writing is the one thing that's really mine. No one has expectations for it but me."

"Your readers don't?"

I waved a dismissive hand. "I mean, they do. But they don't have any idea I'm Kella Harmon. There's not a thing out there about me online for anyone to connect to *me*. No photos. No bio that says anything real. Blair runs my social media, and I don't touch it. That's the way I wanted it. I write the books I want to read, so I don't have to please anyone but me. If people find out, then suddenly there's all this pressure of *their* expectations. And I'm already having trouble stringing two thoughts together since the flood took over my life and brain."

Uncle Dee sipped his wine and absorbed all that. "So why this conference thing?"

I huffed a breath. "Blair. She signed me up for a panel without asking. Per usual. Because she knew I'd say no."

"Ah, ye classic ask forgiveness rather than permission."

"It's literally her favorite tactic. Since the next book in my series won't be out anytime soon, she thought it would buy me some time. And she's probably right. But for the sake of my own sanity, I cannot walk out on that stage as me."

"So we need to make a whole new woman."

"Yes."

He rose from the table with a familiar spark in his eye and crooked a finger for me to follow. "Come on, Buttercup. You know where the magic lives."

I trailed after him through the cozy hall, past framed family photos and a signed poster from his days performing at The Bourbon Belle, until we reached the third bedroom. It was technically a guest room, but no one had slept in there in years.

He opened the door with a flourish, and I stepped into the wonderland of transformation that was Uncle Dee's closet.

It wasn't merely racks of clothes; it was a curated archive of personalities and eras, a rainbow riot of sequins and feathers, leather and lace, glitter and tulle. Wig stands lined one wall like spectators, each one crowned with a different color and cut—sleek bobs, cascading curls, bold fantasy styles dyed in impossible shades. Shoes, organized by heel height and sass level, filled cubbies like a high-fashion armory. And in the corner, a vanity table sparkled with jars of rhinestones, palettes of eyeshadow, and lipsticks in shades that defied the laws of nature.

This was where Uncle Dee became Delilah Devine. And standing here, it was impossible not to believe in the power of reinvention.

My breath caught as I stepped inside, letting the door shut behind me. This wasn't a room; it was a portal. A place where rules didn't apply and expectations could be shed like a second skin. For someone like me—someone who'd spent her whole life being watched, judged, and expected to hold everything together—this room felt like freedom. Like possibility.

He turned to me and framed my face between his palms. "I'll do this for you. I'll help you hide. But someday, baby, I hope you'll let people see the real you. Because you're the real star."

I didn't make any promises, but I grasped his wrists and smiled in gratitude. "Thanks, Uncle Dee."

"Now, step up on that footstool and let me measure you. We've got work to do."

Chapter 6

Ramsey

@BookishDreamer24: OMG! Just spotted a guy in full Soren cosplay at #GARomantasyCon and I'm DYING! 😵 His armor looks so authentic! Getting a pic with him later! 📸 #CrownedInAshAndFlame #SorenForever

@FantasyBookNerd: Two hours until the Romantasy Royalty panel, and I'm already in line! Worth it to see Kella Harmon in person! 🙏 #GARomantasyCon #KellaHarmonFan

@ReadingRavenGirl: This Soren cosplayer at #GARomantasyCon is PERFECTION. Those leather pants should be illegal! 🔥 Anyone else spotted him? I think I'm in love! #HotCosplay #BookBoyfriendIRL

@PageTurnerQueen: My book haul so far is INSANE and it's only day one of #GARomantasyCon! Can't wait to get these signed after the panel! 📚 #BookHaul #TakeMyMoney

"**O**h my God! It's Soren!"

"Can we get a selfie with you?"

Caught off guard for maybe the tenth time in the past hour, I paused. The girls couldn't have been more than nineteen or twenty. Dressed in book-themed sweatshirts that proclaimed *Emotionally Attached to Fictional People* and *Certified Smut Scholar* respectively, the pair of them were practically vibrating as they looked up at me in adoration.

I wasn't unfamiliar with that expression, but getting stopped for something that had nothing to do with football? Yeah, that was new.

Fixing the half-smile I'd been using all afternoon into place, I nodded and straightened, my hand on the hilt of my sword. The girls took up positions flanking me, and we mugged for the camera.

"This is so perfect! Our friends are gonna die. You look exactly like him!"

My hand to my brow in a salute, I gave a half bow. "Ladies."

The sound of their tittering giggles followed me as I strode away.

I was starting to have a few regrets about my choice of attire. Not because I looked like an idiot—there'd been too many excited fans for that—but because only a fraction of the conference attendees were cosplaying. Most were dressed in some variety of reader-centric merch, like these two. Outfits they could wear to Target without getting stared at.

And then there was me, with my bespoke armor. There hadn't been any of Viv's predicted broken hearts or meltdowns yet, but at this point, it was only a matter of time and statistics.

Before being waylaid by anyone else, I joined the throngs flowing into the biggest of the conference rooms, where the panel featuring Kella Harmon would be held. Rows of chairs were arranged in four sections, trailing back from the stage all the way to the rear of the enormous room. Seats were filling up as I worked my way closer to the front. My size definitely worked to my advantage for that, as I towered over most of the attendees, so I saw the open spots. As I wasn't trying to sit with anyone else, it was easier to find a single seat on the end of the third row, on the far right of the stage. I'd have preferred a straight-on view, but the middle sections of seats were already packed, and with the sword, I needed to be on an end so as not to impede anyone else.

The moment I lowered myself to the chair, there was a minor stampede to the seats around me. A trio of elderly women somehow made it to the front of the pack.

The smallest of the three, a bird-boned woman with improbably auburn hair and a sweater embroidered with *Villain Era, Chapter One* in sparkly yarn, batted her lashes at me. "Excuse me, sonny. Can we slip by you right here?"

The manners my mama had drilled into me as a boy kicked in. "Yes, ma'am." I straightened, stepping out of the aisle so the three of them could file by.

Every single one of them managed to trip on the way, such that their hands landed somewhere on my person and needed steadying. I recognized a fake when I saw one, and these three clearly had plenty of practice.

Number two—whose sweatshirt read *My TBR pile could kill a man*—eyed me up and down. "I wonder where I can get one of these getups for Percy?"

"Custom made, I'm afraid," I told her.

The third one—*Book Hangover Survivor*—hummed in approval, her gaze lingering on my leather breeches in a way that had me sweating more than the leather itself. "Worth every penny." She held out a hand in expectation.

Realizing she expected me to literally hand her into the seat, I hesitated before deciding, *in for a penny, in for a pound.* I carefully took her gnarled fingers and helped her the four feet to her seat.

She and her friends lapsed into a chorus of what a "nice young man" I was, and promptly launched into the expected Southern-people form of small talk. "Where are you from?"

Knowing this meant either where I lived now or where I was born, I opted for the latter. No reason to give any extra details that might connect me to the Sentinels. "Little town outside Birmingham. Y'all?"

"Wishful, Mississippi," *Villain Era* said proudly. Then she dove straight into an outright interrogation about my favorite romantasy books. The three of them clearly weren't expecting me to be able to hold my own in the conversation and were delighted to find out that I wasn't "just a hot bod in leather."

"Now tell us, which smutty scenes are your favorite?" Villain Era batted her lashes again, and I struggled not to choke on air as the collective group of women on all the surrounding rows seemed to lean in for the answer.

"Uh..."

Hands clapped twice from the stage. A woman stood with a microphone in hand. "Alright, folks, if y'all can find your seats, we're about to get started. Welcome to the most anticipated panel of the weekend: Romantasy Royalty!"

A cheer rose around the room, and I joined in with a half-hearted clap, still trying to recover from the elderly interrogation squad to my left.

"Our authors today have built worlds we love, villains we thirst for, and heroes we'd happily sell our souls to kiss. Please welcome A.M. Sinclair, Diana Ferguson, and Kella Harmon!"

The crowd went wild, whistling and hollering like we were at a rock concert. I was grateful for my height, as I was still easily able to spot the authors filing in from a door to the right of the stage as the emcee read their bios.

A.M. Sinclair came first. She was all angles and long platinum hair, with a presence that absolutely commanded the room. I wouldn't have been at all surprised if she could press those stiletto heels into service as a weapon, should the need arise.

Diana Ferguson couldn't have been more different in a floral skirt and hot pink sweater. Her sunshiny smile made it all the more surprising that she wrote some of the most bloodthirsty, battle-heavy romantasy out there. It only went to prove you couldn't judge a book—or author—by its cover. Then again, maybe she killed off everyone who annoyed her. That was probably pretty cathartic.

And finally, the woman I'd come here for. Kella Harmon. Her step stuttered only once as she moved onto the stage. Red hair tumbled in soft waves around her shoulders. She was all polish and quiet confidence, in black-framed glasses, and a fitted blazer over a dark, silky top, with slim pants and a pair of bright red heels that belonged on a catwalk. Her lipstick matched the shoes. There was something about the way she moved, the angle of her chin, the shape of that painted mouth, that tugged at the back of my brain, like a piece of a forgotten dream.

Why did she look so familiar? I'd never seen a photo. She

was notoriously reclusive. It was a huge part of the mystery surrounding her online.

Shaking off the question, I watched as she crossed the stage, shook hands with the emcee, and took her seat in one of the armchairs arranged in a conversational grouping. The only sign of her nerves was the fact that she didn't look directly at the crowd. I was pretty sure her gaze was fixed on the center aisle, where no one stood.

I kept my eyes on Kella as the questions began, only dimly listening as each of the other authors spoke about how they'd gotten into writing. Then it was her turn.

"What about you, Kella? How did you get started writing?"

She crossed her legs, her fingers flexing on the arm of the chair. "I actually started writing back in college, after a really crappy breakup. My ex very publicly cheated on me, so I ended up writing a short story where he got horribly devoured by a terrible monster in retribution. That monster was the basis of the narkesh from *Crowned in Ash and Flame.*"

Nothing in that soft, smooth voice betrayed the nerves I saw in her hands. And still as she spoke, that niggle kept insisting I knew her somehow. Which was ridiculous.

Someone from the back of the room shouted out, "Did the ex get away with it? I mean, did he ever pay for it?"

Those red lips curved in unmistakable amusement. "Let's just say he got too up close and personal with Thunder and Lightning."

As the rest of the room puzzled over that, I fought to keep my jaw from hitting the floor. Because I *knew* this story. I was Lightning. Bodie was Thunder. It had been our dual nickname back in our college ball days. I'd been at the bar the night Alia had caught the douchenozzle she'd been dating making out with another girl. Her brother and I had meted out punishment on the cheating ex during practice on the football field. There was no possible way that was a coincidence.

Holy shit. My favorite author was actually Alia Gibson.

As I stared intently at her, I finally saw it, though she'd obviously done something with makeup to subtly alter her face. Plus the wig and glasses. Uncle Dee could probably be credited for all that. No sense in *not* taking advantage of having a former drag queen as an uncle. Finally, Kella Harmon's reclusivity made sense. Alia had always been a huge introvert. She hated being the center of attention. I wondered how she'd even ended up on this panel.

Blair, no doubt. I felt sure she had something to do with it. If anybody in Alia's circle was aware of these books, it would be her. Those two had been thick as thieves since freshman year. She was Alia's ride or die. Not surprising. When Blair had come out to her own family, she'd been brutally rejected. After that, she'd become an honorary Gibson, moving back to Gibson Hollow when Alia did after grad school. The fact that she'd met the love of her life there had been icing on the cake.

As the panel continued with one question after another, I drank Alia in, soaking up the sight of her in a way I hadn't been able to do since college, back when I'd thought we still stood a chance of being... something. Before I had to choose between her and my lifelong dream of going pro. Not that she knew any of that. I'd never confessed my feelings for her.

But I still knew her. I could still read her, and I didn't miss the way she was getting more and more uncomfortable as the questions continued. The tremble in her hands got more pronounced, and the flush in her cheeks brighter.

"Let's talk about next books! Kella, I know I speak for all of us when I say we're eager for news of when the last book in the series will be out."

The flush drained away, and Alia seemed to lose her voice

entirely for a moment. To buy herself some time, she picked up a bottle of water from the small table beside her chair, but her hand shook so hard, it sloshed out before she could actually drink. With a hard swallow, she finally whispered, "I don't know."

Fuck. Of course she didn't. Because her real world was falling apart. She was busy saving a whole damned town and probably hadn't had a moment to even think about the story, let alone write it.

But she wouldn't share that, because it was personal, and almost nothing she'd said today qualified as that.

Instead, she sat there, having a fucking panic attack, while the tenor of the crowd around me began to turn irritable and ugly. A few voices called out, "Come on!" "Tell us something!" "We need to know!"

The mic caught the hitch in her breath.

The pause stretched.

Too long.

Someone hissed out a dramatic sigh.

Another called, "Don't leave us hanging!"

"Give us a date!"

"She's probably blocked," someone muttered behind me, not even bothering to keep it quiet. "She's scared to finish it."

A wave of murmurs followed, cresting on a sharp-edged tide of entitlement disguised as enthusiasm. The fans weren't asking—they were demanding. Like she owed them answers, owed them pieces of herself she hadn't signed up to give. The energy in the room shifted from eager to restless, then restless to ugly. All that devotion, flipping on a dime. And she was still sitting there, cheeks pale now, blinking fast like she was holding something back.

She cleared her throat, started to lift the mic—and faltered. Her lips parted, but nothing came out.

"Seriously?" snapped someone else. "We waited for that?"

The air around me sharpened. Tight. I could practically feel the heat of her embarrassment rolling off the stage.

And that was it.

To hell with this. I wasn't gonna leave her up there to drown.

Chapter 7

Alia

I couldn't breathe.

The crowd had gone quiet in that awful, expectant way that wasn't silence at all. It was pressure. Heat. A thousand pairs of eyes locked on me, waiting for a reply I didn't have. Waiting for something—*anything*—that might make the months of waiting and speculating and rereading worth it.

I had nothing to give them. The idea of admitting my failures in front of them made a pit open in my gut. There was the truth of everything going on at home, but that seemed like an excuse, and I didn't want to give that much of my reality away.

My fingers clenched tight around the water bottle in my lap. Too tight. My palms were damp, and I was sure I looked every bit as rattled as I felt. The flush had drained out of my face, but my ears were burning, and my vision was going swimmy around the edges.

I knew this sensation.

Tight chest. Short breaths. The roar of my pulse in my ears like incoming waves I couldn't outrun.

Panic attack.

Some distant, rational part of my brain slapped the label on it, like naming the monster made it easier to fight. But there was no fighting this. No escaping the stage, the spotlight, or the crowd I was letting down in real time.

This was why I hadn't wanted to be here.

This was why I wore the wig and the glasses and kept my head down and my name hidden.

Because the moment they saw me—really *saw* me—they'd want more. And if I didn't have it, if I couldn't give it to them, this was what I'd get.

Judgment. Blame. The kind of pressure that crushed the words right out of me.

Someone in the back called, "Just say you're blocked!"

Another sharper voice added, "She doesn't even *want* to finish it."

The crowd rumbled again. Every frustrated remark, every disappointed sigh, every disillusioned grump struck me like a blow, wearing away whatever scraps of composure I had left.

Then came the roar.

At first I thought it was the noise in my head peaking, panic tipping over into full collapse. But no—this was real. Audible. Movement in the crowd. Gasps. Screams. A thunder of boots against the floor.

A man charged the stage from the left, dressed head to toe in matte-black leather armor that molded to a body straight out of the pages of a book. Straight out of the pages of *my* book. The helm that showed only his darkly bearded jaw, the sword strapped at his hip—it was all straight out of my first caffeine-fueled draft of *Crowned in Ash and Flame*.

What in the actual hell?

Either I was full-on hallucinating from oxygen deprivation, or the actual, fictional, not-real hero of my book had just stormed into this very real conference hall.

He mounted the stage in a single, terrifyingly graceful leap.

For half a second, the whole room froze as he *growled* at them.

Then he stepped between me and the crowd like a wall of muscle and menace, and scooped me up from the chair like I weighed nothing. I dropped both the water and the microphone. My breath whooshed out as I landed against a hard chest and warm leather.

"Time to go, princess." That dark, rumbling voice and the warmth of his breath ghosting against my ear sent a shiver down my spine that had nothing to do with the anxiety that still had hold of my body.

Maybe I should've asked questions. Demanded answers. Screamed about being manhandled by a fictional figment of my imagination.

But instead, I clung tighter to the edges of his breastplate and let him carry me off the stage.

Because staying meant drowning.

And this? This was oxygen.

The crowd was roaring now as he whisked me offstage. Not in outrage, but in excitement. Phones were up, flashes going off like fireworks. Someone cheered. Someone else shouted, "Best panel ending ever!"

God, this was going to be all over the internet.

I buried my face against his shoulder as he moved, the jostling rhythm of his stride all that tethered me to reality. The solid curve of his arms didn't feel like a stranger's. It was somehow familiar. But none of that made sense. I definitely didn't have some secret colossus in my back pocket. For a wild moment, I wondered if Blair had hired an undercover bodyguard to save me from myself. A just-in-case backup plan.

But fond as my bestie was of making a spectacle, I didn't think even she would've thought of this.

We passed stagehands and volunteers, a few blinking in surprise, but nobody tried to stop us. Nobody even asked a question. Maybe they thought it was part of the show.

My armored rescuer carried me through a warren of hallways until the noise of the panel faded behind us, the echo of his steps bouncing off cement walls. Finally, he ducked into a narrow side hall and shouldered open a heavy gray door into what had to be a storage room. Fluorescent lights buzzed overhead, illuminating metal shelves full of table linens, extra signage, and cords in tangled piles.

He kicked the door shut behind us, and suddenly, belatedly, my brain caught up.

I had been carried off by a masked man in full armor. To a secondary location.

What the hell was I thinking?

This was how the true crime podcast started. Somewhere, my police-chief brother was having a conniption fit via twin intuition alone.

My rescuer gently deposited me into a chair shoved into a corner. Leather creaked as he knelt before me, stripping off his gauntlets and taking both my hands in his massive ones. "Breathe."

Yeah, okay, that seemed like a good idea. I couldn't think clearly to get out of this situation until my heart stopped trying to pound its way out of my chest.

I tried to drag air into my lungs, but my throat locked up in protest.

"Focus on me."

As if I could think about anything else when one of my fantasies had evidently come to life at my time of need. I stared into the dark, shadowed eyes behind the helm, unconsciously syncing my labored breaths to the rise and fall of those broad, armored shoulders. His strong fingers easily encompassed my whole hands, but they touched me with such care, I wasn't afraid. That skin-to-skin connection anchored me, letting me know this wasn't a dream or a hallucination. This man—whoever he actually was—had legitimately saved me from my humiliation in front of all those people.

As the panic finally began to ebb, I tore my gaze from his eyes to take in more details about the costume itself. The runes etched into the helm were a perfect match for the designs I'd put in the book. The chest piece was layered leather in deep slate, with claw-like scoring across the front that looked torn straight from a wyvern ambush. The bracers, the boots, the subtle green beneath it all—details I'd obsessed over in my own writing, now brought vividly to life at what I knew was no little expense. Someone somewhere was very, *very* talented.

"Soren, I presume?"

He grinned, a flash of straight, white teeth through his short beard, which was really all I could see of his face other than the mask. "At your service, my lady."

Damn, that was hot. Then again, I'd always had a thing for men in masks.

I sensed no malice in him, and I couldn't stop myself from smiling back. "This isn't going to turn into some kind of *Misery* situation, is it? Because I promise that's really not going to help my writer's block."

He huffed a laugh that rolled over me like warmed honey. "No. But you looked like you needed a save up there."

"You're not wrong. Agreeing to come here was a mistake."

Sympathy twisted his mouth. "Not much for crowds, huh?" His tone held no judgment, for which I was immensely grateful.

"That's putting it mildly. So, thank you for the intervention. Maybe it'll help distract everybody from the fact that I still don't have a release date for the last book."

I realized my hands were still in his, and his thumbs were stroking the pulse points in my wrists. My heart sped up again for entirely different reasons as a potent punch of awareness shot through me. How could it not, when he was literally my walking fantasy? I couldn't quite stop myself from licking my lips. His eyes followed the gesture, something darkening there.

So, I wasn't the only one aware of this chemistry.

I definitely wouldn't complain. Attraction was a million percent more pleasant to focus on than the panic.

"You... aren't exactly what I pictured as my typical reader."

That smile of amusement deepened. "What? Appreciators of badass fight scenes, terrifying monsters, and deeply emotional love stories can't look like me?"

"I suppose they *can*; they just usually don't." He couldn't possibly have been further from the conference center full of women I'd been hiding from most of the day.

"My *Support Your Local Book Hoarder* shirt was in the wash."

I snorted, trying to imagine what he looked like under all this armor. But my brain continued to snag on all the details. So much had gone into this costume. I was equal parts impressed, flattered, and intrigued.

Needing to get myself more on even footing, I stood. "Whenever I finally get the last book written, I'll have to get you a signed copy as a thank you for the rescue."

Without releasing my hands, he rose to his full height, pulling me to my feet. I tipped my head back, looking up and up and up. Dear God, he had to be at least 6'4". Taller in the boots. Even in my heels, he had at least eight inches on me.

One corner of his mouth quirked. "That'd be awesome. But there's something I'd like even more."

"What's that?"

The other corner of his mouth curved in a flirty smile.

"Well, heroes are frequently favored with a kiss as their reward."

I went brows up, and he immediately backpedaled.

"You can 100% say no, and I will not be offended. It occurs to me that I've dragged you into what amounts to a closet, and that was probably not actually cool. I swear I have no nefarious intentions. It was only a thought."

A thought that held more than a little appeal in the name of drawing out this fantasy. "If I say no to you, I'm pretty sure my best friend will disown me."

There went that quirked smile again. Why did it seem so familiar?

"Can't have that," he murmured.

"No. No, we can't."

Oddly emboldened by the disguise so carefully crafted by Uncle Dee, I stepped into my rescuer, closing the small space between us. He released my hands to curl his around my waist. I slid mine up the planes of that armored chest, a part of my brain filing away the sensation so I'd be able to write about it later. I lifted to my toes, and he met me halfway.

The moment his lips touched mine, I was catapulted back to college, to the last masked man I'd kissed. Ramsey Shaw. My brother's best friend. The guy I'd thought would be a new start after the same terrible relationship that had begun my writing journey. We'd had one evening together at a masquerade party, but in the end, he hadn't known it was me. Or if he had, he'd never pursued it. So my hopes had been dashed, and I'd moved on. But no one else had ever made me feel like he did.

This man did.

Every nerve ending lit up, and I leaned into it, into him, wanting more.

His massive arms wrapped around me, hauling me closer. He angled his head, and I instantly acquiesced, allowing him to take the kiss deeper. A groan rumbled low in his throat. A groan I'd heard before, in a dark parking lot, ten long years ago.

As the taste of him flooded my system, I *knew*.

This wasn't just someone who made me feel like Ramsey.

It *was* Ramsey.

Dressed as the hero from my first book.

The one I'd based on *him*.

Chapter 8

Ramsey

I f I hadn't already been certain that Kella Harmon was Alia, I'd have known from that little whimper of pleasure she made as she pressed closer. That whimper had haunted my dreams for a decade, ever since I cut my own heart out and walked away from her. And now she was right here.

God, I'd missed the taste of her. The feel of her in my arms. I'd only kissed her twice before, at the masquerade all those years ago, but the memory hadn't dimmed. Neither had the chemistry between us. I wanted to devour her. To strip off that neat blazer, peel away that silky top and find her skin with my mouth. To kiss every inch of that body and make her scream— and then do it all over again. For a year or two. Until I absolutely had to come up for air. It took all my restraint not to back her against the nearest wall, so I could give in to a whole host of fantasies that had sprung up since the moment I'd realized it was her on stage.

But she didn't realize it was me.

So I kept a ruthless leash on my lust and took only what she wanted to give, which, in and of itself, left me reeling. She was honey and fire, and I couldn't get enough. Every defense I usually lived with, every wall I erected to put distance between myself and everyone else, simply collapsed at her feet. In that moment, I'd have given her anything she asked.

But I understood Alia Gibson never asked anyone for anything.

When she eased back, I didn't stop her.

Her eyes were glazed, her expression startled, with perhaps a tinge of embarrassment in her cheeks. Apparently, her lipstick was the semi-permanent kind that didn't smudge. Lucky for both of us.

Wanting to put her at ease, I murmured, "That was one hell of a thank you."

"You earned it." With what appeared to be some effort, she stepped fully away from me, and I instantly missed her touch.

I considered ripping off the mask. Throwing all caution to the wind and admitting everything right here and now. For a fleeting moment, I imagined laying all my cards on the table. That it was me here in this costume. That I'd been the one at the masquerade. That it hadn't been a lie. We really had been on the same page. Were still on the same page?

That kiss sure as hell made it seem like we were.

But I didn't know what her relationship status was. Bodie hadn't mentioned that she was dating anybody. But I hadn't come outright and asked, lest I make him suspicious. I doubted she even had the time, given everything she was juggling back home. And she wasn't the sort of woman who'd have given in to my impulsive request for a kiss as a reward if she were tangled up with someone else. But still, there were far too many unknowns. Not to mention, all my reasons for walking away back in college were still valid.

But if this little interlude proved nothing else, it was that none of my feelings had faded one iota. If anything, they'd grown. And that was definitely something to think about.

Alia straightened the glasses and checked her watch. "The panel should be over by now."

It seemed like this fantasy was winding down, too. More was the pity. "I guess you have to go do author things." She'd come here in that capacity. No doubt that included other professional obligations.

"I guess I do." She didn't sound especially keen on whatever they were. After the panel, I couldn't blame her.

But before I could suggest something crazy, like catching the next flight to the Bahamas, she looked up at me behind those glasses she didn't need. "We should probably leave separately. Be less conspicuous."

It had been so long since I'd gotten to spend any real time with her, I was loath to let her walk out of this storage room. I also didn't want to risk anyone else hassling her about the panel. No matter how my rescue had distracted them, there were still readers who were pissy and entitled roaming these halls. She didn't need more of that. "Or I could be your bodyguard the rest of the day. Bounce anybody who looks at you funny."

I'd always had an unreasonable desire to protect her. Not that she was generally any sort of damsel in distress; she was usually so devastatingly capable, no one else ever considered she might need it. But I'd always been able to see the strain she was under, carrying the weight of familial responsibilities. I saw the added weight of the whole town in the faint shadows beneath her eyes, despite the expert use of makeup to hide them.

Her smile was wry. "No offense, but I'm pretty sure that

would only drag more attention to me, and that's the last thing I want."

Well, in my current attire, I didn't have any arguments for that. Even my everyday look would pull more attention than she'd like, simply because of who I was. For better or worse, I was in the public eye. The very last place she wanted to be.

"Fair enough. In that case, I should leave first and make sure the coast is clear. Anybody sees me, I'll lead them away."

"I'd appreciate that."

I hesitated, still not wanting to leave. "I suppose this is goodbye then."

"It is. But thank you, Soren. I won't forget this. Or you."

Right. Time to actually go. Committed to my character, I placed a hand over my heart in the honorific sign from her book and bowed. "Your servant, my lady."

I got one last flash of her grin before I slipped out of the room.

The hallway was empty, but I heard the distant din of voices. I made my way back the way I'd come, checking around corners for hotel staff or over-enthusiastic fans who'd come to track us down in the wake of our very dramatic exit. I saw no one.

Relieved, I worked my way back toward the storeroom where I'd left Alia, ducking into a nearby alcove to wait.

A few minutes later, she slipped out, her hair still a little mussed from my hands, the glasses firmly back in place. She glanced up and down the hall before heading toward the event space.

I didn't move, though every instinct screamed at me to go after her. To pull off the mask, call her name, tell her everything. But instincts didn't change the past. And they sure as hell didn't untangle the knots I'd tied a decade ago.

She'd deserved more than half-measures back then.

Deserved someone who could be there for her. Who could stay with her for the everyday. I hadn't been able to offer that. Not with the league calling. Not with the life I'd shed blood and sweat to earn within reach. Hell, even if I'd been willing to fight that tide, Bodie would've stopped me cold. She was his twin, his heart. And I hadn't been ready to risk losing both of them.

But I wasn't that kid anymore, and the choice was no longer as clear-cut as it had been. Not with everything I felt still bubbling through my veins. Not with the taste of her still fresh on my lips.

Knowing the woman she'd become—the one still fighting for everyone but herself—lit up something in me I'd thought I'd buried. My need to protect her, to be there for her, went so far beyond running crowd control against people who had no idea who she was.

I couldn't undo the choice I'd made back then.

But maybe it wasn't too late to find out if she'd make a different one now.

I'd have to be smart about it. Alia didn't know it was me. That much was clear. If she had, there'd have been more than a thank-you kiss in a storage closet. I wasn't sure if that more would've been a slap upside the back of my head or something more pleasant, but I knew there would've been... something.

And if I was wrong—if she had known it was me at the masquerade—then it meant I'd potentially hurt her in ways I didn't even want to fathom when I hadn't followed up. I didn't know how she'd react if I came clean about that, even if my intentions had been good.

Either way, I needed to get the lay of the land. Figure out where she stood and what her life looked like now. Find out if there was room in it for me.

Only one person could help me figure that out.

Tugging off my helm, I scooped a hand through my sweaty

hair and dug my phone out of the cleverly hidden pocket inside the breastplate of the armor, pleased to see that I had sufficient Wi-Fi signal from the conference center to actually dial out. I found Bodie's name on my favorites list. My thumb hovered for a second before I hit call.

It rang twice before he picked up. "Don't tell me the off-season already has you bored."

I huffed a laugh. "Not precisely. But how would you feel about a working visit?"

He paused. "Come again?"

"I've got some time on my hands, and I figured y'all might appreciate an extra pair with everything going on up there, even if it's simply to haul heavy shit."

"Are you serious?"

Guilt pricked as I recognized the ragged edge in my friend's voice. I should've made it out there before now.

"As a heart attack."

"Brother, we'd be thrilled to have you. Every spare pair of hands is welcome, and yours doubly so. I've missed the hell out of you."

That twinge of guilt wound tighter. "Back atcha. It'll take me a couple of days to wind up what I've got going on, but after that, I'll head your way."

"That sounds fucking fantastic."

I hesitated. "Don't tell anybody I'm coming. Let's keep it a surprise."

"It means Grandma Elsie will skin somebody's hide for not warning her so she can put together a welcome feast."

"I'll sweet-talk her down. She always liked me best, anyway."

Bodie snorted. "You wish. But hey, your funeral."

I laughed. "See you in a few days, brother."

Far more cheerful, I ended the call. It was the start of a plan, anyway.

Stowing my phone, I replaced the helm and set about finding my way through the labyrinthine halls to a side exit.

I'd accomplished what I'd come here to do.

Now my sights were set on a more important mission: winning a real shot with the woman of my dreams.

Chapter 9

Alia

@BookishBadassBabe: OMG Y'ALL I WAS THERE!!! When that knight in ACTUAL ARMOR stormed the stage at #KellaHarmonPanel I nearly DIED! The way he scooped her up like she weighed nothing?? That growl??? #SwoonyMcBroadsword is the hero we didn't know we needed! 🗡️⚔️🫠

@PageTurnerPrincess: Still processing what I just witnessed at #GARomantasyCon That had to be planned, right? The timing was too perfect when she froze up. Either way, whoever cast #SwoonyMcBroadsword deserves a raise because DAMN. Those thighs in that leather... 👀

@FictionFanatic42: Theory: That WAS Soren from the books. Kella Harmon figured out how to bring fictional characters to life and that's why the last book is taking so long. She's busy rescuing hot heroes from the page. #SwoonyMcBroadsword #KellaHarmonPanel

@SpicyReaderGirl: I was literally 10 feet from the stage when it happened! His armor had ALL the details from the books - the wyvern claw marks, the runes, EVERYTHING. No random cosplayer goes that hard. This was 100% the panel surprise they teased. #SwoonyMcBroadsword #MarketingGenius

@EpicFantasyLover: Unpopular opinion: That whole rescue thing felt a little too convenient? Harmon looked like she was having a panic attack, then boom - hot armor guy appears? But also... I'd let #SwoonyMcBroadsword carry ME to a secondary location ANY day. Just saying.

@RomanceReadingQueen: The way he put himself between her and the crowd before carrying her off? THAT'S how you write a protective hero, folks! I'm literally BEGGING someone to drop the armor guy's socials. For research purposes. #SwoonyMcBroadsword #IVolunteerAsTribute

@BookDragonDiva: Y'all I've been to a lot of cons but I've NEVER seen anything like what happened at the Kella Harmon panel today. That man didn't just look the part - he MOVED like a warrior. The whole room went dead silent when he growled. I felt it in my SOUL. #SwoonyMcBroadsword #GARomantasyCon

B y the time I pulled into Blair and Elena's drive, my spine felt permanently shaped to the curve of the driver's seat, and my brain had officially gone gelatinous. Five hours on the road after an already long day, most of it spent replaying a single, reckless, entirely out-of-character kiss on loop, and I still hadn't managed to make sense of it.

It had been a moment. A blip. A stolen breath of fantasy. One I'd have given a great deal to still be in.

I could still feel the press of Ramsey's hands, the whisper of leather and steel, the low rumble of *Time to go, princess* like it had been branded on my eardrums. The way he'd kissed me had left me feeling both fierce and fragile and had short-circuited every ounce of logic I'd ever possessed.

Which, for the record, had never happened before. Not even when he'd kissed me at the masquerade all those years ago.

The porch light glowed warm and golden ahead of me, haloed by the soft flicker of café bulbs strung across the eaves. That familiar teal door beckoned like a sanctuary. Or a trap. Hard to say at this point. The explosion of GIFs in my text thread with Blair proved she'd absolutely heard about the panel. I could've tried to avoid her and gone straight home, but she'd just have cornered me there. Better to get it over with.

I killed the engine and trudged up the steps, my boots heavier than they should've been. Before I could so much as knock, the door was yanked open.

"There she is!" Blair stood back, one arm already extended in invitation-slash-interrogation. "Shoes off, coat on the hook, and prepare to be cross-examined."

I groaned. "Can I at least have wine first?"

Elena's voice floated from the kitchen. "Already poured!"

Of course, it was.

I stepped inside, the scent of cinnamon and clove hitting me like a weighted blanket. For five full seconds, I let myself breathe it in—this house, this chaos, this weird little pocket of safety that belonged to two of my very favorite people. A part of me that had been tense since I'd left town the day before yesterday finally unclenched so I could take my first truly full breath in days.

Then I braced myself again, because Blair was practically vibrating with questions, and I already knew there was no way in hell I was getting out of this night without confessing something. And maybe a part of me needed to share this with my bestie. Part of it, anyway.

Blair's wife emerged with a glass of red in her hand. I wrapped her in a grateful hug, managing not to slosh.

"Have you eaten?" Elena demanded.

I took a sip of wine. "Takeout on my way out of Atlanta."

"Pssh. That was hours ago. I make you something." With an about-face, she headed back to the kitchen.

I knew better than to argue with a Puerto Rican woman determined to feed me. Especially as said woman was an incredible cook.

"We had pastelón for dinner," Blair reported.

"That might make the interrogation worth it." I trailed her back to the living room, where a laptop was open to a paused video that was clearly from the romantasy convention panel.

Elena was the only other person who was aware I was Kella Harmon, and courtesy of spousal privilege. Even if she hadn't known before, I suspected after tonight, there would've been no hiding it.

"Sit, sit." Blair all but shoved me onto the center seat of the sofa, draped a weighted blanket over my legs, and leaned forward to hit play.

The screen lit up with footage from someone's phone zooming in on my face right at the moment the emcee said, "—eager to know when the last book in the series will be out."

The camera caught the slow drain of color from my face, and as the silence spun out, an echo of the panic built in my chest. All I really remembered was the roar in my ears, but a half dozen questions rang out when I didn't speak. In the moment, I'd thought everyone could see me flying apart, but on the screen, I simply sat there, pale-faced and resolute. At least until the battle cry sounded. The camera jostled as everyone looked for the source. It swung back in time to catch the dark-armored figure vaulting onto the stage. The expression on what could be seen of his face as he snarled at the crowd had goose-flesh rising along my arms. I'd seen that face before, the night he'd found me at that college bar, right after I'd spotted my boyfriend making out with someone else. That look said *Come for her, and I will break you and enjoy it.*

Yep, still hot as hell. Not that I'd been in any shape on either occasion to appreciate it in the moment. But seeing it now? Well, my brain fell into a merry little alternate version of how that storage closet interlude might have gone. One that involved stripping him *out* of all that armor...

Blair paused the video seconds before we disappeared offstage. "This has, like, a million views already. You're a literal main character."

I closed my eyes, trying to shake off the lingering reminder of the panic attack. "It was awful."

"Sweetie, you got *carried off the stage* by a dark prince in full armor. It was legendary."

"The internet agrees. There are already T-shirts." Elena set the plate of pastelón on the coffee table.

I groaned. "Seriously, I tanked, Blair. Fully froze. I—T-shirts?"

Elena crossed her legs. "*Where's my #SwoonyMc-Broadsword?* That sort of thing."

Blair waved that away. "We'll show you later. Continue."

I blew out a breath, deciding to let go of that insanity for now. "I had a fucking panic attack on stage."

Her hand curled around mine. "First, I'm so sorry you

experienced that. Second, nobody could actually tell from looking at you. Third, if they could, they won't remember anything but His Hotness swooping in. Literally no one from the con is talking about anything else. Top questions are 'Who is he?', 'Is there a real-life romance happening here?', and 'Where can we find pictures of him in nothing but those leather pants?'"

I slid Blair a sideye. "Top questions from the internet or you?"

"Both can be true. I *do* love *The Witcher*."

"I don't even bat for that team, and I can appreciate how Geralt looked in those leather pants," Elena admitted. "Now eat and take your time telling us the rest."

Between bites of delicious plantain lasagna, I took them through the panel. It wasn't actually what Blair wanted to hear about, but I needed to talk through this part for myself.

"I thought it was gonna be okay, you know? They'd stuck to general questions for all of us. And then blammo. The exact thing I *didn't* have an answer for. I folded. It was like being in the middle of a nightmare because the crowd started to turn on me, and I was powerless to stop it."

My bestie winced. "Shit. I'm sorry. I should never have pushed you into the panel."

"You weren't wrong. But neither was I. And then, while I was busy praying for the floor to open up and swallow me, *that* happened." I waved a hand toward the screen, where Ramsey's broad, armored shoulders were still frozen.

"That *is* Soren he's dressed as, right?" Blair asked.

"Down to the wyvern claw marks on the breastplate. Yes."

"Epic," Elena breathed.

I finished my dinner and set the plate aside, finally turning my attention to the wine.

My bestie fairly danced in her seat. "You can't leave us hanging there, babe. What happened off camera?"

I paused, considering how much to tell her. "He whisked me away to a quiet room and talked me down from my panic attack. The crowd in general might not have realized, but he apparently did." That was another piece that had been circling through my brain the entire drive home. Ramsey had seen me. *Really* seen me, in that way he always had. That had always been a significant part of the horrendous crush I'd nursed all through college and after.

Blair pressed a hand to her heart and sighed. "That's peak real-life romance there. Please tell me he's single, gorgeous, and that you snuck off for a flaming tryst before you came back home."

I arched a brow at her. "In all the years you've known me, have I *ever* struck you as the sort of woman bold enough to sneak off for a flaming tryst?"

"I mean, no, but hope springs eternal. A flaming tryst would do you a world of good."

The alternate version of the storage room began playing through my brain again.

"I did not have a flaming tryst. But I might've kissed him."

Blair let out a squee so loud, I checked the wine glass for cracks. "Tell. Me. *Everything!*"

I immediately wanted to backpedal. "It wasn't a thing. It was a thank you. A moment. I don't even know what he looked like."

She bent forward and screamed into a pillow. "OMG, girl, what *is* it with you and kissing masked strangers?"

Elena held up a hand. "There's obviously a story there."

I sighed. "I went to a masquerade party back in college and met a guy. We had this really incredible night, two earth-shattering kisses, and..."

"And she didn't even get his name, so she never saw him again," Blair finished.

That wasn't strictly true. I'd seen Ramsey plenty after that. But I'd never told Blair I'd known it was him. For some reason, I still didn't want to reveal that now. Because Blair knew Ramsey, and that would make all this more complicated than it already was.

"That's tragic. Did you at least get this one's name?" Elena asked.

"I did not." It wasn't technically a lie. I hadn't asked, and he hadn't volunteered.

Blair flung herself backward against the arm of the sofa. "You've got a type, and apparently it's 'anonymous hero.'"

"Don't start, B."

Elena laughed. "At least your bad decisions are on theme."

I drained the last of my wine and considered asking for another glass.

Blair sat up. "Okay, but real talk. Are you gonna use this? It seems like the inspiration you've been waiting for."

I hadn't finished processing the whole thing in real life yet. I certainly hadn't considered how I might translate any of it to fiction. "My muse is still MIA. If I go looking now, she's going to go haring off to Iceland or something, never to be seen again."

Elena laid a hand over mine. "Then let it percolate. You don't owe anyone anything right now. You're allowed to take a breath."

"For sure," Blair added. "The internet thinks it was a publicity stunt. A brilliant one. Sales are already spiking overall, with a really nice boost to the original series. You've got a cushion."

I loosed a breath. "I hope so. Because the town still needs me more than the book does." That was my reality, for better or worse.

"And yet, you might've just launched the most swoon-worthy new ship on BookTok. They're currently vying between #ArmorDaddy, #MaskedBae, and #SwoonyMcBroadsword."

I snorted. This was exactly the unhinged delight BookTok was made for.

And if the whole interlude had re-ignited my own personal ship, well, at least I'd had a refresher exposure to hero material.

Chapter 10

Ramsey

NOTICE FROM CHIEF GIBSON
January 25

Gibson Hollow residents:

We have visitors in town helping with recovery efforts. Some may be recognizable public figures.

Please respect their privacy.

- No unwanted photographs
- No social media posts about their whereabouts
- No crowding or disrupting their work

These folks are here to help. Let's treat them like neighbors, not celebrities.

Thank you,
Bodie Gibson
Chief of Police

By the time I hit the outskirts of Gibson Hollow, the winter light had gone slate gray, pressing low and heavy over the mountains like a weight no one could quite shake off. The road curved through bare-limbed woods still slick with ice in the shadows, patches of old snow crusting the edges of the shoulders. I'd seen the damage starting three counties back—washed out bridges, whole swaths of roadside stripped bare where the flood had carved through like a knife—but nothing prepared me for the gut punch of the town itself.

The lower end of Gibson Hollow looked like a war zone.

Buildings I remembered from my last visit—quaint little shops with hand-painted signs, the art gallery with the crooked shutters—were just... gone. Torn down to framing, or worse, left as rubble and fenced off with bright-orange mesh. One side of the square had collapsed in on itself, a jagged sinkhole still lined in frozen mud, steam rising faintly where crews had been trying to pump it out. Sandbags leaned like forgotten soldiers against half-rebuilt facades, and signs for relief stations flapped wearily in the icy wind.

Even the people looked different—slower, heavier in their movements. Faces drawn and pale with the kind of tired that didn't come from one bad night's sleep. I saw a woman dragging a plastic sled full of bottled water behind her like it was 1802. A pair of kids huddled in too-thin jackets beneath the awning of what used to be the library, now tarps and plywood.

Yeah, I'd known it was bad. I'd read the stories. Watched the footage.

But this?

This was so much worse.

Guilt that I hadn't made the time to come sooner set up like concrete in my gut. I'd had professional obligations, but I could've done more than send emergency supplies.

You'll make up for it now.

With that promise ringing in my brain, I went to find Bodie.

The police station was a solid, unassuming building tucked into the crook of a hill like it had grown there. Rough-hewn timber siding gave it a log cabin feel, with wide stone steps leading up to a heavy front door. It looked built to last, and apparently it had—one of the few buildings that hadn't taken on water when the Hollow nearly drowned.

Inside, heat hit like a wall, smelling faintly of wood smoke and old coffee. Because, yeah, the Gibson Hollow Police Station had a fireplace. And it was getting used. A radio crackled quietly behind the front desk, manned by a young officer with sleepy eyes and a buzz cut. He looked up, blinked, then did a double take.

Yup. Football fan.

"C... Can I help you?"

I leaned against the counter. "I'm here for Chief Gibson." He'd had that badge for more than a year, and I still couldn't quite get over the fact that he ran the department now.

"He's in back. Office door's open."

I gave the kid a nod and made my way down the short hall, boots echoing on the scuffed wood floors.

Bodie was behind his desk, frowning down at paperwork like it owed him money.

We'd met freshman year at Carolina Southern University, both scholarship players who'd been brought on to knock over defensive linemen like they were dominoes. We'd been damn good at it. Now he looked like someone had carved a mountain into human form and handed it a badge. Shorter than me by a few inches—most folks were—he was still broad as hell. His winter beard had grown in thick. As I watched, he reached up to scratch it, then glanced up and grinned.

"Holy shit."

I didn't even get a word out before he was around the desk, hauling me into one of those no-nonsense guard hugs that locked in tight and hit just shy of a bear tackle.

"You're really here!" Bodie pulled back to look me over, like he couldn't quite believe it. "Damn good to see you."

I squeezed his shoulder. "You too, brother. It's been too damned long."

"Come on." He snagged a department-issue overcoat from the rack and dragged it on. "Walk with me."

After a word to the officer at the front desk, we stepped out into the brittle cold, our breath frosting in the air as we made our way down toward what was left of downtown. The store-fronts we passed were a hodgepodge—some gutted, others half-built, a few with fresh siding or new windows framed in plastic sheeting. Tarps and plywood still outnumbered shingles and glass.

"We've come a long way since September." Bodie's boots crunched over gravel where sidewalks had crumbled. "But there's a hell of a lot left to do."

I nodded. "I can see that. I'm done for the season, and I've got a good back that's not doing anybody any good sitting idle. Tell me where you need me."

Bodie gave me a long look, then nodded once. "We'll have to talk to Alia about that. C'mon. We should be able to catch her at her office."

The bell over the door jingled as we stepped into The Commissary. The scent of frying oil, strong coffee, and something savory—maybe pintos or butter beans—wrapped around me like a blanket, reminding me it had been a hell of a long time since breakfast this morning. The place was buzzing with lunchtime traffic, but it wasn't merely a diner anymore. Donation bins lined the walls, and hand-lettered signs for FEMA assistance, rebuilding crews, and food pantry hours covered one whole corner like a patchwork bulletin board. Crates of supplies flanked the register, and the laminated menu bore as many taped-on substitutions as it did actual options.

Toward the back, Alia was holding court in the corner booth. Bodie had told me she was using it as her temporary office, but it was a whole different thing seeing it in person. Countless manila folders, a stack of legal pads, an aging laptop, and a printer I wasn't sure was from this century were all bracketed by empty coffee mugs. She was listening intently to an older woman who pressed a mason jar into her hands— preserves or pickled something, I couldn't tell.

"This is plenty." Alia hugged the woman like they were old friends. "I'll make the call this afternoon, and you'll hear from me before the end of the week."

The woman gave her a grateful smile and headed for the door.

Alia turned, adjusting her grip on the jar. Then, her eyes landed on me.

The jar slipped.

I moved without thinking. One foot planted, the other already pushing off the tile, I lunged and snatched the jar out of the air an inch before it hit the ground. My shoulder thudded into the leg of a table, and I exhaled hard, heart thudding from the sudden burst of motion, but the jar was safe in my hand. Not even a crack in the seal.

Bodie let out a low whistle. "Still got the hands."

I stood slowly, straightening with the jar cradled in my

palm like it was precious cargo. "Didn't make the playoffs just to let—" I glanced at the contents. "—homemade salsa meet an untimely end."

Alia stared at me, wide-eyed. "Ramsey?"

"Hey, Alia."

For a long moment, I couldn't read a damn thing on her face.

Not shock, exactly. Not happiness or anger either. Only... blank space where something should be. I held the jar out like an offering, half-wondering if this was the moment she'd say something—anything—that would tell me she'd known it was me behind the mask. That the kiss had meant something more than a heat-of-the-moment rescue fantasy.

Then, slowly, she stepped forward and wrapped her arms around me.

The hug was familiar. Automatic. Like muscle memory built from a dozen past ones we'd shared before life got complicated. I closed my eyes for a second and let myself breathe her in—lavender and ink and the faintest trace of cinnamon lotion, always slightly out of season. It had been her mama's favorite. A tiny link to her memory. Everything in me wanted to hold on, just a second longer.

But I didn't.

I stepped back before the moment lingered too long, forcing my face into something casual.

It was strange seeing her like this. No flashy red wig. No glasses. The real Alia. The one who used to fall asleep on my shoulder during all-night study sessions in the library, with her earbuds in and a highlighter in her teeth. Her long, glossy brown hair was swept up in a haphazard twist, and there were traces of exhaustion on her face that the makeup hadn't quite covered. Shadows under her eyes, the pinch of a headache between her brows. She looked like a woman carrying the weight of a town on her back, and doing her damnedest not to let it show.

"What are you doing here?" Her voice held nothing but honest curiosity.

"Came to offer my hands."

One brow winged up. "Aren't they insured for some stupid amount of money?"

"I can still flatten people without them." I gave a lopsided grin. "Seriously. I'm off season, and I've got plenty of time for the foreseeable future. Put me to work."

She stared at me for a long beat, and I couldn't help but search her face again, desperate for even the tiniest sign. A flicker of recognition. The edge of a smirk. Anything that might say: *I knew it was you.*

Nothing.

"You're sticking around for the off-season?" Was there hope in her tone? Wistfulness? That might've been my own wishful thinking.

"Got a trip to see Mama in there somewhere, but yeah. I figure y'all can use the help."

"Well, you're not wrong." She tilted her head like she was already mentally sorting through a list of logistics. "I'll give it some thought and figure out where we can best use you. Where will you be staying?"

"I hadn't thought much about that."

Bodie stepped up beside us. "Crash at my place. Dean's there, since he got back from deployment, but there's room for all of us. Everybody's sort of bunked up where they can, to free up available housing to folks who lost theirs in the flood. Alia moved in with Uncle Dee."

Surprised, I looked back at her. "You gave up your apartment downtown?"

"Other people needed it more. And since I adore Uncle

Dee, it's not a hardship." She reached for her messenger bag and slung it over her shoulder. "Anyway, Bodie, bring him to dinner at Grandma Elsie's, and I'll have an assignment by then. I've gotta get to the high school for a zoning meeting about rebuilding the gym."

And then, like she always did, she was gone in a flash of purposeful motion and boots thudding against tile.

I watched her go, the hem of her coat swinging, knot of hair swaying with each stride. That was Alia. Always moving. Always solving. And not once in that whole conversation had she given me even a hint that she'd recognized me from the panel. Or the masquerade before that.

I couldn't decide if it made me relieved or a little sick.

"I see she hasn't slowed down any since college," I muttered, still watching the door.

"Not a bit." Bodie clapped a hand on my back. "Damn, it's good to see you. C'mon. I'll get you a key."

Chapter 11

Alia

I didn't run the way I wanted. But I did leave with enough polite efficiency and professional polish to make it seem like I had somewhere I absolutely needed to be. Which—technically—I did. The zoning meeting about the gym rebuild was in forty-five minutes.

But no way I could walk into that school board conference room still warm from Ramsey's hug. I was far too rattled, and Gibson Hollow Alia was never rattled. Grown Ass Adult Alia had her shit together. Always. She did not obsess over whether anyone noticed she might've held on to her brother's best friend a second too long. Or whether they'd caught the moment she'd leaned in slightly and breathed him in like he was a giant chocolate chip cookie she wanted to take a bite out of.

Furthermore, she did not refer to herself in the third person.

Get it together, Gibson.

Three days. Three whole days I'd spent trying to get that kiss out of my head. The weight of it. The heat. The way my pulse had skittered when he'd murmured, *"Time to go, princess,"* like he'd been built to say lines exactly like that, in a voice that was somehow comfort and sex appeal all at once.

Now he was here. In my town. In my grandmother's diner. Effortlessly catching salsa jars like it was the final touchdown pass of the Super Bowl.

I turned down Main Street, quick-stepping through the slush toward anywhere that wasn't The Commissary.

I needed five minutes. Ten, tops. Just to get my head on straight.

What the hell was he *doing* here? He said he came to help. And of course, that made some sense. He was Bodie's best friend. He was a good guy. I should have expected it, now that his season with the Sentinels was over.

But *why now?*

Was this merely coincidence? Or did he somehow know?

I'd been in disguise. Had the wig and the glasses for the whole female Clark Kent routine. Uncle Dee had worked his magic to make my face a subtly different shape. But that was all intended to fool people who *didn't* know me well. Had it actually worked on someone who had once known me extremely well?

But then, if Ramsey had recognized me, why wouldn't he have said something then? Had he figured it out after and come here to confront me about it?

God, I was going to drive myself crazy with all this speculation. Nothing at all in our conversation had suggested he knew a damned thing. I'd been analyzing every micro-expression, every nuance of tone in his voice. Not that I was operating at peak efficacy, considering I'd also been actively trying not to visibly freak out at the time. But still

I couldn't go to Blair. Not like this. She'd known about my college crush, sure. But she'd never seen my masked companion from the masquerade. If she had, she'd have figured out it was

Ramsey back then. She'd watched the video of that con rescue approximately eleventy-billion times already. If I showed up this out of sorts because Ramsey Shaw was in town, she was going to do the math and figure it out. Which would lead to a lot of hurt feelings about why I hadn't told her all of it before, and I didn't want to get into *that* either.

That left only one place.

I cut left on Ridgewood, hustled down two blocks until I hit the alley running behind one of the few rows of buildings that hadn't been impacted by the flood. The third door down was unlocked, and I slipped inside, letting the door ease shut behind me with the softest snick. I'd hang out here, in the back of Uncle Dee's vintage shop, Devine Interventions, until I had my feet under me again. He'd never even know I was here.

"Alia Rose Gibson."

I froze, one hand still on the door as I tried to school my features. With a breath, I slowly turned.

The lighting in the back of the shop was a low, golden tone that made everything seem richer than it was. Including the semi-circle of vintage armchairs, which held Uncle Dee and his three closest friends. They looked me over, wine glasses in hand, a tribunal dripping with rhinestones and curiosity.

Miss Bea—aka Madame Bea Dazzle—adjusted her oversized readers, one slippered foot idly stroking the back of Dorothy, her geriatric bulldog, currently snoring and snorting like a buzz saw at her feet. How I'd missed that, I had no idea. Too in my head, I guess.

Miss Glory—known outside her circle as Vanglorious Jones—flashed a smile sharp enough to slice paper. "Sugar, you look like you saw the Ghost of Christmas Past... shirtless."

Damn if that didn't immediately start that alternate fantasy of Ramsey in nothing but those leather pants all over again. Fresh heat rose to my cheeks.

Self-proclaimed snackfluencer Mo'nique Delight set down her charcuterie plate with deliberate care and tilted her head. "You bring snacks or secrets, baby girl? 'Cause one of those is definitely required to crash Sasspatch Society meetings."

Crap. I was so busted.

Uncle Dee steepled his fingers beneath his chin, all glittering rings and calm calculation. "Well, this got interesting."

"Sorry. I didn't mean to interrupt. I'll just—"

"Hold up. You snuck in like the Artful Dodger for a reason." Uncle Dee arched one perfect brow.

At my undoubted deer-in-the-headlights look, Miss Bea patted the arm of the remaining empty chair beside her. "Sit down and tell us what's got you in a dither, darlin'."

Hiding was no longer an option.

Resigned, I crossed to the chair Miss Bea had indicated and dropped into it like my bones had stopped working. "I'm not staying long. I've got a zoning meeting in thirty..." I checked my watch. "Twenty-five minutes. I just needed—" I exhaled hard. "A second."

"From the look on your face, I'd say you need more than that." Mo'nique promptly began building a plate from the magnificent charcuterie board that had already been half-decimated. Were those salami roses?

Since I hadn't gotten a chance to eat more than about a third of my sandwich at the diner between meetings, and had lit out of there like my ass was on fire, I didn't protest the effort. I was too busy trying to figure out how to explain the cyclone of thought still taking over my brain.

Miss Glory leaned in to lay a light hand on my knee. "Sweetheart, whatever it is, it's better out than in."

Mo'nique thrust a plate at me. "Have a brie button. It'll help."

To buy myself some time, I stacked the brie on a cracker and dutifully stuffed it in my mouth. Damn, that was good.

"This is personal," Uncle Dee declared.

"What makes you say that?" I asked around a piece of salami.

"Because if it were business, you'd be fine. Tired maybe, but fine. You, my little sunbeam, are frazzled."

And of course he could see it.

I blew out another long breath. "I am frazzled. I had a blast from my past show up at the diner, and it's left me... off kilter."

All four of them leaned forward in their chairs.

"What sort of blast from the past?" Miss Glory demanded.

"A former lover?" Miss Bea suggested.

"A former husband?" Miss Glory asked.

"This is Alia we're talking about, not you," Mo'nique chastised.

Miss Glory batted her eyes. "The girl has *depths*. It's always the quiet ones who have the secrets you never expect."

She had absolutely no idea.

Before they could go off on more unlikely tangents, I interrupted. "It's nothing so dramatic as that. My old college crush is in town for a while to help out, apparently."

"Oh." Miss Glory sounded disappointed.

"O-o-o-oh." Uncle Dee drew it out into four knowing syllables.

"Don't you say it like that," I protested. "It was a long time ago. I'm fine. Totally fine. I just wasn't expecting him to be here. It was a shock, that's all. And I haven't quite figured out what to do about it."

Uncle Dee's grin went feral. "Well, I can think of a number of things you could do about it."

I pointed at him with a narrow-eyed glare. "Not helping."

"I'm just saying—"

"Nope." I crossed my arms. "This is not a romcom. There are no 'oops, only one bed' situations happening in this town."

Miss Bea tutted. "A shame, really. I mean, with the current housing issues..."

"I'm a grown-ass adult," I insisted. "I will get over this."

They all nodded like they believed me.

They didn't.

Without a word, Miss Glory reached behind her for the emergency throw blanket she always kept draped over the arm of her chair. Mo'nique set a fresh glass of ice water within my reach. Miss Bea pulled a lint roller out of God only knew where and started brushing down my coat sleeve like grooming would soothe me into submission. Uncle Dee leaned back, smug as a cat who'd found a whole pitcher of cream. "Of course you will, baby. But we're going to make sure you're comfortable while you do."

God help me, I loved them.

Even when they were insufferably right.

After a few minutes under the calming influence of blanket, charcuterie, and people who knew how to take care of me whether I wanted it or not, my pulse finally started to slow. The fluttering panic subsided to something manageable—still there, like a kettle left on low, but not boiling over anymore.

"I really do have to go." I set the glass aside and smoothed my hands over my dress pants. "The zoning meeting's legit. I just... might've left the Commissary early to come here first."

Miss Glory gave me a once-over that felt like an X-ray. "You're walking in there composed and collected?"

"As I ever am." I rose and started working my way around the room, doling out hugs. Miss Bea smelled like powder and white tea, and her squeeze was deceptively strong for someone with bad knees. Miss Glory's was theatrical and air-kissed on both cheeks. Mo'nique gave me a full-body bear hug that felt like being enveloped in a heated weighted blanket with a faint aroma of sugar cookies.

I saved Uncle Dee for last.

"Thank you," I murmured as he pulled me in close. "For not making me say more than I wanted to."

"You said what you needed to say." He brushed a kiss to my temple. "We've got you, baby. Always."

I stepped back, already steeling myself. "This is fine. I'm fine. It's not like this is my first time around Ramsey Shaw. I used to spend all kinds of time with him in college, and no one ever knew how I felt."

That earned a round of raised brows, but I forged ahead. "This is nothing but an echo. I've got it under control."

"Of course you do," Miss Bea said in the exact soothing tone reserved for letting you believe a comforting lie.

I headed for the back door again, trying not to let the nervous energy creep back into my limbs.

I was fine.

Totally fine.

So what if my old college crush was back in town three days after giving me the best kiss of my life without even knowing it was me? It didn't matter. I was a professional. I had a job to do. And I'd been keeping this secret for ten years already.

What were a few more days or weeks?

It was fine.

Everything was absolutely fine.

Chapter 12

Ramsey

Sasspatch Society Group Text:

DELILAH:

Did y'all see what I just saw? Our Alia is
SHOOK.

> GLORY:
>
> Girl needs intervention STAT.
>
> BEA:
>
> That child hasn't done anything for herself in
> years.
>
> MO'NIQUE:
>
> So Ramsey Shaw is in town and has our girl
> running scared? Interesting...

DELILAH:

There's definitely more to this story. That
wasn't just old crush nerves.

> GLORY:
>
> Perfect timing. She needs a shake-up.

MO'NIQUE:

She needs to get laid.

BEA:

Mo'nique! (But yes.)

DELILAH:

Are we doing this?

GLORY:

Absolutely. I'll handle the "accidental" run-ins.

MO'NIQUE:

Food situations are mine.

BEA:

I'll read his cards.

DELILAH:

And I'm upgrading her wardrobe. No more hiding.

GLORY:

For Alia!

DELILAH:

Operation Rattled & Rolling begins now!

The Gibson homestead had been in the family since before Gibson Hollow was more than the trading post that had evolved into what was now The Commissary. Perched high on a ridge above town, the original clapboard house was more than a century-and-a-half old, and it had been added onto and repaired a million and one times. The current structure was a massive, somewhat chaotic blend of farmhouse and cabin that nevertheless reminded me of the warm, welcoming chaos of the Gibsons themselves. As an only child, that had been something I'd always appreciated on my trips home with Bodie to visit. It was the kind of place that always had a dog or three and a row of rocking chairs on the front porch.

But as Bodie pulled to a stop in front of the house, it wasn't a dog standing on that porch facing off with his pint-sized grandma, who was armed with nothing more than a kitchen towel.

"Jesus Christ! Is that a bear?"

Unconcerned, Bodie shifted the truck into park. "Nah, that's Ludo."

I cut him a glance. "Is that supposed to be an explanation?"

"Colter's mutt. He's some Newfoundland mix. Judging by the mud on his paws, they're having a standoff."

"What's he mixed with? Wooly mammoth?"

"Jury's still out. I personally think he's part Wookie."

We slid out of the truck in time to hear Elsie call, "Don't you give me those eyes. You'll wait 'til your daddy gets here from work, because you're not coming in my house with dirty feet."

Ludo made a noise that did indeed sound like an angry Wookie as he stomped one big paw.

Side-eyeing the creature I still wasn't entirely sure was a dog, I made my way to the porch. "If I offer to wash his feet, will that get me off your shit list for not letting you know I was coming?"

Elsie waved the kitchen towel like a red cape at a bull, and the beast huffed and lumbered out of her way. She opened her arms wide. "Ramsey Shaw, you get over here and give me a hug."

I did as ordered, folding her into my embrace. Despite the fact that she topped out below my sternum, her hug still felt as if she could lift me off my feet. There was nothing like a Grandma Elsie hug.

"Mmm-mmm. It has been too long! When you gonna bring

me home a nice girl and some great-grandbabies? I got this whole passel of grandchildren, and only one of them has seen fit to make me a great-grandma."

"Uh..."

Before I could think of a reply, Bodie jumped in, slapping me on the shoulder. "That's gonna require him slowing down to find a nice girl first."

Naturally, Alia chose that moment to step out the door. "Perhaps you could let us finish rebuilding the town before you start tasking us with marriage and babies, huh?"

"Hey." That sounded casual, right?

I tried desperately not to stare as her hand automatically went to Ludo's big head for scritches and the corner of her mouth lifted.

"Hey. I see you've met our resident mud lover."

Ludo leaned fully against Alia's legs, almost taking her out with his bulk as he groaned in adoration. I tensed, preparing to catch her, but she only chuckled and shifted her weight as she wrapped her arms around the animal and pressed a noisy kiss to the top of his head. Lucky bastard.

There was a bit of a chaotic shuffle as the two youngest Gibson brothers—Fletcher and Gunner—arrived with Fletcher's dog, Gouda, a lab mix with satellites for ears. As he and Ludo greeted each other like long-lost brothers, I retrieved the bottles of wine I'd brought from Charleston as a hostess gift for Elsie. She escorted me into the house, assuring me I was entirely off dog-washing duty, and I trailed her into the kitchen, where I found their Uncle Dee fussing at the stove over something that smelled of tomatoes and garlic.

"Mama, this sauce is about ready."

"Good. Look who came to dinner!"

He turned, a broad grin stretching across his face as he

wiped his hands on another kitchen towel. "Well, well. Ramsey Shaw, as I live and breathe. It's been a very long time."

"It sure has. Good to see you." I held out my hand, which he promptly took and pulled me in for a back-thumping hug.

The whole Gibson clan were huggers.

When he pulled back, his eyes were bright and curious as they studied my face, like he thought my being here was going to be the best entertainment he'd had in months. I wasn't quite sure what to do with that.

He took the wine out of my hands. "What have we here?"

"Just a bit of a host/hostess gift."

"Oh, this will go perfectly with the pasta for dinner. I'll open it up and let it breathe."

The sound of another engine outside announced someone else's arrival.

Elsie stuck her head out the door. "Colter, you wash your dog's feet and your own before you come in this house."

His voice drifted in from the porch. "Yes'm."

More feet tromped inside.

I stood in the corner of the kitchen. "What can I do?"

"Set the table. Places for nine. Utensils are in the drawer there." Elsie gestured to the big center island.

Relieved to have a task, I gathered up utensils and headed for the dining room, where Alia was setting out cloth napkins. We circled the table, laying places. I couldn't help but notice she looked even more tired than she had when I saw her at lunch, though she was as composed as ever. Before I could think what to say to her, the last of the Gibson brothers strode in. I'd only met Dean once, as he'd been in the Marines most of the time I'd known Bodie.

His gaze slid to me. "Ramsey. Didn't know you were here."

"Hit town today. You got taller."

Dean's serious expression turned to a grin. "That happens in ten years. You got broader."

My turn to smile. "Same."

"Everybody get in here and fix your plate!" Grandma Elsie's order started the inevitable stampede back to the kitchen.

By the time I set my plate down, most of the Gibsons were already claiming their usual spots with the easy choreography of a family that had done this a thousand times. The only seat left was the one on my right—narrower than the others, squeezed in between me and the built-in hutch.

Of course, it was hers.

When Alia approached with her plate in one hand and a cloth napkin in the other, I pushed back from the table and stood to pull out the chair for her. My mama had raised me right, after all.

She blinked in surprise, then offered a soft "Thanks" as she eased in beside me, smoothing her napkin across her lap. The moment she sat, the space seemed smaller. Closer.

I wondered if she was half as aware of me as I was of her. She didn't seem rattled, exactly. More... braced. For my part, it seemed every hair on my arm was aimed toward her. As if I could feel the charge she created merely by being in proximity to me. I felt every shift, every breath.

As the meal kicked into gear around us—laughter, teasing, a never-ending shuffle of bread baskets and bowls—I kept half an eye on her. She answered questions, offered updates, chuckled at Fletcher's impersonation of the zoning chair. On the surface, she was exactly who she'd always been: poised, competent, impossible not to admire.

But her fork barely made a dent in her spaghetti, and every time someone asked her something about the recovery efforts, that tension in her shoulders cinched tighter. She didn't fidget. She didn't complain. But she was wound so tight, I wondered how nobody else noticed. Maybe they were simply used to it.

But I wasn't. And I couldn't stop seeing it. Or feeling it every time her elbow brushed mine and she didn't seem to notice at all.

Fletcher passed the basket of garlic bread down the table. "Colter, you take more than two pieces, and I'm stabbing you with my fork."

"You think I'm scared of your dainty-ass salad fork?"

"It's a dinner fork, you Neanderthal."

Dean reached across me to snag the last breadstick. "What's the over-under on how long before these two knock something off Grandma's wall again?"

Gunner answered around a mouthful of pasta. "Ten minutes. Less, if you bring up that time Colter lost our fantasy league and had to wear glitter body spray to work for a week."

Colter didn't even look up. "And *still* looked better than you at prom."

"I didn't even go to prom!"

"Exactly."

Fletcher groaned. "Can we *not* talk about high school? Some of us have tried to block that trauma."

Dean pointed his fork at him. "Because you wore that tux with the mandarin collar like you were auditioning for a mid-2000s boy band."

Fletcher flipped him off with a finesse that probably did Uncle Dee proud. "Your hairline's still recovering from your basic training buzz cut, bro. Let's not pretend you've got fashion authority."

"Don't make me tell everybody what really happened at the Christmas party last year."

"You swore you'd never—!"

Bodie cut in. "Okay, new rule: No blackmail threats during dinner."

"Seconded." Gunner smirked. "Unless they involve Grandma's rum cake."

"Don't drag her rum cake into this," Colter warned. "That's sacred."

"It gave me heartburn for three days."

"That's because you ate five slices, dumbass."

I was lifting my glass when Dean elbowed Gunner. "Speaking of dumbasses, tell me you're not still simping over that girl from the DMV with the dragon tattoo and the side shave."

Gunner set his glass down with a thump. "She was hot."

"She had a lizard named *Brad* in her purse, dude."

"That's personality!"

"And unresolved trauma!"

That was when Alia cleared her throat. Not loud, and only once, but the response was immediate.

Every Gibson brother at the table froze. Fletcher glanced up and winced. Dean straightened like he was still in uniform. Colter put both hands in his lap like a kid waiting on punishment. Bodie's shoulders inched up toward his ears.

Gunner shrank an inch in his chair and mumbled, "Yes ma'am."

Silence reigned for several long beats.

Alia didn't say a word as she went back to twirling pasta on her fork like nothing had happened.

Grandma Elsie sipped her tea with a satisfied little hum. "Makes me proud every time."

I glanced at Alia again, and she caught me watching and merely blinked at me in innocence, as if she hadn't just deployed a tactical Mom Look without batting an eye.

I knew she'd effectively stepped into the role when their

mother died. She was the eldest, if only by five minutes. We'd never really talked about it, but I found myself wondering what that had really been like for her. Was she okay with it? Did she resent losing whatever was left of her childhood by stepping into that responsibility? No question, she loved her family fiercely, and I didn't think she'd have made any other choice, given the chance. But something like that had to take a toll on a person, and I wondered if the rest of the Gibsons had ever considered what it had cost her, or if they'd all simply accepted her natural competence without question.

Because no one else had said anything, I decided to take one for the team and start the conversation again. "Have you decided where you want me?"

Alia stopped chewing, her face going absolutely blank for five seconds that made me wonder if she was thinking about something other than work.

Maybe that was just me.

Finally, she swallowed. "I'm sorry. I haven't had two seconds this afternoon to even think about it. After the zoning meeting with the school board, I had to talk the county inspector out of red-tagging the south wing of the library, help coordinate volunteers for the supply drive, and figure out what the hell to do about Miss Addie's busted water heater. Again."

"Miss Addie?" I asked.

"Eighty-four, stubborn as a mule, and refuses to move out of her house even though the plumbing's shot, and she's been boiling water on the stove for baths."

I pushed my plate aside. "Let me take care of that."

She blinked at me. "What?"

"I can fix the water heater. If it's salvageable, I'll get it working. If not, I'll help replace it. If someone can hook me up with tools and walk me through what's already been done."

"You... seriously?"

"Did you forget I was a construction management major? You used to quiz me on supply chain vocab and OSHA regs. I'm pretty sure you made me memorize the four types of contracts while we were watching *The Princess Bride*."

That startled a laugh out of her—an honest, belly-deep giggle that loosened something in me that had been coiling tighter and tighter throughout the meal.

"Oh my God, I *did*. Bodie had a convenient camping emergency that kept him away half the semester until that class was over."

My buddy looked entirely unrepentant. "I wasn't about to get looped into that crap. I had my own shit to memorize. And Alia was always the one with all the study hacks."

"They worked. I passed all those classes with A's. Anyway, I've kept my skills up volunteering for Habitat for Humanity during my off-season, so pretty sure I can handle a water heater."

Her eyes lit, and for a second, the tight lines around them faded. "That would be amazing. Thank you."

Fletcher spoke up around a bite of garlic bread. "I've got tools in the back of my truck. You can take whatever you need. If you're short anything, Cooley's Hardware is basically FEMA-adjacent these days. They'll either have it or know who does."

"I appreciate it."

Uncle Dee raised his wineglass. "And if you do good by Miss Addie, she might give you her apple pie recipe. It's been a guarded secret since 1957."

"That's not a recipe," Gunner said. "That's witchcraft."

"Whatever it is, it's worth earning."

Everyone chuckled, and the conversation shifted again, voices rising and falling like waves around the table. Plates passed, forks clinked, and Alia finally relaxed a fraction. Her shoulders dropped, and she leaned back in her chair with the first genuine ease I'd seen all evening.

But she still wasn't eating. Not really.

I didn't call it out. This wasn't the moment. Not here, in front of her whole family. I knew she'd brush it off and tell me she was fine.

But I'd seen too much to believe that. So I filed it away. Every brush of her elbow. Every polite smile that didn't quite reach her eyes. Every bite she pushed around instead of taking.

And I made a silent promise to myself, right then and there: while I was in Gibson Hollow, I was going to do everything I could to make her load lighter.

Even if she never asked.

Chapter 13

Alia

It was barely seven by the time I stepped into The Commissary. The bell above the door gave its usual jingle, and I got a few nods from the early birds already settled in their usual booths or at the counter. Most of them had known me since I was knee high to a biscuit tray, so no one batted an eye when I veered straight for my regular spot in the back corner.

The air was rich with the scents of coffee, bacon, and Big Wade's magic biscuits. From the kitchen came the rhythmic clang of spatulas and the low hum of Wade's voice, carrying the notes of some old school blues number like molasses. Quiet wasn't really the word—his bass could rattle the walls if he wanted—but it was a soundtrack I always found soothing.

I dropped my tote bag on the bench seat and headed behind the counter to pour myself a cup of black coffee. I'd grown up here and spent more time than I could count waiting tables or ringing up meals, so I wasn't about to stand on ceremony in my pursuit of caffeine. The first sip all but scalded my tongue, but I didn't mind. It had become part of my wake-up process.

Back at the booth, I settled in, pulling out my laptop, my current legal pad, and a pile of different colored highlighters. We were down to the triage portion of the week, where I had to figure out what had to be dealt with immediately and what could wait a while longer. If I was lucky, I might find another task or two I could delegate, though those seemed to be few and far between. Seemed like I was everybody's point person for every damned thing.

The curse of hyper-competence.

I could probably offload more than I did, but it would take more time to explain and train someone than it did to do the thing myself. I didn't have the mental capacity for that right now. Now, if we could clone people like Ramsey, who took initiative without my having to organize it, I might could get somewhere.

Dinner last night had been exhausting. I kept waiting for something to blow up on me. But it had become increasingly obvious that I was borrowing trouble. If Ramsey knew something, he wasn't giving any sign of it. Which meant he really was here to see Bodie and help out. The sooner I accepted that and let things get back to the way they used to be when we were friends, the better.

That would be considerably easier if he hadn't been the consistent star of my dreams every night since I got back from the book convention. I didn't need a reminder of the fact that my actual love life had been DOA for far longer than I wanted to admit. I'd been fine with that. Well, okay, not *fine*, but I had bigger priorities right now. I did not need Ramsey dressed as Soren and doing a striptease to "Holding Out For a Hero" stuck on repeat in my brain. That had been last night's dream entertainment.

"You keep skippin' meals like you do, Miz Gibson, and I'm gonna start putting protein powder in your sweet tea," came the rumble from behind me.

I looked up at the rumbling voice to find all six feet four inches of Big Wade Washington with a plate in one hand and a kitchen towel tossed over his broad shoulder. His apron read *GRITS & JUSTICE* in fading vinyl.

Grateful for the interruption, I mustered an innocent smile. "I'm not skipping. I'm pacing myself."

He grunted, unimpressed. "Pacing don't pay your body back when it crashes from caffeine and stress, sugar."

I was really getting tired of being attacked for my judicious consumption of caffeine.

Before I could argue, he set the plate in front of me with a look that dared me not to eat it: two biscuits drowning in sawmill gravy, one of his maple-pecan sausage patties on the side, and a perfectly fried egg perched on top like a crown jewel.

"You've got the heart of a lion and the appetite of a field mouse."

"He's not wrong."

The heart that had eased at settling into the familiar leapt into a gallop again as I spotted Ramsey. How the hell had he snuck in here without my noticing? He stood behind Big Wade, who was one of the few guys in town to actually rival him for size.

He and Big Wade exchanged a look before turning their focus back to me and folding their massive arms with perfect synchronization.

Knowing a silent order when I saw it, I picked up my fork. "I'm eating. I'm eating." To make the point, I cut my egg in half, so the yolk drizzled out over the gravy, and dipped my sausage patty into it.

Big Wade nodded in satisfaction. "I expect that plate to be clean when I come back for it."

"Yes, sir." My gaze slid unerringly back to Ramsey. "You want to join me for breakfast?"

What the hell was I doing? I wouldn't be able to *eat* with my stomach doing somersaults due to his very presence.

"Wouldn't say no. Bodie was up and out early, and the state of his fridge is just sad."

"Any idea what you want?" Big Wade asked.

Ramsey nodded toward my plate. "I'll have what she's having."

"On it." Big Wade disappeared back to the kitchen.

Ramsey was about to slide into the booth across from me when the bell over the door jingled. Mr. Dalrymple from the zoning board made a beeline straight for my booth.

"Oh, Alia, I meant to ask yesterday, did you get a chance to review the easement maps—?"

Ramsey stepped smoothly between us like a human roadblock. "I'm sorry. Miss Gibson won't be available for the next fifteen or twenty minutes. She's eating her breakfast."

Mr. Dalrymple blinked at him like he'd spoken in tongues. I had a hard time not staring myself, but I was grateful. Once Dalrymple got going on anything, I'd never get a warm bite. Hot food had been a rarity since I'd taken over as mayor.

After opening and closing his mouth a couple of times, Mr. Dalrymple narrowed his eyes. "Aren't you Ramsey Shaw?"

"Right now, I'm her breakfast bodyguard. She'll be happy to talk to you in half an hour."

"I... see." He gave me an apologetic smile and backed away. "Right. Sorry. I'll come back."

Once he'd retreated a safe distance across the room, Ramsey finally sat. Given his incredibly long legs, we had to do a bit of a dance beneath the table to make them fit, and I tried not to jerk my own legs away as if he'd burned me.

"That really wasn't necessary."

He looked every bit as unimpressed as Big Wade. "How long has it been since you've had a meal here without interruption?"

I considered. "Well, I'm thirty-one, so... basically since birth?"

The corners of his mouth twitched. "The price of being a Gibson in Gibson Hollow, huh?"

"Where everybody knows my name, my history, and probably remembers what I wore to homecoming junior year. It's part of the charm. Most of the time."

"Yeah, well, I know you. The moment somebody puts a problem in front of you, you won't see those biscuits and gravy anymore, so I say it was necessary. Eat."

I could see a trace of worry in his deep brown eyes, so I softened. "Can't argue with the truth. Thanks."

I took another bite, grateful he wasn't pushing. Grateful for the quiet. For being able to enjoy the hot, delicious food. For the minute to simply *be* without someone needing something from me. Until Ramsey had intervened, it hadn't even occurred to me that was an option. These days, I was always on, always available, always in demand.

He didn't say anything else right away, and maybe that was the real miracle. He didn't fill the silence with small talk or prod me with questions I didn't have the brain space to answer. He just... let me eat. Which might've been the kindest thing anyone had done for me in weeks.

When Big Wade returned with Ramsey's plate, he gave the cook a respectful nod. "Thanks, man."

Big Wade gave me a pointed look and then Ramsey a fist bump. "She's a treasure. Make sure she eats."

"Yes, sir." Ramsey didn't even flinch at the marching orders before picking up his own fork.

For a solid ten minutes, the only sounds were the low murmur of other conversations and the clink of forks on plates. Anyone who even looked like they were considering an approach took one glance at Ramsey's face and thought better of it. The man had the scowl of a linebacker and the jawline of a Greek statue. The combo was a very effective people deterrent.

By the time I polished off the last bite, I was so blissed out from warmth and actual nourishment that I almost forgot I was supposed to be analyzing him. Almost.

He set his fork down and leaned back. "Forgot how good the food is here."

"I forgot what it's like to finish a meal hot. That was magic."

"Big Wade is a wizard."

We sipped our coffee in tandem, and it was... nice. Too nice. In moments like this, it was easy to pretend that nothing had changed between us. That we hadn't spent most of the past ten years with entirely separate lives. That I wasn't constantly dissecting everything he said for signs that he knew too much. I remembered what it was like to just be friends with this man.

After a beat, he eased back in his seat, stretching one long arm along the length of the booth. "So, any chance you still have your Marvel trivia crown, or did someone finally unseat you?"

I'd expected him to ask something about the town or the flood recovery. That was basically the only thing I'd had conversations about for months. So the question made me laugh —a real laugh that pulled all the way up from my belly and felt like it dusted off a corner of my soul that wasn't entirely devoted to mayoral duties or lawyering. "Please. I *own* that title. No one else in this town can tell you the name of Captain

America's high school sweetheart or recite the full dialogue from Stark's first suit test in a cave."

"I never doubted you. You never let me win a single round."

"You would've hated it if I had."

He grinned. "Maybe. You were ruthless."

I lifted my nose in a haughty pose. "I was effective."

He made a show of tipping his coffee mug in salute. "True."

That small memory settled between us like a warm blanket, tugging up other echoes. Nights in the apartment I'd shared with Bodie, me sitting cross-legged on the couch with those OSHA flash cards, Ramsey half-reclined and pretending to study, until I caught him staring. I remembered how he used to look at me. But I also remembered the thousand reasons I couldn't let it mean anything then. Or now.

He hesitated. "Bodie told me about Pepper. I was really sorry to hear you lost her."

The name of my little gremlin of a rescue mutt struck me in the chest like an almost physical blow. I automatically reached up to rub at the ache in my sternum. "It's been nearly a year. I keep expecting to stop...well, expecting her. But I still wake up sometimes thinking I hear her tags jingling."

Ramsey leaned his elbows on the table. "I was sixteen when we lost my childhood dog, Charlie. I swore for years after, I'd catch whiffs of his ghost farts."

That startled another laugh out of me. "That's a new one."

"Never would've thought lingering odors of canine digestive distress would be comforting. But somehow it helped. I remember your Pepper used to hide behind your couch cushions like they were foxholes."

My throat went thick. "She used to jump out to try to scare me, like she was some big bad dog who weighed more than fifteen pounds. I played along so her feelings wouldn't get hurt. God, I miss her."

"I'm sorry. I know she was a big part of your life."

"All the way since law school. Sometimes I thought she knew more about tort reform than I did." I took a sip of coffee to try to dislodge the knot. "The donation you made to the rescue in her name meant a lot."

He shrugged. "Seemed like the least I could do. I know how much you loved her."

I looked down at my empty mug. "I keep thinking I should get another, but…"

"But?"

"Timing. Energy. Stability. Pick one. Everything's been so upside down since the flood. I can't take on anything else that needs me right now."

He nodded like he got it. And because it was Ramsey, he probably did. He'd always seemed to understand me in a way no one else did. That had always been part of his appeal.

I took a breath, determined to get myself back on even keel. "Anyway, thank you. Really."

He gave me a soft smile. "Anytime."

I caught myself looking too long and forced the conversation to safer ground. "So, for today, are you picking up tools from Fletcher or going straight to the hardware store?"

"I got a few things from Fletcher last night after dinner, but I figure it'll be a hardware run either way. I'll need to go by and see what I'm working with first, to figure out whether it's a full-on replacement or if the existing one can be salvaged."

I grabbed a sticky note from my pad and scrawled down the address. "Part of her driveway washed out with the flood, so you'll have to park on the side of the road and hike in the rest of the way. It's not too far. I hope to God you packed some work boots."

"I came prepared. Anything else I should know?"

I bit my lip. "I should also warn you that your skills at

dodging might become necessary, as there's a strong possibility she might try to cop a feel of your ass."

Ramsey snorted a laugh. "Understood. Not my first rodeo there."

I wasn't surprised. He had some of the best buns of all the tight ends in the NFL. Not that I was gonna mention that.

"Right. Good. Do you remember where the hardware store is?"

"Around the corner and down two or three blocks? It's up the way from the community center, right?"

"Exactly. Will or his grandfather will hook you up with whatever you need. Tell him Fletcher sent you."

"Got it." He began pulling out bills to lay them on the table.

"Oh, just don't mention my sister, Everly. I mean, not that you would have any reason to, but... Don't."

One dark brow winged up. "Okay... why?"

"High school sweethearts. Bad breakup when she left for Nashville. He can't avoid seeing the rest of us, but we do our best not to remind him."

"Fair enough. No accidental mentioning of the ex. Anything else you need from me?"

Oh, so many things. Most of them including 'oh, yes there,' and 'more,' and 'harder'.

Praying my face was not reflecting anything going through my brain, I managed, "Nope. That'll do it. And thanks for your help."

With a quick two-finger salute, he stood. "See you later, Alia."

Swallowing the flutter in my chest, I nodded. "Yeah. See you."

I watched him go, trying like hell not to watch too closely. I still didn't know if he knew I was Kella Harmon. I still couldn't read him on that. But I did know he saw more than he let on.

And that? That might be a problem.

Chapter 14

Ramsey

Sasspatch Society Group Chat

DEFCON 1 at The Commissary! Football player just body blocked Dalrymple from interrupting Alia's breakfast. "Miss Gibson won't be available for 15 minutes. She's eating." I'm hiding behind my menu but GIRL. ● ●

DELILAH:

She's actually EATING? Without paperwork?

MO'NIQUE:

Clean plate! She LAUGHED twice. They talked about her dog. He donated to the rescue in Pepper's name. She's looking at him like my chocolate soufflé looks at my spoon.

GLORY:

"Just an old college crush" my sequined behind!

BEA:

Operation Matchmaker is already working.
Dorothy approves.

"Try it now!"

I leaned back on my heels, laying a hand on the freshly installed water heater tucked into a corner of Miss Addie's utility room. It hadn't been hooked up to the electric all that long, but I could feel the faintest hint of warmth radiating from the case.

Nearly a minute passed before I heard her holler back from the kitchen. "Well, I'll be. It's warm! Not hot yet, but it's warmer than I've had in weeks!"

Satisfied, I twisted the valve to allow the tank to fully fill. That would take a bit to heat, but after all her time doing without, even lukewarm water was a victory. In the end, the change out had only taken a couple of hours. I wasn't sure if the original could've been salvaged, but either way, it would've taken time to order the necessary parts for a maybe. *If* I could've even found them. The color and shape of the original one suggested it was at least as old as Miss Addie's famed apple pie recipe. The hardware store had a new one in stock, so I'd elected to swap the whole thing out. All in all, it had been a simple job. One that I'd found surprisingly satisfying.

Standing up with a grunt, I grabbed a rag from my back pocket and wiped my hands as I stepped into the kitchen. The whole house smelled like lemon oil and wood polish, a tidiness that came from decades of habit, not fancy cleaners. There was still a strip of water-stained wallpaper curling up from the flood, but otherwise it was cozy as hell—little curtains with ruffles, magnets on the fridge from every one of her grandkids' vacations, even a velvet painting of Elvis presiding over the breakfast nook like a hip-shaking saint.

Miss Addie turned from the sink, dabbing her hands dry with a floral dish towel. At eighty-four, she didn't even reach my shoulder, but she had a spine of steel and eyes that cut through excuses before they were even spoken. "What do I owe you?"

"Not a thing. I'm happy to help."

"Son, that water heater wasn't free." Those eyes pinned me in place, making it absolutely clear she wouldn't accept charity.

I had to handle this carefully, so she'd accept it without taking insult to her pride. "No ma'am. But I'm not hurting. Consider it a donation to the town and pay it forward."

She squinted at me like she could see through my T-shirt and flannel to the heart of my intentions. Finally, she huffed. "Then you'll sit yourself down while I fix you something to eat. That's non-negotiable."

"Yes, ma'am." I dropped into the nearest chair. I'd learned early that trying to out-stubborn Southern women of a certain age was a fool's errand.

I watched her pull a loaf of what looked like homemade bread from one of those roll-top boxes. She sliced it with a wicked-looking knife and slathered the thick slabs with peanut butter and jelly. In less than five minutes, she set a plate with two fat sandwiches cut into neat triangles in front of me, along with a tall glass of milk that made me feel about ten years old.

"Blackberry jam's from my bushes. Put it up last summer."

I picked up half, took a bite, and nearly moaned. The bread was soft, the crusts just chewy enough, and the jam tasted like sunshine and nostalgia. "I'll deny it unto my dying breath, but these are better than my mama's."

That earned me a delighted cackle. "You flatterer. That's what happens when you make it with love and arthritis."

I smiled around another bite. "Well, arthritis's got some magic in it, then."

We sat in companionable silence as I ate like I hadn't had food in a week, and she sipped something out of a mug that announced *World's Best Great Grandma*. I'd almost forgotten what it felt like to be a regular guy. Football was a rush, sure. Big plays, roaring crowds. I loved the game. But sitting here having done something for somebody who needed it, who wasn't looking at me like I was a star but with genuine gratitude? That was something else entirely.

Miss Addie gave me a long look over her mug. "It's nice... being useful."

I raised a brow, chewing the last bite. Was she reading my mind?

"I retired when Dr. Norris retired himself and moved off to Knoxville. Ran his office for damn near thirty years, and then, just like that, I was an opinionated old woman with nothing to do and nowhere to go."

I drained the last of my milk. "Town like this? I bet there are still plenty of places for an opinionated woman to lend a hand."

She simpered at that, her teeth flashing white against medium brown skin. "Maybe so. Maybe so."

I stood, gathering my tools while she fussed about wrapping up a third sandwich "for the road." I thanked her again, made promises to stop by sometime, and headed back out to my truck, parked at the road.

I tossed my gear onto the passenger side. One job done, and it was only lunchtime. I could probably find somewhere else to make myself useful.

The road back into town curled through the bare bones of Gibson Hollow's winter landscape, all leafless branches and frost-tipped weeds bowing under the wind. The sun hung low and pale, offering more light than warmth. I kept one hand on the wheel and the other wrapped around the last sandwich Miss Addie had insisted I take.

Everywhere I looked, the scars of the flood lingered. Limbs and debris still lined the ditches, piled high and frozen stiff. Tarps in that too-bright blue flapped over rooftops, some rimmed with snow at the edges. There was hot pink tape tied around cracked trees—likely a signal for which ones needed clearing—and temporary signs tacked up with duct tape and hope. *ROAD CLOSED AHEAD, BRIDGE OUT, USE CAUTION: WORK CREW*.

But it wasn't all damage.

Outside one house, two bundled-up kids were rolling insulation into a gutted garage while their mom handed them tools from a milk crate. A teenager in a worn Carhartt jacket was sawing lumber on a pair of cinder blocks in a driveway. Hand-painted signs dotted the route into town: *WE'LL RISE AGAIN, THANK YOU VOLUNTEERS*, and my favorite— *GIBSONS DON'T QUIT*—hanging from the railing of a porch still missing its steps.

Even half-drowned and half-frozen, there was a pulse to this town. Tough and tired, but determined.

And at the center of it—always—was Alia.

I was starting to see how much of this whole machine depended on her. Every question, every task, every damn nail seemed to have her name on it. I hadn't even been here forty-eight hours, and it was already clear: if something needed fixing, they didn't ask who could help—they asked what Alia thought.

And she kept showing up for everyone.

But I could see the seams. The exhaustion beneath her polished surface. The way she kept feeding every ounce of herself into the town, like she was its personal generator. As though if she stopped moving, the power might cut out for everyone else.

It wasn't sustainable.

The truck rolled to a stop in front of the hardware store, engine ticking as I killed the ignition. I sat there for a beat, thumb tapping the steering wheel.

She wasn't going to ask for help. Not even from me. But that didn't mean I wouldn't offer it. Whether she wanted me to or not.

The bell above the door gave a cheerful jingle as I stepped into the warm, dry heat of the hardware store. Inside was organized chaos. Shelves mostly stocked, some half-empty. Handwritten signs taped up here and there: *SPECIAL ORDER ONLY, BACKORDERED TIL FEB, ASK ABOUT OUR SANDBAGS—LIMIT 4.* You could tell the place had been humming overtime since the flood, and still couldn't quite keep up.

Will Cooley stood behind the worn oak counter in a red-and-black flannel, talking a woman through the merits of two different kinds of caulk. His manner screamed infinitely patient. Peak Southern hometown guy to his core, he seemed to be the kind of man who knew everybody's uncle, ex, and alma mater without trying.

He glanced up as I approached. "Back again?"

"Water heater install went off without a hitch." I leaned an elbow there. "Figured I'd see who else needs a hand."

He passed the customer her receipt. "Alia'll know."

I wasn't surprised that was the go-to reply. But I wouldn't be that easily dissuaded. "She probably does. But I'm trying not to give her one more thing to manage."

Will let out a short breath, equal parts laugh and agreement. "Fair. She's the glue holding this place together."

That's what worries me.

"I figure plenty of folks come through here talking about what they need. You hear about anyone else needing a fix—roof patch, door hanging, busted sump pump—send them my way. Anything I can do to help, I want to. Got a pen?"

He grabbed a pen and a notepad, and I scrawled down my name and number.

Will looked at the note, then up at me. That easy smile faded into something quieter. Appreciative. "You sure?"

"Yeah. I've got time. Tools. The rest of mine will be here by next week." I'd have my assistant, Asher, ship them from Charleston. Should've thought of it before I left in the first place. "Might as well put both to work."

He nodded, folded the page, and tucked it into the pocket of his flannel. "I'll keep my ears open."

The voice cut through the low murmur of the store like a gospel solo in a church full of sinners. "Did I hear we have a man with tools who knows how to use them?"

I felt the presence behind me down to the bone.

The newcomer stood inside the doorway, framed by cold air and confidence. Late fifties or early sixties, though age clung to her the way dust might dream of landing on satin. She was tall and stately in a flowy floral duster that looked like it might've been a curtain in a previous life but hung off her like fashion royalty. Big hoop earrings, plum lipstick, and those eyes—sharp, amused, and clearly assessing whether I was worth her time.

She walked like the ground should be grateful to have her.

Will chuckled from behind the counter. "Ramsey Shaw, meet Vanglorious Jones of the Sasspatch Society. Or Miss Glory, if you value your life."

"Pleasure." I offered a nod. "I feel like you must be friends with Bodie's Uncle Dee."

Her smile spread, slow and knowing. "Oh yes, sugar.

Delilah and I go way back. That man still owes me a ride to Savannah and an apology for that barbecue disaster of '03."

My lips twitched. "Dare I ask?"

"He *burned* the ribs and tried to blame the moonshine marinade." She waved a hand, dismissing the memory like smoke. "But that's old business."

I grinned. "Was there something I could help you with?"

"Not me, sugar. But one of my neighbors has a front step sagging worse than my patience on a humid day. If you've got time, I can walk you over."

"Sure thing. I can at least take a look and see what's needed."

"Then come on, baby." She turned on her heel with a grace that would've made a stage director weep. "We'll walk and talk."

And that was how I found myself swept up in the orbit of Vanglorious Jones, Sasspatch Queen. Uncle Dee really did have the most fabulous friends.

The cold bit through my flannel as Miss Glory and I strolled down the sidewalk, boots scuffing against old salt and fresh gravel. The sky was still that heavy, leaden gray that hadn't budged since morning, and a cold that made your bones take notice had settled in like it meant to stay. Snow was definitely coming.

But that didn't stop the town from moving. We passed a pair of teenagers arguing over how to properly lay a tarp across a roofline, a trio of older men digging out a trench along the side of a house, and someone's *abuela* setting out a plate of cookies for volunteers on a makeshift folding table, steam still rising from the Tupperware.

Everyone here was working. Patching. Cleaning. Rebuilding. You could see it in every gesture—they weren't waiting on

FEMA or the state or some savior to show up. They were doing it themselves. Together.

I glanced at the woman beside me, still walking like a queen in catwalk heels even on uneven sidewalk. "So what is the Sasspatch Society, exactly? Is that a real organization, or more of a legend?"

Her regal laugh bubbled up like champagne. "Oh, it's real. The Sassypants Society was what Delilah and the rest of our group called ourselves back when we were all performers in New Orleans. Jazz, blues, cabaret—you name it, we did it."

I raised a brow. "You were all performers?" I'd known Uncle Dee had done a show for a long time, but I hadn't realized there were more of his compatriots up here.

"Mm-hmm. Loud, brash, beautiful women with more opinions than sense some days." She gave me a sideways smile. "We kept the name when we migrated up here and became movers and shakers in Gibson Hollow. When Alia and Bodie and the rest of the kids were little, they couldn't say Sassypants, so they called us the Sasspatch Society instead." Her voice went warm with memory. "It stuck."

"That's pretty adorable."

"Isn't it, though?" Her gaze softened, flicking toward a house with Christmas lights still dangling from the porch rail. "Our Alia's turned into such a go-getter. I don't know what we'd be doing without her."

Instead of speaking, I shoved my hands deeper in my pockets as that settled like a stone in my chest. I kept hearing it. Over and over. From every direction.

Everything's on her.

And it wasn't said like a complaint. It was simply fact. That made it worse.

I murmured, "I get the sense she's not any better at delegating now than she was back in college."

Miss Glory let out a soft hmm, all understanding and no judgment. "She's not one for giving up the reins easily. Not when it's her people hurting."

Yeah, that was Alia. But who worried about her when *she* was the one hurting?

The bungalow was small but tidy, its faded yellow siding showing wear from both time and weather. One of the porch steps was cracked clean through and listing slightly, like it had one foot already in the grave. A small ceramic wind chime shaped like a crescent moon clinked softly in the breeze, and a worn prayer mat sat folded neatly inside the storm door.

Miss Glory stepped up and rapped her knuckles lightly on the doorframe before calling inside, her voice warm and sing-songy like she was summoning someone to tea. "Yasmeen, baby, I brought you a man with tools and a good heart!"

A voice floated back, tinged with curiosity and humor. "It's open!"

Miss Glory turned to me with a flick of her fingers. "Go meet Yasmeen Qureshi. She'll be glad to see you. I've got to get back to the community center—potluck planning committee doesn't run itself. Holler if you need anything."

"Thanks, Miss Glory."

She gave me a look that pinned me with more weight than her smile let on. "You're a good man, Mr. Shaw. We're glad to have you here."

Then she turned and swept back up the sidewalk like it had been laid with the express purpose of carrying her.

I stepped carefully onto the porch, the broken stair creaking under my boot, and leaned through the doorway. "Miss Qureshi? I'm Ramsey Shaw. I'm here to take a look at your steps."

Chapter 15

Alia

@**BookishBree94:** Y'all I've watched the rescue video 47 times and I'm CONVINCED #SwoonyMcBroadsword is a professional actor. The way he LEAPT onto that stage?? That's Broadway training. I'm thinking he's an understudy in some fantasy musical who read Crowned in Ash and was like "this is my MOMENT" 🔥🔥🔥 #KellaHarmon #IdentifySwoonyMcBroadsword

@**FantasyBookFiend:** That armor was WAY too detailed to be amateur cosplay. I'm thinking he's either: 1. A professional costume designer, 2. A LARPer with serious skills, 3. THE ACTUAL SOREN FROM ANOTHER DIMENSION #SwoonyMcBroadsword #ArmorDaddy #KellaHarmonFandom

@**RomanceReaderRita:** The CHEMISTRY in that three-second interaction has me DECEASED. Did you see how he looked at her when he said "Time to go, princess"?? I've never been so jealous in my LIFE 🫠 #SwoonyMc-

Broadsword #MaskedBae

@BookTokTyler: Hot take: #SwoonyMcBroadsword is a former military guy. That tactical approach? The way he assessed the situation and executed the extraction? Pure special forces energy. Also explains the BICEPS. #Armor-Daddy #KellaHarmon

@FictionallyCrazed: I've analyzed his height compared to the stage dimensions, and I'm calculating #SwoonyMc-Broadsword is approximately 6'4" of PURE HERO MATE-RIAL. That narrows it down to... still millions of men, but I'M WORKING ON IT #IdentifySwoonyMcBroadsword

T he lights hadn't blown. Yet.

That fact alone felt like a minor miracle considering how many extension cords were spider-webbed across the community center floor. We were violating more electrical codes than I wanted to think about right this moment. Every table was a different flavor of fix-it wizardry—bike chains getting re-threaded, lamps being rewired, a whole corner dedicated to stitch-and-patch repairs. Somebody even had a soldering gun over in what was usually the arts and crafts room.

It smelled like burnt dust, machine oil, and banana bread. Honestly? Glorious.

"Now this was one hell of an idea."

I turned toward the warm, approving voice to find Mrs. Dailey, one of the substitute teachers from the elementary school, bundled up in a puffer coat with a vacuum cleaner hose slung over one shoulder like a plastic python. She was beaming.

I couldn't help but smile back. "You mean the Fix-It Fair?"

She nodded, shifting the hose to a more comfortable spot. "All these folks with know-how, showin' up to help, for nothing but the satisfaction of being useful? That's community. Pure and simple." She patted the vacuum like it was a cherished relative. "And if somebody can finally get this thing to stop making that awful shrieking noise, I'll be grateful for life."

"I'll put in a good word with the appliance gods." I nodded toward the repair table. "The man in the flannel's got the magic touch."

Mrs. Dailey waddled off in search of salvation, and I let myself breathe for half a second. Not because things were done —God knew they weren't. But because the thing I'd dared to hope might work... actually was.

People were smiling. Helping. Getting their broken pieces looked at and mended—appliances, jackets, maybe even their faith in the idea that we could still look out for each other without expecting anything in return.

Which meant that any minute now, something was going to short out and catch fire.

My eyes lifted automatically to the overhead lights. Still humming. Still holding.

I started weaving my way toward the backup generator access door, just in case. Nothing put a damper on neighborly goodwill like an indoor blackout in January.

I was halfway to the door that led to the backup generator closet, already mentally calculating whether we'd blown past the amperage limit for the building, when Blair stepped neatly into my path like a very stylish roadblock.

"Hey." She dimpled. "You running a power audit or avoiding small talk?"

I huffed out a breath, smiling despite myself. "Can it be both?"

She tilted her head, gave me the once-over in that subtle,

therapist-y way she claimed she'd learned from all her years on the other side of that relationship. "You doing okay?"

I knew better than to lie outright. "Functional."

The dimple wattage faded some. "That's not the same as okay."

"No, but it gets the job done." I tried to sidestep her. She mirrored me, arms crossing as she leaned one hip against the wall, clearly settling in. So much for my stealthy systems check.

Blair scanned the room. "You should be proud. This was a brilliant idea, Alia. People are *glowing*. You gave them a way to help each other. To feel less helpless."

I swallowed down the lump that tried to rise at her words. "Yeah, well, let's see if we make it through the day without tripping a breaker."

She softened, reaching out to squeeze my arm. "It's a win. Even if something blows."

I nodded and tried another pivot. She wasn't having it.

Her voice lowered. "Speaking of things blowing up... have you been online today?"

My stomach dropped faster than a bad date at prom.

"No. And I don't plan to be. If this is about the book panel—"

"It's not *just* the panel," Blair said carefully. "Kella Harmon's on a PR blitz, and #IdentifySwoonyMcBroadsword is trending. Again."

I groaned and pinched the bridge of my nose. "Please don't finish that sentence."

She held up both hands. "Message received. No social media spoilers. But I thought—"

"I know. And I appreciate it. But I can't right now. I haven't been able to think about that train wreck in almost a week, and I'd really like to keep it that way until I die."

Blair laughed, but it trailed off when a louder burst of

laughter erupted from across the room. We both turned toward the sound.

Ramsey, of course.

He was crouched next to a folding table, helping an elderly man troubleshoot the battery terminals on a cordless drill. His flannel sleeves were rolled to the elbow, grease streaked one cheek, and that stupid devastating smile of his was lighting up half the damn gymnasium.

A line had formed behind him. Naturally.

I forced my gaze away and tried to remind myself that I had *other* things to focus on. Like power grids. And emotional survival.

Blair followed my gaze with a grin that was a little too knowing. "How many folks do you think are actually in that line because something's broken, and how many just want his autograph?"

I didn't need to answer. Because she was right. And it was another reminder that no matter how good Ramsey had been this week—no matter how many hours he'd put in rewiring outlets, hauling sheetrock, fixing appliances like some kind of blue-collar Captain America—he was still a public figure. Still the guy who got recognized at the airport—or the town Fix-It Fair—and whose name trended on Twitter for breathing too attractively.

And I wanted nothing to do with that.

Not now. Not ever again. The virality of the con rescue video had cured me of wanting anything in that vicinity for life.

That should have made it easier to accept we'd merely been crossed wires. Twice.

But it didn't.

Because who he was to the world didn't hold a candle to who he was to me.

And damn if every single thing he'd done this week after

that first job, he'd gotten on his own without going through me at all. He was taking things off my plate where he could. I recognized the kindness, and it made me want to weep. Also to ask him to give lessons to everyone else in my world on how to use their eyes and their brains to save some of mine.

My phone buzzed in my back pocket, successfully saving me from getting caught watching Ramsey too long. I fished it out, already bracing for something to be on fire, or canceled, or frozen solid.

Hutton.

I answered on the second ring. "Hutton? What's wrong?"

"Wrong?" My baby sister's voice was bright, teasing. "Why does something have to be wrong?"

"Sorry. Habit." I was already veering toward the side exit. "Let me get outside where I can hear better."

The cold slapped me the second I stepped out, sharp and bracing and *blessedly quiet*. No drills, no laughter, no faint whine of a sewing machine. I pulled my coat tighter, phone tucked between cheek and shoulder, and started walking. I couldn't sit still for this. Whatever it was, I needed motion to meet it.

"So?" I prompted. "You don't call in the middle of a community event unless you've got news. Spill it."

"Okay, but you have to *promise* not to scream."

I stopped short, everything in me bracing hard. "That depends. Is this the sort of news that requires me to buy cake or bury a body?"

"Cake. Definitely cake. Possibly champagne."

Good news. I can definitely use some of that. "Now you *have* to tell me."

Hutton sucked in a long breath and then spilled the whole thing out in a gush. "I got the invite. Kyle Keenan. His next tour. He wants me as one of the opening acts."

My breath caught. "Wait—*what?*"

"I know!" she squealed. "I got the call this morning. His team saw me at that showcase I did at the beginning of the month, and apparently they've been watching my stuff ever since."

"Hutton. That's... that's *huge*. That's amazing. You're opening for *Kyle freaking Keenan!*" God, if Mom were alive to hear this news, she'd be beside herself. Hutton was the only one of us who had any interest in following in her footsteps in the music industry. And apparently she was finally getting her break.

"I *know*. I keep waiting for someone to say it was a prank."

"Oh, sweetie, if it is, I will personally hunt them down and light their inbox on fire."

She laughed, breathless with joy, and it made something in me unfurl. For all the chaos and weight and scraped-together everything of the last few months, this—this was a damn good thing.

I closed my eyes for a beat, smiling. "I'm so proud of you."

"Thanks, sis." Her voice softened. "But... that's not the only reason I'm calling."

Here it comes.

I exhaled slowly. "Okay. Lay it on me."

"Dad's therapists say he's ready to come home soon."

My whole body sagged in relief. "Oh, thank *God*. I'm ready for him to take his job back."

"Yeah, about that..." Hutton's tone dipped. "Home doesn't mean back to normal. He's made a ton of progress, but he's not ready to jump back into all the mayoral duties. Not yet. Maybe not for a while."

I stopped walking and stood there in the cold, my breath fogging in front of me, heart thudding beneath a weight that hadn't left since the day the floodwaters started rising. Because I could hear the thing she didn't say.

Maybe not ever.

"Right." I ruthlessly shoved down the weight of crushing disappointment. "Well. We'll do what we need to do."

"Alia—"

"It's okay." The lie rolled off my tongue easily. I was getting good at it. Everyone seemed to believe me. "Really. I'll talk to the boys and figure out who's free to come get him. Let me know when you want us to make the trip."

"Okay," she said gently. "And... thank you. For all of it."

We talked for a few more minutes—details, travel dates, vague chatter about logistics I'd write down later. I made all the right noises, even laughed at one of her jokes.

Then I hung up and stood still for another minute longer, letting the cold bite deep and hard until the sting brought me fully back to center.

The moment I walked back to the community center, I'd be the one with the answers again.

But out here?

Out here, I could admit I didn't have a clue how long I could keep holding all this up.

I needed a minute. More than that, I needed space. Somewhere that wasn't buzzing with extension cords and questions and the weight of too many people needing too many things I didn't have the bandwidth to give. Somewhere not cold enough to freeze my thoughts but quiet enough to let them settle.

My feet knew where to go before my brain caught up.

Ten minutes later, I was unlocking the side door of the old Gibson Hollow community theater, with its creaky stage and velvet curtains that smelled of dust and memory. I slipped inside, shutting the heavy door behind me, and exhaled into the hush.

This was Mom's space before it became mine. After she died, the Sasspatch Society took over the care and feeding of the building like it was a stray cat she'd left behind. They kept it warm in the winter, patched what they could in the summer, and made sure it stayed a place for stories. A few of them still popped in regularly during the off-season to help with organizing youth theater or storing costume bins in the wings. Usually at least one of them was around to keep me from staying too long in my own head when I wandered in here. Or to keep others out when I needed that.

But not today.

Today, the place was empty. No lights but the cold slant of late morning sun cutting in through high windows, no sounds but the tick-creak of old ductwork.

I padded down the center aisle, footsteps echoing against the concrete floor, and climbed the three low steps to the stage. I crossed to the corner, sat down in front of the old baby grand piano that had been hers, and rested my hand on the closed lid. It was scratched and scuffed from years of use, one of the legs had a shim under it to keep it from wobbling, and the middle C stuck if the weather turned too damp. But it was here. *She* was here. Or enough of her that it made a difference.

"Hey, Mama."

I closed my eyes and told her everything. About Hutton. About the tour. About Dad finally coming home, but not *coming back*. Not the way I needed or wanted him to.

I let the silence settle.

"I'm trying, Mama. I'm trying so hard. And I'm proud of what we've managed. I really am. But I'm also tired. And bitter. And—"

My throat clenched. I pressed the words out, anyway. "—I hate that there's this little part of me that's relieved you're not here to see how messy all of this has gotten. What it's done to us. What it's done to me."

That part of me—that tiny, guilty part—shrank every time I said it out loud. Still hurt, though. Like it scraped something raw beneath the skin.

I exhaled. Then sat back and rested my palms on my thighs. "You'd know what to say," I whispered. "You always did."

I glanced down at my phone. Because what she'd say, if she were here, was probably something like, "You can cry later, baby, but right now you've got work to do."

And damn it, she'd be right. There were at least six FEMA reps I still needed to follow up with, and two senators' staffers who owed me a callback about housing funds.

Nobody was going to magically give this town what it needed because I asked nicely. But sometimes, if you asked loudly and often enough, and with the right pitch in your voice, you could get some traction.

I glanced back at the piano once more. "Alright, Mama," I murmured. "Break's over."

Then I opened the FEMA spreadsheet from my phone, took a breath, and started dialing.

Chapter 16

Ramsey

"Looks like the lever's sticking." I nudged the inner mechanism with the tip of a screwdriver. "Might be gunk from... I don't even want to guess what year."

The woman across from me huffed a dry little laugh. "Probably early Reagan. That toaster's been with me longer than both my exes combined."

I glanced up at Miss Evette. Mid-fifties, sharp eyeliner, faded salon hoodie under a pea coat, nails still immaculate. I hadn't met her before, but I liked her already.

"Well, that explains the mileage." I eased the faceplate off the side. "Let's see if I can give it a little retirement-age tune-up."

She watched me work in silence for a beat, the air between us filled with low hums and distant clatter from the rest of the Fix-It Fair. I'd been elbow-deep in busted appliances and wobbly furniture since lunch. Mostly small things that needed someone to care enough to see if they could still be saved. It took me back and made me grateful for my own humble beginnings. Mama and I had done our fair share of fixing and making do.

Miss Evette shifted her weight, glancing toward the gymnasium doors like she was looking for something that wasn't there. "My realtor said there's still a good market for small homes in towns like this. Especially if they're conventional foundations. Better for flooding, I guess. Don't know how that's true since half the town's wiped out, but I've got an appointment with her tomorrow morning to find out."

I paused at the casual remark. "You're selling?"

She gave a small shrug. "Don't really have a choice. The salon's toast. Took out the whole back wall and most of the dryers. Insurance isn't covering what a rebuild will cost, and even if it did—I'd be starting from scratch. So's everybody else around here."

I didn't have any idea what to say to that. Hell, what could you say? Sorry the flood wrecked your life and your livelihood. Hope this toaster works?

My hands kept moving—out of habit more than anything. I re-threaded the spring and replaced the latch, trying not to think about what it meant to watch someone put a neat little bow on leaving.

"It's just..." She gestured vaguely with one hand. "I had my life set up here, you know? Regulars. Hair shows in Atlanta every spring. A damn shelf of ribbons for updos. Now? My daughter says I oughta come to Raleigh. Start fresh." Her mouth twisted. "I'm almost sixty. I don't want fresh. I want what I had."

The toaster clicked as the lever caught and stayed down.

"Give it a test run?" I gently nudged the toaster back toward her.

She did. Plugging it into the waiting power strip before she pressed the button. Heard the satisfying thunk as the heating element kicked on. Her eyes went glassy, but she covered it with a sniff and a nod. "Would you look at that?"

I cleared my throat. "If you need help loading anything into a moving truck, you let me know."

She gave me a look, something wry and wistful all at once. "I hope you're still here when I come back to visit."

I didn't have a reply for that either.

She packed up the toaster and moved on, and I sat there for a second too long, watching her go. Watching the space she'd leave behind stretch wider.

And suddenly the room was too loud. Too bright. Too full of people who might already be halfway gone.

Alia was nowhere in sight, which wasn't like her. It was possible she'd gotten dragged into another meeting somewhere. Probable, even. But knowing her—really knowing her—I thought it was far more likely she'd reached her limit of questions, of crowds, of being asked for one more thing, and had gone to ground somewhere. Or tried.

I stripped off my gloves, rolled my neck, and gave the lady at the next table a sheepish smile. "Apologies. Station's closed for a bit."

Then I grabbed my coat and circulated the room for a bit, scanning in case she'd simply been caught up with someone or something. When I didn't find her, I headed outside and circled the community center building in case she'd stepped out for some air.

Still, no Alia.

Gunner and Dean were both inside. I could've asked them if they knew where she'd gone, but I didn't want to get on their radar in case they thought it was weird. I could've texted her, but that felt too easy for her to ignore. Not that I wanted to be pushy, but a low-level worry had set up in my gut when I'd arrived last week and hadn't let up. Right now it was screaming that she needed somebody, whether she wanted it or not.

Where do you go when you need quiet, and the whole damn town needs you?

I turned it over in my head. Not the diner. She had an endless stream of clients and townsfolk there. Not Uncle Dee's shop. The Sasspatch Society was many wonderful things, but quiet wasn't one of them. Not even home, probably. Too easy to track down. My brain chased old conversations, sifting through offhand mentions from years ago.

A memory stirred—her voice, soft and a little sad, once upon a time over too many rum and Cokes.

"After Mom died, they donated her piano to the theater. I hated the idea at first. But now... It feels right. Like it's still hers, in a way."

The theater. I knew from my work around town that it was one of the buildings that had survived. It was a long shot. But something in me said it was the right one.

Five minutes later, I was pushing through the side door of the old performing arts building. It smelled faintly of sawdust and velvet, with a hush in the air as if the echo of applause had faded moments ago. The lights were off inside, no voices echoing off the high ceilings. The muted stillness asked you to tread soft and carry whatever weight you brought in with you.

I walked slowly down the main aisle, past rows of scuffed red seats and playbills curled at the corners on the wall. And then I saw her.

For a second, something warm and victorious flickered in my chest that I'd found her.

Alia sat alone on the edge of the stage, her back hunched slightly, one hand curled around the edge of like it might anchor her to the world. Her shoulders shook, and her breath faintly hitched with quiet sobs she didn't want anyone to see.

That flicker turned to ash. I hadn't wanted to be right that she was breaking. That she needed someone. But damn it, I wasn't letting her handle this alone.

She must've heard my step on the boards because her head jerked up, eyes red, face stiffening like she could lock it all down by sheer force of will.

"I'm fine." The thickness of her voice and the quick swipe at her cheeks undermined the instant denial, leaving the lie brittle and useless between us.

"Yeah?" I kept my voice soft. "You want to try that one more time, with less bullshit?"

She tried to laugh, or maybe choke it down. I didn't give her a chance. I crossed the last few feet, stepped up to the stage, and wrapped her in my arms.

She went rigid for half a breath, and I wondered if she'd try to pull away. But then she melted, burrowing into my chest like she was finally letting herself fall apart somewhere soft. Her fists balled up in my flannel, and she dragged in another ragged breath, shaking all over as the weight of everything she'd been carrying poured out in silence.

And I just held her. Because she never let herself do this. Not with me. Maybe not with anyone.

She was letting me be here for her.

God help me, I was so damn glad it was me.

She didn't say anything at first, only curled closer, as if she could disappear into my chest for a while and come back when the world made sense again. I held her with one arm snug around her waist, the other smoothing slow strokes down her hair. Someone to lean on who wouldn't demand a damn thing back.

She cried like someone who hadn't let herself in a long time. No big sobs. Just a long, shuddering exhale of all the weight that had been swallowing her whole. That sort of grief didn't have one clean source. It came from being the strong one for too many people for far too long.

Eventually, the tremors eased. Her breath started to even out, and I felt the soft, heavy press of her leaning into me, letting herself rest.

I didn't say a word. I wasn't about to ruin the miracle of her letting me hold her by pointing out she was doing it.

She drew in a shaky breath against my shirt, voice hoarse when it finally emerged. "I'm so fucking tired, Ramsey."

"I know." I kissed the top of her head before I could think better of it. "You don't have to hold anything up for me. Let me do the holding for a minute, okay?"

Her exhale gusted warm against my chest, something between surrender and relief. She didn't move, and God, I didn't want her to. Not even a little. I would've stayed like that all day and all night if she needed me to. She deserved to lean. To rest. To be something other than the town's unshakable center for once.

We stood there in the hush of the empty theater, the only sound the occasional creak of the old rafters and the ghost of a woman's piano on the air.

"I talked to Hutton today. Dad's coming home soon." The rasp of her voice was soft, ragged from her emotional purge.

I smiled down at the top of her head. "That's good news, right?"

"It is." But her tone told me there was a *but* coming. "He's not ready to take the job back. Not really. He's still got a long way to go. He's... trying. But he's not the guy who can run all this again. Not yet."

I said nothing, only rocked her gently, side to side.

She sniffed, pulled back to rest her temple against my chest instead of burying her face in it. "And I just got off the phone with FEMA again. The funding we were supposed to have in hand weeks ago? It's delayed. Again. Could be another month. Possibly more."

My hand stilled in her hair. "Shit."

"Yeah. How do I tell the council? We're running out of time. Out of money. Out of room to push things back without somebody paying for it. Something's gonna have to get cut. Something important." Her voice cracked. "And it's my job to decide what that is."

I held her tighter as she let out a defeated breath. My palm found its rhythm again, smoothing over the crown of her head. She was unraveling, and I didn't blame her. It was too much for anyone. And she'd been carrying it alone for way too long.

"That'd be a lot for anybody on a good day," I said softly, "and you haven't had a lot of those the last several months."

"No."

She didn't say anything else, just kept leaning, letting me hold the weight of it with her. I knew what it cost her to admit all that out loud. To not have it all together. To not be the calm, collected center everyone else leaned on. Had always leaned on.

The deep, slow-burn ache of wanting to do more than listen set up somewhere behind my ribs. I wanted to fix it. Not the sort of fix that took a wrench or a nail gun and a pile of new lumber, but the kind that would let her shoulders drop an inch because she actually believed she didn't have to do it alone. But I wasn't sure how to go about convincing her of that.

She sniffed again, quieter this time, and I felt her start to pull back—not away, just straightening. She wiped at her face with both hands, like she was scrubbing off the vulnerability.

I had to resist the urge to reach out to wipe the tears away myself. "Have you eaten?"

Her eyes lifted to mine, brows drawn together in confusion at the segue. "What?"

"Food." I eased back to look her in the eye. "Have you had some?"

Her silence stretched between us like a guilty verdict.

"You haven't gotten any better about remembering to eat when you're busy than you were in college. You know, contrary to what you seem to believe, coffee and antacids are not a food group." I reached into the pocket of my cargo pants. A protein bar came out first—peanut butter chocolate. Then a pouch of applesauce. Then a sealed stick of string cheese I'd stolen from Dean's stash yesterday and forgotten to put back. "Here. Take your pick. I'm not above bribing you with snack options."

Alia blinked at the offerings, then at me. "You carry snacks now?"

"I remember how you get when your blood sugar tanks. Seemed worth it to be prepared."

For a second, I thought she might cry again. An unmistakable mix of gratitude and amusement crossed her face as she stared at the snack lineup in my hand like I'd just offered her the keys to a kingdom. Then slowly, she took all three and sank back to sit on the edge of the stage.

Good. It would save me the trouble of gently bullying her into it.

Without comment, I sat next to her, close without crowding her, as she peeled open the protein bar and took a bite, chewing like it took effort to convince her jaw to work. She polished it off faster than I expected, and the applesauce pouch followed like the introduction of food had reminded her she was starving. By the time she was halfway through the string cheese, some color had returned to her face, and I saw some life in her eyes. That stubborn little crease between her brows had eased a fraction.

She shot me a look out of the corner of her eye. "Does this

mean I can consider you my personal walking vending machine?"

"There's a strong possibility."

"Good to know." She polished off the last of the cheese with a faint hum of satisfaction that made me feel like I'd done more than provide a few hundred necessary calories.

Because I wanted to put my arm around her again, I leaned back on my hands, all casual-like. "So, what's the number?"

Alia turned her head to me slowly. "What number?"

"For the FEMA funds. The one you're trying not to think about because, if you do, your brain might short out."

I regretted asking when her shoulders sagged again, but I needed to know.

"It's... a lot."

"How much is a lot?"

She told me.

I let out a low whistle and blinked. "Okay. That *is* a lot."

She winced like the number had sucker punched her again. "Yeah. And that's *just* what we need to cover the next phase. That's not even the long haul."

"Rebuilding a town is an expensive proposition."

"Yeah." Alia drew in another breath, longer this time. Then she pushed up from the stage with slow deliberation. "I need to get back. Or get over to the thing at the school. Or maybe both. I think I triple-booked myself, and I don't even remember which one I was supposed to be at next."

I stood when she did and couldn't stop myself from reaching out. My fingers brushed a smudge of chocolate from the corner of her mouth before I tucked a stray strand of hair behind her ear. Her eyes flicked up to mine, unreadable for a beat, though her pupils had sprung wide at the touch.

I tried not to read too much into that.

"It's gonna be okay."

She looked at me like she wanted to believe it but couldn't quite get there. Then she sighed. "It has to be. There's no other option."

And with that, she turned and walked out, shoulders squaring with each step like she was building the armor back around herself as she walked.

I waited until the sound of the door clicking shut faded behind her. Then, I pulled my phone from my back pocket and scrolled to the contact I needed.

I didn't have all the answers. But I sure as hell had a few resources. And it was time to put them to use.

Chapter 17

Alia

Two days.

That's how long it had been since I broke down in an empty theater and soaked the front of Ramsey's shirt like some overwrought Hallmark heroine. Two days since I'd let myself cry where someone could see it—*on him*, of all people. Two days since I'd admitted how exhausted I was. Let the overwhelming sense of Sisyphean defeat show. Because that was absolutely the most attractive thing to show to the guy who'd been starring in all my nighttime fantasies on the increasingly rare occasions when I could actually sleep.

Worse, he hadn't made me feel weak for it. He'd held me like it was the most natural thing in the world. Like I didn't have to apologize or explain or scramble to shove the pieces back together. And for a fleeting, fragile few minutes, I'd been... safe. Which was almost more terrifying than the crying. Because I didn't depend on other people to feel safe. I was the one who made sure everyone else was.

And now I had that forehead kiss to add to my repertoire of swoon-worthy moments. And that moment when he'd touched

146

my cheek. And absolutely *none* of it was helping me squash the attraction and admiration the man inspired. He now carried *snacks in his pockets for me* to make sure I ate. What did that *mean?*

Hell, he'd make a damned nun question her vows of chastity. I was not a nun—the state of my love life for the last year notwithstanding—and I needed to get a handle on this.

I still hadn't told the town council about the FEMA delay. I told myself I was waiting until Monday. That they'd be too busy with their own families over the weekend. That I needed more hard numbers first. All of which was technically true.

But also? I simply couldn't do it yet.

I needed one damn weekend where I didn't have to be the bearer of bad news. Or any news. Or expectations. Not that there wouldn't be work. There was always work. But tonight was community movie night, and for the next hour and a half, I wasn't the acting mayor or the emergency liaison or the oldest Gibson kid with all the answers. I was just Alia. A person with a blanket I still needed to find a spot for.

The gymnasium had been transformed in the way only small towns could manage. Blankets and fold-up lawn chairs were scattered across the scuffed floor like a post-flood picnic. Somebody had MacGyvered a projector to the basketball hoop. It was slightly tilted, but no one cared. At the opposite end of the room, a giant painter's tarp had been hung as a screen.

The air smelled like popcorn and possibility.

Will had dragged the machine over from the hardware store, and his granddaddy—wearing a bright orange *Movies Make You Smarter* tee over his flannel—was doling out paper bags of fresh popcorn like he was Santa in July. Every kid got a wink and a joke about the calories not counting if you licked the butter off your fingers first.

Laughter spilled through the gym. Real, actual laughter.

Not the brittle kind we'd all been forcing for the last several months. The whole place seemed lighter. Like maybe we'd turned some invisible corner.

I didn't even know what movie had won the online poll. Didn't care. As long as it had a plot and a runtime under two hours, I was sold. The prospect of ninety uninterrupted minutes where no one asked me to fix anything was basically the highlight of my week. Hell, my month.

I spotted my brothers near the edge of the makeshift seating sprawl. Gunner was poking Dean in the ribs with something, and Dean was swatting him away like a gnat, both of them grinning like they were twelve again. For once, I didn't have to step in or referee.

We had some time before Dad came home. Hutton wouldn't be leaving on tour until near the end of March. I could hope and pray he'd make more progress between now and then, but we'd figure out what his return really meant when he got here.

Right now? I was letting myself file that under *Future Problems*.

I spotted a clear patch of floor near the back row—close enough to see, far enough to make a quiet escape if the world started crumbling mid-movie—when I sensed the shift in the air, in my chest, that told me Ramsey was near. I told myself not to look. Not to give in to this subtle awareness I didn't want to name.

"Hey."

Crap.

At the sound of that voice, subtle gooseflesh rose on my arms. I turned to find the object of my fascination looking far too good for someone who'd spent most of the week covered in sheetrock dust and grease. Tonight he'd traded his usual flannel for a simple thermal and a zip-up hoodie, and somehow that made him look even more devastating. Probably because it was unfairly tight across the shoulders. Also, because it reminded me of the hoodie of his I still had from college that had been washed to within an inch of its life but still lived in the back of my closet, where I could pull it out when I needed a wearable hug.

"Hey." I tried not to sound winded. I wasn't prepared to talk to him alone. We'd been orbiting each other the last couple days, side-by-side in groups, never solo. It was safer that way.

Those deep brown eyes searched mine in that quiet, steady way he had of seeing right through all the layers of armor I wore all the time. It unnerved me how he could do that. And how much I wanted to let him.

He jerked his chin toward the side doors near the concession table. "Can I steal you for a sec?"

Alarm bells didn't go off exactly, but something shifted behind my ribs. "Sure."

I followed him into the vestibule off the gym—a narrow alcove with too much echo and a bulletin board announcing events that hadn't happened since before the flood. It was blessedly empty, quiet except for the distant sound of the popcorn machine and someone setting up the speakers in the main room.

Ramsey reached into the inner pocket of his jacket and pulled out a plain white envelope. I reached for it reflexively when he offered it. The moment my fingers closed on the paper, he jerked his back in a move alarmingly redolent of my siblings doing *no takesies backsies* to whoever had drawn the short straw over chores.

"What's this?"

His answer was that frustratingly unreadable look again.

Frowning, I opened the flap, drawing out the contents.

It was a check. A very large check. One that—after I'd blinked a few times to make sure I wasn't hallucinating—I confirmed exceeded the FEMA funding number I'd admitted to him in the theater by a jaw-dropping margin.

My stomach bottomed out. "Ramsey, what the hell is this?"

"A donation." He said it simply. As if the number of zeroes on that check were something anybody in this town would see in their lifetime.

I stared at him like he'd offered me the deed to the moon. "I can't accept this. It's too much."

"It's not only from me." His hands tucked into his pockets, his voice casual in the way people are when they're afraid you'll say no. "I reached out to my team—PR, managers, some of the crew I've worked with for years. Asher, my assistant, reached out to others beyond that. We told them what was going on up here. What the money would go toward. Everybody wanted to help."

I looked back down at the check, my throat closing.

This wasn't a patch job. This was a stopgap miracle.

"I—" I swallowed hard because I was perilously close to tears again, and this was no abandoned theater. "I don't even know what to say."

"You don't have to say anything." He shrugged one shoulder, then reached out to lightly nudge the envelope back toward my chest. "You can deal with it on Monday. Tonight, I saved you the best seat in the house."

My mouth might've dropped open. "You what?"

He smiled then. The impish one. The dangerous one. "Come on."

He led me back into the gym, weaving through the patchwork of seats until we reached a weirdly glorious setup along the side wall—an inflatable sofa, complete with two oversized pillows and a folded blanket that was way more cozy than the one I'd dug out of the backseat of my car.

"I— Is that..."

"Our dorm couch." He grinned. "Or what's left of it. Bodie had it in his guest room closet. I may have ordered a crapton of new patches and a portable air pump online."

Emotion twisted hard behind my ribs.

"You made me a nest." I didn't even try to keep the affection out of my voice. Because of course he did. Because he knew how much I'd loved this thing, and he knew how much I was struggling, and he was trying to help in whatever way he could.

How the hell was I ever supposed to get over this crush?

He held out a hand, palm up. "Come on, Gibson. You've earned it."

I took it because, in that moment, I was powerless to do anything else.

The sofa gave a squeaky little protest as I settled onto it, the cold vinyl clinging to my jeans for a second before it adjusted to my weight. It was exactly as ridiculous and nostalgic as I remembered—like someone crossbred a pool float with a love seat. I'd forgotten how absurdly perfect it was for collapsing into after a long day. Or month. Or year.

Ramsey eased down beside me, and the shift in weight nearly launched me right into his lap. I caught myself with a sharp inhale, narrowly avoiding planting my hand right on his crotch. For one breathless moment, I was an inch away from that mouth I couldn't stop thinking about.

"Sorry. Didn't think about the weight distribution. Let's try this." He took my hand to stabilize me while I straightened, then wedged one of the oversized pillows between us. "There, that should be more comfy."

My face was flaming, but thankfully the lights dimmed

right then as someone hit the projector remote. The screen flickered to life on the opposite wall, the sound janky for half a second before the Bluetooth speaker settled into sync. Someone had queued up a DVD or Blu-ray. I still had no idea what movie it was. Still didn't care.

Around us, laughter bubbled, voices dropped, and the buzz of community softened into the hush of collective anticipation. I draped the blanket over my lap and hugged the second pillow to my chest, half shield, half anchor, letting my shoulders drop by degrees I hadn't realized were even lifted. I loosed a cautious exhale.

Somewhere between the opening credits and the first scene, my body betrayed me. Not a full crash but a slow surrender. My eyelids dipped. My head lolled. The slight give of the vinyl combined with the comfort of Ramsey's presence had my whole system pulling the emergency brake on the week's adrenaline.

I tipped, my temple landing softly against his shoulder. My breath caught mid-inhale, and I jerked upright. "Crap. Sorry, I didn't mean to—"

"You're fine." He said it softly, as if it wasn't the first time he'd been someone's safe place. "Go ahead. Nap if you want." He adjusted slightly, the motion so subtle I almost missed it— just enough to give me more room to lean against him without it feeling like a thing.

And I let him.

I leaned back in, cheek to his shoulder, the pillow still between us, but now serving more as headrest than barrier. His breath stayed slow and even beside me, like it was perfectly natural that I'd curl up next to him like a cat in need of peace.

My eyes fluttered shut again, my pulse finally syncing to something calmer than panic. I didn't know how long it would last. Monday was coming. The crisis would still be waiting. But for tonight, I had a couch that remembered me, a warm shoulder to borrow, and the luxury of pretending—for ninety glorious minutes—that the world could take care of itself.

Chapter 18

Ramsey

Sasspatch Society Group Chat

DELILAH:

••••• Did anyone else see what I saw at movie night? Our girl Alia practically melting into that football player's shoulder?

GLORY:

CHILD. I had binoculars. That man brought back their college couch! THE COLLEGE COUCH. I'm not saying I believe in soulmates, but...

MO'NIQUE:

I brought snacks specifically to watch that show instead of the movie. Did you see how he put that pillow between them? That's a gentleman move if I ever saw one.

BEA:

A gentleman who clearly wants more. My readers don't lie—the way he looked at her when she dozed off! Dorothy and I were taking notes for my next romcom script.

DELILAH:

She's fighting it so hard. Remember how she came in here all "I'm fine, totally fine" after seeing him at the diner? Girl is NOT fine.

MO'NIQUE:

That man had SNACKS IN HIS POCKETS for her. SNACKS. IN. HIS. POCKETS.

GLORY:

Three husbands and not one ever thought to carry emergency snacks for me. I've clearly been doing this wrong.

BEA:

Should we intervene? Or let nature take its course?

DELILAH:

Oh, honey, nature is ALREADY taking its course. Did you see how many people were watching them instead of the movie?

MO'NIQUE:

Town's gonna have a pool going by Monday. I'm putting $50 on them kissing before the end of the month.

GLORY:

That's a sucker bet. I give it a week, tops.

BEA:

You're all wrong. They've already kissed. Mark my words.

DELILAH:

• • • • • • Madame Bea Dazzle with the hot take! Meeting at my shop tomorrow. Bring mimosas. We have PLANS to discuss.

The community center gym smelled like popcorn and feet with a vague overtone of coffee that Grandma Elsie had sent over from the diner this morning to fuel the post-movie night cleanup.

I pushed a broom across the scuffed hardwood, collecting kernels, napkins, and at least one crumpled juice box that was leaking something vaguely grape-scented. The projector had been taken down. Blankets rolled up. A few tired-looking folks were carting stacks of folding chairs toward the side doors, making space for whatever community thing was happening here next. Somebody'd mentioned a potluck later, because this town ran on casseroles and community goodwill.

I didn't mind the work. After two weeks of hammer swings and hauling lumber, cleaning up crushed popcorn felt like a vacation. And at this point, I knew half the people in here by name. Hell, I even got a "Morning, Ramsey!" from Mrs. Callahan, who'd handed me an apple cobbler three days ago and said it was because I reminded her of her third-favorite nephew. Not the first, but I'd take it and another cobbler any day. Given my fondness for all the home cooking that was becoming the only thing I'd accept for payment, I was gonna have to do some serious work to keep my season-ready physique. But that was Future Ramsey's problem.

Bodie showed up with a cup of coffee in one hand and a half-eaten biscuit in the other. "You're here early."

"Figured I'd earn my keep." I swept another pile toward the wall. "And I didn't want to be in the way at your place."

"You're never in the way, man." He squinted over the rim of his coffee mug. "So I gotta ask... where'd you even find that inflatable sofa? I thought for sure it had bit the dust a million years ago."

I straightened, leaning on the broom handle. "It was shoved in the back of the closet in the room you've got me in. I think it might be more patch than original at this point, but I remembered Alia used to love that thing, and it felt like the right call for movie night. Get her to actually, you know... sit down."

"Yeah, she seems to have forgotten how to do that." Bodie kicked a popcorn kernel out of the path of a table being dragged past. "How you like being a human pillow? She was out cold on your shoulder for like an hour."

I felt a muscle tick in my jaw and forced my grip on the broom to stay loose. "She was exhausted. Passed out before the opening credits even finished. I wasn't about to wake her up when she clearly needed the rest." That much was true. Every word.

"Fair point. I think that's the longest stretch I've seen her sit in... Jesus, months? Glad I've got someone else around who can help wrangle her when she's pushing too hard. She always listened to you better than me."

I gave him a pointed look. "That's 'cause I never try to railroad her."

Bodie snorted. "You're sneaky like that. Keep it up."

His gaze drifted toward the side entrance, and something about the way his whole body subtly realigned made me glance over too.

A woman had come in, balancing a tray that looked to be holding at least a couple dozen cinnamon rolls. She was petite, brunette, dressed in jeans and a soft pink long-sleeve shirt dusted faintly with what might have been flour. Even from across the gym, I could tell she brought the scent of sugar and nutmeg.

I didn't recognize her. Which was saying something, considering I'd spent the past couple of weeks doing small repairs and heavy lifting for at least half the town. But she looked like the type of person people automatically liked. Pretty, but in a quiet, Sunday-morning way—like a favorite sweater you didn't even realize you missed until you put it back on.

Bodie handed me his coffee and clapped my shoulder. "I'll catch you later. Thanks again for all the help, man. Seriously. Means a lot."

I barely managed a "Yeah, of course" before he was halfway across the gym, that easy stride of his suddenly more deliberate.

Out of blatant curiosity, I watched him approach her. Bodie had been single for a while, and I hadn't heard him mention any woman in... well, come to think of it, since he'd taken the job as chief of police. Something about his reaction told me this wasn't simple professional courtesy or curiosity. As the brunette caught sight of him, she stiffened. She didn't back away, but she definitely didn't smile either.

I watched in fascination. Back in college, Bodie had been the charming one, always with an easy smile. Girls had eaten it up. But this woman was having none of it. Bodie said something. She answered, but whatever it was landed with the thud of a closed door.

He tried again, and I could imagine his easy tone. She shifted her grip on the tray. He gestured—small, like he didn't want to spook her—and I caught the edge of something in his face. Not regret, exactly. But something in the neighborhood.

I couldn't hear the words, but I knew that look. I'd worn it a few times myself lately. Trying to reconnect with someone who mattered more than you'd realized—until they didn't look at you the same way anymore.

Whatever was going on there, it wasn't about cinnamon rolls.

"God, that's a hot mess."

I glanced over to find Blair, somehow managing to sip coffee, juggle a clipboard, and exude judgment with nothing more than the arch of an eyebrow. I had no idea where she'd come from, but I was learning not to ask. Blair had always materialized where and when she wanted, and odds were high she already had a list of everything I'd touched in this building and a solid opinion about how I'd done it. As Alia's ride-or-die, I'd known her well back in college, too.

She followed my line of sight toward Bodie and the brunette with the now half-empty tray of cinnamon rolls.

"What am I looking at?" I watched as the woman offered the tray to someone other than Bodie with a full, warm smile, while he stood there like a man trying not to sigh too loud.

"That's Emmaline Maddox. Her people have been feuding with the Gibsons since before electricity. Some land dispute back in the dark ages turned generational blood sport. From what I understand, she and Bodie were friends once. Real close. But then he arrested her brother a few years back. He went to prison. That ended... well, pretty much whatever friendship there was."

"Damn. Hot mess seems like an understatement. Appreciate the local gossip drop."

Blair sipped her coffee again. "Just keeping you in the loop."

I watched Emmaline turn on her heel and walk off with military-grade politeness. Bodie stood there a second longer, hand half-lifted like he wanted to call her back and knew it would only make things worse.

She turned those eagle eyes on me then. "Speaking of things worth noting. That inflatable sofa last night. Was that a strategic move or merely nostalgia?"

I shrugged and hoped it looked casual. "I found it in the back of the closet at Bodie's, and I remembered Alia used to love it. Thought it might make her smile."

Blair's expression didn't change. Not much, anyway. But I caught the shift. She was cataloguing. Weighing. I wasn't sure what column I landed in, especially since Alia's bestie was a hell of a lot more observant than her brother.

"She passed out in five minutes," I added. "Didn't even make it past the opening credits. I figured she needed the sleep more than whatever movie was playing."

Blair hummed, a small, noncommittal sound that gave nothing away. I waited for the ribbing. For the eyebrow wag. For the inevitable "So, what are your intentions with our mayor?"

It never came.

Instead, she continued sipping her coffee. "She's been running on fumes for a while now."

Maybe we were on the same page then. "Yeah. I actually wanted to talk to you about that."

Her observant stare turned sharp and more than a little curious, and I had to fight to keep my shoulders from hunching up around my ears.

"I wanted to talk to you about organizing a covert ops food detail."

Her perfectly shaped brows arched. "A what now?"

I kept my tone mild. "You and I both know she's terrible about remembering to eat when she's busy. Always was. This?" I gestured vaguely toward the world. "This is worse than college. I just... I think we could tag-team it. Make sure she's not running entirely on caffeine and willpower. I mean, I know

I could've gone to the Sasspatch Society, but I'll be honest. They kinda intimidate the hell out of me."

Blair's lips quirked in delighted amusement. "Smart man." She sobered. "Anyway, you're not wrong. About any of it. A lot of us try to make her sit down and eat when we get the chance, but it wouldn't hurt to have a more concerted, organized effort."

Relief bloomed low in my chest. This was why I'd gone to Blair. Because she wouldn't make it weird. She'd just get it done.

She nodded once. "We'll work something out. Discreetly."

"Appreciate it." Casting another glance around, I jerked my head for Blair to stay with me, and we began to walk. I kept my voice low. "How's she really doing?"

Blair adjusted the grip on her clipboard and let out a breath through her nose that said *buckle up*. "She's running on adrenaline, caffeine, and sheer Gibson stubbornness. We're all worried about her. But she doesn't let anyone in far enough to help for more than five minutes."

That tracked.

"She sleeps maybe four hours a night. If that. Pretends it's fine. Says she'll rest later. You know how she is."

"Yeah." My voice came out rougher than I meant it to be. "I do."

Because I'd seen it. The way she powered through. The way she deflected. The way her shoulders carried weight like it was oxygen. And I'd also seen the moment she stopped. When she finally let go—for about five minutes—and then patched herself back together like nothing had happened.

"We've got to keep her from burning out. Again."

"Good luck with that," Blair muttered. "It's like trying to keep the tide from coming in with a sandcastle and a soup spoon."

I huffed a breath. Not a laugh, but close. "So we build a seawall."

She looked at me then, brows lifting in surprise, as if she hadn't expected me to mean it quite like that.

I didn't back down. "She's doing the job of five people. From a diner booth. With no insulation, no staff, and no damn gatekeeper. She's going to break herself if we don't figure something out."

"You have an idea?"

"Not yet," I admitted. "But I'm working on it."

Because she deserved more than a corner booth and a twenty-minute lunch she didn't remember to eat. She deserved boundaries. Support. Space to breathe without someone expecting her to hold up the sky. She was holding this whole damn town together and shouldn't have to carry the weight alone.

So, no—I didn't have an answer yet.

But I would.

Chapter 19

Alia

@ReadingRainbowRaquel: I've started a spreadsheet tracking every professional cosplayer who matches #Swoony-McBroadsword's build, and I'm down to 43 possibilities. This is what my literature degree prepared me for. #Detective-Work #MaskedBae

@PageTurnerPrincess: THEORY: #SwoonyMc-Broadsword is Kella's secret boyfriend, and this was all planned to boost book sales. And it WORKED because I just bought the entire series again but in special edition hardcover this time 🫣 📚 #NoRegrets

@BookDragonDave: My girlfriend is STILL talking about #SwoonyMcBroadsword and honestly? Same. That growl he let out before grabbing Kella? I felt that in my SOUL. #ArmorDaddy #RomantasyGoals

@LiteraryLush: GUYS what if #SwoonyMcBroadsword is actually a famous athlete?? He had the build, the confidence, the HEROICS. I'm thinking football or hockey or maybe MMA? The investigation continues! #IdentifyS-woonyMcBroadsword #KellaHarmon

@NovelNerdNancy: What if #SwoonyMcBroadsword is someone Kella knows IRL and this is going to be the plot of her next book?? A real-life rescue by a masked hero?? I would literally throw my wallet at that book 💰📖 #KellaHar-monTheory

The building was part of what locals called Gibson Row—a retail block owned by my family—and was only partly reconstructed. It didn't have heat yet, but it had four solid walls, a roof that didn't leak, and—most importantly—no one else in it. Which made it the best office I'd had in weeks.

I'd dragged in a camp chair, a folding table, and my tote bag full of grant applications, damage reports, and too many FEMA emails. There was a portable heater at my feet that only sort of worked if I didn't move and the extension cord didn't twitch wrong. I could see my breath every time I sighed, which was often, but at least I wasn't being asked where the extra paper towels were or if someone could use the restroom in the back of the diner.

My phone buzzed every three minutes with something new I didn't want to look at. I didn't. Not yet. I was elbow-deep in form submission hell, trying to figure out how to merge three different recovery spreadsheets into one coherent document, when the front door of what would eventually be retail space again creaked open.

I glanced up, fully prepared to politely but firmly send

someone away if they were about to ask me where to stack the donated blankets.

Instead, Elena strolled in like some casually radiant domestic goddess, holding a brown paper sack in one hand and a bottle of tea in the other.

My stomach made an embarrassingly hopeful noise.

"That smells suspiciously like real food." I eyed the bag like it might bite. "Please tell me it's not a trick."

She grinned a grin that said she was a little too pleased with herself, and I was reminded all over again why she and Blair were soulmates. "Spinach and cheese hand pie. Still warm. And peach tea. Figured you'd be about due."

I blinked. "You're the third person in as many days who's shown up with food. Should I be worried?"

"You should be grateful." She offered the bag with the self-satisfied air of someone who knew her food fixed problems. "But yeah. There's definitely a conspiracy."

I narrowed my eyes. "Let me guess. Blair?"

"Wrong." Her smile turned sly. "Ramsey. It was all his idea."

My fingers curled tighter around the edge of the table. That well-aimed dart hit right in the center of my chest. Not a surprise really—given the snack pockets—but something about hearing it out loud made my heart flutter behind my ribs.

I didn't say anything.

Elena didn't wait for me to. She leaned in, gave me a warm, solid hug that I hadn't been aware I needed until she'd already given it, then headed back for the door like this was a casual lunchtime favor and not a calculated strike on my defenses.

"Thank you!"

She waved over her shoulder, then was gone, leaving me with a hand pie, a bottle of tea, and a heart that wouldn't settle.

I stared at the bag for a solid minute, like it might explain itself. Eventually, the hand pie won. I peeled back the wax paper wrapping, took a bite, and groaned. Flaky crust, warm cheese, perfectly wilted spinach, a hit of garlic and something buttery. It was comfort food that didn't judge me for forgetting to eat breakfast. Again.

To be fair, I'd *ordered* breakfast. But per usual, I'd been interrupted seventeen times, and by the time I got to my oatmeal, it was a gelatinous lump that seemed more like something appropriate for patching a tire. That was when I'd decided to relocate literally anywhere else, before I dropped any more of my spinning plates.

I sat back in the camp chair, which creaked like it resented supporting any weight that wasn't emotional, and forced myself to chew slowly. To actually taste the food. To not pick up my phone. To not answer one of the six open emails on my laptop. For the first time in longer than I wanted to remember, I did nothing more than eat. Which shouldn't have been such a revolutionary act. And yet, here we were.

I took another bite, thinking of Ramsey.

Of course, I was thinking of Ramsey. The inflatable sofa had been a punch straight to the memories. That stupid dorm couch that had somehow survived their entire freshman year despite three slow leaks. He hadn't only remembered it. He'd patched it up, hauled it in, set it up like a soft-landing zone in the chaos. With pillows. And a fluffy blanket.

Then he'd saved me a seat.

And when I crashed—because that was a thing I did these days when I sat for longer than two minutes at a stretch—he'd let me rest. Let me lean.

Of course, that made me remember my breakdown in the theater, where he'd let me need something, and be held, without asking for anything in return.

I sipped the tea and swallowed past the lump in my throat that wasn't food.

Everything he'd been doing was helping more than I wanted to admit. More than I knew how to admit. And that scared me a little. Because these feelings were more than attraction. More than the crush I'd nursed for years. They were messy and inconvenient and... really big.

And right now, I didn't have the bandwidth to detangle my own heart when the town was still hanging by a thread.

I needed space. Somewhere quiet, where nobody would ask questions and I didn't have to be anybody's solution for a while. At least for another half dozen hours.

Locking my temporary office, I trekked the few blocks to the theater. Unlocked today. Miss Bea was probably using the lobby as extended workspace again. She always insisted she loved the vibe. The doors creaked when I tugged them open, and I was struck with the scents of old wood, dust, and velvet, threaded with whatever vintage perfume Miss Bea had declared appropriate for early afternoon couture. Which today, apparently, was rhinestones, red lipstick, and a turquoise caftan so loud it could've served as a hurricane warning.

She looked up from the lobby table, where she had a half-dismembered pageant gown stretched out like a crime scene. A scattering of sequins glittered across her sewing kit like fallen stars. Her glasses were perched halfway down her nose, and there was a pearl-headed pin clenched between her teeth like a cigarillo from an old movie.

"Well, hey there, Sugarplum. You look like somebody ran you through the spin cycle and forgot the softener."

"Sounds about right. I wanted a quiet spot for a bit. You mind if I use the piano?"

"Honey, it's your mama's." She flicked her wrist. "Go on.

I'll be out here finishing up this poor dress's resurrection. Needs to be back at Devine by curtain call."

"I won't be long."

"Mmmhmm. I'll lock up if you're still in a fugue state when I head out. No one's interrupting you today unless they come bearing cobbler or a confession."

I leaned in and gave her a quick side-hug, one arm around her glittering shoulders. "Thanks, Miss Bea."

Inside the theater, the quiet was weighted. Like a breath held. A silence that wrapped softly around you and said, *You're safe here. Let it out.* Or maybe that was my own projection.

I crossed the dusty floor slowly, my boots making barely there echoes against the boards. Up ahead, Mama's piano was tucked on one side of the stage, beneath the heavy velvet curtains she and Uncle Dee had sewn themselves "to class the place up" when I was little. They'd had the best time gilding this place like one of the grand theaters of old.

I climbed the steps, pausing to turn on a couple of stage lights before I strode over and pressed my hand flat to the closed lid. It might've been my imagination, but it seemed as if warmth—or possibly just memory—bled into my palm. After a moment, I settled on the bench, lifting the lid with a soft creak. The strings inside hummed faintly, like they recognized something was coming.

But not yet.

"Hey, Mama," I whispered.

The keys were cool beneath my fingertips. I let my hands rest there, the weight of memory pressing heavier than my own fingers.

"I miss you." The words were like a pressure valve loosening in my chest. An exhale after holding my breath for too long. "Nothing new there. I'll always miss you."

I stroked the keys the way she used to stroke my hair. "I'm

holding on, but it's hard." My voice cracked on the last word. I closed my eyes and let the stage swallow the sound.

"There's been some relief lately. Ramsey's here. And it's not the same as college... but it is."

He'd never been my person. Not really. Not in any official way. He was Bodie's, and I was the bonus friend. But he kept showing up. Not merely for the town. For me. Quietly. Consistently. Without being asked. Without expecting anything in return.

"He keeps doing the work. Taking care of people." I paused as my thumb ghosted over middle C. "Taking care of me." That admission came out softer, as if it didn't want to be caught in the open lest someone recognize that I wasn't actually unbreakable.

"What am I supposed to do with that? I'm the one who takes care of everybody else. That's what I do. I don't know how to accept someone doing that for me."

My hand drifted to the side of the piano. I could still picture Mama's hands there, moving with that graceful certainty. She'd always known how to lead from the background. To offer strength in a way that never made you feel weaker.

"I don't want to get used to it," I admitted. "Because this isn't home for him. He's got a life and a job hours away."

And yet. He was here.

"I kissed him," I murmured. "Did I ever tell you that? At the masquerade. Years ago. He didn't know it was me." That still made me feel fourteen kinds of foolish. A state that hadn't been improved by the more recent repeat I'd had at the book convention.

"I thought I imagined the connection. But I didn't. I know I didn't. Still, I didn't know what to do with how I felt then." I huffed a laugh that didn't hold a trace of humor. "I don't know what to do with these feelings *now,* either. I can't escape them. I can't escape *him.*" My throat tightened. "And I don't know that I want to."

The words echoed in the quiet, bouncing back at me with more weight than I'd expected, reverberating through my chest. When had I gotten to the point that the impossibility of a real relationship with Ramsey had stopped being a deterrent to all the things that came with him? Probably somewhere between the protein bars and the inflatable sofa. I was so tired of fighting what he stirred up in me. So tired of denying that I wanted him on every possible level.

My fingers found their places through muscle memory and long-buried instinct. The melody rose slowly—soft and yearning—threading through the empty theater like a secret too old to forget.

It was the song we'd danced to that night. The one he'd probably forgotten.

But I hadn't.

And as the notes poured out of me, steady and aching, I let myself feel it all. The memory. The want. The impossibility. The hope.

And then I began to sing.

Chapter 20

Ramsey

I had the answer.

Not a workaround. Not a temporary Band-Aid slapped over a bullet hole. A real, honest-to-God solution. It wasn't quite finalized, but it was solid as a concept. A way to give Alia a space that was hers. Not borrowed or jury-rigged or cobbled together between lunch rushes at the diner. A place where she'd actually be able to *breathe* and work.

My hands wouldn't stop moving. I'd already tried to shove them into my jacket pockets twice, but they kept twitching like they had something else to build.

I needed to tell her. *Now.*

So I headed to the diner, practically humming with the need to see her reaction. That tilt of her head when she was trying not to smile too big. The way her eyes softened like I was a damned hero before she rolled them at me. I wanted all of it.

Which was probably getting ahead of things. It was equally likely she'd be pissed at my high-handedness and say no. Because this wasn't something directly for the town that she couldn't refuse. This was unequivocally, unarguably, for her.

And okay, it was big. But damn it, I had the means to do this, so why the hell shouldn't I?

But her booth was empty when I shoved through the door. Fine. No big deal. She was probably at the community center. I did an about-face before Grandma Elsie or anybody else had a chance to catch me, and hoofed it over, heart still thumping with excitement. But Alia wasn't in the committee meeting I busted up in the middle of.

That's when the buzz in my chest shifted. Not panic. Not yet. But that low-grade static that said *something's off*. She didn't just vanish. Not with this many people relying on her. Not with a dozen half-fires still waiting to be put out.

Muttering apologies, I stepped back outside, running a hand over the back of my neck, and took a breath.

She might be in a meeting somewhere else. God knew she had a million of those. But somehow, that didn't feel right. My gut sent me toward the theater. If she wasn't there, I'd hit up Devine Interventions and see if Uncle Dee had any notion where she'd gotten off to.

My boots pounded the pavement faster than my thoughts could catch up.

The heavy glass door creaked open with a tug. Miss Bea was front and center in the lobby, wrapping a garment bag around something shiny enough to cause temporary blindness. Or maybe that was her caftan. Rhinestones winked under the house lights, her earrings catching the gleam like miniature disco balls.

She didn't even glance up. "If you're here to ask my opinion on plum versus aubergine for eveningwear, I'm out of patience and pearls."

I cleared my throat. "Not here for fashion advice, I swear."

That earned me a quick glance. "Well, that's a shame. You'd look fine as sin in a deep jewel tone." She zipped the bag with one decisive motion, then turned to face me fully. "You look like you're chasing something, sugar."

Self-conscious, I rubbed a palm over the back of my neck. "Have you seen Alia?"

She tilted her head and smiled, slow and knowing, but not unkind. "You didn't hear it from me, but she's inside. Alone. And she wants to stay that way, so if you're going in there— make sure it's worth it." Her voice was velvet-smooth and edged like a blade.

My breath hitched. Not from nerves exactly, but from the weight of what I was carrying. Of what I might finally be ready to hand over.

"I wouldn't be here if it wasn't."

Miss Bea nodded, satisfied. "I've got a hem to finish and a martini waiting. I'm locking up." She slung the garment bag over her shoulder like a weapon, then swept past me in a cloud of vintage powder and sass, heels clicking like punctuation marks.

The door clicked shut behind her, and I was alone in the hush.

Except it wasn't hushed. Behind the doors to the theater itself, faint strains of music sounded. Soft at first. A handful of piano notes, unspooling like thread through the quiet. I moved toward it without thinking, keeping my steps light as I reached the house doors and pushed them open, like the sound might shatter if I came in too fast.

The theater was bathed in gold and shadow. Dust hung like glitter in the lights onstage. And at the far end of the room, at her mother's piano, sat Alia. Singing.

Her voice—Christ, her voice—wrapped around me like a wire pulled taut. Fragile and sharp and stunning.

I stopped dead inside the house doors, because I recognized the song before the second line left her mouth. "When You Say

Nothing At All." That song had always been ours. Even if we'd never said it out loud. Even if we'd let a decade pass without touching that truth. It belonged to that one night at the masquerade. The one where we'd danced slow in the shadows and kissed like the world might end. She was singing it like she remembered too.

Her eyes were closed, her fingers moving over the keys as if they were an extension of her. Every line she sang carried something low and aching and heartbreakingly beautiful.

God, she could sing.

In theory, I knew all the Gibsons were musically talented. Their mama had been a country singer before she'd given it up to raise her family. But knowing and hearing were two different things. Alia couldn't simply carry a tune. She wouldn't just blend in with the family harmony. She had a voice that made the air around her feel sacred.

And I'd never heard it before.

Not once.

Thirteen years of knowing her. Of loving her—quietly, stubbornly, stupidly—and I had never known she had this in her. Even if I hadn't long since fallen for this woman, just hearing her like this, I'd have laid my heart at her feet, like a knight offering fealty. I knew this was it. The end of the road of pretending. I had to tell her, no matter what the consequences.

The last note lingered like a held breath, and in the silence that followed, she didn't move. But I did. Slow and careful. My heart was beating so hard it thumped in my ears. And maybe I should've waited. Given her a moment to come back to earth, to tuck all that rawness away. But I'd waited too damned long already.

"That song always reminds me of you." My voice came out steadier than I expected, heavy with everything I hadn't said for a decade.

She jolted like I'd fired a gun, nearly toppling right off the piano stool before catching herself with a sharp grip on the edge of the bench.

"Jesus, you scared me." Her voice was breathless. Defensive. "What are you doing here?"

I took a step closer—slowly, because I wasn't entirely sure she wouldn't bolt if I moved too fast. But I didn't stop. Couldn't.

The air between us buzzed like a live wire.

"Why that song, Alia? Why now?" There was no accusation in it. But no way out either. The truth was finally pushing its way to the surface, whether we were ready or not.

She stared at me like she was weighing a thousand answers. Her throat moved as she swallowed. Her fingers still gripped the edge of the bench, her knuckles showing white. When she finally spoke, it was so quiet I barely heard her. "You told me not to forget you. I never did."

The floor tilted beneath me. I sucked in a breath, sharp and uneven, like air might fill in the cracks her words split wide open.

I remembered saying it. Not just the words, but everything wrapped around them. The silk of her mask. The tumble of curls. The way her hand had felt in mine. How she'd looked at me like she *knew* who I was, wanted me, and I'd believed it could be a beginning for us.

I stepped closer, boots whispering against the plush carpet of the aisle as I approached the stage. The creak of the stairs underfoot barely registered over the pounding in my ears. "You knew it was me?" My voice rasped like sandpaper. "Why didn't you say anything?"

She looked up at me, eyes wide. Her fingers tightened on the edge of the bench like it was the only thing keeping her grounded. "I didn't think you recognized me."

The stunned laugh that tore loose from me was more broken than bitter. "Alia." I shook my head. "I'd know you anywhere. With a mask and an evening gown, or a wig and glasses and a whole new name."

Her blink was slow, like her brain was catching up in real time. "You knew it was me at the con, too?"

My gaze snapped to hers, locking in. "You recognized me there, too?"

She lifted her chin, a wry twist to her mouth. "You're bigger than ninety-nine percent of the population. You don't exactly blend in. But I wasn't sure... not until you kissed me." Her exhale felt like a blade being unsheathed. "Why didn't *you* ever say anything? Either time?"

And just like that, it was all laid bare. Everything we hadn't said sat between us, thick and electric. All these years, we'd both known, and we'd done nothing. I'd hoped she really had given in to the fantasy and thought I was someone else. But that was cowardice, because I hadn't known how to face her when I didn't think I was in a position to give her what she deserved. And because of it, I'd hurt her. I saw the lingering traces of it in her eyes.

There was a pause—long and thick and knotted with all the time we'd lost. Ten years of could-have-beens pressed down on my shoulders like an overloaded Olympic bar. I hadn't moved. Didn't think I could. Until the silence got too damn loud for me to stand.

"I wanted to. God, I wanted to so damned badly. But back in college..." I hesitated. Swallowed. "Bodie convinced me not to."

Her eyes snapped to mine, sharp and narrowing. I'd seen that look a hundred times, but never pointed at me. Not like this. "My brother warned you off me?"

"No. Not like that." I shook my head fast, stepped in before that spark turned into a wildfire. "He never knew. I didn't tell him. But after you broke up with the douchewaffle, Bodie said something that stuck. That you deserved someone who stayed."

I looked down, letting the truth strike the floor between us. But she deserved eye contact for this, so I forced my gaze back to hers. "I was getting drafted. I couldn't be that for you. So I let you go."

That was the moment I saw the bloom of hurt flare hard into anger.

Alia stood so fast the piano bench scraped across the floor. She stalked toward me with a purposeful fury I'd once seen her unleash in a courtroom, before she'd moved into family law. And I stood there, because I deserved every bit of whatever she was about to dish out.

"Did it ever occur to you to actually talk to me?" she demanded. "To ask what *I* wanted? Because you decided for both of us without taking me into account at all."

I opened my mouth. When nothing came out, I closed it again and tried to force air into lungs that didn't seem to want it.

"I... never thought of it like that. I wanted you to have the world."

Her voice went soft then. Not gentle. This wasn't a mercy. This was steel under silk. Something forged in the fire of too many years spent holding it all in. "I just wanted you. Which is what I'd have told you if you'd bothered to ask. Would I have preferred someone who could be there with me day in and day out? Sure. But I'd have taken part-time with you over settling for less with someone else."

Her confession spotlit something I hadn't realized I was still holding onto. This rewrote everything. Every single story I'd told myself about why I'd made the choice I did. And now, all I saw were the years. All that empty space that could've been filled with her. With us.

Regret echoed through every beat of the pulse still ringing in my ears. The pain of everything we'd lost because I'd effectively taken the choice away from her. But with pain came clarity.

I wouldn't make that mistake again. And maybe she wouldn't want to give me another chance. Everything she'd said had been past tense. I wouldn't blame her if she considered me a shit bet after all that. Maybe this would mean I'd lose her for good, even as a friend. Might even lose Bodie, too.

But I knew if I didn't try, I'd regret it for the rest of my life.

Resolved, I stepped closer, erasing the last of the space between us short of touching her. "I can't change what I did back then. But I want to change now. No more masks for either of us. No more hiding what we've both been avoiding."

My throat tightened, but I didn't back down. Not this time.

"I want you, Alia. I've always wanted you. And I'm yours... if you still want me."

Chapter 21

Alia

Sasspatch Society Group Text

🔔 ALERT 🔔 Football Adonis just burst into the theater looking for oᴜr girl. Man's got that "about to confess his undying love" face. I'm evacuating!

GLORY:

SHUT. UP. Is this finally happening?! I've been waiting since she first mentioned that "college crush" :GIF of Mᴵchael Scott from The Office "Oh my God, it's happening! Everybody stay calm!":

MO'NIQUE:

Do we need snacks? I can be there in 10 with an emergency charcuterie board.

DELILAH:

Nobody moves! Nobody goes near that theater! I'll handle any strays at the door.

BEA:

Already locked up, sugar. Told him if he was going in, it better be worth it. That boy looked READY 🔥

GLORY:

I'm redirecting the costume committee meeting to my place. No interruptions!

MO'NIQUE:

I'll tell everyone the sound system is down for maintenance

DELILAH:

Operation Let-Them-Kiss is officially in progress. Updates required IMMEDIATELY after.

BEA:

Dorothy and I are taking strategic positions across the street. Will report developments 🕵️

GLORY:

Ten years of pining. TEN YEARS! If they don't figure it out now, I'm locking them in the prop closet myself.

"I want you, Alia. I've always wanted you. And I'm yours... if you still want me."

Ramsey's words washed over me, soothing the temper that had sparked over the fact that—well meaning or not—he'd taken my choice away all those years ago.

He was giving it back now.

I could either focus on the gut punch of the lost years, or I could take what I'd wanted all along.

If the flood had taught me anything, it was that life was too short to wait.

I launched myself at him. He was too damned tall for me to kiss easily without heels, and I didn't want to waste another moment. He didn't even stagger as we collided. Those big, strong arms wrapped around me and lifted like I weighed nothing. Our mouths crashed together, a fever of desperation. There was nothing careful or sweet or slow here. This was years of deprivation and longing finally detonating.

I wrapped my legs around his waist, glorying in the groan that dragged from deep in his chest as he shifted his hold to get a firmer grip on my ass. I didn't hate that one bit because I wanted to feel those massive hands everywhere.

Nipping his bottom lip, I broke the kiss to murmur, "Stage left."

"Huh?" He didn't understand. And why should he? He'd never been backstage, and all the blood had clearly left his brain already.

"Stage manager's office. Sofa. Door. Lock."

Something feral lit in his eyes, and I loved it. "Which way is left?"

On a delighted laugh, I pointed.

Ramsey turned us in that direction and made good use of the fact that he was one of the fastest tight ends in the league. He stumbled through the door, kicking it shut before pressing me back against it and taking my mouth again. I whimpered, clutching at his shoulders as we warred to get closer.

"Alia. God, you have no idea..."

"Do too. Five steps straight back."

He didn't ask why, only followed orders. I miscalculated the length of his stride, and at four and a half he stumbled, his arms tightening around me as we tumbled onto the couch. It was ancient, with who knew how much dust trapped in the wales of corduroy that was probably older than I was. I didn't give a damn. It was a horizontal surface and our best shot at privacy.

I tugged at his black henley, revealing a drool-worthy swath of his washboard abs before he gently curled his hands around my wrists.

"Are you sure?" He wasn't objecting. I could feel the evidence of that where I straddled his lap.

Releasing the shirt, I shifted to frame his face between my palms. "Honestly, you are the only thing I've been sure of in a long time."

Eyes softening, he combed his fingers through my hair to cup my nape, drawing me forward for another kiss. I melted against him, settling more firmly against the bulge behind his jeans. And didn't that just light up every long-neglected atom of my libido? A pleased hum vibrated in his chest as I shifted against him. He pulled me closer, rocking up in a way that had me gasping against his mouth. My hips found his rhythm, chasing the delicious friction that was so much less than I wanted, but still so very good. My fingers fisted in his shirt, anchoring myself as I followed my pleasure, my tongue warring with his to the rhythm pulsing between my legs.

The quick, sharp flash of peak left me bowed and gasping. There was no room for embarrassment, no room for anything but the need already coiling inside me again. I pulled at his shirt. "This. Off. Now."

He let me go to drag it over his head with one hand, in that way guys did that was so inexplicably hot. Then I got my first view of his naked chest, and holy hell. Reverently, I skimmed my hands over the ridges of muscle, smiling as he twitched under my touch.

"Remind me to thank whoever designed your training program."

His eyes darkened. "The only one you'll be thanking is me."

The possessive edge to his tone made me absolutely giddy. "I can work with that."

Because I understood he was letting me take the lead here, I stripped my sweater up and off. I didn't want any more questions about how far I intended this to go or if I was certain. I had a moment of self-consciousness when he stopped moving to stare.

Shit. What bra was I wearing? *Please let it not be the totally stretched out, should have tossed it three years ago, but spent too much money on it in the first place to pull the trigger one.*

I glanced down. Plain black. Nothing outstanding, but nothing embarrassing either.

Ramsey's hands tightened at my waist. "Alia Rose, you are stunning."

"Oh." That was all I could manage before he was kissing me again.

I felt the change in tone instantly. The lingering glide of his tongue, the slow skim of his hands up my back, calluses lighting little fires along the way. Those talented fingers made quick work of releasing the clasp of my bra, drawing it off and leaving me naked from the waist up. He explored the bared skin of my back and shoulders, mapping it with his fingertips as he began trailing kisses along my jaw and down my throat.

"Um." It came out as more of a squeak than I'd intended. "What's happening here?"

He smiled against my throat. "If you have to ask, I'm doing it wrong."

His thumbs traced the sensitive skin on the underside of my breasts, and I hissed. "No, you're doing it very, very right. But... did we hit the slo-mo button?"

"You have somewhere to be?"

"The answer to that is almost certainly yes. Not that I could tell you where if you held a gun to my head."

Ramsey lifted his gaze but didn't stop the slow, rhythmic stroking. "Do you want to stop?"

"I might cry if you do, and that would be mortifying."

He huffed a half-laugh before sobering again. "I've waited for you all my life. I'm taking my time with this."

"Oh." Well, God, what was I supposed to say when he said something like *that*?

Turned out it didn't matter, because the next thing I knew, his hands were fully cupping my breasts, and I lost all capacity for coherent speech. Yeah, he could keep doing that as long as he wanted. Every pass of those rough thumbs over my nipples shot a bolt of pleasure straight to my core. As need spooled tighter, I began to rock again.

"Need more, princess?" It was the voice again. The one he'd used at the con when he'd rescued me from my nightmare. That black velvet rasp that made me want to give him anything.

I forced myself to meet his hooded gaze. "You know I do."

His lips twitched. "At your service, my lady."

All the yes to that.

Abruptly, he scooped me up, tipping me back to the sofa. Before I'd even adjusted to the new view of the ceiling, he was tugging off my boots, then coming for my jeans. I wriggled my hips, helping him drag them off, along with my underwear. The kiss of the air was cool against my flushed skin, but that was nothing against the heat in his eyes as he knelt before me like some kind of supplicant.

His hands settled on my thighs, a warm, welcome weight. "You remember back in college, a few days before the masquerade? You weren't going to go, but Blair came over to convince you. She said you deserved to be worshipped."

I more remembered something in her speech about being a

goddess of vengeance, but there was a dim memory of something about being worshipped. "Yeah?"

"I've been thinking about this ever since."

My breath wheezed out on a slow exhale.

I was never ever, ever getting over this. He was about to ruin me for anyone ever again. And I was so here for it.

"Well then, let's see what you've got."

With a flash of that devastating grin, he settled between my legs.

What he had, as it turned out, was the capacity to turn me into a quivering pile of pure, mindless pleasure. I lost count of the number of times he drove me up and held me at the edge before driving me even higher. My hands fisted in his hair as I gasped and writhed against his mouth, desperate for release.

"Ramsey, please!"

At last, he eased one thick finger inside me, finally filling the ache he'd dragged out for what felt like hours. He shifted, curled, and struck some spot inside me that set off stars behind my eyes.

By the time my vision cleared, he'd shed his jeans and rolled on a condom. He was beautifully built, every inch of muscle honed to perfection. From those gorgeous shoulders to the sharp cuts of muscle at his waist that made me want to drool, he was a product of years of excellent training and nutrition. An athlete at the top of his game. But I'd admire that later. Right now, I needed him.

I opened my arms, and he joined me on the sofa. There was nothing elegant about the shifting we had to do to rearrange limbs and make ourselves fit. There was gasping, a banged elbow, a few laughing swears. Then he curled my leg around his waist and notched himself at my entrance, and I forgot any awkwardness or discomfort because we were finally here.

I reached up to touch his cheek, and he turned his head to

brush a kiss in the center of my palm. Then he pressed into me. Only an inch or so, but I gasped.

He froze. "Okay?"

"Yeah. Don't stop."

As he'd promised earlier, he took his time, rocking into me inch by slow inch, as my body adjusted to his girth. He was big... everywhere, so it took a while, but eventually he was fully buried inside me, and oh God. I had no idea it would feel this incredible to be so full. I tightened my legs, flexing my hips to take him just a fraction deeper.

He groaned. "You keep that up, this won't last nearly long enough."

I tightened my inner walls around him. "There's always time for another round."

Ramsey choked out a laugh, even as he thrust again, making me gasp.

"Oh God, do that again."

He did. Over and over, gradually picking up speed until we were lost to the glory of skin on skin. Sensation built with every thrust, and the world narrowed down to the two of us, our bodies moving in sync, the sound of our ragged breaths filling the small office.

His eyes locked onto mine, as if I were the only thing he could see, the only thing that mattered in that moment. "Let go, princess." That low growl sent shivers along my skin. "You can let go. I've got you."

I'd never been good at letting go, at shutting off. But for him, I did. I released the fear, the doubts, the endless to-do lists that had been weighing me down for months. I let go of the past and the what-ifs and the could-have-beens. I let go of everything except the sensation of Ramsey's body in mine, the taste of his lips, the sound of his voice.

The orgasm barreled into me like a freight train. Waves of

pleasure crashed over me, drowning out everything else but the groan of his release. For a long, shuddering moment, Ramsey held himself above me, his arms shaking as we rode out the aftershocks. Then we collapsed in a tangle of limbs and sweat-slicked skin. He rolled so he wasn't crushing me, tucking me close, so I didn't fall off the edge of the narrow couch. I wilted against him. After multiple orgasms, I was more relaxed than I'd been in literally years, so I was content to stay this way for an eternity or two.

His hand stroked down my spine.

"You keep that up, I'm going to fall asleep," I murmured.

"Bet I could wake you up again." He wriggled his hips against me, making me giggle.

My watch began to vibrate.

With a tone of suspicion, he glared at it. "Is that a call?"

I squinted at the screen, then grinned. "No, I just hit my active zone minutes for the day. So much better than the gym. Not that I've seen one of those in six months."

With a snicker, he cuddled me closer, pressing a kiss to my bare shoulder. "I'd definitely take this workout any day."

Laying my hands on his chest, I peered into his face. "I need to ask you something, and I need you to be honest with me."

"Anything."

"Did you pack the armor?"

His laugh rolled out full and rich this time. "I didn't. That wasn't something I wanted to explain to Bodie."

Holding in a pout, I settled again. "No, I imagine he'd give you eternal shit about it." Thinking back to what I knew now, I frowned. "Wait, did you know who I was when you came to the con?"

"No. I just really love your books. I didn't know it was you. Not until you mentioned Thunder and Lightning."

What were the odds that he'd even *read* my books, let alone loved them enough to spend what had to be a small fortune on a costume? "And you showed up dressed as Soren?"

His broad shoulders twitched in a shrug. "He's my favorite."

I pressed my lips together.

Ramsey gently gripped my chin. "What?"

We'd had mind-blowing sex. We were together now in some form or fashion. I could admit the truth.

"He's you."

Ramsey blinked. "What?"

"I based him on you."

A grin of pure, unmitigated delight spread across his face. "Really? Why?"

"Because you were always my hero."

He tightened his arms around me, pressing a kiss to my temple. "I'm sorry for walking away at the masquerade. I got the call for the Charlotte Combine, and I couldn't miss that."

Of course he couldn't. That exclusive regional training session was where he'd first been exposed to pro scouts. It was the thing he'd been working toward his whole life at that point. I hadn't held that against him.

"I figured that much out on my own when Bodie told me where you'd gone. But I thought when you got back that we'd..." I trailed off. "Well, when you never said anything, I assumed you didn't know it was me."

"You could have said something."

I pushed myself up to peer into his face. "And put you in the awkward position of having to let me down gently if you were disappointed that it was me? No, thank you. I didn't need that mortification, and I valued our friendship too much."

His fingers curled around my arms, firm, but not bruising. "I would never in a million years be disappointed it was you.

I'm sorry I hurt you by not talking to you about it. I never would've wanted you to doubt yourself."

I snorted. "Oh, well, you don't have the market cornered on that. I doubt myself all the time."

"You are the most terrifyingly capable woman I've ever known. And I include my mother in that."

"Being terrifyingly capable has nothing to do with my ability to doubt myself." I snuggled in for another moment, then pulled away on a sigh. "I need to get back to the real world. I still have so much to do. And I don't even know what I missed to be here."

"You work too hard."

"Story of my life. Someone's got to do it." With one last brush of a kiss, I rose and began to dress.

Ramsey sat up on the sofa. "Was this a onetime thing for you?"

I looked back at him, my bra still dangling from my fingers. "God, I hope not."

The tension bled out of his face. "Good. Not for me either." He stood, dispensing with the condom and dragging on his jeans. "How do you want to handle this? I know I'm not exactly the easy hometown local guy you can just start dating."

That was the absolute truth. Even here, he was a celebrity. I couldn't forget that. But I was no longer willing to let that be a deterrent to being with him. We'd figure it out.

Still...

"For now, can we keep this quiet?" Realizing how that might sound, I rushed on. "I'm not worried about how my family will react."

Ramsey hooked a finger under my chin. "You sure about that?"

"*Yes.* Uncle Dee is going to have kittens, Grandma Elsie adores you, and my brothers will... Well, I don't actually know what my brothers will do, but I'll handle them when the time comes." I curled my fingers in his belt loops and stepped closer. "It's not like I think you're some dirty little secret. But I want something that's mine. Something I don't have to share with the world or my family."

His lips curved, and he brushed a kiss to my temple. "Okay. I'll follow your lead on this."

"Are you sure? Is it going to make things weird for you?"

"Am I going to be trying not to picture you naked at dinner while I'm sitting across from all five of your brothers? I mean, hell yes, that'll be weird. But I'm a big boy. I'll manage."

"Thank you."

We both resumed pulling on clothes.

"So, your family doesn't know about the author thing?"

"No. Well, Uncle Dee does now, because I needed his help with the makeover for the con, but everyone else, no."

"Why not? The books are awesome." He looked truly baffled by the secret.

Melting a little more at his instant and unquestioning support, I crossed to pull him down for another kiss. "You are very sweet. That's a conversation for later. I promise. For now, I need to go figure out what I can salvage of the afternoon. See you at dinner tonight?"

"Yeah." He laced his fingers with mine and pulled me in again for another kiss. "I need one more to tide me over."

One more turned into three before I finally managed to slip out the side door of the theater, leaving him with orders to wait a bit and go out the rear. I knew better than anyone that keeping a secret in a small town was tantamount to mission impossible, but I wanted to hold this beautiful chance with him close to the vest for a bit longer.

Chapter 22

Ramsey

@BookishBaeBae: Y'all, I've watched that rescue video 83 times and I'm CONVINCED #SwoonyMcBroadsword knew exactly who Kella was before he stormed that stage. The way he looked at her? That wasn't just a fan. That was a MAN ON A MISSION. #KellaSwoonyTheory

@RomantasyQueen5000: THREAD: Evidence that Kella Harmon and #ArmorDaddy have a secret relationship: 1. The precision of that rescue—he knew EXACTLY when she needed saving, 2. The way she didn't even flinch when he picked her up, 3. That protective growl wasn't acting, folks #KellaSwoonyConspiracy

@BookFlickFairy: Theory: Kella Harmon's writer's block is because she's been busy having a torrid affair with #ArmorDaddy and can't focus on fictional men anymore when she has the real thing at home 🔥🔥🔥 #RealLifeRomance

@SeriesEnder: Conspiracy theory: What if the whole panel disaster was staged to generate buzz for the final book? That rescue was too perfect, too cinematic. Marketing genius if true. #PublicityStunt #SwoonyMcBroadsword

@RomanceReaderDaily: You can't convince me that the way #ArmorDaddy carried her wasn't PRACTICED. Those two have definitely been in each other's arms before. The body language doesn't lie! #BodyLanguageExpert #KellaSwoony

@ReadersAnonymous: The final book is taking forever because she's busy LIVING her happily ever after with #SwoonyMcBroadsword instead of writing one. And honestly? I respect it. #LiveYourBliss #RealLifeRomance

B y the time I pulled up to Grandma Elsie's, I could already hear the war cries.

Or maybe they were whoops of victory and vengeance echoing off the porch railings, but it had all the tactical sound and fury of a backyard militia on a sugar rush. I barely had one boot on the top step before a bright orange Nerf dart zinged past my ear and thudded against the doorframe.

Inside, absolute chaos reigned.

Blair launched herself over the back of the couch with an agility that said she either had a parkour background or was fueled by competitive spite. Gunner was crawling military style across the rug, his blaster balanced on his shoulder like a sniper rifle. Fletcher—half behind a wingback chair—called out coordinates like a squad leader in a war movie. And darting between them all, like a pint-sized, candy-colored assassin, had to be Oakleigh, Colter's eleven-year-old daughter. Her ponytail bounced, her eyes laser-focused as she fired shot after shot with deadly accuracy. Kid had game.

Ludo barked once in alarm, ducked behind the ottoman, then promptly stole a dart and ran off with it. Gouda was happily dart-dodging like this was the best day of his life.

And right in the thick of it, laughing with her whole body, was Alia.

I stopped cold for half a second, watching her. Barefoot. Blaster in hand. Hair falling out of its clip. Her eyes were shining, and her smile was wide and unapologetic.

The sight of that smile sparked one of my own. I hadn't seen her like this in years. Not without the weight of the world pressing between her shoulder blades. Well, other than naked with me on that sofa a few hours ago.

A dart smacked me square in the sternum.

"Y'all seriously didn't think to recruit me?" I raised my hands in mock betrayal as I stepped inside. "I feel like LeBron watching March Madness from the bleachers."

"Ooooh!" Oakleigh crowed. "Somebody get him a blaster!"

Blair tossed one my way without even looking. I caught it, rolled behind the couch, and immediately took a shot at Gunner. It struck him in the temple.

"Friendly fire!" he yelped, but went down dramatically clutching his heart.

I grinned. "Rookie mistake."

It didn't last long. I got about two shots off before Oakleigh popped out from behind the piano, aimed with zero hesitation, and nailed me right between the eyes.

I staggered backward, clutching my face like I'd been mortally wounded. "You got me," I groaned. "I die with honor."

"Victory is mine!" Oakleigh declared, striking a pose with her blaster held high.

Colter beamed like a man watching his kid win Olympic gold. "That's my girl." They exchanged a high five.

"She's a menace." Blair's tone was entirely proud as she flopped onto the couch and fanned herself. "A glitter-slinging, Nerf-wielding terror. I've trained her well."

"I noticed." I rubbed my forehead and wondered if I'd been publicly executed by an eleven-year-old.

Dean and Bodie came in a beat later, too late to save me.

"What'd we miss?" Bodie scanned the battlefield strewn with darts, pillows, and the wounded.

Oakleigh didn't even blink. "Dessert selection rights. I won."

Dean raised both eyebrows. "That so?"

"Fair and square," she announced, just as Fletcher tried to sit up and got clocked with another dart from Blair. "You snooze, you lose."

Dean shook his head. "She's vicious."

Bodie was already reaching for her. "Don't care. She still gets the noogie penalty."

Oakleigh screamed with laughter as both her uncles descended in a joint tickle-and-noogie attack that would have made lesser kids beg for mercy. She held her own like a champ, though she shrieked and kicked like a rabid pixie. The whole room was warm with laughter, boots thunking against hardwood, the scent of something delicious baking in the kitchen curling through the air.

And through all of it, I stood there, still grinning, still holding a blaster, and thinking, *This.* This noise. This family. This lightness in Alia's eyes as she leaned her hip against the arm of the sofa, hair pulled back, cheeks flushed from laughter. I wanted every disorganized, Nerf-fueled second of it.

She wasn't wearing anything special—jeans, boots, and a soft, oversized sweater in a deep burgundy that made her skin look even warmer under the light. Nothing flashy. But all I could think about was how she'd looked earlier that day, stripping that same sweater over her head as she straddled my lap. The way her breath had stuttered in my ear. How I'd taken her apart over and over until she hadn't been able to hang on to any of those burdens dragging her down.

My dick twitched, volunteering to do the job all over again. *Down, boy.*

I dragged my gaze away before someone clocked me for staring too long.

It didn't help. The memory of this afternoon lived right there beneath my skin, just waiting to bite me. I'd told her I could handle it, and I'd meant it. I'd wait as long as she needed.

But God. That didn't make it easy.

There were no corners in this house to hide in. No safe space to sneak a kiss or hold her for a second longer than polite. She was living at Uncle Dee's. I was still bunking with Bodie. And Alia had made it clear she wasn't ready for front-page gossip.

This thing between us was still only ours.

I didn't resent her for that. I understood that this wasn't a simple thing. I came with professional baggage that would be hard for her to handle. If she wanted me as the secret thing that was hers and hers alone, I was fucking honored to be that for her.

Still... Every time she laughed, I wanted to bottle it. Every time she tucked a curl behind her ear, I wanted to kiss the spot her fingers touched. And every time she looked at me, I had to remind myself not to cross the line she'd drawn.

Just breathe. Be patient. Be the man she deserves. And maybe don't stare like you're remembering the perfect curve of her breasts in your hands while her entire family is in the room.

Grandma Elsie saved me from myself by calling a ceasefire and demanding dart collection before we were allowed to get dinner. As we were all hungry, we made quick work of corralling foam ammunition before we piled into the dining room. Another leaf had been added to the table, and I found myself wedged between Oakleigh and Fletcher, with Alia directly across from me. The temporary truce established by the Nerf war was apparently over. We hadn't even made it through the first round of passed plates before the noise level doubled. This wasn't a polite dinner. This was verbal bumper cars with cornbread and beans flying backup.

Gunner stabbed his fork toward Fletcher's plate. "You gonna eat that cornbread or just admire it?"

Fletcher pulled the wedge closer. "This is strategy. I'm saving it to mop up the gravy."

Bodie snorted. "Gravy's on the far end. By the time it gets to you, there won't be anything left to sop."

Dean reached for the dish. "Shut up and pass it."

"Don't you dare skip me," Alia warned, eyes narrowed.

I kept my head down but still watched her from across the table. She was relaxed, leaning on one elbow, the tail of her hair falling over her shoulder as she traded jabs with her brothers like she'd never carried the weight of them all on her back.

"This pork roast is ridiculous." Blair pointed her fork like it had something to prove. "Elsie's out here making the rest of us look like sad, beige food influencers."

Grandma Elsie arched a brow. "Excuse you. Sad beige food made this country."

Alia choked on her tea. "She's not wrong."

Uncle Dee waved one ringed hand. "Gimme the collards before Blair tries to gentrify them with sriracha."

"That was one time!" Blair protested.

"I don't forget trauma."

Oakleigh grinned as she shoveled mashed potatoes onto her plate like a tiny champion. "Blair puts pickles on pizza."

"Sweet pickles," Alia clarified, legitimate horror in her voice.

"Okay, traitor." Blair held her hand to her chest. "I thought we were family."

Elena patted her hand. "You thought wrong. I warned you about the pickles."

"You're Puerto Rican. You love pickles!"

"Not on pizza, *mi amor.*"

Fletcher leaned toward me. "If you're smart, you'll stay quiet until dessert."

I lifted both hands in truce. "I said nothing."

"Good instinct," Dean said. "You make eye contact too long, and next thing you know, Oakleigh's challenged you to a push-up contest."

"I will win," Oakleigh announced without looking up from her plate.

I didn't even bother to fake bravado. "I don't doubt that."

Alia snorted, her gaze flitting to me, quick and bright. For half a second, everything else blurred. I knew what her laugh sounded like when it was only us. When it was low and breathless against my neck. I knew what it felt like when she curled against me after, soft and safe and mine, and my hands itched to touch her.

I cleared my throat and turned to grab the butter before I could embarrass myself.

"Colter, stop hoarding the mac and cheese," Gunner griped. "That bowl is not your emotional support companion."

"You try dealing with three sixteen-hour shifts and a broken HVAC system and tell me carbs aren't therapy."

"Man has a point." Uncle Dee raised his glass. "To carbs. And to not punching the city council in the throat this week."

A raucous round of "Hear, hear" followed, along with forks clinking and Oakleigh's quiet, "I thought that was the Sasspatch Society."

"We should be, sugar," Uncle Dee replied. "We'd get things done so much more effectively."

Blair nodded. "And stylishly."

Uncle Dee clinked his glass to hers.

Alia's laughter slid across the table and settled under my skin. She passed Oakleigh the potatoes, called out Fletcher for trying to claim seconds before thirds were up for grabs, and fed Ludo a green bean when he begged too hard to ignore. I watched her and thought again that I'd wait forever to be the man who got to sit across from that smile.

"Y'all hear Miss Evette sold her house?"

Blair's question brought the whole table to a sudden halt. Forks paused. Chairs creaked. Even the dogs stopped trying to beg and sat up like they understood the weight in the air.

And I realized that, between the confessions and the resulting best afternoon of my life, I'd never actually gotten the chance to tell Alia the thing I'd gone to find her for in the first place this afternoon.

Shit.

Gunner blinked. "She listed it? I didn't even know she'd gotten that far."

"I don't think she even got a sign in the yard." Blair glanced around. "According to Tasha over at the post office, it's already a done deal. Miss Evette came in this morning to fill out a change of address form. Said the buyer even paid for the movers. They show up tomorrow."

"Wait, what?" Dean leaned forward, looking genuinely thrown. "She up and sold it like that?"

Fletcher frowned, arms crossed. "To someone local?"

Blair shook her head. "Out of town, supposedly. Nobody knows who, and Miss Evette wouldn't say."

My jaw tightened mid-chew. Nope. Not the time. Not the place.

Colter set his glass down with a dull thunk. "That's what worries me. What if some outsider came in and pressured her? People are struggling here. Maybe they made her an offer she didn't think she could refuse."

What I'd done was give her twenty percent over market value—in cash—and offered to cover moving expenses so she could start that new life in Raleigh near her daughter with a decent nest egg. It had been a win for both of us, and in the end, she'd been grateful not to be caught in some long, drawn-out waiting game.

But I didn't want to bring that up here and now. If I did, I'd be stealing yet another choice from Alia—publicly this time—and she deserved the space to process what I'd done in any way she wanted to, whether she was going to rip me a new one or be grateful.

So I kept eating, staring at my plate as if it held all the answers.

Fletcher leaned back, brow furrowed. "Think it's some out-of-town developer?"

Blair made a face. "God, I hope not. If that turns into one of those soulless corporate vacation rentals—"

"Maybe don't borrow trouble until it comes knocking," Alia suggested. "It's equally possible it might be a new neighbor who'll be a valuable member of our community."

Uncle Dee sighed. "Fine, then I'll wait so I know whether to provide the Jell-O salad of menace or a proper welcome casserole."

She shot him a fond look. "I would expect nothing less.

Now, in more celebratory news, the water station is finally running properly on *real power* again instead of generators. The inspector cleared us this afternoon."

"Hot damn." Colter did a fist pump. "It's about time."

Conversation shifted to other positive updates around town for the rest of the meal, and I was saved from accidental evisceration or exposure. We all cleared the dishes, and the Gibson siblings engaged in the ritual Rock Paper Scissors competition to settle dish duty.

Once he'd been cleared, Bodie clapped a hand on my shoulder. "C'mon. Let's head back to the house. You owe me a beer."

I hesitated for a second, wanting to say goodbye, to maybe catch her eye. But Alia didn't look over, busy laughing at something Blair said while trying to stop Oakleigh from sneaking another scoop of cobbler.

So I nodded. "Yeah, alright." There wasn't much else I could do.

We said our general goodnights and filtered out onto the porch with leftovers in foil and dogs underfoot. Bodie tossed a casual wave to the rest of the crew as we split toward our trucks.

The drive back to his place was quiet. Only me and the low hum of the engine and the thing I hadn't said sitting like a rock in my chest.

I'd meant to tell her today. I should've. Hell, I'd gone looking for her with that exact plan.

But then everything happened.

We had happened.

Now the clock was ticking. I'd done a thing—one I still believed was the right move—but the longer I waited, the more it started to feel like a lie by omission.

I didn't want her to find out from someone else. And I

really didn't want her to think I was trying to steamroll her into anything.

Tomorrow. The first chance I got, when it was the two of us without an audience. No pressure.

I'd tell her everything. And hope like hell she took it the way I meant it.

Chapter 23

Alia

Gunner and Oakleigh lost Rock, Paper, Scissors, so they were on dish duty. Elena was deep in conversation with Grandma Elsie about some crochet pattern, and the rest of my brothers seemed to have largely scattered, with Colter and Fletcher taking the dogs out, and Bodie disappearing with Ramsey. I'd overheard something about a beer.

Which meant I wasn't going to get a goodbye. Not the kind I wanted, anyway.

I was disappointed, but it wasn't like Ramsey could have given me the goodbye we both wanted under the circumstances, so this was probably for the best. If he got his mouth on me again, chances were, I'd climb him like a tree, and I wasn't prepared for that explanation to my family.

Still, that didn't stop the pang of it. The quiet ache of wanting his hand on my back, his mouth near my ear. I wasn't ready for public affection, but getting nothing seemed almost like punishment.

It had been hard enough not to stare at him all through

dinner and imagine having him for dessert. Which, judging by the way my brain kept replaying this afternoon, meant I'd officially turned into one of those women who couldn't focus with sex on the brain. I wasn't sorry. I was... preoccupied. A lot.

Blair looped her arm through mine. "My girl and I are going upstairs. Anyone who follows risks a glitter makeover." She began to drag me up the stairs.

Oh God. She knew. She had to That level of smug only came from discovery.

"Should I be worried?"

"I'm not using glitter on you unless you ask nicely."

Which meant she was definitely on to something.

But she was practically vibrating with excitement as she hauled me into the furthest bedroom at the end of the hall and shut the door.

The excitement was infectious. "What? What? What?"

Blair leveled a finger at me. "You had sex."

Yep. She knew. Dead woman walking. I froze like a deer in the headlights. "What?"

My bestie clapped, bouncing like a kid on Christmas morning. "You had sex!"

I stared at her, baffled. "How would you even know that?"

I mean, sure, I felt like I'd been walking around with a neon sign over my head, but I was at least trying to keep it on dim.

I'd been home. I'd showered. My hair was not still a mess from Ramsey's hands.

Oh God. Had someone seen us sneaking out of the theater like teenagers after curfew?

Had I missed some obvious tell? Lipstick smeared? Shirt buttoned wrong? God, please let it not be that obvious.

"Because you, my lovely, look relaxed for the first time in like a year. Longer, really. And if I were a betting woman, I'd say the lucky man is Ramsey."

And there it was. Laid out like it was obvious. Because apparently it was.

I tried. I really fucking tried to maintain my poker face. I wasn't good at lying to her. I never had been. She saw straight through me like glass. Blair had known me too long and too well, and I simply hadn't been prepared for her to blindside me like this.

She squeed, dancing in place like "She's a Maniac" was blasting on the internal playlist constantly scrolling through her head.

I grabbed her hands. "Quiet!"

And even though the door was closed, I lowered my voice and looked around like one of my siblings was skulking beneath the bed. Because knowing my family? Someone probably was.

"We are keeping this on the down-low right now because I don't want to deal with my nosy-ass family." I didn't want to share him yet. This was still new, still mine. Still a thing I wasn't ready to offer up for public consumption.

She dragged me over to the edge of the bed and down. "Tell. Me. Everything. How was it?"

"I... it was..." Electric. Explosive. Quiet and devastating in the best possible way.

Remembering everything we'd done on that couch, I pressed my hands to my heated cheeks. "It was really, really good."

"Yes, girl! You so deserve that! How did this happen? I remember you always had a bit of a thing for him back in college."

I blew out a breath, knowing it was time to confess. "It was more than a bit of a thing. It was a whole lot of a thing that's never really gone away." It had lived in the quiet corners of me all this time. I'd gotten good at ignoring it.

Blair clasped her hands over her heart. "Now you're finally

getting a shot with your college crush. Oh, I love that for you. Honestly, I thought he had a thing for you back then, too. He used to watch you in that quiet way he has. But then he never did anything about it, and I thought maybe he had some weird bro code objection because of Bodie. But then he showed up here a few weeks ago, and maybe he thought he was being subtle, but girl, he was not. He's been eyes on you since he got to town."

That startled me. "He has? Do you think Bodie's realized?" Because that would be bad. Very, very bad. I needed more time to figure out how to talk to him in a way that wouldn't fracture their friendship.

"For all that he's an otherwise reasonably intelligent man, your twin is dumb as a box of rocks on this front. I don't think it's ever occurred to him that Ramsey could see you as anything but a sister."

Thank God. At least I had some more breathing room.

"Good. I'll deal with him when it's time, but right now, I just want to enjoy this." For once.

"Girl, I hope you enjoy that man's fine ass in every conceivable position, as often as humanly possible."

I laughed. "There's an appealing and unlikely idea. Privacy is in somewhat short supply." Tragically. Criminally.

"Where even were y'all?"

"Stage manager's office of the theater."

Her eyes rounded. "Oh. Solid choice, honestly. But I can see why you wouldn't necessarily want that as a continued rendezvous point."

"We'll figure it out." We had to. Because not touching him again was not an option.

She squeezed my hands again, grinning from ear to ear. "Oh, I'm so freaking excited and happy for you! Nobody can say you don't have a type. But at least you got this one's name."

I'd confessed part. It was past time to confess the secret I'd kept locked up for years, because saying it out loud would've made it too real. Too sad.

"I never needed to ask his name."

The words fell like a whisper between us, and I let them hang there, waiting for her to connect the dots.

When she did, her jaw dropped open and her eyes peeled wide. "No! Are you saying—? It was him? At the *masquerade*? *And* he's Swoony McBroadsword?"

I nodded, flooded with an odd sort of relief at giving that truth its moment to breathe.

That sent Blair off into paroxysms of glee so huge, she had to leap up and dance around the room again.

"Oh my God, ohmygod, ohmygod! I can't even... Wait! So, did he know it was you? He had to have. He wouldn't have been at the party otherwise."

"Yeah. Turns out he did."

She sank back down on the bed. "Honey, why didn't you ever tell me this?"

"Because nothing ever came of it, and I convinced myself he didn't realize. Or if he did, that it was a onetime thing, and he didn't want to do anything about it. And I guess I just... felt stupid. Like I'd blown the whole thing out of proportion."

Her hand squeezed mine, hard. "You have never been stupid a day in your life. And we have a viral video of him performing a hero-worthy rescue of you to prove it. But why *didn't* he do anything about it back then?"

I sighed. "The noble idiot. Bodie—who knows nothing of any of this—said something to him about how I deserve some-body who stays. Ramsey knew he was likely getting drafted, so he convinced himself it was better for me if he let me go."

Her mouth opened, then closed again, along with her eyes. "Why are men so stupid? Didn't even ask what you wanted."

"That's what I said. But maybe it was for the best. I have no idea if we'd have survived all the early years of his career, while I was in law school. We wouldn't have seen each other much. And I'd have hated everything that goes along with his celebrity." I still wasn't thrilled about it. But for now, we had the bubble of secrecy and however long he was in Gibson Hollow. There was time left to figure things out.

"Well, he's here now, and he clearly decided to do something about it. *Has* been doing something about it since he got here. You think I haven't seen him taking things off your plate wherever he can? Keeping freaking snacks in his pockets for you because he knows you forget to eat when you're busy?"

"Yeah, that one kinda did me in."

"As it should! There's something about a man who wants to make sure you're fed. If I hadn't been sure he was interested in you before, when he came to me with that idea, that cinched it."

"Thanks for that, by the way. It's definitely helped."

"You are, of course, very welcome. We all want to help however we can, and you're not great at accepting that. Except, apparently, from him."

"Part of that is because he doesn't ask. He sees what needs doing and does it. I don't have to spend any mental energy figuring out who or how to delegate a thing. So much of my brain is full of logistics, and handing things off to people involves trying to communicate all of that. And since I don't have a Borg mind to send the instructions directly to their brains, it often seems easier to do the thing myself. He didn't wait for permission. He didn't treat my competence like a barrier to helping me. He just... helped. Without making me feel guilty for needing it."

Blair fixed me with a deeply unimpressed stare. "We're

gonna talk about that later. Right now I'm too happy for you to call you out on how that's bullshit."

"I'm glad you're happy for me. I'm happy for me." For once, I was genuinely, breathlessly happy. Not simply not-miserable. Not merely functioning. Happy. "But I need you to keep quiet about this. Like your-birth-name-before-transition quiet. I'm serious, B."

"Why the gag order? Is it because you're worried about the family? Because I'm pretty sure Grandma Elsie would be planning the wedding, and Uncle Dee will lose his damned mind."

"Because we're complicated."

"Why is this complicated? You like him; he obviously likes you."

"He is a very public figure, and I want no part of that. I just want him." Wherever he went, he was *seen*, and I didn't know how to do that and not panic. "So right now, that's what we're doing. The rest will come later." Maybe. Hopefully.

"Okay, fine. Even though I want to squee to high heaven, I will keep this under my hat because you, my love, deserve something good in your life. And from the way that you're glowing, he is very, very good."

He really was, and for once in my life, I wasn't going to feel guilty for taking something for myself.

Chapter 24

Ramsey

The sun hadn't even crested the horizon when Alia slipped out of Uncle Dee's house and into my truck. She wore skinny jeans with tall boots, a sweater, and a blazer, which I'd learned meant she probably had meetings later. I felt doubly bad for the early hour.

"Thanks for meeting me so early. I hated to ask, but the last few days have been kinda insane, and I needed to see you."

My plans to snag her for a full confession about my purchase of Miss Evette's house got delayed by a burst pipe turning the community center basement into a wading pool. I got pulled in, along with Fletcher and some of his crew, to reroute plumbing and save what we could before mold became the next disaster. By the time we came up for air, two whole days had passed, the movers had come and gone, and I'd only seen Alia long enough to essentially wave as she'd dropped off food from the diner for the work crew.

I wanted to do this the right way. Not because I thought she needed saving, but because I'd seen what it looked like for a woman to carry too much for too long. My mother never asked for help either. I learned early on that, if you paid close attention, you didn't have to be asked. It was obvious what needed doing.

Her hand came to rest over mine on the seat between us. "It's fine. I wanted to see you, too. A little lost sleep is worth it."

"I brought coffee."

She reached for the to-go mug on her side of the truck. "Because you are a smart, thoughtful man."

"Hang on to that thought." Putting the truck in reverse, I backed out of the drive.

"So, where are we going exactly?"

"It's a surprise."

I felt her side-eye from across the cab. "Surprise like a romantic breakfast picnic at sunrise or surprise like you've booked me for a public appearance without my asking?"

"Um... not either of those." Though I mentally bookmarked the idea of the breakfast picnic for later.

"Blair is still not off my shit list for the latter. Although, maybe I should relent, given I think that's partly why you're actually here."

"Ah. So she's behind your appearance at the book convention. I'd wondered."

"She's the reason I have a writing career at all. I'd have kept it all to myself. She self-published the first one without telling me."

"Bold. Very Blair. And I bet it went over like a ton of bricks when you found out."

"Yeah. It's the only *real* fight we've ever had. It's irksome that she wasn't wrong, but I *hate* being pushed into things."

I forced myself not to wince. I really, *really* hoped I was not about to be filed under the heading of pushing her into things and fucking us up before we'd even really begun.

"Does anybody besides her and Uncle Dee know about the whole Kella Harmon thing?"

"Elena, but only because of spousal privilege. Otherwise, no. Blair's run my marketing essentially from the beginning, and she's damned good at it."

"I'd say so. And I know you well enough to understand why the pen name and all that. But that still doesn't explain why you haven't even told your family."

"That's... complicated."

I didn't press. Whatever that word carried, it wasn't only about writing. It was about all the weight she'd taken on and the ways she hadn't let herself put any of it down. I'd lived in a world of pressure for a long time, but hers was different—quiet and constant, the kind that wore grooves in a person's soul.

"I didn't know I'd fall in love with writing. It was something I did for myself as stress relief when I'd rather have been shot than write one more brief in law school. But it's *fun*."

"Nothing wrong with fun. That's exactly why I read them."

"It's why a lot of people read them. Lucky for me." She sipped again. "I went into family law because I see value in helping people. It's something I was raised with. Both the responsibility and the privilege of being a Gibson here in Gibson Hollow. This is our town, and I don't take that lightly."

"I sense a 'but' coming."

"It's been very rewarding on a lot of levels. I've done good work. But the reality is, I was burning out even before the flood. And the books have been sufficiently successful that I was going to close my practice and write full time."

"That's incredible!"

"I think it would have been. But then the flood happened, Dad got hurt, and I'm the one who ended up picking up the pieces. Again."

The first time had to have been when her mom died, but I

didn't want to press on that particular wound. I turned onto Oak Ridge Drive, a mile north of town proper. "That doesn't mean you can't still go full-time writer. It only means now isn't the best time."

"It's hard to imagine there will ever be a good time. The whole town needs what I bring to the table, and doing anything else feels selfish."

She said it like an immutable fact, like her needs would always rank second or third behind someone else's crisis. It made me want to take her hand and tell her that saving a whole damn town didn't have to come at the cost of saving herself.

"You are the least selfish person I've ever met."

I meant it. I'd seen this play before—different cast, same plot. My mom never let herself come first either, and I'd watched the way it wore on her, quietly, steadily. It didn't make her a saint. It made her exhausted. And she still showed up for everyone. Exactly like Alia.

She shrugged that off as if it meant nothing. "It's a moot point, anyway. My creative well has reached Death-Valley-level dry."

"I know you value your privacy, but you've had more than a lot going on. Your readership would understand if you told them."

"After I froze at the panel, I feel like anything I say at this point will sound like an excuse."

I knew when to cut my losses. Filing all that under the heading of *Stuff To Circle Back To Later*, I pulled into the driveway.

"Are we waking someone *else* up before the ass crack of dawn?"

"No." Putting the truck into park, I turned to face her. "I need to tell you something."

Wariness and confusion flickered over her face. "Okaaaaay."

"I'm the one who bought Miss Evette's house."

Her head whipped toward the small, two-story clapboard house in front of us. "You bought a house? Here? Why?"

It was still too dark to really read her reaction, but I worried she'd think I was pushing too fast, making assumptions.

"To be very clear, I did this before us."

Her brows knit together. "Okay?"

I waved a hand toward the house. "This is going to be your new office."

The pause that followed was way too long. "I'm sorry?"

"Look, you've been working out of The Commissary for months, and it's taking its toll because you can't get any privacy. You can't get everything you need done because there's no gate-keeper. There's no nothing. You can't even eat a meal in peace without a bodyguard. You need a space. This is a space."

"How... what... Why did you not tell me this?"

"To be fair, I was coming to tell you, and then I got distracted by the naked and everything else. And I didn't want to say anything at dinner when it came up until I'd had a chance to talk to you first."

"Okay, yeah. Fair. But... I don't even know what to say to this, Ramsey. It's a whole house."

"I mean, not like a giant house. About eighteen hundred square feet, all told. It'd be closer to twenty-three hundred if I finished out the attic above the garage." It was on the maybe list. Depended on what happened in the future.

"You can't buy me a house."

Relieved that I'd seen this part coming, I shook my head. "I didn't buy you a house. I bought a property. I expect you were paying rent on your previous office space. You can pay me rent.

We'll arrange whatever's fair on that front. I knew you'd never accept it as a gift, even though I would happily give it to you."

"Yeah, well, you have that correct. But, Ramsey, really?"

"Yes, really. This gives you somewhere to work with a fucking door. And for the record, I have a new gatekeeper in mind for you. She might or might not work out, because she's not exactly a legal secretary, but she sure as shit can control who walks into your office and doesn't."

"Who's that?"

"Miss Addie. She said she ran Dr. Norris's office for like thirty years, and she's bored to death with retirement. I have no doubt whatsoever that she can do what you need in terms of controlling the flow of people who can get to you."

"Okay, I have to admit, that's kind of brilliant. But this is a whole-ass house. I do not need a whole-ass house for my office."

"Well, that comes to the second part of all of this, which really wasn't so much a thing until everything else happened with us. But it's getting rather crowded over there with Bodie and Dean. This way I can turn the second floor into an apartment as a place for me to stay while I'm here. Which also solves the issue of giving us a place with some privacy. Win-win-win."

When she didn't immediately tear a strip out of me, I crossed the fingers of the hand she couldn't see.

"So, let me get this straight. You've bought a house for me to use as an office. And for us to basically have a love nest?"

"I mean, the love nest was secondary and not part of the original plan, but it seems sensible at this point." When she only stared at me, I caved. "Please don't be mad. I'm just trying to help."

Huffing an enormous sigh, she shoved out of the truck.

Shit.

I slid out of the driver's seat and watched her pace half a dozen steps away before doing an about-face and coming back.

"You're mad."

"No. Maybe a little." Another huff. "You are the kindest, most generous, most observant man. And I don't know what I did to deserve you."

It bothered me that she didn't think this was just something she could have. That she needed to do anything at all to deserve any of this. To merit having someone show up for her in ways that counted.

As she had not ordered me to pack my bags and high-tail it out of town, I edged a few cautious steps closer. "You don't have to do anything to deserve me." *That's not how this love thing works.* But it was way too soon to be throwing that around, no matter how long I'd felt this way. "Will you take this as your office?"

She looked up at the house. "Well, I guess, since you have the keys, you should at least give me a tour. Behind a door that locks, so I can give you my answer."

Hell, yes.

"I can make that happen."

In the pale pre-dawn gray, I led her up the two steps to the front door and let us inside. The electricity was still on, so I switched on the light. "There's this entryway here. A front sitting room to the left, which'll make a good reception area. Room for a desk there. Over here, these two sliding pocket doors open up to the dining room. It's got these great built-ins. I was thinking that'd work for your office. Room for books and a desk and a couple of guest chairs for clients. Kitchen back here, and a half bath under the stairs."

She trailed me up the stairs, which had seen better days, but a good sanding and fresh paint would perk them up.

"Three bedrooms up here, one bath. Built back when it was no big deal for a full family to share a bathroom. But that's not a problem for me. Everything looks kinda tired and worn, but that's nothing some elbow grease and new paint won't fix."

There was still some furniture scattered on both floors.

"Is Evette coming back for the rest?"

"She said she was downsizing to an apartment in Raleigh and didn't need a whole house worth of furniture. So she took what she wanted and sold the rest with the house. There's the sofa downstairs, the table in the kitchen, and this extra bedroom set she said actually belonged to one of her ex-husband's family that she kept out of spite. She said she wasn't planning to take it into her new life."

I pushed open the door on the spite furniture. It was nothing special. A lowboy with a matching mirror that barely hit me above the navel, and a full-size bed that I'd hang off even if I lay diagonally. But it was bigger than the sofa in the stage manager's office, and I'd optimistically put on fresh sheets I'd found left behind in the hall closet. I guessed the bed she took was a different size.

"I'll be ordering my own for the primary bedroom, but..."

Alia's eyes sparkled as she turned to me. "It's a bed. In a house. With blinds. And a door that locks."

"It is all of that." I hooked both her hands with my forefingers, drawing her close as I'd wanted to for days. "So, what's your answer, counselor?"

She tipped her head as if considering. "I believe I said it quite a few times the other day at the theater."

"Did you?"

"Mmm. Maybe you need a refresher."

"Maybe I do." I nudged the blazer from her shoulders, catching it before it landed on the floor. "Checking before we get started here... what *time* is the meeting you dressed for this morning?"

"Not until ten-thirty."

I carefully laid the blazer on the lowboy. "Perfect." I nudged her back until she sat on the bed, then reached to unzip the boots. "These are incredibly sexy."

"Personal favorites. Uncle Dee calls them bitch boots. I wear them when I intend to take no shit."

"I like it." I set the pair of them neatly aside and stripped off her sweater, giving a low hum of appreciation at what was beneath. "I like this, too." The lacy blue confection offered up her breasts like a gift.

"I put it on hoping you'd get to see it."

"Does the bottom match?"

"I guess you'll have to unwrap me to find out."

Chapter 25

Alia

"You definitely have to get a bigger bed. Here, I'll move so you can rearrange."

Ramsey's arms clamped tight around me, keeping me exactly where I was, still splayed across the top of him. "No ma'am. You'll stay right there."

"But all the blood's going to rush to your head like that." His head was hanging off one side, while his feet stuck off the far side of the other.

"I can assure you there is no blood in my head whatsoever in this moment. I'm fine."

Laughing, I pressed a kiss to his chest. "Thank you for doing all of this."

"It was my absolute pleasure, and if you'll give me fifteen or twenty minutes to rehydrate, I'll happily do it all over again."

"Not that." As lingering aftershocks continued to flutter through me, I reconsidered. "Although, yes, that. I meant everything else. Not only the snacks and the meal train. You show up, Ramsey. More than that, you pay attention, and you take action. Do you have any idea what that means to me? Nobody thinks about the mental load of always having to be the one to delegate, to manage everything. *Not* having to expend that energy because you just *get it* and get it done is worth so much more than you can know."

Somewhere, he found the muscle strength to lift his head and wriggle around until he was mostly on the mattress and could look more directly at me. Eyes soft, he brushed the hair back from my face. "I learned to pay attention early. You already know my mom raised me on her own. Worked three jobs at times to make sure I had what I needed for football. Camps, gear, travel. She never once complained, but I saw the toll. And it wasn't always about football. A lot of years, it was the basics. Keeping food on the table, a roof over our heads, clothes on our backs. And you've seen me. Some years I outgrew my clothes almost faster than she could get new ones."

He paused, gaze unfocusing like he was thinking back. "I learn how to fix stuff because we had to make do. We learned from books, YouTube, neighbors. I worked construction in the summers as soon as anybody would hire me on. The contractor thing was always going to be my backup plan, because there was never any guarantee that football would be forever. Hell, even now, it's not forever. I've probably got another good five years or so, assuming I avoid major injury. I'll still be in my mid-thirties. A lot of people at that age still don't know what they wanna be when they grow up."

Didn't I relate to that? I'd poured all this time, energy, and effort into my law practice, and I wanted to go write stories for a living. The dream was still there, even if my creativity had abandoned me.

"The point is, I see everything you're doing for everyone but yourself. And I get it. I do. I just want to take some of the weight off where I can."

Emotion thickened in my throat, because even among so

many people who loved me, they didn't recognize this in the same way he did.

I pressed another kiss to the big heart that was slowly thumping beneath me. "I really wish we could stay here all day so I can properly express my gratitude, but the sun is actually up, your truck is in the driveway, and it's not Miss Evette's car, so we're already on borrowed time that no one has stopped by to be nosy and find out who bought the place. We need to get dressed."

He snagged one of my hands, lavishly kissed my knuckles. "There will be more time. I'm not going anywhere."

For now. He still had that five years or so of career to go back to in a few months' time. But that was on the list of things I wasn't thinking about right now. I was determined to stay in the present as much as possible and simply enjoy what we had for as long as we had it.

I slid off him and off the bed and reached for the matching lacy blue panties that were motivating me to place an online order for more, as soon as humanly possible. Before I pulled them on, Ramsey stood and tugged me in again, pressing all his gloriously naked parts against all of mine as he cupped my ass with those delightfully massive hands. The proximity was giving me all sorts of ideas that were going to get us both into trouble.

"So, you'll take the office?"

I chuckled. "I thought I made that answer abundantly clear."

"Well, there were a lot of yesses in there, but also a lot more please, there, harder, and faster."

I poked him in the abs, which was about like jamming my finger against a brick wall. "Yes, I will take the office, and the love nest."

"Good. I'll get a bigger bed and some other furniture ordered." He drew me in for a lingering kiss that told me he had more of those terrible, wonderful ideas himself.

"Work," I groaned. "I have it."

"Right. Adulting. Not adult time." Reluctance in every move, he released me and reached for his jeans. "In the meantime, I need to go tell your brother before he finds out from somebody else, and it gets awkward."

When I froze, bra in hand, he rushed on. "Not about us. I'm fine with keeping that quiet as long as you want. I mean about me having bought this place without mentioning it to him first."

"Why *didn't* you talk to him about it?"

"Because I was afraid he was going to tell me no. I was afraid *you* were going to tell me no."

"What would you have done if I had?"

He shrugged. "I mean, there's a housing crisis around here. I absolutely would rent it to somebody who needs it for a completely reasonable rate. Hell, I can still do that. The place still needs some work to be an apartment, but it could be done."

"Right now, I think it can wait. I'm willing to be selfish enough to want the love nest part of this equation."

"Three cheers for that."

We finished dressing, and I took a few minutes in the bathroom to tidy the hair that he'd utterly wrecked. Messy bun it was.

Downstairs, I took another glance at the proposed office space. "I need to figure out what I've got in storage from my apartment that can be brought in to make this work for the short-term."

"We can go by the storage whenever you're ready, so you can get things moved and set up as quickly as possible."

"And I need to have a chat with Miss Addie. I'll see if I can squeeze that in later today. I think she—" I broke off as a noise sounded. "What's that?"

We both went silent, listening to the sort of scraping, scratching from under the floor.

"Sounds like something's under the house." Ramsey made for the door. "It's a conventional foundation. An animal may have gotten up under there."

Outside, we circled the house until he found the hinged section of siding that was effectively a door to the crawlspace. Retrieving a flashlight from his truck, he got down on his knees and peered inside.

"Nothing obvious from here. I'm going in for a better look."

"Are you sure you want to do that? We do have skunks."

"Then hopefully I'll spot it before it has a chance to spray me. If I need to set a humane trap for something, better I have an idea what I'm trying to snag." He disappeared under the house.

A string of muttered cursing and a thump told me he'd probably banged his head or elbow or something. "You okay?"

"Fine."

He moved deeper under the house, and I heard him making little cooing, clicking noises.

"Can you see it?"

"Yeah."

"Is it a raccoon? A possum? A cat?"

"Nope, none of the above." Another few minutes passed before he emerged, knees and front of his shirt filthy, with a tiny, equally filthy dog in the palm of his hand.

I took one look at those mismatched blue and green eyes and melted. "Oh, my God! Puppy!"

"I don't think it's quite a puppy. Maybe one of those miniature weenie dog things."

Heedless of the mess, I reached for the dog. It was trembling, from fear or cold. Possibly both. I thought its coat was brindled, but it was hard to tell beneath the dirt. "I didn't know Miss Evette had a dog."

"If she did, she surely wouldn't have left it behind. The news would have been all over town if it was missing, right?"

"That's a good point. I don't know anybody with this breed of dog." Cuddling the animal closer, I headed back for the front door of the house. "We should give her a bath and get her something to eat. Call Miss Evette and ask if she knows anything about this."

"Yoo-hoo!"

At the sound of the voice, we both turned to find a sixty-something woman trotting up the drive, a basket in hand.

"Good morning! Oh Alia! I didn't expect to see you here."

"Good morning, Mrs. Crowder." *And thank you for not being fifteen minutes sooner.*

"I saw the truck and thought I'd be neighborly and bring by some biscuits for the new owner."

Ramsey offered an easy smile. "That'd be me. Ramsey Shaw."

"Beverly Crowder. I live down the road and across." She offered him the basket. "These are for you, then!"

"The blue house?" He accepted the basket, lowering a nose to sniff. "These smell fantastic. Much appreciated."

"Will you be moving in?" Her eyes were bright with curiosity.

"Actually, the property's going to be split. The downstairs is going to be Alia's new law office. Upstairs, an apartment."

Smoothly done, sir.

"He was squeezing in a tour before my workday. So much to do, we had to start early." As soon as the words were out, I wondered if I was over-explaining.

223

"Oh, well, I'm sure that will be much better than trying to keep up with things down at the diner." Mrs. Crowder zeroed in on the bundle in my arms. "And who do we have here?"

"I was hoping you might be able to tell us. We found this little girl up under the house. Do you have any idea who she might belong to?"

"No, I don't think I've ever seen her before. Tiny little thing. I wonder if she's who's been getting into my trash bags. I thought raccoons—you know how they are—but maybe not."

"We're gonna get her cleaned up and post on the town Facebook page in case somebody recognizes her. It was good to see you, Mrs. Crowder." I headed for the front steps.

Ramsey lifted the basket. "Thanks again for these. I'll get your basket back to you."

Mrs. Crowder lifted a hand in a wave. "No rush. Enjoy!"

Inside, I unearthed some dish soap beneath the sink, while Ramsey went to hunt up something to dry the dog off with.

"We're gonna get you all fixed up, little one, and find your mama or daddy."

Those eyes settled on me, then swung hopefully to the basket of biscuits. Her little nose twitched.

I didn't need to bathe her to realize she was almost certainly hungry. "Let's start with water first." I ran some into my cupped palm and held it for her to drink. Her little pink tongue darted out to delicately lap at the water. "Good girl."

Ramsey came back with another sheet. "Not ideal, but it'll do."

I set the dog in the sink to strip off my coat. The moment she was free of my hold, she leapt onto the counter and scampered over to the biscuit basket.

Ramsey was faster. He rescued the biscuits before she managed bury her nose in them. "After your bath."

She fixed him with the Look.

"Okay, maybe a tiny bite first."

Laughing, I scooped her up again. "Oh, man, you're toast. Don't have kids. They'll run all over you." Checking to make sure the water was warm, I wet our would-be biscuit thief down. She howled in miserable protest, at least until Ramsey snuck her a morsel of biscuit over my shoulder.

I gave him a look in return. "Really?"

"You're saying you can resist that sound?"

"Fair."

Through a series of additional biscuit bribes, I managed to get the rest of the dirt and muck washed off. Turned out, she had a brown and cream dappled coat. Using the sheet Ramsey had found, I dried her off as best I could, then set her down with the remains of the biscuit he'd been decimating for treats. She pounced on it as if she hadn't eaten in weeks.

My heart squeezed. "You are the cutest little doll baby. Obviously, we have to call her Biscuit."

The dog's little tail wagged, though she didn't slow down on the biscuit one bit.

"Naturally." Ramsey took in my now wet sweater. "You're gonna need to change."

"Worth it. It's past eight now. Do you want to try calling Miss Evette to see if she knows anything about this dog?"

"Sure, I'll do that. Why don't you grab a biscuit for yourself before our guest here eats the whole basket?"

"Don't mind if I do." In the end, I took two because we'd worked up an appetite before we found Biscuit beneath the house.

He came back a few minutes later. "Miss Evette says she doesn't know anything about it. Said she heard something under the house off and on for the past few weeks, but like you, she thought it was a possum or something. Couldn't find anything when she looked. She didn't know anybody in the area who had a dog like this."

I scooped Biscuit up to nuzzle her. Belly full of bread, she settled in my arms, eyes drooping shut. "Well, she couldn't have been on her own for very long, right? She's so little. I mean maybe not a full puppy, but not fully grown either. She can't be more than about eight pounds. Precious little angel baby."

Ramsey looked at me with expectant eyes.

"I'm not keeping her. I know we have to post a picture on Facebook, and that we'll probably find her owner in a day or two. But I can enjoy puppy cuddles until then."

"Uh-huh." He said it in a tone that told me he didn't believe me a bit. "Well, in the meantime, you have a meeting, and I need to talk to Bodie. Why don't you take the picture, get the post made, and I'll keep Biscuit while you take care of whatever's on deck for you today. I'll pick up supplies. Obviously, she can't live on biscuits alone." He stuffed half of one in his mouth and chewed. "No matter how good they are."

He was right. I could get away with a lot of things at The Commissary, but bringing an animal into the restaurant was not one of them.

I fished my phone out of my purse and took a selfie with Biscuit. Then I kissed the tip of her sweet little nose and reluctantly handed her over to Ramsey. The sight of her fitting more or less in the palm of his hand made my ovaries explode.

Okay, tiny dog plus giant man is somehow a big turn-on. Things I didn't know about myself.

I made myself post the photo on the town's Facebook page, saying where she'd been found and asking anyone with information to contact me. Her owner would probably be found by dinner.

"C'mon. I'll take you back to Uncle Dee's so you can change and grab your car."

"It's probably safer if you don't have a dog in your lap while you drive."

With a grin of pure indulgence, he handed the puppy back to me, and let me keep my delusions.

Chapter 26

Ramsey

"Don't pee in there, okay?"

From her perch in the hood of the sweatshirt I'd put on backward, Biscuit licked my chin in answer. Okay, I could concede she was really damned cute. I wasn't quite in the same danger of falling as Alia was, but I probably wasn't far off.

I'd been by the house, but as expected, Bodie had already left for work, and Dean was out with Gunner working on another bridge. So, after changing into some clean clothes, I headed back into town to the police station, hoping to find my buddy there.

Officer Buzz Cut—who I'd learned over the past few weeks was actually Tyler Clark—looked up from the front desk. "Can I help—you?" He trailed off at the sight of the passenger in my hoodie.

"Hey, Tyler. Bodie in?"

"In his office."

"Great." I didn't wait for an invitation before I headed on past him down the hall.

Bodie was wrapping up a phone call when I stepped into the doorway. His brows drew together as he spotted me and hung up the phone. "What in the hell is that?"

"A dog."

"Are you sure it's a dog? 'Cause it looks awfully small to be a dog."

"It's one of those miniature dachshunds, I think." Absently, I reached up to rub a knuckle over the top of her head. Biscuit pressed into the touch with a happy groan.

"And where did it come from?"

I settled into one of the chairs across from Bodie's paper-strewn desk. "Well, about that, she was underneath the house that I bought."

He blinked. "I'm sorry, what now?"

"I'm the one who bought Miss Evette's house."

In an expression alarmingly reminiscent of his twin, Bodie's brows drew together. "And you didn't tell me this... why?"

"I wanted to talk to your sister first, because I bought it so that it could be her office."

My friend sat back in his chair, soaking that news in. "You bought my sister a house."

Yeah, definitely had to right this ship before he started making assumptions that were, while correct, not something Alia wanted to deal with right now. "I bought an investment property so that I could lease her space to have an office. It happened to be the one that was available. Perhaps not the most ideal, but it was an option. And I was able to help Miss Evette out because she wanted to take care of things quickly. This way she avoided all the realtor and expensive closing fees, and she's in a nice position to start her new life in Raleigh near her daughter."

"Uh-huh. And how did Alia take all this?"

"About like you'd expect, but she eventually came around

to the notion. She'd never admit it, because she wouldn't want to offend Grandma Elsie, but she's tired of working at a booth in the diner."

Bodie angled his head to concede the point. "It's been less than ideal."

"We've got to go pick up some furniture from the storage unit later. I figured you or one of your brothers could help with that, and we could go ahead and get things started for her. But on our way to leave the house after touring it this morning, we found this little gal." I gently booped Biscuit's nose, and she promptly began to gnaw on my finger. "Alia is supposed to be posting pictures on the town Facebook page to see if we can find her owner."

"I've never seen her before. I feel sure I'd remember seeing something that damn tiny. Like, dude, she basically fits in your pocket."

"Yeah, she seems to like it in there pretty well." After a pause, I admitted, "There's more."

"What's that?"

"I'm going to use the upstairs of the house basically as a base of operations, as an apartment, while I'm here. Not that I don't appreciate you letting me crash at your place, but you've got to admit we're all on top of each other. And I wouldn't mind having my own space. I need to have some of my gym equipment brought in, so I can squeeze in some workouts between all this other stuff, because I'm going to be here for the long haul. This makes more sense than living out of a suitcase."

Bodie studied me with that even cop's stare. "You're really going to stick around until pre-season starts?"

Forcing myself not to squirm under that look, I kept my voice even. "That's the plan."

I waited for the questions. For the why? The suspicion.

Instead, Bodie's grin spread wide. "Well, damn, son, this

will be the most time we've gotten to spend together since college."

Relieved, I answered with a grin of my own. "It's the least I can do to help."

"We sure appreciate that."

"In the meantime, can you put me in touch with the vet? I want to get Biscuit checked out."

"Biscuit?"

"She really likes them."

"I'm not gonna ask. Anyway, yeah, I can absolutely do that." His lips twitched. "Are you planning to keep her if nobody claims her?"

"Consider me temporary custody. Alia fell in love with her on sight. She doesn't want to let herself get her hopes up, in case we do find the owner. And I get that. Pepper was her shadow, and losing her gutted Alia more than she lets on. She doesn't say it, but I know she's still not over it. But man, if you'd seen her face this morning? This is her dog. I'm only keeping her until she acknowledges it."

Armed with the number to the vet's office, I stepped out of the police station. Sunlight struck me square in the face. Followed by a blinding flash I instantly recognized as a camera.

"Hold it right there, sweetheart."

I froze on instinct, braced to pound some paparazzi if necessary. Biscuit popped her head up from my hoodie like a damn periscope.

Miss Glory swept forward like a storm front in stilettos, sunglasses already perched, camera phone poised like she was born to it. "There she is. That's the one."

She snapped again as Miss Bea materialized on my other side with a plastic shopping bag and a leash that glittered. "Hold still, baby, we need to see if this fits." Before I could react, Biscuit had been scooped from the pouch with surprising efficiency, and Miss Bea was fastening a pink rhinestone collar around her neck like she was crowning a pageant queen.

"Wait, what is happening—?"

Miss Bea settled a now bedazzled Biscuit back into my hoodie pouch.

"Turn this way, sugar," Uncle Dee directed, snapping a photo like this was his job. Maybe it was. The man had quite the history. "Chin up. Hoodie out. Show the branding. Yes, perfect."

Mo'nique popped the hatch of a car parked at the curb and pulled out what looked suspiciously like a pink pet carrier, a tiny dog bed shaped like a cupcake, and an entire reusable grocery bag full of supplies. "We figured you'd need the essentials. Starter pack's all ready."

"I—wait—hang on." I made a circular gesture, trying to rewind the chaos. "We're watching her until the real owner shows up."

Miss Bea gave me the sort of look reserved for toddlers who insisted they weren't sleepy. "Sweetheart, if this dog had a real owner, we'd know them. You think someone in this town could keep a secret like that little cutie?"

"She would've been claimed by lunch yesterday." Miss Glory snapped another photo with her phone. "Now tilt her up like Simba. The light's better on her left side."

Feeling railroaded, I curved protectively around Biscuit. "I didn't agree to a photoshoot."

I should've been irritated. Should've drawn a line. But there was something about the sheer force of their joy—saying no would've been like kicking a puppy. A sequined, rhinestoned puppy wrapped in community and cupcake-scented chaos.

Biscuit put her paws on my arm, and I'd have sworn she preened for the camera.

"No one ever does," Uncle Dee said cheerfully, "but this moment demanded documentation."

"What moment?" I asked, already regretting it.

Four knowing smiles hit me in unison.

Mo'nique handed me Biscuit's carrier with the gravitas of a passing torch. "Instagram handle is @MascotOfMayhem. We've got it live with the soft launch. You and Alia'll get the login by end of day."

"I—how do you even know—?" It had been less than two hours.

Miss Bea brushed invisible lint off my shoulder. "Baby, we know everything that goes on in this town."

I could tell they absolutely believed they did. But there was *no way* they knew about Alia and me. About the theater. About this morning. No way. We'd been careful. Hadn't we?

The group of them smiled serenely, sneaking kisses on Biscuit's snoot, before disappearing in a cloud of perfume, like a quartet of glittery chaos agents.

I scooped Biscuit up and looked her in the eyes. "Tell me the truth. Were they in on it all along?"

Her answer was to lick my nose.

"Right. Well, one way or the other, we did need starter supplies. I hope you like pink." I scooped up everything the Sasspatch Society had brought and tucked it under my arm to take to the truck. "Let's go get you a clean bill of health, Mascot of Mayhem."

Chapter 27

Alia

Sasspatch Society Group Text

GLORY:

🔔 EMERGENCY MEETING 🔔 Operation Office Glow-Up is a GO! Miss Evette's old place is about to become our girl's legal domain, and I am LIVING for it.

MO'NIQUE:

Already pulling together a charcuterie-themed welcome basket. Question: too much if I shape the salami like law books?

BEA:

Darlings, I've got three lamps from my attic that would be PERFECT for her space. That poor child's been squinting at legal papers in diner lighting for months!

DELILAH:

Can we just take a moment to appreciate that RAMSEY SHAW bought our girl a whole damn building? Man didn't just bring flowers; he brought REAL ESTATE.

GLORY:

I told y'all that boy was smitten! Nobody buys "investment property" with that look in their eyes.

DELILAH:

Operation needs a timeline. She's moving in next week. I vote we surprise her with the full makeover while she's at that zoning meeting.

GLORY:

And some strategically placed throw pillows for the upstairs "apartment." 😏 You know, for "back support."

MO'NIQUE:

GLORY! 😂

BEA:

Well, the man did think of everything else...

DELILAH:

Meeting at my shop tomorrow, 9am sharp. Bring coffee, ideas, and your best matchmaking energy. Our girl's finally getting her happy ending whether she admits she wants it or not!

G olden morning light spilled through the freshly cleaned windows of my new office and glinted off the surface of the massive old desk that used to belong to Lou Anderson's great-uncle, the judge. The moment he'd heard about the new office, he'd been delighted to offer it up and get "that battleship" out of his spare room. I'd been more than happy to accept. Biscuit snored in the footwell under it, dead to the world in the utterly ridiculous cupcake-shaped bed, complete with pink frosting and embroidered sprinkles, that the Sasspatch Society had given Ramsey. It was one of three beds now. She had another purple fluffy one in my room at Uncle Dee's and a Sentinels' themed one for when she stayed with Ramsey. Over the past week, we'd been trading her off, depending on schedules.

Across the hall, Miss Addie was already humming what sounded suspiciously like "Highway to Hell" as she laid out a tray of fresh coffee and something homemade and probably sugar-drenched beside the classic Mr. Coffee machine. No Keurig on her watch, as she insisted, "That's not real coffee." She'd been here since 7:30. By the time I'd arrived at eight, she'd already filed the last of my bankers' boxes into the refurbished cabinets, wiped down every surface, and color-coded the brand-new digital calendar that now ran like an actual system across my synced devices. With alerts. With buffers between appointments. With actual conflict resolution.

I hadn't done any of it. She hadn't asked.

Miss Addie called herself my secretary. I called her my office dragon. It was an already well-earned promotion, and she wore it like armor.

Maybe the last book in my series needed a wise, ancient, take no shit dragon matriarch...

The front door creaked open as I took my first sip of coffee.

Blair swept in, holding a potted plant that looked suspiciously like a snake plant had been forced to live in a designer purse. In her other hand, she carried a gift bag in my favorite shade of blue. "Welcome to your new kingdom, Counselor. Or do we just call you Boss Lady now?"

"That depends." I set my mug down as she leaned in for a one-armed hug. "Are you bringing tribute?"

"For you, an office-warming plant that allegedly even *you* can't kill. For Biscuit—" she fished into the bag and pulled out a chew toy shaped like a gavel, "—justice is served."

"Please tell me that doesn't squeak, or she can't keep it during work hours."

"Officially work compliant," Blair assured me.

From her domain across the hall, Miss Addie looked her over once, then nodded a short, almost approving hello.

"You should see what Addie's already done." I led Blair into my inner sanctum, where Biscuit emerged with a stretch and a yawn before trotting over, little tail whipping in delight as she looked at me with those mismatched eyes in the universal puppy signal for "Up!"

Scooping up my furry companion, I continued the tour. "She turned my disaster zone into a fully functional law office in three days. The files are actually filed, the cabinets organized, the calendar synced. I didn't even *ask* for digital integration—she just did it. With color codes. And labels."

Blair whistled in a suitably impressed tone. "So... an office dragon?"

"Official title," I confirmed.

"Wait. Were the walls always this color?"

"Nope. Apparently, Ramsey roped my brothers into painting. Surprise reveal. I found the drop cloths and the receipts in the trash yesterday."

Blair didn't say a word, but one of her eyebrows arched like a slow elevator. Given I was fluent in Blair Young eyebrow-speak, I understood everything she wasn't saying about Ramsey.

I pretended not to see it and gestured toward the other additions. "The Sasspatch Society brought those lamps." They were a fun and funky collection, each one screaming the personality of the person who picked it out. "And the artwork's from local artists. Uncle Dee found the rug in Grandma Elsie's attic. I didn't expect any of it to work together, but somehow it does."

"Gonna admit you like it yet?"

Instead of answering, I shrugged and watched the morning light dance across the desk. But I smiled.

Blair set the plant down on the corner of my desk and offered the chew toy to Biscuit, who clamped it happily between her teeth. I held onto it so she could gnaw from her perch in my arms.

"Still no word on the original owner of the cutie pie?"

I shook my head. "Not yet."

She didn't miss a beat. "You're not going to find them."

I wasn't ready to agree, so I let the silence stretch, full of all the things I wasn't ready to admit out loud. That I'd missed having a dog. Something soft and small that depended on me out of love, not because I was the only thing standing between it and disaster. A reason to go outside, to get up in the morning, to come home. A tiny heartbeat that didn't ask questions or need anything except presence and cuddles.

I nuzzled the soft fur on top of her head.

Blair scrolled through her phone. "She's already got more followers than my last three posts combined. That selfie you posted to the town page? Someone made it into a meme. You've got thirty thousand followers on her account, and I think two of the fan edits are in German. Or is that Dutch?"

"Honestly? She might be the only thing that could get me on social media willingly." She wasn't officially *mine,* but how could I *not* share her adorableness with the world?

Blair smirked. "Noted."

Miss Addie appeared in the doorway, tablet in hand and eyebrow already raised. "Your 9:30 is here."

Blair winked. "Duty calls." She gave Biscuit a final ear scritch, then looked at me with that particular brand of friend energy that said, *I see you, I know what you're not saying, and I'll let you have your moment. For now.*

With a swish of her ponytail and the click of designer boots, she was gone.

I smoothed my blazer with suddenly clammy palms, let out a breath I hadn't realized I was holding, and went to greet my client.

Time to get to work.

The morning moved in a blur of back-to-back appointments. A young couple trying to make sense of a real estate contract with more holes than sense. An older gentleman with a box full of papers and a list of things he wanted squared away, "before my kids start fighting over my fishing boat." A property line dispute that hinged on a rickety shed, a defunct fence, and a healthy amount of neighborly spite.

Biscuit stayed curled up under my desk for most of it, occasionally emerging to nuzzle a hand or plop her little paws on a knee. She had an uncanny ability to show up at the right moment—especially when the nerves kicked up or the tears threatened. By lunchtime, I was half-convinced she had been an emotional support dog in a past life.

Every single person who came through the door said something kind.

"This place feels warm. Like someone actually cares what happens here."

"I heard Ramsey Shaw's the one who bought the building. That true? Nice of him to invest in the community like that."

"Funny how he and your brother've been thick as thieves since college. You'd think they were related, the way they carry on."

I smiled when I needed to. Nodded, made polite noises, and gave exactly nothing away. But inside... yeah. I was glowing.

The office felt real now. Mine. Biscuit's tiny huffs and soft feet on the floor were a balm I hadn't known I needed. And the fact that she went home with me sometimes, and with Ramsey other times, was a rhythm I'd started to settle into without even noticing. A gentle tether. Quietly domestic. Cozy, in a way I hadn't dared want.

Miss Addie poked her head in as I finished writing up notes from my last client. "Alia, there's a pair of gentlemen here with clipboards and a truck who say they've got furniture for Mr. Shaw."

"Oh, I'll call him. Ask them to wait a minute?"

With a nod, she disappeared, and I dialed Ramsey.

He answered on the third ring, background noise full of hammering and what might've been a circular saw. "Hey. Everything okay?"

"Everything's great." I was surprised to realize I meant it. "Are you expecting furniture today?"

"Oh, shit, yeah. I forgot to tell you." He blew out a breath. "I'm elbow-deep in replacing a busted banister right now. Can you point them wherever makes sense? I trust you. If you're in the middle of something, have them dump it and I'll sort it out later."

"No, I can take care of it." It gave me a strange warm fuzzy in my chest to have the assignment.

They'd brought more than I expected. A full bedroom suite in warm wood, with simple lines, and the sort of clean aesthetic that looked effortless but wasn't cheap. A new dining table, too. Sturdy, not flashy, but definitely an upgrade on the one that had been two steps away from kindling. An entertainment center with a predictably man-sized TV, and a pair of armchairs I instantly wanted to curl up in with a book and a blanket.

None of it said temporary.

Ramsey wasn't the type to need much. I knew that about him. He'd lived in Charleston for years with what he called "functional furniture," which mostly meant stuff that served a purpose, not stuff that made a place feel like his. He'd never been one for nesting. He could make anywhere livable. But this? This wasn't merely livable.

This was intentional.

I directed the layout—bedroom first, then had them set up the chairs and entertainment center in the second bedroom where he'd moved the second-hand sofa. The dining table went into the kitchen, and the delivery men kindly hauled the old one out to the curb for garbage day.

I wandered upstairs after the delivery crew left, Biscuit padding along beside me like a tiny bodyguard. The back bedroom now held actual furniture. The California king bed wasn't made yet, but that didn't matter. The frame was substantial. Good lines. The dresser matched. So did the nightstands. No rug yet. No lamps. A man's version of move-in ready.

Biscuit tried to hop up onto the mattress and slid off again with an undignified squeak. I scooped her up into a cuddle. "I'm sorry, baby. I'm sure he'll get you some stairs."

Holding onto the dog, I took a slow walk through the room, fingers trailing along the edge of the dresser.

Ramsey hadn't said anything. No big declaration. No "I'm staying" conversation. I knew he still had his career in Charleston.

But this? This was the type of furniture you picked when you were planning to wake up here. Not for a night or two. Not to crash between jobs. It wasn't permanent. This house wouldn't be a forever home for him. But it was something. A start.

It was the first time in a long time I'd looked at a space and seen potential instead of pressure. Not a future I had to plan or control. But one I might get to *want*.

Downstairs, Miss Addie's voice floated up the stairwell. "Your two o'clock is here."

"Right." I glanced once more around the room, then patted Biscuit's rump. "Let's go, squish."

I let her down, and she trotted toward the stairs. I followed, steadier than when I came up, and starting to believe in this thing we were building together.

Chapter 28

Ramsey

By the time I'd polished off my second beer and scavenged the last slice of pepperoni, the house was humming with raucous conversation and memory. Laughter bounced off the old plaster walls, mingled with low music from a Bluetooth speaker that had gotten buried under a throw pillow. The unmistakable scent of frozen pizza filled the air, because no one in this town had managed to reopen the local pizzeria yet, and college instincts die hard.

The upstairs living room looked nothing like the half-furnished bachelor cave I'd expected to throw together. The new chairs had that broken-in-by-someone-else vibe already, softened by a couple of ridiculous throw pillows with hand-stitched football puns. There was a cozy-looking lamp in the corner I was pretty sure had once belonged to somebody's meemaw, and a rug under the coffee table that I couldn't stop stepping on because it felt too damn nice to have been thrifted. Which meant it probably had been, because the Sasspatch Society had been here.

I hadn't even heard them come in. Ninja-level accessorizing.

They'd done the same thing to Alia's office. One minute it was functional; the next it was curated. And while none of it was stuff I would've picked on my own, I couldn't bring myself to care. They weren't wrong. The space was warmer now. More homey. Even if that wasn't what this place was supposed to be.

"Hey, remember when Ramsey tried to grill in the dorm courtyard and set off the building fire alarm?" Blair grinned around a mouthful of crust.

I pointed my beer at her. "That was *one time*."

Bodie snorted. "One time too many. We were almost banned from having open flames within a five-mile radius of campus housing."

Alia shook her head, biting back a laugh. "What almost? You *were* banned. *I* only got a strongly worded email from Residence Life."

"A *good* sister would have put her pre-law skills to work for both of us," Bodie insisted.

"Rules exist for a reason, and behavior has consequences." The sparkle in her eye took all the prim and proper out of the statement. "And honestly, you both deserved to be punished for the crimes committed against those bratwursts."

"Here, here!" Blair lifted her beer.

I leaned into the rhythm of verbal sparring with people who'd known me for years. "How were we supposed to get better without practice?"

Alia and Blair exchanged a look before both bursting out, "Read the instructions!"

Bodie snorted. "Instructions are for weenies."

As he and his sister continued to rib each other, I looked around the room, taking in where Bodie sprawled in one of the chairs with a beer balanced on one arm of it like a coaster. Blair sat cross-legged on the floor in fancy boots, double-fisting paper plates and gesticulating her reply with so much animation she nearly flung a slice of supreme across the room. Alia was settled at the other end of the couch, with Biscuit snoozing on the cushion between us. I couldn't stop looking back at that soft, quiet smile she only wore when she wasn't trying to keep up a front.

Yeah, this is what home feels like.

It was different from anything I had in Charleston. Not better, just... older. Rooted. This wasn't merely comfort. It was a history that went bone-deep and needed no explanation.

I must've gone quiet too long, because Bodie nudged me with his foot.

"What?" I asked.

"You're lookin' all sentimental. You about to cry or something?"

"I was thinking how much I've missed this. The shorthand. The history. I didn't realize how much until I had it back."

Bodie sat up straighter, narrowed his eyes. "Jesus. Are you drunk or pregnant?"

Blair rolled her eyes. "Let the man have his feelings, Bodie."

Alia raised her glass in mock salute. "Mark the day. Ramsey Shaw went soft in public."

That got a round of easy laughter. Nobody meant it as a dig.

Before I could fire back something halfway witty, Bodie's radio crackled to life with a burst of static and a voice I couldn't quite make out.

He groaned like it physically hurt, but peeled himself up. "Duty calls." He clapped a hand on my shoulder as he passed. "Small town. Never really off duty."

"Slice for the road?" Blair asked.

"Nah, y'all keep it. See you tomorrow."

And then he was gone, leaving the rest of us in the sort of quiet that only settled when you've known each other long enough to not need to fill it.

Blair stretched her arms over her head and got to her feet with the fluid grace of someone who definitely hadn't eaten half a pizza by herself. She brushed off imaginary crumbs. "Well, that's my cue to go home to my stunning wife and leave you two lovebirds alone."

She threw me a smirk as she said it—eyebrow arched, mouth twitching, the full force of the Eyebrow of Doom. That one move had taken down pledges, professors, and one particularly persistent guy from her freshman bio lab who didn't understand that no meant *no*.

I froze. Not visibly, I hoped. A micro-stutter in my spine. Because there was *no way* she could actually—

"She figured it out at dinner that first night." Alia said it casually, like it wasn't a nuclear statement.

Blair smirked. "I've got eyes, don't I?"

I opened my mouth, ready to say something—anything—but she cut me off with a raised finger and a knowing nod. "Don't worry, Shaw. Lips are sealed until you two are ready to make it Gibson Hollow official. And I want props for not even telling my beloved."

"All the props," Alia agreed.

Then Blair leaned in to press an exaggerated air kiss toward each of us, gave Alia a warm squeeze on the shoulder, and aimed a final wink at me as she swept out of the room like a Broadway exit on a hardwood stage.

A minute later, the front door shut, and Biscuit sleepily sat up and looked around, clearly wondering where everybody had gotten off to.

In the warm hush of post housewarming-party calm, Alia looked at me like she already knew what I was thinking.

That quiet stretched between us, comfortable. I let it settle for a beat, trying to gauge her mood.

"The night's still young."

Alia huffed a laugh. "Maybe for our college selves. These days I start thinking about sleep at seven-thirty and weighing the consequences of late caffeine."

I grinned. "So... you're saying you're tired?"

The glance she shot over the rim of her glass that was all spark and no quit. "No. I'm saying I want the quiet. *You.*"

That struck me. Not heat, though there was always plenty of that between us. This was something warmer. Deeper. As if I was one of her safe spaces. I'd worked hard to give her one in the literal sense, but being one of her chosen people? Yeah, that was a gift I wasn't going to take for granted.

"Good." I set my drink down. "Because I've got a surprise."

She lifted one perfectly skeptical brow. "Surprise?"

"I know how you feel about those, but come with me."

I held out a hand. She took it without hesitation and followed me down the hallway, past the lingering smell of pizza and laughter, into the back bedroom where I'd shoved half my life into place.

She shot me a look as we crossed the threshold. The one that said *if this is headed where I think it is, I'm not stopping you.* And yeah, it was headed there eventually. But first... I had something better.

I picked up the box on the dresser. It was nothing special. Plain brown cardboard. But inside was something a lot more special. I set it down on the mattress next to where Biscuit had climbed up the miniature stairs at the foot of the bed to sniff all the way around the package.

"What is this?"

"Open it."

She raised a brow but didn't hesitate. Lifted the flaps, peeled back the layer of packing foam—and frowned in curiosity when she saw the matte black case inside.

"Keep going."

She pulled out the case and unlatched the sides, tipping back the lid. Her hands stilled. "No way." She lifted the foam inside, and her whole face lit up at the sight of the helm nestled inside. "You had the armor sent?"

"I had the armor sent."

She looked up at me like I'd given her front-row *Hamilton* tickets. "Are you serious?"

"I'm extremely serious."

She lifted the helm from its case and ran her fingers along the curve, with a gleam in her eye that was part awe, part mischief. "Would it bother you if I asked you to put it on?"

I smirked. "Thought you might."

She didn't even try to hide the way her eyes lit up. "You need a minute?"

"Ten, tops. You wanna take Biscuit out while I get battle-ready?"

As if on cue, the pup trotted down her steps to the bedroom door like she knew her role in this little production. Alia trailed after her, but not before giving me one last look over her shoulder that said, *this is happening* and *don't make me wait* all at once.

I ducked into the bathroom with the case, heart kicking up in anticipation.

Ten minutes later, I stepped out of the bathroom, helm already in place, armor cinched and strapped and gleaming under the warm overhead light. Chest plate, bracers, the works. And, yeah, the leather pants. Because let's be honest, they did half the heavy lifting in this scenario.

Alia was just setting Biscuit on her Sentinels bed in the corner when she turned and saw me.

She froze, her gaze dragging from boots to helm, slow and deliberate, and then she let out a low whistle that did unholy things to my blood pressure.

"This," she took a step closer, voice breathier than before, "will never, *ever* get old." Her eyes sparkled as she added, "I'm sorry, but this is your permanent form now. No take-backs."

I laughed, low in my chest. "That so?"

"Oh, absolutely." She reached out and ran a hand up the leather bracer on my forearm like she was checking the grain. "I'm gonna need to write a strongly worded petition."

I'd gotten a high the first time, back at the con—watching her face when I stepped in as the fictional hero she'd created. That flash of stunned disbelief, the magic of it all crashing into her in real time, despite the panic attack. It was something I'd never forget.

But this... this was different.

This time, she knew it was me. And still, she looked at me like I'd come to life all over again. I'd never wanted anyone more. Not only in bed, but in every way. I wanted that look from her every day. To be her hero for always.

She was still looking at me like I'd handed her the moon and dared her to dream bigger. Not because of the gear—though, yeah, she was clearly not immune to the leather pants—but because it was me wearing it. Me showing up for her. Me trying, even when I wasn't sure what came next.

And right then, in that quiet, holy kind of moment, I didn't want to wait. Didn't want to go slow or be patient. I wanted to move forward to what I hoped and prayed we both wanted, deep down.

So I unsheathed the sword, the weight of it oddly familiar and grounding in my hand.

Alia's brows lifted, amused, like she thought I was about to do some showy pose or quote one of her books.

Instead, I dropped to one knee and held out the sword across both palms. "I'm offering you my sword, my life, and my heart. A lifetime of devotion. If you'll have me."

Her breath caught. Her smile faltered—not in fear, but in surprise. Real, raw, heart-clutching surprise.

"This isn't a stunt." My voice came out a lot steadier than I felt. "Or a joke or a moment. I know it might seem fast, but it's not. Not really. It's been twelve years. And if we'd gotten out of our own way sooner, I think we'd have been here a long time ago."

In stunned silence, she stood there, watching me, eyes wide and shining.

"The thing is, I don't want to waste another minute. I love you. I've always loved you, and I want to build something with you. A life. A home. Hell, a kingdom, if that's what you want."

The silence between us felt suspended in time, and right this moment I was really hating her poker face. Because I knew I was probably freaking her out, springing this on her, I rushed to add, "You don't have to say yes right now. I'm not asking for an answer tonight. I know you weren't expecting this. But I wanted you to know where I am. What I want. Take as long as you need to think about it. The offer stands."

I kept my eyes on her face, the weight of the sword balanced across my palms like a vow.

Alia stared at me like she was trying to recalibrate reality. Because yeah, this *wasn't* what she'd expected after pizza and party banter and that whole detour into cosplay-induced lust. I hadn't planned it either. But kneeling here now, sword across my hands, waiting for something—*anything*—from her, I couldn't regret it. Because I'd meant every damned word.

Then she stepped forward, slowly lifting the helm from

my head. Her fingers were careful, almost reverent, like she understood exactly what this moment cost me. What it meant.

She set the helm aside on the dresser without breaking eye contact, then cupped my jaw with one hand, her thumb brushing across my cheekbone. "You really know how to pull focus." Her murmur was soft. A little awed. A bit shaky. "I don't know what I thought your surprise was gonna be, but it definitely wasn't a medieval proposal with leather pants and heartfelt declarations."

I huffed out a breath that could've been a laugh if it weren't stuck in my throat. "Sorry. I'm a go big or go home guy."

Her smile tilted. "Yeah. I noticed."

She didn't say yes. Didn't say no either. Instead, she leaned in and rested her brow against mine. "Let me think about it, okay?"

"Okay." What else could I say?

Her fingers curled against my jaw. "Maybe I can't give you a yes right now, but I can give you this: I love you, Ramsey. I'm in this with you. And I want to be *sure* when I say yes, because Gibsons don't go in for temporary."

Hope and joy roared to life in my chest as the air shifted between us, subtle but seismic, cracking open something tender. Instead of trying to fill it with jokes or noise or more words, we breathed for a moment, her forehead still against mine, her hand still warm on my face, the sword balanced between us.

Finally, she glanced down and huffed a breath that was almost a laugh. "So... how exactly do we get you out of all this?"

That broke the tension enough for me to grin. "Carefully. There's a whole harness situation under here."

"Does that mean I'll need tools?"

"Just patience."

"Mm." She leaned back and slid her hands down to the buckles at my shoulders. "Not my strongest suit."

The next few minutes were spent with her helping me out of the gear. She paused often to brush fingertips over the leather, admiring as she'd wanted to do that day at the convention. Then she did the same to me, stoking fires with her touch as she stripped away every piece of armor, literal and emotional, until I stood in nothing but skin and the soft glow of the bedside lamp.

She stepped in close, wound her arms around my waist, and rested her head on my shoulder. The quiet intimacy soaked into me.

"You knocked me flat tonight." Her voice was so soft, I could hear Biscuit's snores from the corner of the room.

I trailed a hand down her hair. "Didn't mean to. But I don't regret it."

"Good." Her gaze lifted to mine. "Because I don't regret this either."

She kissed me, and everything else fell away. There was no rush, no performance. Just her. Just me. Choosing each other again and again in every touch, every breath.

And when we finally sank into each other in the dark, it was with the surety of something built to last.

Chapter 29

Alia

The cold drizzle had been falling all afternoon, a steady soaker that made the world feel quieter than it really was. It beaded on the front windows like a curtain of tiny jewels, streaking occasionally when the wind shoved against the house. I'd lit the good candles, the ones that smelled like bergamot and bergamot-adjacent things, and the whole place carried that cozy, barely floral warmth that made me want to curl up in fuzzy socks and my favorite sweater and forget the outside world existed. And tonight I was sharing that cozy with my bestie.

Blair stepped inside with a dramatic shiver, shrugging out of a coat that had definitely seen more glamorous days. "This rain can go straight to hell."

I reached for the coat. "Could be worse. At least it's not snow."

She made a face. "Yet. That stretch of sixty-degree days we had earlier this week had me thinking about flowers."

"You didn't give in, did you?"

"No. Elena restrained me from making a pilgrimage to the

nearest garden center, citing the Great Flower Debacle of two years ago. Fucking late season snow. There should never be a freeze after Easter, damn it!"

"We could start a petition with Mother Nature, but I'm pretty sure she's menopausal, and it won't help."

From his spot on the couch, Uncle Dee lifted his mug in lazy salute. "Tea's hot. The sass is hotter."

Blair eyed the e-reader in his other hand. "How far have you gotten?"

Uncle Dee grinned, smug as sin. "Darling, I've finished them *all*. Working my way through round two."

I hung Blair's coat on the rack near the door. "All of what?"

He looked downright triumphant. "Your books, sweet cheeks."

Stunned, I could only blink. "Wait, what?"

He patted the cushion beside him like I was the one who needed to sit down. "All of them. Every Kella Harmon title I could get my hands on. I laughed. I cried. I blushed myself into turning on the AC in the dead of winter."

I covered my face with both hands. "Oh, God."

Naturally, Blair was delighted. "He's bucking hard to take over as president of your fan club."

"I don't have a fan club."

Blair arched a knowing brow. "Actually..."

Uncle Dee wagged his empty mug at me. "How do you write kisses like that and still blush when somebody says the word nipple out loud?"

My whole face lit up like a fire truck because—not only had he said it—but now I was thinking about *my* nipples and that thing Ramsey did with his mouth and well, *great*.

"Uncensored access to your author brain is a trip." Blair kicked off her boots. "And I love that you're part of Team Kella now."

Uncle Dee clutched his chest like the world's most dramatic romance reader. "It's gonna come down to a Kella Harmon trivia showdown, and I. Am. Ready."

I had no idea how to feel about his effusive enthusiasm. No one in my family had read my books. At least nobody who knew I'd been the one to write them.

Setting the e-reader aside, he stood, pressed a smacking kiss to the top of my head, and made for the door. "You ladies have a fabulous evening. I'm off to Sasspatch dinner. Don't wait up."

The door clicked shut behind him, leaving the house extra quiet.

"Well, that happened." I scrubbed a hand over my still heated cheeks. "Tea?"

"Absolutely. Where's the Mascot of Mayhem?" She trailed me into the kitchen while I put the kettle on.

"With Ramsey tonight. He's got plans to trounce Bodie in *Madden* and wanted her as his good luck charm. He even got a tiny Sentinels jersey for her."

"I hope you got a picture of *that* for her socials."

"I didn't, but I'm sure he will."

Spying the neat tray of iced butter cookies in the shape of books, she arched a brow. "Are those Emmaline's cookies?"

"They are."

The other brow followed. "And to what do I owe this treat?"

"They're part apology, part thank you."

"For?"

"Handling everything for my author life."

"I mean, that is what you pay me for."

"Yeah, but I've been a pissy, uncooperative nightmare lately. I'm really sorry about that."

Her lips quirked. "Grump wrangler is on my business card."

"No, I mean it. You've kept the entire author side of my life afloat, while all I've wanted to do is shove it in a locked closet and pretend it didn't exist. I've said no to almost everything you've suggested, and I haven't been as appreciative as I should be. Without your hard work and dedication, Kella Harmon would have fallen off the map."

Blair softened, reaching out to lay a hand on my shoulder. "You've had a hell of a year. You don't owe me an apology for surviving it."

"Still, I wouldn't have without you. So I wanted to do this to say thank you."

She pulled me in for a hard hug, and I squeezed back.

"You're my ride or die. Always. But I will never turn down Emmaline's cookies." So saying, she grabbed one and took a bite that ended on a near pornographic moan. "Why are these so *good?*"

"I believe the answer is butter, butter, more butter, and sugar."

"Thank the goddess for that."

The kettle whistled, and I doused our tea with boiling water.

I passed Blair her mug and settled across from her at the kitchen table. "In the spirit of being more cooperative—what's the update on all the things?"

Her eyes gleamed with a dangerous delight that meant she'd been waiting for this opening. She pulled her tablet from her purse, tapping to wake the screen. Half a dozen swipes later, she began reeling off data as if this whole thing had been planned all along. "Well. Sales are still steady. Preorders on the special edition hardcovers are strong—thank you, TikTok unboxings—and the reader engagement spike after the mystery man rescue video has yet to calm down."

I groaned. "Swoony McBroadsword strikes again."

"Oh, honey. The fandom is frothing. You've created a monster."

I snorted. "I'm only the damsel. *Ramsey* created the monster."

"Not on purpose, maybe. But on brand? Absolutely."

"Not sure if I should be flattered or afraid."

"Both. Definitely both. They're convinced he was a plant. Half the subreddit is sure you hired him as some guerrilla marketing stunt."

I frowned over my tea. "What, like I'm secretly rolling in Disney-level promo budget?"

Blair held up a finger. "Speaking of Disney—there's a whole sub-thread dedicated to the theory that the man in the armor was an AI deep fake, and that you're secretly in cahoots with Marvel."

"Oh, my God."

"And then there's the Henry Cavill camp—"

"No."

"They've cross-referenced his Comic-Con schedule and built a conspiracy board."

I laughed into my tea.

"Pedro Pascal is the backup theory. 'Because obviously we all want him to be our soft king.' That's a direct quote."

"Valid. But still no." I grabbed one of the cookies and bit in, barely restraining myself from repeating Blair's performance as the sweet, buttery goodness melted on my tongue.

"Oh, and my personal favorite—someone thinks it was Jason Momoa in disguise. Like he cosplayed as his own bodyguard to sneak in unnoticed."

I choked on the cookie. "What even is the logic?"

"There isn't any. There never is." She tapped again. "Then you've got the Estonian blacksmith-slash-model theory. That one comes with a Pinterest board of cheekbone comparisons."

"That feels like too much effort."

Blair shrugged. "Passion knows no bounds."

I peered at the screen. "And 'The Vanishing Várdur'?"

"I cannot make this up. It's some Aragorn cosplayer from a Ren faire circuit who vanished from the internet in 2019 and is now their number one contender."

I stared at her. "People are *so* weird."

"People are *invested*. You've weaponized their collective thirst."

I blew across the top of my tea. "It wasn't intentional."

"Doesn't matter. It's effective." She scribbled some notes to herself and plucked another cookie off the plate. "Now, in the spirit of cooperation, do you have anything you'd like to share with your fandom?"

The rest of the cookie bought me time to formulate my answer. "Well, maybe not something to share with the fandom, but with you. I actually wrote something."

My bestie froze, wide-eyed. "You did?"

"I mean, just a chapter. An entirely new beginning, because when I opened the WIP earlier this week, I couldn't even remember where the hell I'd been going with it. But it felt good."

With a soft squee, she pounded her feet on the floor beneath the table. "Okay, okay. Not gonna jinx it. But I'm lighting a candle later."

"It doesn't mean anything yet. It might dry up tomorrow. Dean left for Nashville this morning. He'll get back with Dad tomorrow, and then... who knows?"

Reaching out, Blair covered my hand with hers. "Baby, it means everything. Even if it's only a spark right now, that's more than you've had in months."

"True. I'm treating it like a wild animal and not looking it directly in the eye, lest I scare it off."

"Seems sensible." With another squeeze of my hand, she let me go and sipped more tea. "Sooo... is this creative breakthrough at all related to a certain tight end's continuing campaign to sweep you off your feet?"

I snorted into my tea. "You make it sound like he shows up with rose petals and a boombox every morning."

Blair didn't even blink. "Please. That man's mere existence is a grand gesture."

My lips curved, unbidden. She wasn't wrong. Not when I was still thinking about that sword and the look in his eyes when he'd held it out to me like it was his whole heart. Not when I couldn't stop replaying the way he'd whispered, *Take as long as you need to think about it. The offer stands.* Like I was worth waiting forever for.

Instead of taking the bait, I stared into my cup like the swirl of steam might hide the softness I couldn't quite keep off my face. "Things are going... very well."

Blair narrowed her eyes like a hawk who'd spotted prey. "Very well, huh?"

I shrugged. "What do you want me to say?"

"That you're finally being worshiped the way you deserve and getting multiple orgasms in lots of interesting places as often as humanly possible."

I choked on my tea. Because *yes*, thank you, storage room at the community center. And also, how dare she be so spot on?

The grin that spread across her face could only be described as feral. "That right there is answer enough, and I couldn't be more delighted. You deserve all the romance and sexy times he can bring. And whenever you're ready to go Gibson Hollow official, I will be ready to squee the loudest."

Oh, she thought she was loud now. She hadn't even heard the proposal story. I hadn't told a soul—not even her. Not because I didn't want to. But because I hadn't given him an answer yet. I was still hugging the question close, like the spark of a story I didn't want to breathe on too hard. The kind that flickered quietly in your chest, waiting to become something more.

And maybe, just maybe, I was getting to the point where I really believed it.

Chapter 30

Ramsey

Everett Gibson walked into his mama's house like he hadn't spent the last six months in and out of hospitals being put back together with enough hardware to set off TSA. Sure, he was moving slowly, and I recognized the faint lines of pain around his eyes and mouth as he did it, but that signature Gibson grin was still locked and loaded, aimed at the man waiting for him in the doorway.

"If I go home, am I gonna find everything redecorated, Dee?"

Uncle Dee arched a perfectly sculpted brow and kissed him square on the cheek. "Please. I would never undo Rosanna's masterpiece. She'd haunt me with a vengeance."

Everett chuckled and thumped his brother's back. "Damn right she would."

The two of them stood there for a second, arms still looped around each other, both smiling in that way family does when they've been to hell and back and are damn grateful to be home. Then came big hugs all around, like Everett was a soldier returned from war—which, to be fair, wasn't too far off.

Multiple surgeries and hellish PT to learn how to walk again after having his pelvis broken in three places and his shoulder completely rebuilt were no joke.

He got to Alia last and didn't rush it, pulling her in and holding on long enough that I saw the breath hitch in her chest before she let it out slow against his shoulder. She didn't talk much about what this meant to her. She didn't have to. I'd seen it in the way she'd cleaned the windows that didn't need cleaning and baked three versions of the banana pudding to make sure it was perfect. I'd benefitted from the rejects.

She was a fortress most days, but today I was seeing her soft underbelly.

Blair got her own rib-cracking hug and a teasing, "You still putting up with my girl?" that made her laugh and say, "Only because she pays me in baked goods."

Then Everett turned to me and offered a firm handshake, eyes crinkling at the corners. "Appreciate you being around, son."

I gave him a firm squeeze back. "Wouldn't be anywhere else." And that was the damned truth.

That was about all the mush Everett would willingly tolerate, apparently, because the second Grandma Elsie bustled in from the kitchen with a dish towel flapping in one hand and purpose in her eyes, he held up both palms. "Mama, I'm fine."

"You are not fine. But you're here, which is better than the alternative. Now sit down before I put you there myself."

"Time limit," he muttered. "You've got five minutes before I start charging you for all this fussing."

Elsie folded him into her arms, despite the fact that he towered over her by almost a foot. "You'll take what you get and like it."

He hugged her back and sniffed. "Is that your pot roast I smell?"

"And all the fixins. Plus banana puddin'. Your favorites."

"Aww, you do love me."

"It's not every day my firstborn comes home after being duct-taped back together for being a hero."

That one made Everett look down and rub at the back of his neck like the compliment itched. "Your firstborn is hungry, Mama. How soon's dinner ready?"

"As soon as you get yourself seated, which won't happen if you keep jawin' in the doorway."

There was a shuffle of movement as all the brothers made space, forming a loose perimeter like they might have to catch him. Everett waved them off with a glare that didn't hold much heat.

"Y'all make me feel like I'm ninety."

Colter smirked. "You're walkin' like John Wayne after a long day in the saddle."

"Keep talkin' smart, and I'll make you carry my plate."

Once he was settled at the table, and we'd all followed suit, the vibe eased back into familiar banter and clatter. I took my usual spot, so I could keep Alia in my periphery without being so close anyone would get suspicious.

Everett leaned back in his chair and turned his attention my way. "Tough loss at the end of the season."

"Yeah." I nodded, happy to take the brunt of the small talk for a bit. "It was."

"You got a plan for next year?"

I didn't miss a beat. "Always do."

That earned a satisfied grunt and a sip of sweet tea.

The scent of pot roast hit full force as Grandma Elsie and Uncle Dee started ferrying in dishes, and the table filled fast. Along with the pot roast, there was cornbread and mashed potatoes, green beans with little bits of ham hock, a behemoth platter of deviled eggs, and the banana pudding set on the dining room sideboard like a promise. Classic Gibson spread. The kind that required multiple passes, a second stomach, and at least one post-meal nap.

Plates were filled, glasses passed, and then everybody dug in with a gusto only found in big Southern families and small-town funerals. For a few minutes, the only sounds were happy hums as we all partook of an incredible meal.

Then Everett looked at Alia with a serious expression. "Everybody's been keeping me updated about everything you've done for this town while I was away. I don't even have words."

Alia didn't glance up from her plate, but I caught the faint pinking in her cheeks. "I didn't do anything that anybody else wouldn't have."

"Bullshit." Every fork at the table paused for half a breath as Everett continued, "You saved this place."

She tried for a laugh, but it didn't quite make it out. "I did my part."

"Your part?" Dean echoed. "Ali, come on. You were down at the courthouse every day for a month straight sorting out the property records alone."

"Filed for damn near every FEMA claim in the county," Gunner added.

Bodie pointed at her with his fork. "Negotiated the new power grid install and the community center remodel."

Fletcher piped in between bites, "I heard from one of the city engineers that if it weren't for your grant paperwork being airtight, they would've lost the federal match money."

Colter shook his head. "She's being modest. Again."

Across the table, Alia's shoulders hunched a little, her fork moving methodically across her plate like she could pretend all the praise wasn't aimed directly at her.

But it was. And she deserved every damn word of it.

Everett only nodded, watching her the way fathers do when they're having big feels and don't know how to say it without making a mess of things. "I'm proud of you, baby girl."

She glanced up, eyes shining, and managed a small, quiet smile.

There was so much love at this table, it practically vibrated off the walls. It thrummed under everything—undeniable and bone-deep. And even if they didn't always say it right, didn't always *see* her right, they loved her. Fiercely. And I knew that was why she was willing to do anything for any of them. They were her heart.

Everett set his glass down with a sigh. "All right, so... now that I'm back, I guess we need to get my meds schedule sorted. They shifted things up right before I left Nashville. There's a bunch that have to be taken at stupid o'clock in the morning, and a few others spread through the day. I have follow-ups at two clinics next week—orthopedic in Asheville and a neuro consult up in Boone that they're having to move times for. And apparently my disability paperwork's been kicked back again."

Dean cut in, helpful as ever. "You want me to drive you to the Asheville one?"

Everett nodded. "That'd be great. But I'll need to make sure they don't double-book me with Boone."

He looked to Alia, not even hesitating. "Think you could help wrangle that? My brain's still foggy from pain meds, and I don't want to screw it up."

Alia gave a tight smile. "Yeah, I can do that."

Across the table, Fletcher wiped his mouth on a napkin. "While you're at it, can you follow up with Public Works? They still haven't sent the drainage reports for the west end of town, and it's about to become a mudslide if we get another week of rain."

"And the Chamber's meeting on Tuesday," Bodie added.

"They're expecting you to chair it again. Somebody needs to finalize the agenda."

"You mean me." That curve of her mouth couldn't really qualify as a smile.. "Got it."

Gunner added, "And the engineer emailed again about that floodplain reassessment. They want confirmation from the mayor's office before they can move forward."

Her jaw twitched in the smallest tell. "I'll reply tonight."

I watched her shoulders pull in a fraction. The pencil she kept tucked near the phone was already in her hand, scribbling notes in the margins of her napkin. Every request was met with a quiet, unflinching yes. Not because she had the time. Not because she'd offered.

Because they asked.

Because they always asked.

Because she always said yes.

And maybe they didn't mean anything by it. Maybe it didn't even register as piling on. But I saw what it was doing to her. How each new ask pulled her further inward. How she got smaller with every task tacked onto her already-overflowing plate.

They didn't see it. But I did. And I was already starting to burn.

Alia pushed back from the table, slow and smooth, like she didn't want to draw attention. "I'm gonna refill the mashed potatoes." She gathered the bowl even though it was still half full.

Nobody questioned it. But I knew that voice. That tone. That was her *I'm at capacity* voice. The one she used when she was seconds from unraveling and determined not to let a single thread show.

I watched her disappear through the archway into the

kitchen, and something in me simply snapped. "What the hell is the matter with you?"

Every fork froze. Every conversation stopped as if I'd pulled the emergency brake on a moving train.

"You're all so quick to celebrate everything Alia's done—like that list of miracles just happened—but the second she sits down, you hand her another one. And another. And another." My gaze swept the table, sharp enough to draw blood. "She's been carrying the weight of this town, this family, for months—some of it, years—and it's like not a single one of you stops to ask how much more she can take. She's not a machine. She's not some endless resource you can tap until she breaks."

Nobody said a word.

I leaned forward, fists clenched on the table. "You think because she hasn't said she's overwhelmed, she must be fine? She's not. She's just too damn used to being the one who holds it together while everybody else falls apart. She's been doing that since she was *sixteen*. And the worst part? You all got used to it. You just let her. You just *keep* letting her, without even thinking about it."

Colter opened his mouth and then closed it again.

Good. Let it sink in.

"You're supposed to be the line that protects your quarterback—not the goddamn pile-on after the snap." I didn't shout. I didn't need to. The words echoed like thunder in the silence that followed.

Then I looked at Uncle Dee. At Blair. "They've been in the trenches with her every step of the way. The rest of you? If you're not offering help, you need to get the hell out of her way before you break her."

A breath hitched, and I knew without turning that she'd heard it all. I looked toward the kitchen, and there she was.

Alia stood in the doorway, frozen. Bowl of mashed potatoes

in her hands like a shield, like she'd meant to do something normal and got sideswiped by everything she'd overheard. Her eyes were glassy, wide, locked on me like I'd ripped open something she hadn't realized was bleeding.

"Alia—" I said her name on instinct, breath catching halfway through.

She didn't answer. Didn't say a damn word as she came back into the room, each step slow and purposeful, like some choice had already been made. She set the bowl down on the table with deliberate care.

Then she kissed me.

Not a whisper of a kiss. Not something gentle or tentative. This one came from the center of the storm. A collision of hope and heartbreak, of finally letting go and grabbing on tight. Her hands found my jaw, then slid back into my hair like she needed an anchor, and I gave her everything I had.

The room disappeared. All I could feel was her. All I could hear was the blood roaring in my ears and the low, quiet sound she made right before she pulled back—like the fight had gone out of her shoulders for the first time in months.

Her eyes met mine, full and clear.

Her voice didn't waver as she said the one word I'd been waiting for.

"Yes."

Chapter 31

Alia

This man.

This kind, fierce, wonderful man had stood up for me. Said the things I hadn't been able to make myself say—ever—because I didn't know how to do it without hurting the people I loved most.

No matter how complicated our situation, how could my answer be anything but yes?

The certainty of it vibrated through me like a plucked string. He was my person. The one who'd held my heart for years, earned it over and over with all his tiny, thoughtful gestures that had been saying he loved me all along.

God, I loved him. The joy of it shot through me like fireworks, and I saw an answering spark in his eyes, as a smile of understanding spread across his face and his hands came up to curl possessively around my wrists.

"What is happening?" Gunner's voice sounded oddly small, far more like the baby brother I remembered than the man of twenty-six.

Right. My hands were still threaded in Ramsey's hair, my

lips still tingling from his, and I was still reeling from the decision I'd made. Other than Blair, no one here was actually aware of our relationship, and I'd effectively detonated a secondary bomb in the middle of family dinner.

I had some explaining to do.

Dropping my hand to curl around Ramsey's nape, I shifted to face my family, who all stared with varying degrees of shock. Probably an even split between everything he'd accused them of and the fact that I'd kissed the bejeesus out of him at the dinner table. For some reason, that made me want to laugh.

"What's happening is that I kissed the most observant, emotionally intelligent, straight man in the room. Who, not coincidentally, I just agreed to marry."

Blair let out a squee so loud the neighbor's husky start howling in reply.

Uncle Dee pumped his fist and stuck his hand out to Grandma Elsie. "Pay up."

Grandma scowled. "Dang it. I had another month in the pool."

Nope, I wasn't even gonna ask about that.

My brothers all started talking over each other.

"What the hell?"

"*Married?*"

"Are you serious?"

All except Bodie, who didn't say a thing. He only sat there, looking like he'd been pole-axed. Shock and betrayal vibrated from him through our twinsense.

"Why didn't you tell us?" Colter demanded.

I arched a brow. "Why didn't I tell my *five* over-protective brothers about my love life? Really? You can't think of any good reasons?"

An embarrassed flush began creeping up from his neck, which gave me an unreasonable amount of amusement. As the oldest, who'd been parentified at a young age, I seldom tortured my siblings, but it was nice to confirm it was still fun.

"I get why you didn't tell them. But why the hell didn't either of you tell *me?*" Bodie's voice was quiet.

Ramsey sucked in a breath to answer, but I squeezed his nape.

"Because I asked him not to. So if you want to be pissed at somebody about this, be pissed at me."

Ramsey's arm slid around my waist. "I did actually come to talk to you about this."

"When?"

"When I got back from the Charlotte Combine."

Bodie's mouth opened. "That was *ten years ago.*"

"Yeah."

"Exactly how long have you been in love with my sister?"

Ramsey didn't hesitate. "Twelve years, four months and—" He did some counting on his fingers. "—sixteen days."

It was my turn to frown as I did the math. "Your birthday?"

He looked up at me with a smile. "Freshman year. It was the first birthday I'd ever spent away from my mom, and I was homesick as hell. You snuck my phone to get her number, called her up to get her meatloaf recipe, and made it for me in the dorm kitchen."

I stared at him. "It was meatloaf? Really?"

"It wasn't just meatloaf—although it was damned good meatloaf. You gave me home when I was missing it most."

From somewhere behind me, I heard Blair give an alarmingly watery sniff. "Oh, that's the sweetest."

I curled a bit of the hair at Ramsey's nape around my finger, feeling warm and fuzzy myself. "You never told me that."

One big shoulder twitched. "Never came up. But for the record, if you get a hankering to make my mama's meatloaf again, I wouldn't turn it down."

I grinned. "Noted."

Bodie's brain was still exploding. "So all these years, you two...?"

Ramsey shook his head. "No. Because you remember what you said to me that day?"

My brother struggled. "Shit, no. It was a decade ago. I remember talking about the combine and your draft prospects."

"It was after she ditched the cheating asshat. You said—and I quote because it's been burned into my brain ever since—'She deserves better than what she's had. No more football players, man. Half the team are dogs, and the good ones—guys like you —you're gonna be headed for the pros. Always gone. Never around. She needs someone who's there, you know?'"

My brother had said *that*? No wonder Ramsey had backed off. Damn it. Why, oh *why* couldn't he have simply talked to me *first*?

Bodie scrubbed a hand down his face. "Fuck, man, I wasn't talking about *you*. I never thought... I had no idea..."

"I wasn't offended, man. I agreed with you. So I didn't say anything."

"Meaning you both effectively took the choice away from me about my own life. Which I'm still annoyed about, by the way. And that is why I asked him to keep it quiet. Because I didn't want to give anyone else the chance to pick it apart or offer opinions that weren't wanted before I'd even had a chance to figure out what I wanted. And what I want is Ramsey. It's always been him. I can't pinpoint the precise moment. Just a thousand little things that all add up to the fact that he sees me. He always has." I fixed my brother with a look. "I don't know exactly when you stopped seeing me."

I watched Bodie flinch and softened my tone. "I'm not trying to take potshots at you. But he's not wrong about anything he said."

"Why didn't *you* say anything?"

"Because no one has ever asked." I blew out a breath, leaning in as Ramsey's arm subtly tightened around me. "When Mom died, everyone fell apart. *Everyone.* Someone had to hold it all together. I stepped up. And I kept stepping up. So much so that I became the default for everyone. Functionally, I became the new mom. I took on the mental load of keeping up with all the things for the family. I didn't stop, even when I was off at college and law school. And when the flood happened, when Dad got injured, no one asked if I wanted any of this. I basically got voluntold and voted in as interim mayor. Because I'm a Gibson, and no one handles disaster better than me." I flashed a humorless smile. "Classic case of living to regret being excellent at my job."

I hated all the looks of discomfort and horror around the table, but I couldn't regret that Ramsey had broken the silence on my behalf.

"Look, this isn't how I intended any of this to come out. But y'all, I'm tired. I have been spread so damned thin for so long. I barely sleep. I've been so busy with so many demands, I've barely been able to eat until someone took it upon himself to make sure that I could." I squeezed Ramsey's shoulder. "I can't keep doing what I've been doing for much longer."

Some weight slid off me with the admission. I hadn't realized how much keeping all this in had been dragging me down.

The silence that followed felt like standing in the eye of a storm. Still. Too still. My family—so loud, so full of opinions and elbows and elbows *on* opinions—had gone quiet. And for a second, I wished I could take it all back. Tuck the words back in. Rebuild the wall.

But Ramsey's hand was still curved around my waist. I wasn't alone anymore. I didn't have to rebuild that wall. I only needed to trust that he'd be that for me when I needed it.

Grandma Elsie was the first to move. She reached up to lay her hand on my arm. "Sweet girl, I didn't know. I should've." Her voice was thick with regret. "I've been so worried about Everett, I didn't see how heavy everything's gotten for you. And that's on me."

Dean nodded solemnly beside her. "Same. You've always had your shit together so hard, I guess I forgot to ask if you wanted to." He scrubbed a hand over his face. "That's not right. I'm sorry."

"I didn't mean to dump this on y'all." That wasn't exactly fair to me, but all the looks of self-recrimination from my family were killing me. "I just... I've been carrying it so long, I stopped realizing how much it weighed."

"You shouldn't have had to." Colter's voice was low. "You're right—we let you. We took advantage without meaning to." He gave a slow shake of his head, his eyes glassy. "That's not who I want to be. I'll do better. We'll do better."

Fletcher rubbed a hand across the back of his neck. "I didn't realize what all you were handling. I swear I didn't. But you've always been the one who kept it together, and I guess I forgot to check if you were falling apart inside." A muscle jumped in his jaw as he met my gaze. "You won't have to do this alone anymore."

Gunner was blinking too fast, jaw clenched like he was mad at himself. "I—I didn't mean to pile on. None of us meant to. I figured... you'd say something if it got to be too much."

Ramsey let out a quiet huff at that, but he didn't say a word. He didn't have to.

"I knew you were carrying a lot." Dad's voice was rough. "I saw it. But I didn't realize exactly how much you'd taken on. And I should have." He looked at me, eyes soft, filled with something that made my throat burn. "You were already doing too much before that water ever rose. Then I got taken out of commission, and you... you picked it all up. No hesitation. You've been holding this town together with grit and spit and that Gibson spine, and I've been proud as hell of you. But, baby girl, I hate knowing I didn't see the cost."

Tears welled, and I blinked them back hard.

Dad leaned forward, bracing himself on his good arm. "You don't have to carry everything now. You hear me? Not for me. Not for this family. You've done more than your share. We'll figure the rest out together."

Bodie, still reeling, finally stood up and came around the table. His voice cracked when he spoke. "I should've seen it. We all should've seen it." His eyes searched mine. "You don't have to keep proving anything, Alia. Not to us. You've done more than enough."

It meant something to hear all this from them. Even though there was a big gap between saying and doing, it was a start. "I'm not asking you to fix it all today. I just needed to stop pretending everything was fine when it wasn't."

Bodie nodded and pulled me into a tight, almost-too-hard hug that said everything he couldn't yet.

Ramsey didn't let go of my hand. He did, however, look at my grandmother and uncle. "Can we talk about the fact that you two apparently were *betting* on us?"

The collective tone of the room shifted, and I was grateful for the break. "Yeah, what did you mean you had an extra month in the pool?"

With an expression of total innocence, Uncle Dee kicked back in his chair. "Oh, honey, this pool's been going since y'all were in college. It's been updated a dozen times, but once Ramsey decided to stick around a while, we figured y'all would finally quit dancing around each other. Mama thought it would take longer. I was banking on nature taking its course sooner rather than later."

Several of my brothers choked at that.

"I mean, y'all have both been terribly obtuse all these years," Grandma Elsie pointed out.

I stared at them both. "Y'all *knew?*"

Grandma waved her hand. "Like I said. Obtuse."

After a long moment, I huffed. "I can't decide whether I should be insulted or not."

Blair finally shoved back from the table and practically danced around to our side. "Can we bypass the insult and focus on the happy? You're freaking *engaged!*"

Her squeal startled the dogs into a flurry of barks outside, and she didn't even pretend to care as she threw her arms around both of us. "Do we get a ring yet? Is there a ring? I want pictures. I need a post. Oh my God, is it too soon for a hashtag? Should I workshop one?"

I laughed. "Slow your roll. There's... not a ring. Yet."

"Actually..." Ramsey fished around in his pocket and came out with a tiny velvet box.

My gaze bounced from the box back up to his face. "When on earth did you have time to do this, too?"

His smile was mysterious and smug. "I have my ways. And also the world's best assistant, who met me on the outskirts of town to deliver it once the jeweler was finished with the commission. Asher insisted on hand delivering it himself."

The word *commission* snagged in my brain. Then he opened the box, and the breath left my lungs.

Nestled inside was a ring so personal, so impossible, it stole whatever words I might've had. The twisting band of rose gold curled like ivy, holding a deep green sapphire between two delicate crescent moons. But it was the finer detail that caught me—tiny sigils and starbursts carved along the sides. Not random. Not generic.

Mine.

From my books.

My words, turned solid and shimmering and somehow secret. He wasn't saying a thing, and I loved him for it.

My eyes stung, breath catching in my throat. I looked up at him, blinking hard. "You..."

Ramsey took the ring out of the box and slid it onto my finger like it belonged there. Like I belonged with him.

Because I did.

Tears welled up, blurring everything but that quiet, steady look on his face. He lifted my hand to his lips and kissed my knuckles without fanfare.

Emotion built so fast it threatened to drown me, and I did the only thing that made sense. I wrapped my arms around his neck and kissed him like he was the only real thing in the world.

When we broke apart, breathless and still wrapped in each other, the room around us started ticking again.

Colter stood up and clapped his hands. "Okay, now I'm calling for a toast."

"Damn right," Uncle Dee said, already reaching for the good bourbon.

Gunner raised a hand. "Do we have champagne? This feels like a champagne thing."

Grandma Elsie snorted. "This is a bourbon family. Sit down."

Bodie leaned in close and muttered, "You're gonna have to tell me where you found that thing."

Ramsey smiled. "Not today."

Dean passed out a collection of mismatched glasses—mason jars and juice cups. I didn't care. They could've handed me a boot, and I'd have drunk from it.

Colter raised his glass. "To Alia and Ramsey. For pulling off the biggest secret relationship in small-town history, and still managing to outdo every soap opera in the process."

"To love," Grandma said with a knowing twinkle. "Even when it's slow as molasses and needs a cattle prod."

"To not being boneheads anymore," Fletcher added.

Everyone laughed.

Blair raised hers last. "To the people who see you—really see you—and love you, anyway."

Ramsey looked down at me, and in that moment, I knew. No matter what came next, I wasn't carrying it alone anymore.

Uncle Dee smacked the table. "Engagement party."

Blair squealed. "Yes! Saturday! We need streamers. And cake. And I already have, like, four Pinterest boards. I'm thinking fairy lights. Or maybe lanterns. Should we have a theme?"

Ramsey groaned. "What have I done?"

Heart light and full, I tipped my head to his shoulder. "Joined the family."

Chapter 32

Ramsey

The community center didn't remotely resemble the place where I'd helped bail water and reroute plumbing a few weeks ago. Tonight, it was glowing. Twinkle lights laced across the ceiling like a net of stars, and the whole room shimmered with warmth and color. The Sasspatch Society had done their thing—tablecloths in bold colors, centerpieces made from late winter blooms and glittered pinecones, and garlands that somehow managed to be both over the top and exactly right.

I gave Alia's hand a squeeze. "They didn't hold back."

She leaned into me, smile slow and unrestrained. "Would you expect anything less?"

Not from them, no. The Sasspatch ladies didn't do anything halfway, and tonight they'd turned potluck into art. The row of tables along the wall overflowed with crockpots and Pyrex dishes, everything labeled in careful handwriting on gold edged notecards. And in the middle of it all was Mo'nique's handiwork—elegant little hors d'oeuvres on tiered trays, some kind of bacon-wrapped miracles vanishing as fast as people could grab them.

Someone's cousin had rigged a DJ booth in the corner, lights pulsing like a high school prom on a budget, and the music was bouncing between Sam Cooke and Taylor Swift without missing a beat.

I'd managed a sport coat and dress shirt, leaving the tie behind. Slacks, not jeans. Not a full suit. Asher had been dead on with that assessment when he'd dropped off the clothes, along with the ring. Judging by the mix of denim and sequins in the room, we'd nailed the unofficial dress code: one step above everyday, with enough excuse to seem like an occasion.

Alia wore this deep green dress that made it hard to focus on anything else. Elegant, soft, and a bit daring in the way the back dipped low, exposing her shoulders and spine. I didn't think she knew how beautiful she was, which only made it worse. Or better, depending on how you looked at it. I had serious plans for peeling her out of that dress later and exploring every inch until we were both blissed out on plea-sure. Which we were free to do now that she no longer had to leave early in the name of keeping our relationship a secret.

Everybody knew.

Everybody.

Which I'd been getting fresh reminders of everywhere I went the past few days. In between jobs, I'd been fielding congratulations, handshakes, and honey-coated warnings to take care of their girl from pretty much everyone I met. Because it had become cry*stal* clear that the citizens of Gibson Hollow considered Alia theirs, and they loved her.

As such, it seemed like the whole damned town had turned out in full force for tonight's engagement party. It was a cele-bration in the truest sense. The first real one they'd had cause for since the flood. The second we stepped fully inside, people turned, smiles broke out. Hugs started before we'd made it five feet.

"Congratulations!"

"We're so happy for you!"

Alia laughed and dove straight into the sea of outstretched arms. I shook hands, took a few slaps on the back, and tried to keep up. It was loud and warm and overwhelmingly kind.

And in the middle of all of it, I got to hold her hand.

No more hiding. No more secrets. She was mine. And I finally got to show it.

I slipped my arm around her waist, let my hand settle at the curve of her hip like I'd wanted to a hundred times before and hadn't let myself. Not in public. Not where anyone could see. That weight of restraint—the constant awareness, the second-guessing, the what if someone noticed—was simply gone. And I hadn't realized until this moment how much tension I'd been carrying because of it.

She turned her head toward me, eyes bright, lips parted in a smile I wanted to memorize.

So I kissed her. Right there in the middle of the community center, with people still streaming in and calling our names and the music shifting to something slow and crooning in the background. I bent my head and kissed her like I meant it—because I did—and the world didn't end. No one gasped or fainted. Miss Addie didn't cluck her tongue. A few people outright cheered. And Alia laughed into my mouth like this was the best damn idea I'd ever had.

Freedom had never tasted so sweet.

"You're really enjoying this." She murmured it against my lips, body still flush against mine.

"I really am." I brushed a thumb along her cheekbone. "You have no idea how many times I wanted to do that."

Her smile turned softer, sweeter. "Yeah, I think I do."

We moved together through the crowd, hand in hand, occasionally pulled aside for another round of congratulations or a memory someone had to share right that second. But even with all the people and noise and food and music, I kept touching her. My hand on her back. Her fingers threaded with mine. That low ache of wanting her close now replaced with the joy of getting to keep her close.

We found the Sasspatch Society near the punch bowl, where Mo'nique was scolding someone for daring to rearrange her appetizer tiers.

Miss Glory saw us first. "Well, look who's finally arrived." She swept in with a dramatic flair that somehow didn't disturb a single sequin. "Do y'all always show up this late to your own parties, or is this a new hobby?"

"Traffic was terrible," Alia deadpanned, then leaned in to kiss her cheek. "You outdid yourselves. Thank you."

"Don't thank me," Miss Glory said, preening anyway. "Thank her." She pointed to Mo'nique, who looked halfway to a meltdown over someone putting the pigs in a blanket next to the caviar tartlets.

"They were not meant to mingle." Mo'nique turned on us with a dazzling smile. "But for you, baby, I'll forgive it. Congratulations. Both of you."

She pulled Alia into a fierce hug, kissed both her cheeks, then grabbed me by the lapels and tugged me in for one, too.

"You break her heart," she whispered, voice low and fierce in my ear, "and I will ruin you."

"Yes, ma'am."

She pulled back, inspected me like I was a cake fresh out of the oven, then nodded, satisfied. "You'll do."

Miss Bea beamed and fanned herself with a napkin she'd folded into a swan. "It's so nice to see good things finally happening to good people."

Uncle Dee appeared next, sweeping Alia into a full twirl before settling her back on her heels. "You are luminous, my darling. Absolutely radiant. Now." He turned to me, lips pursed. "Let's see if the ring matches the dress."

"I've had it on for days," Alia teased.

"I know, and you've been hiding it from me, which is rude. Let me admire."

Alia extended her hand, and he inspected it like it was crown jewels.

"Well." He pressed a dramatic hand to his heart. "He's got taste. You may keep him."

I smirked. "Generous of you."

Uncle Dee grinned. "Don't get cocky, sweetheart. You're on probation."

The whole exchange had me smiling so hard my cheeks ached. These people—they weren't merely friends. They were family. Chosen, fabulous, and fiercely loyal. They'd put this together for her, but they'd welcomed me right into the fold like I'd been theirs all along.

"Ramsey."

I turned toward my fiancée—damn, that felt good to think— and found her watching me with an expression that was secretive and more than a little smug. It was a look that said she'd planned something. I narrowed my eyes. "What?"

Looping her arm back through mine, she grinned up at me. "For once, I get to surprise you."

"You already said yes. I'm not sure how you top that."

Instead of answering, she turned me gently toward the entrance.

My mom stood in the doorway, framed by the twinkle lights and smiling so wide, I probably could've seen it from Alabama. She looked good—better than good. Travel-tired but radiant with happiness, in a neat navy sheath and pumps.

"Mom?" My voice came out hoarse. "What are you doing here?"

She held her arms wide. "Did you honestly think I was going to miss my only son's engagement party?"

I didn't walk—I launched. Crossed the room in three strides and wrapped her up in a hug that lifted her clean off the ground. She let out an exaggerated oof and laughed like I hadn't heard her laugh in way too long.

When I set her down, Alia had joined us, slipping in close with that soft smile of hers that was every good thing I'd ever wanted in this life.

"You did this?" I asked.

Mom reached out to squeeze her hand. "She did. Arranged the flights, sent her brother Dean to pick me up at the airport, even made sure I had a proper place to stay with Elsie. I got in this morning and spent the day hiding out at Devine Interventions helping get ready for the party. Half of those food labels were me."

I kissed Alia again. Couldn't help it. Not with this warm, overwhelming pressure in my chest that kept building every time she looked at me.

Mom wiped under her eye, subtle, but not really. "I knew she was the right one from the moment she called me for my meatloaf recipe back in college."

Alia laughed. "Seriously? I had no idea that meatloaf was so powerful."

Mom winked. "Took y'all long enough to get here."

I pulled Alia in close. "Yeah, we've been getting that a lot."

"Better late than never." Mom turned as another voice cut through the music.

"Come on, Natalie, I need your opinion on whether fondant is ever worth the trouble." Grandma Elsie had appeared like a tiny, determined storm cloud and was already looping her arm through my mom's. "And I need a co-conspirator who knows how to keep secrets."

"You found the right woman." Mom grinned. "Lead the way."

They vanished into the crowd, already deep in a conversation about wedding venues and seasonal flower availability, probably roping in every woman in the tri-county area with an opinion.

"Excuse me, loves. I need to borrow the bride here for a minute." Miss Bea appeared at Alia's other elbow and immediately began towing her away toward what looked like a cake tasting table that had magically appeared.

And suddenly, I was standing alone by the drink table, grinning from ear to ear and feeling like the luckiest man alive.

I picked up a glass of sweet tea and spotted Bodie making his way over, his face set in the lines of stoic cop instead of best friend. Not exactly reassuring. Between one thing and another, we'd both been kept busy since the last family dinner. There'd been no chance to talk to him one on one, and I was concerned about how he was *really* taking the reality of me and Alia together.

I straightened, set my tea down, and braced.

He came to stand beside me without a word, arms crossed, scanning the crowd like he was casing the place. We didn't look at each other as we stood shoulder to shoulder, not quite touching, staring out over the party like we were guarding a perimeter instead of navigating whatever this was between us now.

After a minute, I couldn't stand the silence. "I'm sorry I didn't tell you. Not just now. Back in college. How I felt about Alia."

His jaw ticked. "I made the assumption you were another

brother to her. You always protected her like you were. But I guess that was coming from somewhere else."

"I never wanted to disrespect that. Any of it. You, your family... her."

He nodded once. "Don't know how I would've handled it back then, anyway. I was an overprotective idiot even before the badge. Still am, some days."

I let out a breath that wasn't quite a laugh.

"It's just..." He shifted, still not looking at me. "It's been a lot. Shifting my whole damn worldview a bit. I mean, you've been in our lives for over a decade. And somehow, I missed all the signs."

"I worked really damned hard not to show it. But I love her, man. I've loved her for years."

"I can see that now." He finally glanced at me. "I only feel like a dumbass for not noticing sooner."

I shrugged. "We've all had a lot going on."

He gave a grunt of agreement, then looked back toward where Alia was laughing with Miss Bea and two little girls in sequined dresses. "You two have got some stuff to figure out."

"We know." I smiled, watching her. "We'll get there. Right now we're rolling in the happy."

"She deserves all the happy she can get." There was a softness under the steel of his voice that made my throat tighten.

"I'll do everything in my power to make her happy for the rest of our lives."

"That's all I can ask for."

We stood there a second longer before finally turning toward each other at the same time.

"We good?" I asked.

His mouth lifted at one corner. "We're good."

We pulled each other in for one of those back-thumping

man hugs that said we're fine without requiring either of us to get emotional about it.

Bodie stepped back. "Welcome to the family, man."

And this time, I was the one who had to blink hard and swallow twice.

The music had shifted again, easing into something slow and sweet with a smoky sax and soft harmonies. I glanced across the room and found Alia exactly where I'd left her—head thrown back in laughter at something Miss Bea had said, her hands full of cake samples, glitter catching in her hair from one of the Sasspatch garlands. She looked like joy personified.

My joy.

"Excuse me, I need to go grab my fiancée."

I crossed the room, weaving through conversations and careful not to get pulled into another round of congratulations before I reached her. "Mind if I cut in?"

At the touch of my hand on her back, she turned, eyes lighting up the way they always did when she saw me. "Thought you'd never ask."

"Dance with me."

She passed her cake plate to the nearest person—might've been Miss Addie, might've been a stranger—and stepped into my arms like she had all those years ago, when we'd both been hiding behind masks.

The DJ didn't make any announcements. The crowd shifted to give us space. Made room. And then we were moving together in the center of it all, like this whole night had been leading here.

She fit against me perfectly. One hand in mine, the other resting over my heart. Her cheek brushed my jaw.

"I didn't think it was possible to be this happy," she whispered.

I held her closer. "Get used to it."

We swayed, slow and easy, like the rest of the world had melted away. But every glance, every grin, every misty-eyed look from the people surrounding us settled over us like a warm blanket. They weren't here for a party. They were here for us.

The song faded, and with a clink of glass, someone called out, "Let's raise a toast to the happy couple!"

A chorus of cheers rose up as glasses were filled, and attention turned our way.

Blair was somehow already standing on a chair, glass of punch raised high. "To Alia and Ramsey. May your love be bold, your fights be short, and your bed never be cold."

Laughter rolled through the crowd, warm and loud.

Mo'nique dabbed at the corner of her eye with a linen napkin. "To laughter that lasts, friends who meddle, and kisses that say more than words ever could."

Uncle Dee was softer, but no less moving. "To family. The kind you're born to and the kind you find. May you always know the difference—and hold fast to both."

More glasses lifted. More cheers.

Alia pressed her forehead to mine, eyes shining. "They really went all out."

"They love you. How could they not?"

"They love you too." She brushed her lips against mine. "Even if you are technically on probation."

"I'll take it. As long as I get to keep you."

Chapter 33

Alia

I had Biscuit on my lap, the scent of garlic and something buttery wafting through the kitchen, and no place I needed to be except right here at Ramsey's kitchen table. Which was a minor miracle, honestly.

It had been one of those days that started with a printer jam and ended with a zoning board complaint about a rooster named Elvis, and I'd half expected to come home and face plant. But Ramsey had beaten me there, rerouted me to his place, and declared I was officially off duty. Then he'd kissed me stupid and pointed me to the kitchen table like I was royalty, and he was honored to feed me. Which, okay, I wasn't arguing with. Puppy cuddles and someone else figuring out the details of dinner? Yes, please.

He moved around the kitchen barefoot, in ripped jeans and a henley with the sleeves pushed up, whistling off-key to whatever Motown mix was playing low from the speaker by the fridge. Every so often, he'd glance over at me and grin like he couldn't believe I was real. Which was hilarious, considering I was wearing mismatched socks and had Biscuit draped across my thighs like a fur-covered paperweight with attitude.

My phone buzzed again, lighting up with another wave of notifications. I resisted the urge to silence it entirely. Between Ramsey's terrifyingly efficient assistant, Asher Armitage, and Blair, we hadn't posted anything about our engagement ourselves, but between the official release, the town grapevine, and the never-sleeping beast that was social media, the news had spread like wildfire.

And people had opinions.

Mostly good ones, thankfully. Congratulations from pretty much everyone I'd ever known and half the people I hadn't. Texts, DMs, even a couple of emails from professors I hadn't seen since law school. Old sorority sisters were crawling out of the woodwork like we were planning a reunion, all of them full of exclamation points and comments about how happy I looked, and how Ramsey's arms were as swoony as they remembered.

I wasn't entirely sure how to respond to that last one, so I sent emojis and hoped they'd interpret them correctly.

I scrolled through a thread of heartwarming chaos, my phone buzzing every time I tried to set it down. At some point in the past week, Marcus—the Sentinels' quarterback—had sent us a bottle of champagne with a handwritten note that said, *Looking forward to meeting your good luck charm next season! Congratulations!*

I scooped Biscuit up and went to peer around my fiancé's shoulder. "Does champagne go with whatever you're making?"

Ramsey looked up from the skillet, eyes dancing. "Technically, no. But it's our engagement. I'm pretty sure that means we get to make our own rules."

"Even if that rule is 'bubbles pair well with shrimp and grits'?"

"Especially if it is."

He leaned in and kissed me lightly, as if it was a reflex, and I melted a little on the inside. I was still getting used to this. Being able to give in to this easy affection and the urge to touch or kiss him whenever I wanted.

My phone buzzed again. I glanced at it, saw three more messages roll in, and let out a low whistle. "Okay, I did not expect this many people to care."

"Is it weird that they do?"

"No." I hesitated. "Yes. Maybe. I haven't heard from some of these folks in years. Like, since graduation. It's kind of surreal."

"Good surreal or bad surreal?"

I thought about it. "Mostly good. Just... loud. I hope they don't all expect an invitation to the wedding."

Ramsey glanced at me. "You want a small one?"

"I mean, small is relative. My family alone makes what I consider a large gathering. But I really don't want some massive social event of the season that becomes about appearances instead of us." Realizing I hadn't consulted him at all about what he wanted, I winced. "Do you want something bigger?"

Hooking one arm around my waist, he pulled me closer. "I want whatever makes you happy. I'm getting everything I want the moment you say 'I do'. Whether it's us and a justice of the peace on a beach somewhere, or every Gibson in a three-state radius. Here, taste this." He held out a spoon with a bite of shrimp and grits, and I closed my eyes as it hit my tongue. Creamy, spicy, perfect.

He watched me like he lived for my reaction.

"Mm. Okay. You win. Bubbles with dinner it is. I'll be happy to report back to Uncle Dee that you mastered his recipe."

"Score."

The doorbell rang like it had a personal vendetta, followed by the unmistakable sound of Blair letting herself in with all the grace of a hurricane in heels. Biscuit barked and wriggled to be let down. I barely had time to sit up before Blair came barreling into the kitchen like she'd been launched from a cannon, wild-eyed and breathless, phone clutched in one hand like it might combust.

"Y'all. The internet knows."

I blinked. "Knows what?"

Blair pointed dramatically—at me, then at Ramsey, then did some wild flailing gesture that was probably meant to indicate the entire cosmos. "They figured out that Mr. Football over here is Swoony McBroadsword."

Ramsey, midway through stirring the grits, paused. "I'm who now?"

Blair groaned like we were personally torturing her. "You know—fantasy dreamboat? The sword-wielding, emotionally constipated, deeply noble love interest Kella Harmon fans have been thirsting after since you carried her off that panel stage like the hero of a paperback come to life?"

He looked to me, bewildered. "I did what now?"

"Oh my God." Blair slapped both hands over her face, muffled a scream, and dropped them again with a dramatic sigh. "Ramsey. Babe. The fandom has been speculating about your identity since the convention. There are threads. There are fan edits. There's fan art, Ramsey. Shirtless, leather-pants clad fan art. And now—*now*—it's full meltdown mode on Book-Tok, Bookstagram, and Twitter. Yes, I know it's called X now, but that's dumb and I refuse. Someone connected the dots."

I stared at her.

Ramsey opened his mouth, closed it again, muttering, "Why am I the one with the dumbest name?"

Blair ignored him, scrolling furiously on her phone before

thrusting it out like evidence for a grand jury trial. "Okay. So it starts here."

She flipped the phone around to show us a BookTok post already clocking a few hundred thousand views. The caption read: *Y'all. My boyfriend solved the mystery of Swoony McBroadsword and I'm not okay.*

Blair pressed play on the video. A girl in a Kella Harmon T-shirt was talking fast, eyes wide with disbelief.

"So I'm rewatching the Romantasy Royalty panel, right? And Kella—aka my queen—makes this offhand reference about a cheating ex and Thunder and Lightning. And my boyfriend—who was, like, not even paying attention—whips around and says, 'Wait. Thunder and Lightning? That's Bodie Gibson and Ramsey Shaw from CSU. Everybody called them that.'

"Y'ALL.

"RAMSEY SHAW.

"Former tight end for the CSU Ravens. Current star for the Sentinels.

"HE IS SWOONY MCBROADSWORD."

The rest of the clip was mostly her spiraling and flailing at screenshots of Ramsey in both his football uniform and the custom-made armor.

"But that's spurious logic. Just because they identified Ramsey as Lightning does not automatically equal him being Swoony McBroadsword."

Ramsey stared at the screen. "I am really not prepared for that name to catch on."

Blair gave him a pitying look. "Sweetie. It never had a chance not to. Anyway," she turned to me, "stop using your lawyer logic. That's not how BookTok works."

I rolled my eyes. I mean, this wasn't good, but it wasn't the worst. Ramsey was already out in the public eye. This outed one of his hobbies that might've been slightly embarrassing, but it wasn't a crisis.

Blair scrolled. "Now, here's where it starts getting messy. Someone in the comments goes, 'OMG, I remember those two. Didn't they level some guy at practice for cheating on one of their sisters?' And then another account confirms it—says she was dating one of the defensive linemen back when. Swears it was Jeff Barrett, and the girl he cheated on was Bodie Gibson's sister."

My stomach dropped. "Oh, no."

Blair was already moving on. "And then someone finds a clip from that exact game week—the pair of you absolutely demolishing Barrett in a scrimmage—which I still have fond memories of, BTW. The caption is basically: 'When your teammate messes with Thunder's sister and Lightning brings the pain.'"

Ramsey frowned. "Somebody filmed it?"

Blair ignored him. "So now they've connected Ramsey to the fandom. And they've named me, because hello, you're my best friend, and I've posted engagement photos like a normal person. Which means the next person goes, 'Wait, is Alia Gibson actually Kella Harmon?'"

I slapped my hands over my face. "No, no, no—"

Blair pulled them right back down. "Oh yes. Because someone else found your old sorority photos. Someone else found the CSU yearbook archive. And then—bam—some genius posts the side-by-side."

She swiped some more, then turned the phone again.

Left side: me at the convention in my Kella wig and glasses. Right side: me in the engagement photo, laughing up at Ramsey, wind in my hair and sunlight everywhere.

Same mouth. Same smile. Same dimple.

"No," I whispered.

Blair gave me a sympathetic look. "The cat is not merely out of the bag, babe. The bag has been incinerated."

I couldn't look away. It wasn't only the photos or the captions or the endless scroll of comments. It was the way they looked at them—at me. Like I was a puzzle to solve. A secret to crack open.

I set the phone down. Carefully. Like it might bite.

My chest felt too tight. Not panic exactly, but... something crowding up under my ribs. I rubbed at the spot like that might help, but it didn't.

Ramsey turned off the burner. "Alia."

I didn't answer.

He was beside me a moment later, lowering into a crouch so he could see my face. "Talk to me."

"I'm fine." My voice sounded flat. Off. "Just... overwhelmed."

His brows pulled together. "By what they're saying?"

"No. Yes. I don't know." I shook my head, trying to clear it, to *name* this thing building inside me, but the words didn't come easy. "It's not that they're being mean. They're not. It's—"

I pressed the heels of my hands to my eyes, breathing through the crush of it. "This was supposed to be mine. I wrote those books in a tiny apartment with a space heater and a busted chair. I built Kella from nothing. She was safe."

Biscuit rose up and pressed her front paws against my leg with a whine, and I scooped her up, cuddling her close. "They're treating the stories like evidence. My fantasies like facts. As if my whole life is up for inspection now. Like if they dig hard, they'll find all the answers. And maybe that's fair. Maybe that's what happens when you publish under a pen name and then fall in love with a human embodiment of a fantasy hero." I tried to force a laugh and failed. "But it doesn't feel fair."

Ramsey wrapped an arm around me. "You don't owe them anything. Not your past. Not your pain. Not even your name."

I nodded. I wanted to believe that. But the tightness didn't ease.

Because even if they didn't mean harm, they had my name now. And there was no stuffing it back in the bottle.

Chapter 34

Ramsey

They'd shoved the tables in The Commissary back against the walls and circled up the chairs like we were about to hold an intervention instead of a secret reveal. Outside, the afternoon sun filtered through the blinds in sleepy stripes, but inside the diner, it was quiet. Intimate. Family only. Because Alia knew she had to give away another piece of herself, revealing her author career to the rest of the Gibson clan before they found out some other way.

She fidgeted beside me. At least, as close as she ever got to fidgeting. Tracing her thumb over the knuckle of her opposite hand. Those breaths that weren't quite deep enough to be normal. The way her shoulders stayed too tight, even when she tried to force them down.

I curled my fingers around hers, not to still her hands but to try to make her feel safer. Anchored. After a moment, her hand flexed and held on. Small mercy, that. After everything, I was done pretending not to reach for her.

Uncle Dee perched on a stool near the counter, legs crossed, coffee in hand like he was holding court. Grandma

Elsie held a legal pad in her lap, because apparently she'd been elected note-taker for whatever they thought this was. And the Gibson brothers had spread themselves out like a defensive line—Colter, Fletcher, Dean, and Gunner all clustered together with expressions ranging from curious to slightly concerned. Everett had his elbows on the table, bracing for more bad news. Blair, who actually was aware what was going on, looked like she'd been mainlining espresso and was braced to whip out some secret hacker skills. Bodie sat in the corner, arms crossed, watching Alia with the same quiet intensity he always did when he thought she was about to make a hard call.

"Y'all didn't have to clear your schedules." Alia aimed for light, but her voice carried the weight of someone halfway to bracing for impact.

"Are you kidding?" From the laptop on one of the tables, Everly chimed in, her voice slightly tinny through the Bluetooth speaker.

Hutton leaned in beside her. "You never call a full family meeting. What's up, sis?"

Blair took a breath, clearly about to launch into full press conference mode, but Alia held up a hand.

"I need to say it myself."

The room seemed to suck in a collective breath.

She tucked her hair behind one ear, gaze fixed on the floor, much as it had been during her panel. "I've been keeping something from y'all."

When she didn't go on, I squeezed her hand again in support.

"Oh my God, you're pregnant!" Hutton exclaimed.

Alia's head snapped up, whipping toward the screen. "What? No! Why would you—?"

"I mean, you're sitting there hanging on to Ramsey's hand

like it's life support, and he's looking like he's ready to pound anybody who says anything less than supportive."

She wasn't wrong.

"To be clear, we would all be delighted to be uncles again," Fletcher said.

A chorus of affirmations sounded around the circle.

"Thank you, but no. Jesus. I am unequivocally *not* pregnant. Christ, don't wish that on me. I'm still on hiatus after raising you." Alia scrubbed a hand down her face and blew out a breath. "Uncle Dee isn't the only one with another identity."

Gunner blinked. "Come again?"

"I've been writing under a pen name for almost ten years."

Bodie leaned forward. "Wait, like novels?"

She nodded. "Fantasy romance."

Colter made a low whistle. "You out here writing about dragons and sex?"

Alia flushed. "Not dragons. Not usually."

Blair couldn't hold it in. "She's Kella Harmon." She announced it in the tone of someone who expected everyone else in the room to understand the gravity.

Dead silence.

Then Everly breathed, "No shit."

Hutton was next. "That name's been all over BookTok. You're a big deal, sis!"

Alia gave a sheepish shrug. "I never meant for anybody to know. It was always supposed to be anonymous. But some people online figured it out after the engagement announcement."

Blair, of course, couldn't let it rest at that. "She's so popular she could quit her day job and still funnel enough money into the town recovery to make a serious difference."

Alia shot her a glare that was mostly exasperated and only slightly betrayed.

"How much are we talking?" Dean asked. I didn't think it was meant to be rude—merely curiosity. A "how big is this bomb you're dropping?" sort of question.

Alia hesitated. Then she named a number high enough to make me blink. Enough to make Everett let out a low "Well damn," and Grandma Elsie adjust her glasses.

"Wait, wasn't there, like, a big viral video recently?" Gunner pulled out his phone. "I'm sure I saw something..."

"I've got you." Blair turned her tablet and pressed play. Because of course she had it already cued up.

The video was only a minute or so. Somebody had clipped it from an audience angle, grainy but dramatic. It started with Alia in the chair, blinking into the stage lights, clearly struggling. If you knew her, you'd see the tight clutch of her hands, the paleness around her mouth, the way she wasn't quite breathing right. But the crowd hadn't seen that. Hell, even the panelists hadn't seen it.

What they did see was me, charging the stage in full armor like a damn boss fight had kicked off.

A low rumble of voices broke out around the room as I appeared on screen—black leather gleaming under the spotlights, sword strapped at my hip, all grim purpose as I vaulted the stage and crossed to Alia. I heard a few gasps in real time, even from the family.

The moment I scooped her into my arms, the room on the video lost its mind.

"Damn," Dean muttered.

Everly, from the laptop speaker: "Okay but—*that's* how you make an exit."

Alia buried her face in her hands with a muffled groan.

Fletcher let out a low whistle. "You really committed to the rescue fantasy, huh?"

"Can't lie." Gunner grinned. "That entrance was metal."

Colter elbowed him. "Pretty sure it was leather."

"Wait for it," Blair added, gleeful. "This is the part where the fandom dubbed him Swoony McBroadsword."

"What?" Bodie turned to her with a gleam in his eye that said this was never, ever going away. "They *what now?*"

She grinned like Christmas had come early. "It's a whole thing. There are edits. Slow-mo rescues. Dramatic music. One person dubbed in his 'Time to go, princess' line over a scene from *Gladiator*. I'm not saying I've saved them. But I've saved them."

Uncle Dee gave an approving nod. "It's giving very 'step aside, peasants.' Iconic."

I shrugged, letting them rib me. "I did what needed doing."

They kept laughing, tossing jokes back and forth like a football at Thanksgiving. And I let them, because every second they focused on me was another second Alia didn't have to explain herself.

But I could feel her shrinking beside me.

Not small exactly—but pulled tight. Wound up. Waiting for the moment the teasing would tip from funny into too far.

I squeezed her hand again.

Still here, baby.

Let them laugh at me—so they wouldn't look at her like a spectacle.

Fletcher leaned forward, arms braced on his knees. "So what does this mean? Like... are you going to be famous now?"

Alia let out a breathy little laugh and rubbed the back of her neck. "I don't know. Probably not. Maybe for a hot second. We'll see." She sounded like she was trying really hard not to sound too hopeful. Or too afraid.

Blair snorted. "Y'all, she already is! *New York Times* and *USA Today* bestseller."

That earned another "Damn" from Dean, and a "No shit" from Bodie.

Alia's shoulders were still tense, but that braced, brittle expression she'd worn walking in was starting to ease because the floor hadn't dropped out from under her after all. As if she were starting to believe they weren't going to look at her differently. "I mean, y'all always knew I was a nerd."

"Sure," Fletcher said. "We just didn't realize how *marketable* your nerdiness was."

That got a round of chuckles, a couple of smiles. Colter reached over and clapped her on the back. Grandma Elsie made some quiet note on her legal pad that probably said something like "secret billionaire."

Then Uncle Dee uncrossed his legs and stood, walking over to where Alia sat. He leaned down and kissed the top of her head. "We got you, sugar."

Her eyes turned shiny for a second before she blinked it away.

How could she not have understood that this whole room of people loved her, no conditions, no reservations? Perhaps now she'd be more comfortable with the idea of people seeing and knowing all of her. Because the whole of her was fucking amazing.

She sniffed and stood up, smoothing her hands over her jeans. "Okay. Well. Now that my soul's been laid bare, I've got a zoning board packet to review and a client meeting at four. So —thanks, I guess, for not disowning me."

After another round of hugs, we stepped out into the late afternoon light, the air starting to cool. Long shadows stretched across the sidewalk in front of The Commissary, and for half a second, it seemed like we might actually get a quiet moment to ourselves.

Alia let out a long breath, probably the first full one she'd taken in hours, and twined her fingers with mine again. "That went better than I thought. Nobody threw anything. Nobody cried. Hutton only mildly embarrassed me."

Yeah, the pregnant thing had thrown me, too. But I didn't dare mention it out here on the street, lest someone overhear and run with the rumor. The prospect of kids and family was probably something we ought to discuss at some point, given her remark that she was on hiatus. She'd effectively raised her seven siblings. If kids of her own weren't something she wanted, I was fine with that, too. Spending the next sixty years making up for lost time seemed like a fantastic way to live to me. But we had plenty of time for that discussion down the line.

"They were proud of you." I tipped my head to look at her as we started down the street. "Hell, I'm proud of you for telling them. I know that was hard for you to share."

She glanced up, still a bit misty from everything, but her smile made it all the way to her eyes this time. "Yeah? Even after the Swoony McBroadsword thing?"

"Look what it's brought me. But even if we weren't us right now, I'd storm that stage again tomorrow if it meant you didn't have to face that crowd alone."

The smile grew warmer. Softer. A flicker of her finally—finally—starting to let the tension unwind from her shoulders.

She leaned into my side. "Thanks for not making me do this by myself."

"Never." I meant it.

Click.

We both heard it at the same time. A metallic snap that didn't belong in this town. Followed by another.

Then the shouting started.

"Alia!"

Flash.

"Alia Gibson! How long have you been hiding your identity?"

Flash. Flash. Flash.

A pack of bodies exploded from behind the line of parked cars—four, maybe five of them, cameras raised like weapons. Voices barked out questions over each other like gunfire.

"How does it feel to be Gibson Hollow's dirtiest little secret?"

"Are the books based on your real trauma?"

"How do you justify writing erotica while claiming it's empowering?"

"Did your fiancé know who you really were when he proposed, or was that part of the marketing?"

"Are you planning to monetize your hometown next?"

Alia froze beside me, as if her brain short-circuited, dropping her right back into the worst version of her fears. Her whole body locked up. Her fingers chilled in mine.

I moved in front of her without thinking, my arm sweeping out to block the flashes, the questions, the hate disguised as curiosity.

"Back off," I barked. "Now."

They didn't.

One of them—too close, too loud, too smug—shoved forward with his camera already rolling. "You think your mama would be proud of how you've turned her name into a joke?"

Alia flinched.

And I saw red.

I grabbed the camera and shoved it back into the guy's chest until he stumbled. "You want a headline?" I growled. "Try this: Paparazzo learns what happens when you come after someone's girl."

He came at me again—just a step, just enough. My fist lashed out, fast and sharp. The guy crashed like a ton of bricks, bleeding from the mouth. The other cameras caught every second.

Flashes exploded again, brighter and faster now, like blood in the water.

Behind me, Alia's breath hitched—shallow and too fast. She whispered, "No, no, no..." like this was her worst-case scenario come true.

Because it was. And I'd just made it real. Made it worse. Because I hadn't held on to my temper.

The flash of a badge cut through the chaos like a lightning strike. "Back the hell off!"

Bodie's voice cracked like thunder, slicing through the wall of shouting and camera clicks. He strode forward with the full weight of his badge and his fury behind him, gunmetal gray eyes fixed on the paparazzi like he was deciding which one to cuff first.

Behind him came the cavalry. Colter, Dean, Gunner, and Fletcher—all of them moving in hard and fast, instinct snapping into formation. Colter went left. Dean and Gunner cut across the front. Fletcher flanked the rear, all broad shoulders and clenched fists. Not one of them hesitated.

"Get those cameras out of her face," Dean snapped, teeth bared.

"You heard him," Fletcher growled. "This is your cue to get gone."

Gunner was already reaching for Alia, trying to pull her behind the wall of them, but she didn't move. She couldn't. She was frozen—gutted.

Still. So damn still.

Then Blair's voice cut through from somewhere nearby, sharp and furious. "You want a story? You're about to get one. These heels are registered weapons. Keep filming!"

One of the photographers who hadn't already bolted dropped his phone mid-recording.

Another muttered something about lawyers.

But none of them wanted to tangle with this. With a police chief, four angry brothers, a mouthy best friend, and half the town starting to close in from down the street.

They started to scatter, shouting over each other, filming as they ran, trying to salvage something out of the wreckage. But it didn't matter. The damage was done. The cameras had already gotten what they came for.

Alia didn't say a word. Not one.

Her arms were tight around herself, fingers clenched white at the crook of each elbow, body locked like it had forgotten how to move.

I stepped in close—slow, like she was a wounded animal—and gently reached for her, hands brushing her upper arms. "Alia, baby, are you hurt?"

She shook her head, a tiny, brittle motion that barely counted. Her eyes met mine—glassy, stunned, like she hadn't quite made it back into her body yet. Then a single tear traced down her cheek, silent and devastating.

Not fear.

Not even shock.

This was something deeper. Rawer. A hollowed-out kind of hurt.

"They tore it all open," she whispered. Her voice barely made it past her lips. "Everything I've tried to keep safe... they ripped it all apart."

She wasn't trembling. She was shaking apart. Her arms tightened around herself like she could still hold the pieces in place.

Bodie stepped closer, voice low, sure. "You're not alone in this."

I wrapped both arms around her, pulling her tight against me, fury burning in my chest but held back by the need to keep her upright.

"I've got you," I said, close to her ear. "We're leaving. Right now."

Because she'd given the world a piece of her, and it had chewed her up in return.

I'd be damned before I let it take one piece more.

Chapter 35

Alia

I didn't remember getting into the truck.

One second I was clinging to Ramsey like he was the only solid thing in a world that had cracked wide open, and the next, we were pulling away from The Commissary, and my body curled tight against the passenger door as if I could disappear into the seams.

Ramsey's hand hovered between the gearshift and my knee, not quite touching me. Like he wanted to offer something—comfort, contact, anything—but wasn't sure if I could take it.

I wasn't sure either.

"They're gone." His voice was firm and low, meant to be a reassurance. "The press scattered. Your brothers made sure."

I nodded. Or maybe I just blinked. It was hard to tell the difference from inside this skin.

He drove three more blocks in silence before saying, "Let's get you home."

He meant his house. His space. Safe, warm, quiet.

But everything inside me shrank from that—because I couldn't go be someone's anything right now. Couldn't hold conversation or comfort. Couldn't let him see the rest of me unravel.

"Mine," I whispered.

He glanced over, registered the tone. The one I hadn't used in so long, I barely recognized it. The one that meant I was holding on by my fingernails, and one more thing was absolutely going to break me.

He nodded. "Okay."

And turned toward Uncle Dee's house. My house.

Ramsey didn't say much on the drive. One hand on the wheel, his focus split between the road and me. The tension radiated off him, as if he were holding himself in check by sheer will.

When we pulled into the drive, neither of us moved at first. The engine ticked as it cooled, a faint metallic sound too loud in the stillness. He got out, rounded the front, and opened my door like the act itself might shatter something.

I didn't wait for his hand before I climbed out, climbed the stairs, and unlocked the door with fingers that didn't feel like mine. He followed quietly, a shadow at my back.

Inside, I let everything slide off. My coat. My bag. My shoes. The keys clattered onto the little narrow little catch-all table in the entryway.

Then nothing.

I stood in the hush of the front room, the edges of everything were too sharp, too bright.

The numbness wasn't peace. It was pressure. Something big and broken was dammed up behind a wall. It thrummed in my bones, but I didn't dare touch it yet. Couldn't risk even testing the gate of it without crumbling. It wasn't safe. I hadn't come this close to the threat of it since my mother died.

Behind me, Ramsey moved. Down the hall, I heard the quiet click of the kettle. The familiar rustle of the throw blanket from the couch. Gentle, grounded things. Human things. He didn't say a word, but I understood he needed to do something. To comfort me. To make it better.

But even he couldn't fix this.

When he settled the throw around my shoulders, I something deep inside begin to quake.

"I need space, Ramsey." My voice was hoarse from holding too much in.

He froze mid-motion, his hands tugging the blanket around me.

Arms still wrapped tight around myself, I lifted my gaze to his because I needed him to understand this. "It's not you. I just... I don't know how to do this. Not with someone watching."

His expression didn't shift much, but something behind his eyes went soft and aching. Still, he nodded. "Okay. I'll be here. Whenever you're ready."

I understood what that cost him. What I asked of him. And still, this man that I loved pressed a soft kiss to my temple. The warmth of his lips made that thing in my chest quake harder.

"I love you. No matter what." With another soft squeeze of my shoulder, he walked out, leaving me in the quiet to fall apart in my own time, exactly as I'd wanted.

I didn't move for a long time.

Long after the door clicked shut behind Ramsey, and I stood there, wrapped in a throw blanket I barely registered, in a body that seemed like someone else's. The silence buzzed in the hollows of my bones and left too much room for everything I didn't want to think.

At some point, I fumbled for my phone. My fingers barely worked, but I managed to text Miss Addie and ask her to reschedule my four o'clock. No explanation. She wouldn't need one. She'd already know.

Probably the entire town already had heard everything.

I dropped the phone onto the console table and drifted toward my room like gravity had gotten selective and inconsistent. Pulling open the bottom drawer of my dresser, I reached past the folded pajama pants and the socks that never stayed matched. My fingers found the soft, worn cotton by memory.

Ramsey's hoodie.

Threadbare and frayed at the cuffs. It hadn't smelled like him in years. Not really. Maybe it never had, and my brain had simply decided it should. But I'd had it since college, when he'd walked me home after I stumbled upon my cheating asshole ex at that bar, making out with someone who wasn't me. I'd conveniently forgotten to give it back. It had seen me through every all-nighter. Every migraine. Every heartbreak I'd never admitted.

I buried my face in it now, breathing in the ghost of a comfort I didn't quite believe I deserved, and tugged it over my head. The fabric swallowed me whole. I let it.

I crawled onto the bed and curled onto my side, hugging my knees beneath the too-long hem like it would help me disappear.

God, it had all happened so fast.

One second I was sharing a secret with the people who loved me, and the next, I was flayed open on the street. Stripped bare by strangers with cameras and venom and no goddamn humanity. Not curious. Not even all cruel. Merely... indifferent. Like I was a character they got to bend into a headline.

And of course, it was worse because I was a woman. Of course, they came after my trauma, my work, my grief. They didn't ask questions. They made accusations with question marks at the end. Twisted everything they'd managed to dig up and shoved it in my face like it was fair game. Because I was public now. Because I'd stepped over some invisible line, and that made me theirs. Something to commodify and exploit.

It didn't matter that I hadn't posted about my life. That I'd never once invited them in. They found a way to make it my fault anyway.

Like I knew they would.

I must've drifted. Not sleep, exactly—but a long stretch of nothing behind my eyes. The kind where the air gets thick and time slips sideways. I didn't hear the door open. Didn't register the sound of footsteps on the hall runner. But suddenly Uncle Dee was there, filling the doorway with all his big-hearted presence and quiet knowing.

His eyes landed on me curled up in Ramsey's hoodie, and he didn't say a word as he came to sit on the edge of the bed, taking me in like the truth was written plain across my face.

"You look like you've been hit by a bus made of assholes."

A bitter laugh punched out of me like a hiccup, too sharp to be real humor, but still something.

Uncle Dee didn't push. He sat, one hand resting near my hip, not touching, not crowding, just... there. Solid. Familiar.

"I fought so hard," I whispered.

"I know, baby."

"I didn't want any of this. Not the attention. Not the spotlight. I wanted to tell stories. To give people something to hold on to the way books held on to me. But they—" My throat closed up for a second. I swallowed hard. "They ripped it all open. Dug up pieces of me I didn't even know were still raw. And twisted them like I'd asked for it."

He stroked a hand over my hair. "You didn't. You never did."

"No one ever let me grieve." My voice cracked with the admission. "Not really. When Mom died, everybody else was shattered. And I had to keep going. Keep the house running,

312

keep the peace, keep my shit together so no one else broke worse. And I did it. I handled it. But I never got to fall apart."

Uncle Dee's gaze didn't waver. "You didn't get to fall apart then. Doesn't mean you can't now."

I blinked against the sudden sting behind my eyes. "I don't want to fall apart. I want to burn it down." I wanted blood and vengeance and a chance to take control in a way the world seldom allowed.

His smile was proud and the tiniest bit feral. "Use it. Turn it into fire. That's what you do, baby."

Uncle Dee pressed a kiss to the top of my head and slipped out as quietly as he'd come in.

After he left, I lay there for a minute in the echo of his words, in the quiet that followed the door clicking shut. My breath came steadier now. It wasn't easy or calm, and that raw, shaking place inside me hadn't healed. But it had stopped trying to hide.

And something else had ignited instead.

I shoved the blanket off and swung my legs over the edge of the bed. My body still felt wrung out and hollow, but there was a thread of steel running through the emptiness now. I followed it to my desk on the other side of the room, where my laptop was buried under a small mountain of legal paperwork I'd brought home. I swept the lot of it into a haphazard pile and set it aside, opening the lid.

The screen flared to life. The cursor blinked against the book file I'd left open after last week's surprise chapter. Waiting for what came next.

I shoved the hoodie sleeves back from my hands and cracked my knuckles.

Then I opened a brand new file and started to type.

No outline. No plan. Just blood and teeth and grief sharpened into something weaponized. The first sentence snapped onto the page like a match strike. Then another. And another. The fury poured out of me, molten and righteous, shaping itself into story.

I had no way to stop them from twisting my real life into whatever headline they wanted. No way to shield the people I loved from every blow.

But here—on the page—I was sovereign.

And I was done playing nice.

Chapter 36

Ramsey

I was pacing again.

Didn't mean to. Didn't want to. But three days of silence had me strung so tight, sitting still wasn't an option. Not when every instinct I had screamed to do something. Fix it. Help her. Get to her.

Except I couldn't. Because Alia wasn't letting anyone in.

Not me. Not her brothers. Not even Blair.

She'd had Miss Addie cancel all her appointments. Hadn't said a damn word about mayoral responsibilities—though the rest of the Gibsons stepped in without question. Bodie had taken on scheduling. Blair was fielding calls. Hell, even Fletcher had begun coordinating volunteers. They'd all pulled together to cover the load she usually carried like a champ.

And me? I hadn't heard a word. Not a text. Not a breadcrumb. Not a whisper through the damn door.

I muttered under my breath, hands clenched and steps echoing too loud across the hardwood. "I can't fix this. I can't even reach her."

Biscuit let out a soft woof and padded after me, her nails

tapping out a worried rhythm. Ears down, tail swishing low, eyes locked on me like I was the one in trouble.

"Yeah, yeah." I made another useless lap through the living room. "I'm spiraling. I know."

She huffed and jumped up onto the couch with a grunt that was cuter than it had any right to be, then stared at me until I gave in and dropped beside her with a groan. My elbows braced on my knees, and I scrubbed my hands over my face like I could scrape off some of the helplessness clinging to me like sweat.

One hand drifted down to Biscuit's back. She leaned into the touch, then climbed into my lap with all the grace of a tiny sack of potatoes and flopped down, staring up at me with those soulful, mismatched eyes.

"Yeah, okay," I muttered into the soft fur behind her ears. "Breathing. Breathing's a thing."

She sighed like I was the idiot in this relationship. Which, fair.

My pulse settled by degrees, enough to stop my damn leg from bouncing. Enough to remind me that pacing the floor didn't make time move any faster. That waiting sucked, but pushing would only make things worse.

Then came the knock.

Three sharp raps on the front door, followed by the creak of it opening without permission, which meant Blair. Because of course it was.

The familiar cadence of boots on stairs confirmed my suspicion. Blair always moved like the world was hers by right. But the second, heavier set told me she hadn't come alone. Bodie moved through the world like he was ready to fight it.

Biscuit lifted her head from my lap with a soft woof, ears perking as Blair breezed into the living room like she'd been invited.

"Don't get up." She hurled her oversized bag onto the armchair.

Bodie followed behind her, stiff and silent. His jaw was locked tight, hands flexing at his sides like he was one more piece of bad news away from punching something. I understood that all too well.

Hope flared in my chest anyway—stupid, reflexive. For a second, I thought they knew something. Had seen her. Heard from her.

I shifted, careful not to dislodge Biscuit. "You want something to drink? I've got—"

Blair cut me off with a wave. "We're good."

Bodie shook his head and moved to lean against the wall, arms crossed.

Blair looked me over as if checking for signs of damage. "Any change?"

And there it went. Hope crushed flat under those two words.

I sagged back onto the couch, letting my hand rest lightly across Biscuit's back. "Uncle Dee says the trays are still coming back empty, so she's eating. Probably writing. But she's not talking to anyone."

"Not even you?" There was something raw behind the question. Something that said he'd hoped I was the exception.

I shook my head. "I told her I'd be there when she's ready. I meant it."

Biscuit nosed at my jaw with her pointy little snout, then curled herself tighter against my thigh like eight pounds of ride-or-die reassurance. I scratched behind her ears and breathed past the knot in my chest.

Waiting was the right thing.

It didn't feel like doing enough.

Blair didn't move from her sprawl in the armchair, fingers

tapping a lazy rhythm against the armrest as if trying to convince herself everything was fine. "She'll come out of it. She always does. She's made of tougher stuff than half this damn town."

"She's never shut down like this." Bodie's voice rasped low. "Not even when Mom died."

My hand rested on Biscuit's back, the soft rise and fall of her breathing the only thing tethering me.

Blair's fingers paused for a moment, then resumed their rhythm, slower now. "She's been through worse than this."

"Not like this," I said quietly. "Not in front of the whole damn world."

Nobody argued.

For a moment, the only sound was the slow whoosh of the ceiling fan and Biscuit's even breathing. The silence was heavy. Tired. We were all worried. All trying to believe Alia would come through this the same way she always did. But we'd never seen her vanish like this before. Not from us.

Blair finally sat forward, elbows braced on her knees, her voice softer. "She's not broken, Ramsey. She's trying to hold the pieces until she can breathe again."

I wanted to believe that. God, I did. But the longer this stretched, the more I worried that this hurt, this exposure was too much. That she didn't trust me to protect her. That maybe I *couldn't* protect her the way I wanted.

That I'd lose her.

Bodie exhaled, slow and sharp, like he'd been holding something back for too long. "So what happens next time?" he said, his voice a low growl. "You think this dies down? You think it won't happen again?"

The idea of Alia having to face any of this shit ever again made me physically ill. No, I wasn't willing to put her through that. Not for anything. My jaw clenched so hard it ached. "I'll retire. If that's what it takes to keep her safe. I'll walk away."

Blair didn't even blink. "No. You won't."

"Watch me."

"Don't have to." Her voice remained calm and maddeningly certain. "Because if you did, Alia would never forgive herself. She wouldn't want you to give up your dream because of this."

She was right. Alia wouldn't want that, and the knowledge had my chest pulling tight with things I had no idea how to say. But wanting and reality weren't always on speaking terms.

I shot to my feet, one hand supporting the dog, and dragged the other through my hair. "So what the hell am I supposed to do?"

Biscuit gave an indignant huff and head-butted my shoulder like I'd personally offended her. I glanced down to see her tiny brows drawn in judgment, all eight pounds of her glaring up like I was the disappointment here.

Blair's mouth curved. "Even the dog knows you're spiraling."

I dropped back onto the couch, muttering under my breath. "This is what spiraling looks like quiet."

Blair raised a brow. "Then thank God for the mutt."

Biscuit huffed again, louder this time, and flopped back into my lap like the world's smallest, most judgy therapist.

Blair's voice dropped, not quite soft, but not as sharp as usual. "You keep trying to fix it *for* her. And I love you for it. I do. But this?" She leaned forward, elbows on her knees, hands folded tight. "This isn't yours to fix."

I looked at her. Really looked. And for once, she wasn't hiding behind sarcasm or sass. There was grief in her eyes. And guilt. And that same helpless frustration clawing through my chest. I hated how much of it I understood.

"I can't do nothing." My voice was hoarse from holding too much in. "I'm sitting here, knowing she's hurting, and I can't even get to her."

"You're not doing nothing," Blair said gently. "You're waiting. You're giving her space. You're trusting her to come back when she's ready. That's love, Ramsey. The real kind. Not everybody gets that."

Biscuit gave a soft chuff like she agreed.

"Still doesn't change the world outside that door." Bodie didn't look at either of us. "Doesn't stop the next asshole with a camera or a clickbait headline."

He wasn't wrong. The silence in the room turned brittle.

"No." Blair straightened. Braced. "But that's the part we can do something about."

She pulled her phone out of her bag and started scrolling, her mouth twitching like she couldn't quite contain a smile. "You haven't seen any of it, have you?"

I frowned. "Seen what?"

She turned the screen to face me. "This."

The hashtags registered first—#ProtectOurPrincess, #SupportKella, #WeStandWithKella—scrolling past in waves of purple hearts and dragon emojis and fierce, unwavering support.

It kept going. Fanart of Soren and Meriel. Screenshots of quotes. Videos of readers holding up her books, crying and laughing, talking about how she'd saved them in the worst moments of their lives. Posts calling out the reporters. Defending her. Shouting her name like a battle cry.

And then there was the thread.

A reader who'd lost her husband two years ago. Said she hadn't been able to get out of bed for weeks until she picked up one of Alia's books on a whim. Said it reminded her that love could still exist. That stories had the capacity to hold the pieces of you when you didn't know how to keep breathing.

"She needs to see this," Blair said again, quieter now.

I blinked hard, my throat thick. "Yeah," I rasped. "She does."

Blair's eyes sparkled. Not with tears—Blair wasn't one for easy sentiment—but with something fierce and electric. "She will. But I think there's something else we can do. Well... you can do."

I lifted a brow. "Name it."

That grin stretched across her face. Mischievous. Devious. Absolutely certain. "You're not gonna like it."

From my lap, Biscuit let out a long, theatrical sigh and snuggled deeper into my hoodie like even she knew Blair was about to wreck my day.

Chapter 37

Alia

I woke up in what could only be described as a nest of my own making. And not the cozy, birdsong-and-decorative-pillows kind. No, this was full feral: blankets tangled like seaweed, notebooks scattered across the bed like I'd tried to write my way through the apocalypse, and somewhere under the comforter, the faint, telltale crinkle of a granola bar wrapper.

Everything ached. My back, my neck, the crick in my hip from sitting weird too long—and don't even get me started on the state of my hair. I was hot and cold at the same time, clammy in a way that said I hadn't showered in... a while. The hoodie I wore had stopped smelling like imaginary Ramsey or detergent and started smelling like *me*, which was rude, honestly. Treasonous.

Light stabbed in through the curtain gap like a vengeful god. I hissed and pulled the sleeve of said treason hoodie over my face, momentarily convinced I was dying. But then my stomach growled with a long, low, almost pathetic sound that suggested I might actually still be alive.

Barely.

I pushed upright with the groaning majesty of a woman twice my age, limbs creaking, brain foggy. My room looked like the inside of a writer's mind after a hurricane. Half empty mugs of cold tea. An ocean of crumpled sticky notes. At least four mechanical pencils without tips. A tray from Uncle Dee sat on the nightstand with the remnants of... something involving cheese. Probably.

My phone was dead. Completely black-screened. I had no idea where my charger was. Possibly buried under the landslide of plot outlines at the foot of the bed. So I grabbed my laptop instead, blinking blearily at the boot-up screen like I'd never seen one before.

The time popped up first. Then the date.

I stared at it for a solid thirty seconds before the full weight of it registered.

Two weeks.

Two.

Weeks.

"What the actual hell." My voice came out scratchy and wrong. Like I hadn't spoken aloud in days.

Because I hadn't.

My pulse kicked. Panic, thick and sharp and immediate. What had I missed? Had I tanked a deadline? Was there an angry email from a FEMA rep sitting in my inbox? Had someone taken over my mayoral duties? Had there been—I don't know—another flood?

Where was everyone?

Why hadn't someone come to drag me out of this cave and into the light?

Why—

I stopped. Breathed.

There probably hadn't been an apocalypse without my knowing.

No one came... because they didn't need to. Because they understood. Uncle Dee had kept me fed. My people—my family—had circled the wagons and done what needed doing.

They hadn't pushed. They'd protected my space.

The guilt spiral started to loosen. Not all the way. But enough that I could hear myself think.

Sort of.

Which was right about when the knock came.

The sound didn't startle me. Uncle Dee's trays of food came like clockwork, always with a gentle tap and no expectations. A ghostly room service.

I shuffled to the door, hoodie sleeves half covering my hands, socked feet silent on the hardwood. I didn't bother checking the mirror. I didn't actually want to know what I looked like. Two weeks without leaving my room would have taken a toll.

I opened the door expecting tea and toast.

Instead, I got sequins. And judgment.

The full Sasspatch Society stood in a semi-circle of fabulous condemnation, Uncle Dee front and center like the ringleader of a very sparkly intervention. Miss Glory was in full drag—hair piled high, lashes longer than my will to live, lips a lethal shade of red that said she had thoughts and wasn't afraid to weaponize them. Mo'nique stood beside her with a Tupperware container the size of a carry-on bag and the serene expression of someone convinced food would fix at least part of this mess. Miss Bea clutched a floral tote with the ominous weight of consequence. Whatever was inside wasn't forgiveness.

And Uncle Dee? He gave me that narrow-eyed once-over that somehow managed to be loving and exasperated all at once. "Darling," he said, voice velvet-wrapped steel, "you've been alone long enough. This is an intervention."

Miss Bea tilted her chin toward me with the solemnity of a judge passing sentence. "If you want to keep that sweatshirt, surrender it now to be laundered. Otherwise, it dies today."

Miss Glory sniffed. "Honestly, if the smell doesn't kill it, I will."

I blinked at them, still barefoot and blinking like a mole seeing daylight for the first time in a decade. "...Hi?"

They did not say hi back.

Uncle Dee stepped forward, took me gently by the elbow, and turned me toward the bathroom with all the tender insistence of someone about to steam-clean a haunted house. "Shower. Now. We'll handle the war zone you call a bedroom."

I looked down at myself. My hoodie was so stretched it hung off one shoulder. My leggings had holes in both knees. I couldn't remember the last time I'd worn a bra. Or pants with a zipper. Or literally any expression of basic human hygiene.

"Right," I said faintly. "Yeah. Okay."

Miss Bea raised the tote. "Towels. Clean clothes. A detox face mask. And your favorite body wash. I'm not a monster."

They didn't give me a choice.

Miss Bea hummed a funeral march while stripping my bed, her movements disturbingly efficient. She snapped the fitted sheet off with a flourish that sent a puff of dust and glitter into the air—where the glitter came from, I couldn't say. But with her, it was always lurking.

"I was going to clean up," I mumbled, half-ashamed, half-dazed as I looked around at the room that had become my hermit hole. Crumpled snack wrappers. Sticky mugs. Notebooks stacked like miniature architectural disasters. A vaguely suspicious bowl that might've once held soup. Or cereal. Or regret.

Miss Glory waved a manicured hand. "Honey, no one's got time for guilt today. This is triage."

Dee herded me gently but firmly toward the bathroom. "Shower. Now. I will ward the door shut if you try to escape."

"I wouldn't dream of it," I muttered, but he was already making arcane gestures that might have been dramatic flair or actual spellcraft. Hard to tell with Uncle Dee. He did have that pet interest in hoodoo.

I shut the door behind me, peeled off my clothes, and caught a glimpse of myself in the mirror.

Oh. Oh no.

My hair had become a sentient entity. My skin was dull and blotchy. I had ink on my neck—literal ink—and what might've been crumbs or ancient granola stuck to my collarbone. My eyebrows looked like punctuation marks drawn by someone in a moving vehicle.

I took a breath.

Then I stepped under the hot spray and stayed there contemplating every decision that had led me to this moment. I washed my hair three times. I exfoliated like I was shedding a second skin. The face mask Miss Bea gave me tingled in a way that suggested either healing or punishment, but I didn't question it.

By the time I emerged—clean, damp, wrapped in the fluffy robe my beloved uncle had somehow smuggled into the bathroom—I felt almost... human.

My room had undergone a miracle in my absence. The bed was remade with fresh, soft sheets. A clean set of comfy clothes was laid out—leggings without holes, a soft T-shirt that smelled like lavender instead of despair, and fuzzy socks that looked new. The garbage was gone. The mugs had vanished. The notebooks were stacked neatly on my desk like I hadn't been writing like a madwoman.

It was eerie. And kind. And overwhelming.

Still towel-drying my hair, I padded down the hall and found them all in the living room.

Mo'nique was holding court from the sofa, examining a lineup of hair products with the intensity of a surgeon. "She needs moisture, not volume. Look at the breakage."

Miss Glory sipped from a crystal glass of something amber and judgmental. "Her eyebrows are salvageable, but it's going to take patience and a good pencil."

"I have a stencil kit in the car," Bea said cheerfully.

Dee spotted me and smiled. "Well. Someone's officially risen from the dead."

They looked at me like I'd returned from war. I supposed I sort of had.

Mo'nique rose from the couch in a cascade of jewel-toned silk and handed me a plate stacked with snacks—cheese cubes, apple slices, those little crackers that cost way too much but taste like heaven when you're starving and haven't seen a real meal in longer than you care to remember. "You need sustenance before you faint on us, baby."

Miss Bea tilted her head and beamed at me like a proud, slightly terrifying aunt. "Look, she's human again. Miracles do happen."

"I'm still deciding if I'm insulted or flattered." The cracker in my mouth muffled most of my complaint. I sank onto the couch with all the grace of a melting snowman, the clean clothes and food making me feel almost civilized. My legs were still a little wobbly, as if I'd just climbed a personal Everest.

Uncle Dee sat beside me and wrapped an arm around my shoulders, letting me lean into him. I didn't realize how much I'd needed the hug until he buried me in it.

"Thank you," I whispered, throat thick. "For feeding me. For not pushing. For letting me be a disaster."

His hand rubbed gentle circles on my back. "Sweet girl, you earned the right to fall apart. I was just here to make sure you didn't forget to come back."

My eyes stung. I blinked fast.

"It's a good thing you came up on your own today." His tone had gone dry. "Bea was about to deploy glitter ordnance."

Bea didn't even blink. "Something radical was required. I had plans."

"Industrial fans and everything," Miss Glory muttered from her perch with a smirk. "We were taking bets on how many ounces of biodegradable shimmer it would take to lure you out."

I took another bite of cheese to buy myself a second before I had to respond. "Do I even want to know what I missed?"

The four of them exchanged a look. And that never meant anything good.

Miss Glory picked up the remote like she was unsheathing a sword. "Sit. Eat. Watch."

That was all the warning I got before the TV came to life, casting its glow across the living room like some sort of divine revelation. The screen flickered through a few loading screens, then—

Oh.

Oh.

It was my face.

Or rather, my pen name's face.

A header with #ProtectOurPrincess in looping script. #SupportKella trailing below it in bold block caps. The background was pink, glittery, and somehow already branded like someone's Etsy shop had exploded in my honor.

"I..." My brain short-circuited.

Miss Bea made a satisfied sound. "Wait for it."

A carousel of social posts started playing—like a slideshow

of feelings. Fanart of Kella and Soren in various dramatic poses. Paintings, digital renderings, even a crochet doll version of them that made me wheeze.

Then came the videos.

Clips of readers—some tearful, some furious, some absolutely savage—calling out the paparazzi for stalking and ambushing me. Others holding up their favorite books with captions like: "This woman saved me when no one else could." "Her stories gave me hope after my miscarriage." "I was going to give up writing until I found her."

A shaky phone video of someone saying, "I started reading Kella Harmon when I was in chemo. I read every single book in the waiting room. I wouldn't have made it through without her."

I blinked. Then blinked again. My throat went tight. My vision was blurry.

"I don't..." I swallowed hard. "I don't understand."

Mo'nique perched beside me, gentle and glowing. "Romancelandia protects its own, sugar. They didn't simply clap back. They detonated."

Uncle Dee's voice came from behind me, strong and fierce. "And they mobilized like a militia with glitter for you. Those asshats didn't know what hit 'em."

Another scroll popped up with a compilation of social media takedowns so brutal they probably required a body count. Twitter threads, Instagram reels, TikToks full of righteous fury and reader love. There were memes. Fan-edits. One reel had over half a million likes and was set to Taylor Swift's "The Archer." I almost blacked out.

"They did all this?" I whispered. "For me?"

Miss Glory arched one razor-sharp brow. "You think you write those kinds of stories and don't build an army?"

"I didn't even tell anyone who I was."

"You didn't have to." Bea's voice was quiet now. "They felt it."

Mo'nique smiled. "And when the internet found out? They lit up like a holy damn bonfire."

My hands were shaking, plate forgotten in my lap, crumbs sticking to my fingers. My hoodie sleeves—it was a different hoodie now, clean and soft—seemed to constrict around me.

I curled into the couch cushions, overwhelmed. "I don't know what to do with this."

Miss Glory sipped from her glass. "Start by believing it's real."

Dee added, "And know that this is only the beginning."

I wasn't sure what that meant.

But I was about to find out.

Miss Bea's eyes gleamed. "Oh, honey." That level of glee was usually reserved for unwrapping a scandal.

The screen changed. And there he was. Ramsey. My Ramsey. In full Soren regalia.

The camera caught him from the side at first—armor gleaming, the swoop of the shoulder pauldron unmistakable. And then he turned. Looked straight into the lens. Unmasked.

"Hi." He spoke in that same devastating soft growl he usually reserved for me. "I'm Swoony McBroadsword—also known as Ramsey Shaw."

I choked on a sound that wanted to be a laugh and a sob at the same time.

The video cut to footage of Gibson Hollow. Not only the destruction from the flood, but the rebuild. The grit and sweat and stubborn hope of it. Flooded streets. Buckled pavement. Waterlines stained into siding. And then: hands. So many hands. Cleaning, hauling, hammering. Sasspatches in sequins hauling debris like divine punishment. Miss Glory directing traffic like a pageant queen turned drill sergeant. Kids chasing bubbles near a community meal tent. Uncle Dee in full drag reading to children in the park, tiara glinting in the sun.

And Ramsey's voice over all of it.

"*This* is what Kella's been dealing with. What she's been carrying—quietly, fiercely, and without asking for help. She kept us afloat. She's the reason we're still standing. If her stories have ever meant something to you—if they helped you through anything the way they've helped me—I'm asking you now: help her back. However you can. Time, money, prayers, sharing the word—whatever you've got to give. This is our moment to show up."

Before he even got to the end, I was sobbing. A full-body, soul-evacuating grief mixed with wonder and gratitude, crashing down all at once. I curled forward, undone by the sheer emotional weight of it, and immediately found myself encased in a cocoon of arms and warmth and tissues. Someone rubbed circles between my shoulders. Another hand found mine and squeezed.

"He didn't stand by," Miss Glory murmured, soft and awed. "He stood with you."

I tried to speak. Couldn't. Tried again. "Did anyone..." My voice cracked. "Did anyone come?"

They exchanged a look. The kind that held so much and said everything.

And then Uncle Dee, smiling through her own glassy eyes, said gently, "Oh, baby. You might want to see for yourself."

I was already half up and moving before the words finished leaving her mouth, but I only made it three steps before a perfectly manicured hand landed in front of my chest like a velvet traffic stop.

"Maaaaybe change first." Bea's eyes raked me from head to toe. "Or at least brush your hair."

Glory arched one sculpted brow. "Yes, let's face your

public in something other than a wrinkled hoodie and trauma pants."

I looked down at myself—fuzzy socks, oversized tee, and the leggings that, while clean, I hadn't realized were inside out. My hair was probably still damp and frizzing in all directions.

"...Point taken."

They didn't follow as I padded back toward the bedroom, but I could still hear Mo'nique behind me, already plotting touch-up options like a pit crew prepping a race car.

"Leave the hoodie," Uncle Dee called gently. "But bring the fire."

Oh, I was bringing it. Right after I found pants with a zipper.

Chapter 38

Ramsey

I'd lost track of how many days I'd been doing this.

How many early mornings and late nights had blurred into the rhythm of hammer and saw and the constant bark of "watch your damn fingers" echoing up and down Main Street. Sweat had soaked through my T-shirt hours ago, sawdust stuck to my skin like a second layer, but I was beyond caring.

It was the only thing keeping me sane.

If I stopped moving, I'd think. And if I thought, I'd remember that it had been two weeks since I'd seen Alia. Two weeks since I'd touched her. Two weeks of waiting outside a wall she wasn't ready to open yet. So I kept moving.

I threw everything I had into this rebuild. Into the blueprint Blair had sketched in that deceptively casual tone of hers, like she wasn't handing me a lifeline. Into the concept I'd taken and run with.

When she first pitched the idea, I figured we'd be lucky if a couple dozen folks showed up to help. A few readers, a handful of contractors. Enough to scrape by.

Instead, they came in droves.

Romancelandia rolled in like a damn cavalry. Fans, friends, strangers—people who'd read Kella Harmon and decided her stories had saved them, and they wanted to return the favor. And they didn't only send money, though there'd been plenty of that too. They came here. With tool belts. With trucks. With skills and time and a willingness to sweat.

So now there were people everywhere. Up on scaffolding, hauling lumber, painting trim. The once-shattered line of retail spaces along Main Street was whole again, fresh paint gleaming in the sun. New framing was already rising on the next block over.

And on the green, beyond the square, the skeleton of the amphitheater curved like a promise. The bones of the story garden were set, winding paths that would, in a few months' time, become a maze of wildflowers and quiet corners.

All of it for her.

I wiped my forearm across my forehead, smearing a streak of grit and sweat, and stepped back to take it in. It still wasn't finished. Not yet. But it was getting there.

It had to be right.

For her.

For the woman who'd had everything ripped open in front of the world and still, somehow, stood tall enough to hold this town together.

If I couldn't reach her yet, I'd at least build her something to come back to.

The organized chaos around me had become background noise over the past couple of weeks. Volunteers shouting for more supplies, the steady thunk of hammers and nail guns popping like popcorn, Blair giving somebody grief about safety goggles. Nothing out of the ordinary.

Ihad no idea what made me glance up, but when I did, I

thought my brain had finally cracked from exhaustion. Because Alia was there, strolling down the sidewalk that led past The Commissary. Had I conjured her out of pure wanting?

My gaze raked over her, drinking her in like a man parched, cataloging every detail, irrationally checking for physical injuries, though of course she had none. She still looked tired, but there was color in her cheeks, and she seemed steadier. Lighter than when I'd left her standing in her uncle's house.

And then I met her gaze. Clear. Unwavering.

Something in my chest gave way.

I hadn't realized I'd been holding my breath for fourteen straight days until it punched out of me all at once. I wanted to run to her—God, every muscle in me ached to—but I made myself stay where I was. Because she was looking around, taking it all in. The rebuilt storefronts. The crowd. The life that had kept going outside her walls. She needed a second for that.

So I stood there and let myself really look at her.

She was here, and my chest loosened enough to breathe again.

It didn't take long for the crowd to notice her. A ripple went through the square, subtle at first. Heads turning, murmurs rising above the rhythm of pounding and cutting. Then came the voices, full of warmth and enthusiasm.

"Welcome back, Alia!"

"We love you, Kella!"

Nobody rushed her. Nobody crowded. This town, these people, somehow understood that whatever she needed right now, it wasn't hands grabbing or bodies closing in. So they just called out from where they were, offering soft smiles and quick waves, letting her know she'd been missed without demanding a damn thing from her in return.

She blinked, slow. Like she wasn't sure what to do with it, all this affection, all these people rooting for her. Then she raised a tentative hand. At the answering cheer, a startled smile tugged at her mouth, and she tried again, a little steadier this time.

I stayed where I was, every muscle in me coiled tight, afraid that if I moved, I'd break whatever spell had brought her back to me.

She stopped in front of me, close enough that I saw the shine in her eyes, the way her breath hitched like she'd been holding it the whole way here.

Shit. Tears. Panic shot through me as I second guessed everything I'd done without asking.

"Alia—"

I didn't get any further. She launched herself at me, all soft, fierce momentum, and I caught her hard, hauling her in until there was nothing between us. My world narrowed to the scent of her hair, the press of her face against my neck, her fists knotted in my shirt like she was afraid I'd disappear.

"I'm sorry." Her whisper was ragged and breathless against my throat. "I missed you. I can't believe you did all this."

I let her slide down and cupped her jaw, tipping her face to mine. "Hang on."

I couldn't have this conversation yet. Couldn't do anything but kiss her. There was nothing sedate or careful about it. Everything I'd been holding back came crashing out at once. She met me halfway, fingers curling tighter, mouth answering mine like she'd been starving for this too. I had sufficient presence of mind left to hear the cheers and catcalls around us.

I braced, waiting for Alia to stiffen or pull back. Instead, she laughed against my mouth, a bit shaky but still bright. Something in me finally unclenched and settled.

Easing back, I pressed my brow to hers, arms still wrapped tight around her. "God, I missed you. How are you?"

"Better." Her hands were still fisted in my shirt, as if she couldn't make herself let me go either.

I was totally fine with that. Especially as it angled her hand just right to show my ring glinting on her finger.

"I'm sorry for disappearing and shutting you out. I couldn't —I didn't know how to breathe with all of it pressing in."

Sometime during our time apart, I'd gotten past being upset that she hadn't wanted me with her for all of it. It hadn't been about me. Hadn't been about us.

I smoothed a hand down her spine. "It's okay. You're here now. That's the only thing that matters."

"The Sasspatch Society dragged me out of my cave. They showed me everything. The fans. The hashtags. Your video." She sucked in a breath and tipped her head back, and her eyes were shining again. "I didn't know... I didn't know people could be that good. I didn't know you—" She bit her lip like she needed to slow the flow of words. "I don't know how to thank you for what you've done here."

I tightened my arms around her, because there weren't words big enough for the things I wanted to tell her. And right now, I didn't need them. Not when her heart thumped against my chest, not when she was here, holding on like she didn't plan to let go any time soon.

I eased back to meet her gaze. "Wanna see?"

"Yeah."

Her fingers laced with mine, and together we walked slowly through the square. People looked up from their work as we passed, but nobody stopped us as we passed the row of rebuilt storefronts—fresh paint, glass polished to a shine. Places that had been gutted by the flood now stood whole, ready for life again. At the end of the block, the green opened up in front of us. The old sinkhole was gone, filled and reinforced. In its place rose a curve of new stone seating that would hold an audience.

"What on earth?" Alia took it in, her eyes wide.

"Welcome to Gibson Hollow's very own mini-amphitheater. It'll host shows during the good-weather months. Music. Plays. Can you imagine a Sasspatch musical revue?"

She laughed. "It will be *epic*."

I slowed, turning us to gesture at what stretched beyond the amphitheater. "This part's specifically for you."

Wooden stakes and flags marked the looping paths—beds laid out like a labyrinth, winding through what would soon be wildflowers, native herbs, and trees. Places to sit and read. Quiet pockets to breathe. Every turn, a different little escape.

"This part was my idea," I told her. "I wanted to give you a place that wasn't about rebuilding walls. Somewhere for people to just... be. To get quiet again."

Her brows drew together as she took it in. "What is it?"

"A story garden." I pointed. "Those stakes mark out the paths. It'll all be native plants—dogwoods, herbs, wildflowers that'll come back on their own year after year. Benches tucked into little corners. Places to walk when your head's full or sit when you need to breathe. And there'll be markers—little plaques—with favorite quotes from books woven all through it."

Her gaze swept over the green again, slower this time, like she was already picturing it grown in.

"I figured..." I rubbed a hand against the back of my neck. "You've given everybody else a way to escape. You deserved a place here that could do the same for you."

She blinked fast and tightened her grip on my hand. "Ramsey..."

"I wanted you to have somewhere that safe to land," I added, softer.

Her eyes came back to me, bright and a little wet. "It's

perfect." Then she smiled, and the expression on her face made every late night worth it. "But just so you know, you're that safe place for me. I don't need to do it on my own anymore."

Her words landed with a weight I wasn't ready for. It was what I'd wanted. The thing I'd needed and put aside because she needed something different. For a second, I only stood there, trying to hold myself together with her hand in mine.

I cleared my throat. "None of this would've happened without your readers. They showed up because of you."

She drew in a breath that sounded like courage. "I want to meet them."

"You do?" After everything that had driven her behind those walls, that was a big damn step.

"They came all this way. Seems a shame not to say a proper hello."

I tightened my grip on her hand. "Come on."

I led her across the green toward a young woman stacking brushes into a bin. She wasn't more than twenty, with paint on her arms and that exhausted-but-proud smile I'd seen on half the volunteers these past couple of weeks. She straightened when she saw us coming, eyes going wide when she realized who was with me.

"Alia—" I kept my voice gentle. "—this is Hannah. She came all the way from Dallas to help out."

Hannah's hand flew to her mouth. "Oh, my gosh. I—I don't even know what to say. Your books... they got me through my mom's cancer. Through losing her. I used to read them to her when she was too tired to hold a book, and after... after she was gone, they were the only thing that made me feel like I could keep breathing. You don't know how much you mean to me."

Alia's face softened in a way I hadn't seen in weeks. She let go of my hand only to pull the girl into a hug. Not the awkward, polite kind—just a warm, solid hold like she had all the time in the world.

"Thank you," Alia whispered. "For telling me. For being here."

Hannah sniffled and laughed at herself at the same time. "I just wanted to give something back. You saved me."

They pulled apart slowly, both brushing at their faces. Alia glanced at me over Hannah's shoulder and smiled. And right there, I knew she'd found something she hadn't been sure still existed.

Chapter 39

Alia

Ramsey drove. I hadn't even argued, partly because I was still figuring out what to say when we got to Grandma Elsie's for dinner, partly because I'd been too busy loving on Biscuit to care. She'd launched herself into my arms the second I'd stepped through the door to Ramsey's house, eight pounds of squirming indignation and relief, and now she was curled against my chest like she'd been glued there. I buried my face in the top of her silky little head and breathed her in like I could make up for every missed cuddle all at once.

"I missed you, baby girl." I cooed and scratched under her chin until she snorted. "Did he even let you sleep in the bed? Or did he make you rough it on the cupcake?"

"She owns the bed now. You'll have to fight her for your spot." Ramsey's tone was dry as the gravel crunching under the truck tires.

Biscuit huffed like that was her cue to confirm, and I kissed her head again, smiling into her fur.

By the time the truck turned onto the long gravel drive to

Grandma Elsie's, the yard was already a jumble of headlights and chrome. Vehicles parked nose-to-tail wherever they'd fit, spilling over into the grass and up against the fencerow.

I swallowed hard, rubbing my thumb over Biscuit's tiny ribs. "Looks like the whole clan's here."

Ramsey glanced my way. "They've been waiting for you." There was no judgment in his tone, no hint of what sort of reception I should expect.

The old farmhouse glowed against the encroaching dusk, windows spilling golden light across the yard. Porch boards groaned under Ramsey's boots as we climbed the steps together, Biscuit still cradled in my arms like a security blanket.

The wall of scent reached me first. Roasted chicken. Mashed potatoes. Biscuits. Everything that said home.

The expected avalanche of sound came next. The living room was packed shoulder to shoulder. Every Gibson within shouting distance had crammed themselves in. Dad sat next to Grandma Elsie on the couch. Bodie loomed behind them like a watchdog. Blair and Elena sprawled in one of the oversized armchairs, long legs crossed, and Gunner and Fletcher shared the loveseat. Colter and Dean had taken up the wall, as if by leaning they were somehow holding it up, and Uncle Dee was planted on the ottoman, posture deceptively loose.

And in the middle of it all, they'd dragged out a single empty chair.

Grandma Elsie patted the air toward it. "Come on, sugar. Have a seat."

Anxiety blotted out the scent of good food as I glanced around the circle. "This looks like an ambush."

Blair smirked. "If you run, we might make it one. Otherwise, it's just a family meeting."

With Biscuit still clutched tight, I sat. Every muscle in my back braced for the lecture, the guilt trip, and the list of things I'd let slide while I hid from the world.

But none of it came.

Grandma Elsie folded her hands over her lap. "There are some things we need to say to you."

The words made my throat close up, panic and apology spilling over before I could stop them. "I know I should've—"

One look from her—sharp as a tack and unyielding as iron-wood—shut me up cold. It was the sort of look that made even grown men sink back in their chairs. I clamped my mouth shut and held Biscuit closer, her little heartbeat a rapid flutter against my ribs.

"We didn't mean to let everything all fall on you," she said softly. "But we did. And we're sorry."

The words shook me. Sorry? That wasn't what I'd prepared for.

Bodie was the next to speak, his big frame stiff behind the couch. "I thought you had it handled. Because... you always do." He rubbed the back of his neck, eyes fixed somewhere above my head. "I didn't stop to think about what that was costing you."

Dad cleared his throat, voice already thick. "I'm supposed to be the one taking care of you, baby girl. Not the other way around. And I... let that get away from me a long time ago."

Gunner leaned forward, elbows on his knees. "We kept showing up at your office like it was the town help desk." He grimaced. "Dumping stuff on you 'cause you'd know what to do."

"And you organized everything," Fletcher added. "The fundraisers, the repairs, hell, even the schedules we damned well should have been organizing for ourselves."

Colter's voice was quiet. "And we let you. Because you're good at it. And because we didn't think about the cost."

One by one, they all said their piece without excuses, taking quiet, unflinching ownership of all the ways they'd handed me their weight and expected me to carry it.

It was too much. Too much honesty, too much love, too much of what I hadn't let myself want. My vision blurred as I looked from face to face, seeing only a sincerity I felt in the aching knot in my chest and the way Biscuit nudged up under my chin like she understood.

"I know," I started, "I know I bailed, and I left you all to—"

Blair held up a hand. "Ah-ah. Before you start down that road, let's be real clear about a few things."

I shut my mouth. Biscuit's head popped up at the sharpness in her tone, but Blair's smile softened as she started ticking things off on her fingers like this was a quarterly report.

"Miss Addie has the office locked down tighter than Fort Knox. She's handling scheduling, filing, calls—the whole nine. I stop in when she needs me, so nothing's piling up there. Dean's now the FEMA liaison. Which, let's be honest, he's better at anyway because he's not as nice as you when arguing with bureaucrats. He's getting results. Paperwork for the city is split between him, Colter, and your dad."

I blinked. "Wait, you've—"

She kept going, steamrolling right over me. "We also delegated all the rebuild tasks. Committees for each area—business district, housing, green space. Every single thing that doesn't need your signature has been claimed."

Bodie crossed his arms, voice firm as bedrock. "We're not dumping it back on you, Alia. We've got it covered."

Dad leaned forward, elbows on his knees. "And we're gonna keep it covered."

I looked at him, at all of them, this circle of people who'd just... taken care of it. The way I'd been taking care of things for them for years. It took me a minute to find my voice.

"I don't know what to say. I still have responsibilities—"

Dad's hand came up, palm out, gentle but firm, stopping me mid-sentence. "Honey, I say this with all the love in the world. It's time for you to run away from home."

That startled a laugh out of me, shaky and confused. "What?"

"You've held this place together for so long." He leaned forward until I couldn't look anywhere but straight at him. "Since you weren't even out of high school, it's been you. Keeping the wheels on, making sure everyone else stayed upright. You've done more than your share, Alia. More than any one person should."

The lump in my throat swelled until I couldn't swallow around it. "Somebody had to."

"And you did." His expression softened, a smile creasing the corners of his eyes, proud and sad all at once. "But it's your turn now. You get to go live your life. You've earned that right a hundred times over. So if you want to stay, fine—we'll make room. But if you want to chase your dreams, if you want to go and build something of your own, you do it. Knowing we've got this. We'll be okay. You need to be okay."

For so long, everything I'd done had been about keeping things from breaking. Keeping everyone else steady. No one— not once—had ever looked at me and said, 'You can go. You can live your own life. We'll hold the line for you'

I blinked hard, the room going soft around the edges. Words didn't come. Not yet. There was too much to untangle, too much in the way my chest ached with the weight of what he'd handed me.

A warm weight settled on my shoulder, steadying me. Ramsey. He'd been behind me the whole time, quiet as a shadow while my family poured their hearts out, and now his hand anchored me in a way that made it easier to breathe.

"We haven't talked through all of it yet, but... I figure we'll split time."

I tipped my head back to glance up at him.

"Charleston as a home base during the season, and here whenever we can swing it. However you want to do it." His thumb brushed once against my shoulder, the barest touch. "But I know you. You're not going to fully leave. You love this place too much." The corner of his mouth tipped up, his dark eyes full of understanding. "And that matters, too. To me."

That got me right in the soft spot behind my ribs. Because he wasn't trying to coax me one way or another. He understood me. And he was already building a life around that truth.

Relief rolled over me like a tide, so different from the weight that had been crushing me for weeks. This was so much lighter.

I swallowed, my voice barely there. "You're really sure?"

Dad smiled, though I could still see some sadness at the edges. "You've earned it, sweetheart."

That undid me. A laugh bubbled out at the same time as the tears I couldn't hold back anymore. I grabbed Ramsey's hand like a lifeline, lacing our fingers so tight my knuckles ached, and still I didn't want to let go.

Blair shoved a tissue into my free hand. "You look like a raccoon." But there was nothing but affection in the tone.

Across the circle, Uncle Dee sighed dramatically and fanned himself. "Lord, what am I gonna do with that big house when you move out? I might have to get me a cat."

A watery laugh escaped me as I glanced around the room at every face, every open smile. For the first time, I let myself believe that I really was allowed to have a life that was purely mine.

I drew in a long, shaky breath and let it out. "Okay."

The word barely left my mouth before the whole room

seemed to exhale with me, a soft ripple of relief that turned into motion. Arms came around me from every direction—Dad first, then Blair and Bodie and everybody else piling on until it was a mess of hugs and shoulders bumping, and Biscuit wedged like a furry heat pack in the middle of us all.

When it settled into a quieter tangle, Ramsey bent down, his mouth close to my ear, his voice meant for me alone. "Wherever you want to go, I'm going too."

I tipped my face up to his, a small grin tugging at my lips even through the damp tracks of tears. "We're gonna need more bookshelves."

That earned a quiet laugh against my hair, and I leaned into him as the noise in the room mellowed into a warm hum of smiles, quiet conversation, and the type of glow that only came when something heavy finally lets go.

For the first time in a long time, it felt like peace.

Epilogue

Ramsey

The event space was small by pro football standards. Hell, it was small by high school gym standards. It definitely wasn't intended for a crowd this size, but it buzzed like a live wire. Charleston humidity had a way of clinging to people, even indoors—frizzing hair, wilting clothes— but no one seemed to care. The line snaked out the door, curling down the sidewalk, a mix of readers clutching well-loved books, tote bags sagging with swag, and that electric anticipation that hit me right before a championship game.

Only this wasn't my stage.

The staff behind the signing table moved with the efficiency of a pit crew to keep up, stacking fresh boxes of Alia's books, sliding copies to her for signatures, then whisking them away before the next wave of fans stepped up. The room was shoulder-to-shoulder full—more of a literary tide than a crowd —and yet somehow still seemed intimate. Cozy. Like everybody here was in on the same secret: Kella Harmon was theirs, and tonight she wasn't hiding.

I stood a few paces off, to the side of the little stage they'd set up, armor catching the soft house lights. Full Soren kit, minus the helmet. It had started as Blair's idea—a wink to the fandom—and now it was mine. A statement. Not because I'd ever shied away from the public eye, but because this was Alia's world, and I wanted everyone in it to know I belonged here with her.

No one looked at me and saw a football player tonight. They saw Soren. Her Soren.

And I'd never been prouder to play the part. Especially as I well knew exactly how this would end when we got home. My wife really *did* have a thing for these leather pants.

She was in her element. No wig. No glasses. No hesitation. Just Alia—whole and unarmored in a way I'd rarely seen outside of private moments.

Viv had designed the outfit she wore in exchange for autographs on her entire Kella Harmon collection. The dress was simple, a deep blue gray that hit somewhere between storm and ocean, and a leather corset that I'd come to appreciate as much as she loved my leather pants, paired with boots and the wide leather cuffs Alia adored. They made her look like she could sign a stack of books and go straight into battle. Her hair fell loose around her shoulders, soft waves catching in the stage lights, and she held herself without an ounce of pretense.

Confident. Relaxed. Herself.

Part valkyrie, part Wonder Woman. All mine.

She laughed with a reader leaning over the table, answering questions as she signed, leaning in to listen when someone got quiet. Every person in that line was seen, and she made it look effortless.

And I couldn't stop watching her.

No shrinking from the cameras this time. No ducking her head like she needed to hide behind the name Kella Harmon—

though she'd kept it for branding. No apologies for taking up the space that had always been hers.

I'd always known she was extraordinary. Always seen this in her, even when she couldn't. But standing in this space, I was floored all over again. She'd always been this person.

Now the whole damn world got to see it too.

My thumb found the gold band on my hand without me consciously seeking it out. For a second, the bookstore fell away.

I saw Alia as she'd been a few months ago, barefoot in the grass behind Grandma Elsie's house, walking toward me on her dad's arm like the sun had decided to come home. The Sass-patch Society sat in the front row of tulle-draped lawn chairs, all of them in the biggest, most ridiculous hats they could find, dabbing at their faces like a bunch of glamorous fountains. Blair had one hand pressed to her chest and the other flapping a tissue around as she tried to get the words out without bawl-ing. The rest of the attendees had been made up of Alia's siblings and my mom. Small. Intimate. Exactly as she'd wanted.

And Alia—my wife—had smiled at me like there was no storm in the world that could ever touch us again.

That smile still lived in my chest like a live coal.

And I was looking at it now.

A girl of about sixteen practically bounced up to the table with a stack of dog-eared books clutched to her chest.

"Oh my gosh, I've been waiting all day for this!" She beamed. "These are my comfort reads. My mom keeps stealing them, so I had to bring all of them for you to sign."

Alia laughed, reaching for the top copy. "That's the best kind of book theft. Which one's hers?"

"This one." The girl slid a copy forward. "She says she's borrowing it, but it's been in her nightstand for a year."

"Then I'm signing it to both of you." Alia scribbled. "And putting '*Property of*' really big, so there's no confusion."

The girl giggled, clapping a hand over her mouth. She didn't rush the kid. Didn't let the line or the noise hurry her along. She gave that girl her full attention, made her laugh as they chatted about favorite characters, and sent her back into the crowd like she'd been handed a piece of magic.

Halfway through the line, a twenty-something woman came up with a notebook tucked under her arm, a tad wobbly with nerves but determined. Alia nodded toward the notebook with a smile. "You came prepared."

"I... yeah." The girl set it down gently. "I started writing because of you. I wanted to tell you that."

Alia's brows lifted, her whole face softening. "That's the best compliment I've ever been given. What's it about?"

"Uh—dragons," the girl said, then blurted, "but not like yours."

"Good." Alia leaned closer, dropping her voice like a co-conspirator as she signed the offered notebook. "Make them your dragons. And when you finish it, you better bring it back so I can be the first one in line to read it."

The girl blinked hard, trying not to lose it completely, and left hugging her notebook as if it were made of gold. Alia smiled after her, like she knew exactly what she'd handed over. And I stood there off to the side thinking, not for the first time, that there wasn't a camera in the world that would do this justice. Watching her make every single one of these people feel like they mattered—that was the difference. Back in January, she'd been bracing for the next blow. Now she was loose. Engaged. Fully present.

I leaned a shoulder against the column near the stage, arms folded, taking her in.

This was the woman I'd seen from the start. The one who

built a life out of grit and love and pure willpower. The one who'd held her town and family together, who'd carved out time for her words even when the world wanted to take everything from her.

I didn't kid myself that the world had gotten any kinder. There would always be noise. Always someone ready to take a swing. But looking at her now, laughing with her fans, at ease in the middle of all this chaos? I knew she didn't need me to run interference anymore.

She had armor of her own now.

Mine just happened to match.

The line kept moving, a steady tide of books and faces, until there was a brief lull—a gap in the current. And in that quiet pocket, she glanced up.

Our eyes met across the room. That smile—the same one that had walked barefoot down a grassy aisle and tied her life to mine—struck me like a shot to the chest.

She didn't need to say a thing.

I smiled back and tipped my head in a mock bow, because I'd always be her knight, even if she didn't need one.

Her grin deepened, and then the next reader stepped forward, and she went right back to work, fully herself.

The phone buzzing in my pocket was jarring in a way that had me fishing it out to check the screen. Blair sent regular updates, but she'd have just hollered across the room if she needed something. This was Bodie.

BODIE:

Can you be back in the Hollow day after tomorrow?

My brows drew together. That was... abrupt.

RAMSEY:

Why? What's wrong?

I watched the bubbles appear, disappear, then appear again. Whatever he was typing, he was thinking about it.

BODIE:

I need you to stand up at my wedding.

I stared at the screen, dead still for a beat while the noise of the signing swirled around me. Wedding? To *who*?

I glanced back at Alia. She looked up in that moment, caught me watching. She flashed another smile, then tipped her head toward me as if asking what that was about.

I huffed out a laugh and shook my head, mouthing *later*, before looking back at my phone.

I didn't know what the hell my best friend was up to, but I had a feeling whatever was coming next in Gibson Hollow would be its own sort of storm.

And as always, I'd be ready.

* * *

Choose Your Next Romance

I know you're dying to know what's going on with Bodie. Be on the lookout for his book, Hero, Unexpected, coming November 14th. Preorder your copy today!

Once upon a time, Emmaline Maddox was my best friend. The girl I found in the woods, bruised and too proud to ask for help. The one I brought tea and peanut butter sandwiches, just to see her smile.

But that was a long time ago—before life got messy. Before I put her little brother in cuffs and watched her shut me out with a look that guts me still.

Now she's about to lose everything she's fought for because of some outdated clause in a will and a family feud older than indoor plumbing.

I shouldn't care. But I do.

So I offer her the only thing I can: a fake marriage to make sure she gets what she's earned. She says yes, even though I know she doesn't trust me. Not anymore.

I've never stopped wanting to protect her. But what if this time, I want to keep her too?

In a town built on second chances, sometimes the most unexpected hero is the one who's always been there.

In the meantime, you can get another gander of Alia and Ramsey's happily ever after (obviously with Biscuit) straight to your inbox. Grab your copy right here: https://books.kaitnolan.com/fl7o6fvczp

Other Books By Kait Nolan

A complete and up-to-date list of all my books can be found at https://kaitnolan.com.

GIBSON HOLLOW
SMALL TOWN SOUTHERN ROMANCE

- Hero After Midnight (prequel)
- Hero Ever After (Alia and Ramsey)
- Hero, Unexpected (Bodie and Emmaline)

KILTED HEARTS
SMALL TOWN CONTEMPORARY SCOTTISH ROMANCE

- *Jilting The Kilt* (prequel)
- *Cowboy in a Kilt* (Raleigh and Kyla)
- *Grump in a Kilt* (Malcolm and Charlotte)
- *Playboy in a Kilt* (Connor and Sophie)
- *Protector in a Kilt* (Ewan and Isobel)
- *Single Dad in a Kilt* (Hamish and Afton)

- *Kilty Pleasures* (Jason and Skye)

SPECIAL OPS SCOTS
SMALL TOWN MILITARY SCOTTISH ROMANCE

- *One Fine Night* (prequel)
- *Before Highland Sunset* (Alex and Ciara)
- *Beyond Highland Sunrise* (Callum and Parker)
- *Beneath Highland Stars* (Finley and Saoirse)

BAD BOY BAKERS
SMALL TOWN MILITARY ROMANCE

- *Rescued By a Bad Boy* (Brax and Mia prequel)
- *Mixed Up With a Marine* (Brax and Mia)
- *Wrapped Up with a Ranger* (Holt and Cayla)
- *Stirred Up by a SEAL* (Jonah and Rachel)
- *Hung Up on the Hacker* (Cash and Hadley)
- *Caught Up with the Captain* (Grey and Rebecca)

RESCUE MY HEART SERIES
SMALL TOWN MILITARY ROMANCE

- *Someone Like You* (Ivy and Harrison)
- *What I Like About You* (Laurel and Sebastian)
- *Bad Case of Loving You* (Paisley and Ty prequel)
  Included in *Made For Loving You* (Paisley and Ty)

THE MISFIT INN SERIES
SMALL TOWN FAMILY ROMANCE

- *When You Got A Good Thing* (Kennedy and Xander)

- *Til There Was You* (Misty and Denver)
- *Those Sweet Words* (Pru and Flynn)
- *Stay A Little Longer* (Athena and Logan)
- *Bring It On Home* (Maggie and Porter)
- *Come Away with Me* (Moses and Zuri)

MEN OF THE MISFIT INN
SMALL TOWN SOUTHERN ROMANCE

- *Let It Be Me* (Emerson and Caleb)
- *Our Kind of Love* (Abbey and Kyle)
- *Don't You Wanna Stay* (Deanna and Wyatt)
- *Until We Meet Again* (Samantha and Griffin prequel)
- *Come A Little Closer* (Samantha and Griffin)
- *Just Wanted You To Know* (Livia and Declan)
- *A Love Like You* (Juliette and Mick)

WISHFUL ROMANCE SERIES
SMALL TOWN SOUTHERN ROMANCE

- *To Get Me To You* (Cam and Norah)
- *Know Me Well* (Liam and Riley)
- *Be Careful, It's My Heart* (Brody and Tyler)
- *The Matchmaker Maneuver* (Myles and Piper prequel)
- *Just For This Moment* (Myles and Piper)
- *Wish I Might* (Reed and Cecily)
- *Turn My World Around* (Tucker and Corinne)
- *Dance Me A Dream* (Jace and Tara)
- *See You Again* (Trey and Sandy)
- *The Christmas Fountain* (Chad and Mary Alice)
- *You Were Meant For Me* (Mitch and Tess)

- *A Lot Like Christmas* (Ryan and Hannah)
- *Dancing Away With My Heart* (Zach and Lexi)

WISHFUL MOMENTS SERIES
BITE-SIZED WISHFUL ROMANCE

- *Once Upon A Coffee* (Avery and Dillon)
- *Once Upon A Rescue* (Brooke and Hayden)
- *Who I Am with You* (Dinah and Robert)

WISHING FOR A HERO SERIES (A WISHFUL SPINOFF SERIES)
SMALL TOWN ROMANTIC SUSPENSE

- *Make You Feel My Love* (Judd and Autumn)
- *Watch Over Me* (Nash and Rowan)
- *Can't Take My Eyes Off You* (Ethan and Miranda)
- *Burn For You* (Sean and Delaney)

MEET CUTE ROMANCE
SMALL TOWN SHORT ROMANCE

- *Once Upon A Snow Day*
- *Once Upon A New Year's Eve*
- *Once Upon An Heirloom*

SUMMER FLING TRILOGY
CONTEMPORARY ROMANCE

- *Second Chance Summer*
- *Summer Camp Secret*
- *The Summer Camp Swap*

About Kait

Kait is a Mississippi native, who often swears like a sailor, calls everyone sugar, honey, or darlin', and can wield a bless your heart like a saber or a Snuggie, depending on requirements.

You can find more information on this *USA Today* best selling and RITA ® Award-winning author and her books on her website http://kaitnolan.com.

Do you need more small town sass and spark? Sign up for <u>her newsletter</u> to hear about new releases, book deals, and exclusive content!